# GOD'S
# VINDICTIVE
# WRATH

**Charles Cordell** has been a career soldier and diplomat on the ground in the Middle East, South Asia and North Africa. He has seen humanity at its best, its worst and its most desperate. His novels draw both on time spent on the fraying margins of civilisation and studies of the great political and religious crises of 17<sup>th</sup> century Europe.

*God's Vindictive Wrath* is the first novel in the *Divided Kingdom* series, which chronicles Britain's Civil Wars between 1642 and 1653.

# GOD'S VINDICTIVE WRATH

CHARLES CORDELL

**MYRMIDON**

Myrmidon
Rotterdam House
116 Quayside
Newcastle upon Tyne
NE1 3DY

www.myrmidonbooks.com


First published in the United Kingdom by Myrmidon 2022

This novel is entirely a work of fiction. Other than the obvious historical
figures, the names, characters and incidents portrayed in it are the work
of the author's imagination. Any resemblance to actual persons, living or
dead, events or localities is entirely coincidental.

A catalogue record for this book is available from the British Library.

ISBN 978-1-910183-31-1

Set in Minion Pro by
Falcon Oast Graphic Art Limited,
www.falcon.uk.com

Printed in the UK by CPI Group (UK) Ltd, Croydon, CRO 4YY

1 3 5 7 9 10 8 6 4 2

I do not stand at your grave and weep.
You are not there. You do not sleep.
You are 'a thousand winds that blow.
. . . the diamond glint on snow.'
Yours are the darkest of nights and the dawn
    'purple views' on the road to Buncrana.

# Contents

## PART TWO: THE ROAD TO LONDON

## PART THREE: BRENTFORD

## MAPS

# Character Notes

## THE KING'S ARMY

**Lord Grandison's Regiment of Horse**

Capt Sir John Smith*  the last bannerette to be knighted on the field of battle

Cpl Jock Nisbet  fought in Bohemia, Germany and Flanders

Ralph Reeve  stepson of Mr Reeve* gentleman of Westleton, Suffolk

Luke Sherington  son of Thomas Sherington*, yeoman of Westleton

Clement Tooley  son of Katherine Tooley*, a widow of Westleton

**The King's Lifeguard of Foot**

Sir Edmund Verney*  Knight Marshal and the King's Standard Bearer

Robbie Needham  Derbyshire free-miner and convict with Robert Sellars*

**Sir Thomas Salusbury's Regiment of Foot**

John Benion*  tailor of Newtown, Shropshire

Hywel Lloyd  herdsman of Cyffylliog, Denbighshire

**The King's Train of Artillery**

Mr George Merrett*  younger brother of the scientist, Christopher Merrett*

| | |
|---|---|
| Mr Nicholas Busy* | professional gun captain |
| Cuthbert Cartington* | conductor of the King's train of artillery |

## THE ARMY OF PARLIAMENT

### The Parliamentarian Horse

| | |
|---|---|
| Col Sir William Balfour* | fought in Holland and at La Rochelle |
| Capt Nathaniel Fiennes* | captain in Balfour's Horse |
| Capt Robert Viviers* | captain of a troop of horse under Colonel Goodwin |
| Francis Reeve | son of Mr Reeve*, gentleman of Westleton, Suffolk |

### Denzil Holles' Regiment of Foot

| | |
|---|---|
| Lt Col James Quarles* | experienced veteran soldier |
| Capt William Bennett* | London merchant related to Edward Bennett* of Virginia |
| Thomasine Bennett* | wife of William Bennett |
| Sgt Nehemiah Wharton* | London apprentice and letter writer |

### Lord Brooke's Regiment of Foot

| | |
|---|---|
| Capt John Lilburne ('Freeborn John')* | company captain and radical pamphleteer |
| Anthony Sedley* | Birmingham ironworker |

* denotes a character known to history.

# Part One
# Edgehill

*Edgehill with Bones looked white,*
*with Blood looked red,*
EDWARD BENLOWES *LOVE'S SACRIFICE*, 1652

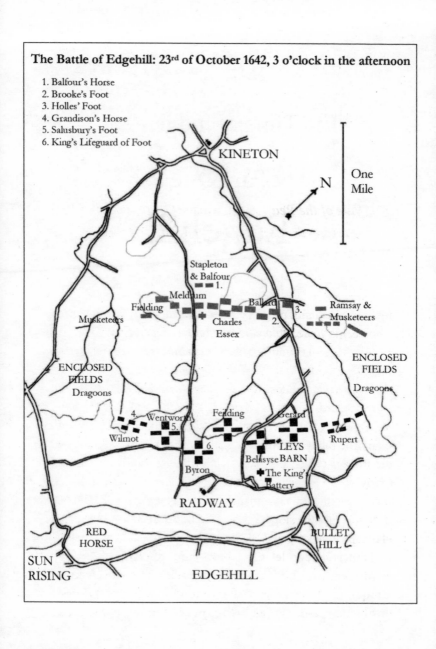

# I

# The Time of Judgement

*Francis Reeve*

*Vale of the Red Horse, Warwickshire, England*
*Sunday the 23rd of October 1642, one o'clock*

Bible in one hand, pistol in the other, the preacher sat astride a horse, his voice lifted to God's light and a clear sky.

*'And there went out another horse that was red! And power was given to him that sat thereon to take peace from the earth; that they should kill one another. And there was given unto him a great sword!'*

A growl of ascent ran through the ranks of godly horsemen. The bible reading was well chosen: John's *Revelation* of the End of Times, of God's wrath, the great destruction and Christ's final judgement. Across the vale, cut into the rich red earth, was the ancient image of a horse, a great primal beast etched across the slope of Edgehill. Beneath it stood the army of an apostate king and his French witch.

Francis Reeve let the power and resonance of God's word wash over him. He needed its reassurance, to feel its armour, to let God's fervour fill the ache within him before this battle against sin and the army of the Antichrist. *Lord,*

3

*let this preacher fill Thy servant with the strength to do Thy bidding, with the strength to overcome the heathen, to build a New Zion in Thy name. Let Thy chosen army cleanse this land of sin, purge it of the forces of Hell that stand before us.*

*Oh Lord, Thou knowest I have sinned. Satan lured me into temptation, into wickedness. Images of flesh haunt me, burn my soul. My so-called friends led me on an immoral path. They lied, cheated, corrupted me. I do not need them. They only caused me pain. I forsake them and my family. Christ and the Bible are my only companions now.*

Damn his father for the ungodly sot that he was. He had never understood, never loved him. The shit blamed him for his own mother's death, said that she had died because he was a bad and sickly child. Now the old fool was ruined, blinded by drink, lost in his crumbling house, in pain and unending sorrow. He should have turned to God.

But Francis had always loved her. He loved her so much. She was kind and beautiful, soft and warm with her gentle hands and lullabies to sooth him when he was ill. He had just wanted to kiss her goodbye, tell her he was sorry for being sick. But they would not let him see her, kept him shut in his chamber, cold, alone.

The memory chafed like an open sore. But he had to keep the thought of her alive, to feel its pain, until he could be with her again. He would not be alone for eternity. God had saved her from the slaughter in Europe; carried her safe to England to be his mother. Now she sat with Christ. He too had been saved by God. He was chosen. He would be gathered in to sit beside her again. He closed his eyes, bent his bared head and let the preacher's sermon fill him with the Lord's fire.

'And I say to you, oh brethren, is it not remarkable that

God has ordered this, our great battle, be fought here in the Vale of the Red Horse? Is it not a fit reference to that red horse revealed by the Spirit of God? For the rider is War, the second horseman! The red horse, God's vindictive wrath! The great sword, the great destruction to be made! And peace taken from the earth? Peace taken from the wicked and idolatrous.

'Before you, brethren, is the host of the wicked, an army of profane cavaliers and Romish idolaters. They are banded here together in this place, against God and His truth. Thus, say I, here is truth! For are ye not the righteous and true army of our Parliament? Do ye not ride the red horse of this vale, so named? And have you not been given a great sword? The sword of just revenge!

'For now is the time of judgement! The base caballeros of Rome have defiled and slaughtered the righteous brethren of Germany, Bohemia, the Low Countries. . . of all Europe! They have set loose the heathen, in league with the Devil, to rape and murder in Ireland. But here is the place of reckoning! For are you not chosen to take peace from them?

'I tell you, ye must ride with God's vindictive wrath! Ye must reap a great destruction upon this wicked host, this army of Satan! Ye must do God's work and cleanse this land of wickedness, purge it of pestilential sin! Ye must destroy this Babylon, and them that have drunk of her filth and of her fornication! *For the great day of His wrath is come. And who shall be able to stand?*

'The way may be strewn with thorns and ye may march between fiery mountains. But we shall prevail! God will make good his promise to cover your heads on this day of battle. For yours is the righteous and pure path! And we shall build a New Jerusalem! Let the judicious and godly judge! Amen.'

'Amen!' Francis joined the ardent assent, his horse tossing

its head, stamping at the sudden power of God's praise rising from the ranks of horsemen.

Surely God had sent this worthy preacher – the pilgrim, Hugh Peters, brought him back from Salem and the wilderness of New England to fill them with His purpose. *Oh Lord, let all Thine army feel the zeal and righteousness of Thy cause this day*. The incantations of a psalm lifted to the hills above, a foot regiment singing, as if in answer – a sign, surely.

But damn his half-brother! Ralph and the sinners that rode with him would destroy God's Kingdom on earth. He, Francis, was chosen to do God's work, to purge England of their curse. If it meant killing fellow Englishmen, then so be it. He would be saving them from their sinful ways and God's retribution. If that meant that he must kill his brother, he would. Ralph was a sinner beyond redemption.

Ralph was handsome and carefree, adored by all. While he had been sick, ugly – shunned. Now the immoral bastard lay with the whores that followed the cavalier host. Ralph had always been a sinner. Francis had to stop him. He had to stop him before he corrupted Susanna with his licentious ways and his sin, before he polluted her. He had to stop Ralph before he infected all with his sin, damned his family for eternity, excluded them from the Kingdom of Heaven.

The memory of her kissing Ralph still burned. But worse was the humiliation, her rejection. He tried to escort her home, away from the drunkenness, the banal leering revellers. But she turned from him, ran to join Ralph in the Midsummer ring-dance. The heat rose beneath Francis's well-tied collar, rose at the memory of her laughter, at her excited clapping as his bastard brother leapt through the bonfire.

Accusation and anger flared the day after, the day he, Francis, left home. Ralph announced he would fight for the

King. He was still drunk. He only did it to get the old man to give him money, to cheat him of his love. But the old fool believed him. With tears in his eyes, he gave Ralph his old rapier. The sword was meant for him, a true son, not for a bastard wastrel. It was his. Ralph had stolen it from him, just as he had stolen his father's love, blinded the old man, turned him away from his own son, poisoned his mind with sin.

He wished he could have been there to see them read his letter. It told how he had joined the godly army of Parliament, that Hell awaited Ralph and those who served in Satan's host. It must have sent the old man into one of his dark moods filled with drunken anger, violence and despair. It served them all right.

Francis pulled on his helmet and buckled its chinstrap. The lobster tail, cheek guards and barred visor wrapping him in their protective steel. It meant the end of any connection with home. It also meant expulsion from Cambridge. He had openly denied the authority of the dons, the bishops and their perverted dogma. There could be no going back. He would be a martyr first.

He, Francis Reeve, would cleanse his family of its heathen half-brother. He would cut out its malignant sin. He would bring Susanna back to the righteous path. He would prevail. Come the Day of Judgement, he would be gathered in to his mother and the Throne of Grace.

# II

# The Day of Battle

*Ralph Reeve*

*Edgehill, a quarter past one o'clock*

Ralph Reeve stood high in his stirrups and looked down into the vale. Stretched before him were two armies. Immediately below, ranged along the base of Edgehill, stood the King's army. Beyond it, across the vale, stood a second – an army raised by his Parliament. They faced each other separated only by a few open fields and a shallow brook.

Lark song hung high in the air as the land held its breath in the bright autumn sun. For a century and a half there had been peace. Here in this corner of Warwickshire the communal fields and commons had not yet been broken up, hedged in, enclosed. The land was still farmed in the old way. The great open fields formed a gently rolling plain of stubble, plough and harrow, ridge, furrow and common pasture – a perfect battlefield.

Each army made a glorious display in the sharp cool air. Sunlight danced upon burnished steel. It glanced off blade, pike head, barrel, armour and horse harness. Like a pair of jewelled harlequin's ribbons laid across the landscape, their bright chequered colours shifted and sparkled in the sun. But this was no parade or review of county militia. Both armies were drawn up for battle. For the past weeks, they had manoeuvred, each unsure of the other's position, strength or intent. Now, they faced each other in the very heart of England. Neither could simply march away. Each had come to save their homes, their families, their souls, their very being. They had to stand and fight.

Had it really come to this? Everyone knew that the world had to change. The old ways of government, order and religion were broken. Collapsed trade, failed crops, a climate out of kilter, plague, vagrants and riot ran unchecked. Some foresaw chaos written in the night sky, royal Saturn defied by Mars and fierce Aldebaran, all England eclipsed in a blood moon. Others saw God's wrath and the End of Times. The hint of an Easterly breeze spoke of winter, of cold, want and hunger. It also whispered of war. A war that had ravaged Europe, raised Scotland in covenant, raped, burned and flayed Ireland. Both sides had answered a call to arms to save England. Now only an English mile separated them.

Across the vale, the Parliamentary foot were drawn up along a slight rise, a chequerboard of twelve big battalions, each a phalanx of pikes flanked by wings of musketeers. A brigade of horse stood on either flank. Two more regiments of armoured horsemen waited to the rear in reserve.

But why did he feel so numb? He had been desperate to catch sight of this rebel army for weeks – to corner them, to rout them in glorious battle. Now they were in front of him, he felt no hatred for his enemy. This too was an English army, not some foreign invader.

The strains of a psalm rose faintly from the ranks opposite. Was Francis amongst them? Was his brother with one of those battalions? He had promised his mother to look after him, always. Now he couldn't even do that. He had failed his mother and driven his brother away with his own blind fool-ishness. Francis had not come home from Cambridge. In his place came an angry letter that renounced their family, told of how he had joined God's army to fight apostasy and that he, Ralph, would die a sinner. Their father had not recovered from the betrayal. God only knew what their mother would have felt.

Perhaps Francis was right. With a shiver, Ralph relived the moment he had been found with his master's wife; the scream-ing daughter, the old cuckold's raised stick, the bitch's denial and accusation, the door slammed behind him. Jesus, what a fucking mess! There was no going back. No forgiveness. He was a sinner beyond redemption. He had been cast out.

'If you ask me, they don't look much like a load o' frowsy rebels.'

Christ, but Clem was right. Lost in his own thoughts, he had forgotten his two companions.

'I thought we was supposed to be chasin' a bloody rabble. Each o' they there regiments have got matching coats an' all. They're a bugger sight smarter than our lot. An' there's more o' they than we.'

The blunt truth was typical of Clem's down-to-earth Suffolk approach. Clem had always been there, dragging him from the frozen marsh or pulling him back from a tavern fight. God only knew how much he depended upon Clem, how he had begged his father not to dismiss him. If only Clem had been there in London. Perhaps things would have been different.

'Ralph, should we try that perspective glass?' Trust Luke to think of it, his earnest friend, Luke who was always ready to help with a whispered answer or note at school.

'Of course! I'd forgotten the damned thing.' Ralph pulled the device from the sash around his waist, studied it for a moment. He put it to his eye. Distant images grew, wavered and blurred, refusing to focus. Then he had it. 'My God! This is extraordinary.'

'Tin't natural if you ask me.' Clem stared into the distance.

Luke sighed. 'Clem, what's not natural?'

'God made man with eyes to see. Don't need no bloody perspect glass. Tin't right to go messing about with such nonsense.'

'It's an instrument of natural philosophy, Clem.' Luke shifted in his saddle. 'One o' the great benefits of our age. Perfected by the extraordinary genius of Signor Galileo Galilei. An instrument developed according to mathematical principle, method and philosophical reason. We're most fortunate t' have the use of Lord John's fine example o' this physiologic wonder.'

'That may be, Goodman Sherington, but I say tin't natural.' Clem leaned forward to pat the neck of his horse. 'An' philosophic don't put food in your belly, do it, my beauty?'

'One day, Clem. . . one day it might just.'

Ralph tried to hide his smile as he concentrated on the view before him. Over every company of foot and troop of horse, a standard twitched in the gentle breeze; on them the badges of the great families of England mixed with slogans and religious symbols of every faction and party. Finally, he found what he was looking for, near the centre: the orange standard of the house of Devereux, of the Earl of Essex, Captain-General of the Parliamentary Army.

'There! Do you see him?' He pointed in triumph. 'The Earl of Essex! Well, the King has finally cornered his bird.'

'Might I?' Luke indicated the glass.

'Of course. See what you make of him.'

But Luke seemed more interested in the rest of the rebel army. 'Clem's right. Each o' their regiments has a full ten companies. And every battalion must be a thousand strong. Some of ours are barely four hundred men. And they stand eight ranks deep to our six. They're well equipped, too. Some of our poor Welsh have only cudgels and staves.' Turning to face him, Luke looked even more grave than normal. 'Ralph, this is no peasant rabble. At least one o' their horse regiments is all armoured cuirassiers. And they've more cannon.'

'Do they?' He should have taken in such detail.

'Yes. There are guns between every tertia.'

He had been foolish, stupid to use the glass only to look for Essex. 'That may be, Luke, but we have the King and right on our side!'

Fuck, now he sounded stupid! He didn't believe it himself. He didn't know what he believed. Perhaps that was part of his problem. He felt no belief, no attachment. He didn't feel he belonged to any cause. What did that make him? Was he just a mercenary? He'd volunteered to soldier because there was nothing else left, because he had failed at everything else, not because he was filled with conviction. He had never felt certain. It had been the same as a child at school, ever since his mother died. He wanted to find his place, his purpose in life, but always felt lost. No matter what he tried his hand at, he never truly felt he was on the right path. Perhaps he never would.

He had joined the King's army to appease his father more than anything else. God knew he had to do something to regain the old man's trust, something to make amends for his failure in London – for being cast out, for his shame and his lost indenture. He could just as well have followed Parliament's call.

If it came to battle, would he have the moral strength to fight? Could he kill another man without conviction – in cold blood? Would that not make him a murderer? He had volunteered to be a soldier because there was nothing else left. But could he see it through? Was he capable of killing? Or would his nerve desert him, leave him a failure once more? How would he face his father again? He could not return home. He could not fail this time.

Fuck, but he envied Luke's certainty. Luke had considered the options, determined that the King offered the best hope against chaos and the mob. He wished he had Clem's faith in Church and Crown. Perhaps he even envied his brother's puritanical zeal. Instead, he was lost in uncertainty. Empty. Numb. He let Luke and Clem fill the void.

'Well, are they just a-goin' to stand there?' Clem asked. 'I hain't much notion on the ways to fight a battle, but I reckoned to more than just standing about.'

'I don't think it'll be long now, Clem.' Luke pointed. 'Look. . . there on that flat ground half way up the slope. . . They're wheeling the last o' the King's cannon into place.'

'They must have had a bugger of a job gettin' them heavy guns down that there slope. Mind, they've got some beautiful strong hosses.'

'Well, yes. But you see how Essex has formed his regiments up in the Dutch style for defence. I think he's standing firm and will wait for us to attack him.'

'So, he wants we to charge he and all o' them there pikes and great guns?'

'Um, yes. Well, our foot are drawn up in brigades – in the mode of the great Swedish king, Gustavus. That'll be Prince Rupert's doing. He must favour attack and soon, afore the day ends.'

A single shot cut the air – faint, far off. Another. The crackle of musketry, puffs of white smoke amongst the hedges and thickets on the edge of the battlefield.

Luke had the glass to his eye again. 'Our dragoons are clearing away rebel musketeers. They'll be trying to secure the flanks – for our horse to charge.'

It had started. The battle had started.

'Well, I don't mind if we sit here and watch.' Clem gathered up his reins. 'But I thought we was to fetch that there perspect glass to Lord John. Not that I'm missing Corporal bloody Nisbet – right shit he is. But, seeing as them is down there and we is up here. . .'

'Clem is right, Luke.' Ralph sat up. 'Do you see our troop?'

'Prince Rupert has the right wing of horse. We should be somewhere amongst the left. Yes, there. I can see Lord John's standard, in the centre of the left wing – in the forward squadron.'

*Fuck!* The day of battle had truly come. The day he had waited for. One day of bloodletting to purge the nation of its sickness. One day to regain his honour. And they would be in the front rank.

A yell rose from amongst the King's foot, a great roar as the two thousand men of a foot brigade shouted in unison. High on the ridge above they felt it, felt the power of the war yell, its raw violence coursing through them. A knot of horsemen approached the next brigade, preceded by a crimson banner; the King was making his way through his army. They were cheering their sovereign, their Captain-General, brigade by brigade.

Turning in his saddle, Ralph could not help but grin with excitement at Luke's calm nod, Clem's beaming smile.

'Well, I reckon this'll be a mite bigger than Ipswich fair.' Clem grinned at his own jest.

14

Ralph threw back his head and let laughter burst from him, let flow the frustration, the uncertainty of the morning. He would not miss the great battle. He, Ralph Reeve, orphaned bastard, failed merchant's apprentice and lowly trooper with no prospects, would fight in the front rank of the King's horse. He would be there. They would be there.

God it was a beautiful day, perhaps the last of the year. Soon winter must come. Perhaps this would be his last. If it was, it was not a bad day to die. Just let him die with honour.

He stuffed the perspective glass back into his sash and urged his horse forward, over the edge to descend the escarpment. 'Come on! I want to be there before the King!'

# III

# For Justice

*Robbie Needham*

*The King's Lifeguard of Foot, half past one o'clock*

Like others in the ranks beside him, Robbie Needham was a free-miner. A big man from Castleton, he and cousin Hal had joined the King's Lifeguard at Derby, six weeks before. He didn't want to leave Derbyshire. He'd always loved the Peak Country and there was nothing better than working their own mine. But, the last years had been hard graft, with only debt, hunger and sorrow to show.

Robbie stood in the third rank of pikes. Behind him were another three ranks. Before him, beyond the front rank, was the King. Mounted on a fine white horse, black velvet over armour, a flash of ermine at his collar, the King stood before his Lifeguard and the Royal Standard they carried.

'Friends. . . soldiers. . . I look upon you with joy and behold as great an army as ever any king had, standing with high and noble resolution to defend your king, your church and the people of England.' Robbie barely understood half the words the King spoke in front of his regiment. The courtly wording was unfamiliar, odd-sounding. No matter, he got the meaning well enough. 'I thank you for your devotion and your desire to hazard your lives and fortunes with me in our cause, so freely offered in the urgent necessity of these times. I see in you that no son can forsake his father, as no subject can renounce his lawful king. But I attribute all this unto God, the justness of our cause, and the will of the people.'

Robbie ha'd loved Annie. She was his garland lass. Everybody knew they would wed when he could find a lode and start up on his own. But Lord pissing Rutland and his bastard hirelings changed all that. Grasping bastards like Rutland would destroy free-mining for good if they weren't stopped. Like others, he was forced off the best lodes by Rutland, his lawyers, backers and fellow Members of pissing Parliament – rich gits who sank new deep-mines like High Rake. They brought in unskilled outsiders from town and city – hirelings to cave for penny wages.

'We have marched long in hope of meeting no enemies to oppose us,' the King continued. 'But matters are now to be declared by swords rather than by words. My resolution, with much grief, is to try the doubtful chance of battle. I do not desire the effusion of blood. But, since Heaven hath presented it, we must accept this opportunity of winning an honourable victory. Your conscience and your loyalty have brought you here to fight for your religion, your king and the laws of your land.'

Robbie wasn't sure about conscience and loyalty. But he was here to fight for justice, his rights to a fair living and an end to leeches like Rutland. They'd fought back, him, Hal, Rob Sellars, Will Ashford, Annie's da' and a hundred others. They'd stood at the Barmote, in a court of law, marked their names to petition. They'd marched against the tithe and against the unfair price Rutland paid for their hard-won ore: nine shilling a load for ore worth twenty-two. But Rutland turned his hired villains and dogs on them. It were pitched battle, free-miner against hireling.

They'd won the day. But Rutland hunted them down one by one. Dragged from their cottages, Robbie, his uncle, Annie's da' and others were left to rot in Derby gaol. He watched Annie's da' die in that cell, a broken old man. It was like all hope was snuffed out in him. The poor sod owed money, a few farthings for firewood he'd had on credit. Rutland took his cottage, threw Annie and the bairns out on the moor.

'You shall meet with no enemies but traitors, radicals, dissenters, levellers, and the factious that would make laws as they want in your name – those who desire to destroy both church and state. They would use their position and privileges to their own ends, while the common man is left to suffer. They have already condemned you, the true people of England, to ruin for being loyal to our cause.'

He'd looked for Annie when he got out. But it was too late. He found her in a clapboard ale shack amongst the mud, filth and hovels of Hucklow, her bonny frame puddled by a grinning, pox-ridden hireling from High Rake Mine, while others waited their turn. He'd broken the bastard's fingers, batted others, smashed a barrel and chairs, before he pulled Annie from them to carry her and the bairns home.

Rutland's clerks said she owed Rutland money, that she was a whore. They threatened him with Derby gaol again. And then the scrofula came, her fine neck thick with it, bloated in a weeping boil of puss like some rank lover's bite; her blood addled, her body sold to keep the bairns from starving out on the slag heaps. There were tears at what might have been. And then she was gone. They found her on the moor up by her da's old mine, her skin washed clean in the rain, a garland bloom clutched tight in her hand.

'You may think my endeavour is to defend our royal person. But know now that I will stand to and endure the hazard. I promise to live and die with you, our people. The immediate action of this battle makes me speak briefly. Know that your king speaks unto you with as much love and affection as ever any king of England had for his army. In a word, your king bids you take courage in this our cause. And may Heaven make you victorious!'

The King had listened to free-miners. He understood his people. He'd promised to put an end to it; to curb Rutland and the other privileged bastards in Parliament and city. That was good enough for Robbie. The King was on their side – on the side of the people. He would fight for the King's promise to give them back their rights and their way of life.

He was glad to shout allegiance with the others of his brigade. In one great yell they shouted their cause. 'For God and for t' King!' The warrior's roar felt good after all the waiting. It felt strong.

Gradually, the cheer was replaced with the clatter of equipment as men regained their place and stance. He tightened his grip on the heavy ash pike shaft, its steel head quivering in the air eighteen feet above.

Cousin Hal turned from the rank in front. 'Worreh he say, sirrey?'

'Buggered if I know, rightly.' Robbie leaned on his pike. 'It were somert about them'll bein' dissenters, levellers and Parliament tossers. And us bein' brawn and 'eaven make us victorious. Any road, I reckon we'll be off right soon.'

But Robbie wanted to hear more, to know what was happening. He looked past his cousin straining his ears to catch what was said between the King and Sir Jacob Astley, the army's veteran Sergeant-Major-General of Foot.

'I see that our foot is ready, Sir Jacob?'

'Sire, they are as ready as they will be.'

'Then we will take our place with our Lifeguard.'

A barrage of concern followed from the King's entourage. They begged him to withdraw, to command from the high ground, with the artillery.

The King raised a gloved hand. 'A king's place is at the head of his army. Come life or death, we will bear you company upon this field. We will march with our Lifeguard.'

Only one dared speak now. 'Sire, your intention is noble indeed.' It was Prince Rupert, the King's nephew. 'But you are our cause. If you are lost, all will have been in vain. The army will not march until it sees you safe.'

Robbie did not hear the King's reply. In its place he felt rather than heard the low rumbling shriek of a cannon ball, its iron bulk ripping a path through the cool air overhead. The vibration of its passing was followed by the dull thump and billow of yellow smoke from the Parliamentary line. For the briefest moment, the two armies stood in shocked silence. But the still broke as the horizon filled with a blur of starlings, crows and lapwings rising from the fields, shrieking and yelling their outrage into the sky.

The rebel gunners must have seen the Royal Standard. They could see the royal party. There was no mistake: they had fired at their king. Their aim was good for line. They did not yet have the range so that the ball passed overhead to bury itself at the foot of Edgehill. But they had fired on their sovereign.

Again, Rupert spoke up. 'Sire, I beseech you! Allow us to do your bidding in the sure knowledge that you are safe.'

A second gun sent its ball thundering towards the King. This time its trajectory was lower. Tearing a deep gouge into the gentle slope in front, it ricocheted up and over the royal party before skipping on to follow the first. Its shrieking passage left a hail of stones, earth and dust, whinnying horses and unsettled courtiers.

The dust barely settled before the air was filled with the scream of iron as all thirty cannon along the Parliamentary line hurled their fire at the King's army. The noise of their bombardment rolled into a near continuous thunder. A young lieutenant in the next brigade was thrown through the air, the first to fall, his arm and shoulder ripped away in front of the King.

Robbie heard nothing more as the King was shepherded away to join his own battery of cannon. Prince Rupert watched him go before wheeling his horse towards the left wing and spurring it into a canter.

# IV

# To Bind their Kings with Chains

*Anthony Sedley*

### *Left of the Parliamentary foot, a quarter to two o'clock*

Anthony Sedley had listened to the growing crackle of musketry as the battle opened on either flank. Now the Parliamentary cannon added their thunderous roar in a great barrage across the front. It had begun. There was no going back.

They had openly defied their King, his taxes and commissions of array. They'd banded together, protested, risen up, stood in armed revolt, seized his royal carriage and his silver. Now they attacked him with fire and shot. This was rebellion. This was it. Now was the time when the common man would take back his natural rights.

Anthony was a nail-maker, his strength and conviction hardened in the sweat, dust, hammering noise and brotherhood of a Birmingham iron-forge. Burns flecked his arms and marked his face in a livid scar. Barely more than a boy, he'd taken his father's standing at the forge when the old man died – a good strong man ground down to die of exhaustion.

But the scar that burned deepest was the memory of his

daughter coughing her life out of consumption in their damp, rat-infested hovel. His little Maid Marian – his hope and dream of something pure, something better – a gaunt, dry corpse flecked in her own blood and spittle.

There was no charity, no apothecary and no priest for those who racked out their last days in that shitting slum. The hundreds living there were abandoned by town and parish, their lives no better than slaves. He was ready to fight for freedom, for his children to live and die free from bondage and godforsaken squalor.

He was a leveller. He believed in the rights and freedoms of the common man. *Shit on the tyranny of privilege and oppression that enclosed common land.* Damn the bloody gentry and merchants that controlled towns and villages, growing fat on their rents and profits while craftsman and labourer suffered failed harvest, raised prices and closed markets. It was time for change. And he'd sworn over the white heat of the forge to fight for it.

His father had fought enclosure. He'd been with Captain Pouch when three thousand gathered to pull down the fences and let the people back onto their ancient lands. But they were armed only with spades. They could not stand against the militia. The so-called gentlemen evicted them with dogs, guns and the noose. Well, now Anthony and those with him were armed with musket and pike. This was no riot. This was war.

But he was also a realist. Some of the younger soldiers did not share the same zeal. They were keen enough to run amok in the streets of Birmingham, Coventry and London, shouting their rebellion, ready to join the army in the heat and excitement of that summer. But were they ready to face the King's army in battle?

Some had joined to escape long indentures, others to simply have a coat on their back, a pair of shoes and five shillings a month in their pocket. A few ran from the constable. They were all as quick and cocky as any town lad. But they could also be sullen and downhearted when life or weather turned against them. Now they stood silent, facing the King's army. Would they stand now that the sport was over; now they faced reality; now they faced battle and a rebel's noose?

Anthony was a file leader, responsible for the seven young musketeers drawn up behind him. With the files beside them they formed eight ranks capable of hammering out a continuous volley fire, rank by rank, fire, reload and fire again. He thought of each man in turn, a mix of craftsmen, day journeymen, apprentices and the vagrant sweepings of the street. Not perfect, but they were his file, his band of merry men. But would they stand and fight? Would they stand firm when the King's cannon fired on them? Feet shuffled in the earth behind him.

'Alright lads, not long now. Each still got a match burning?' Immediately behind him stood Harry Fowler, a hard Aston lad, often in trouble with his fists. Good in a street fight, but on a battlefield? 'Harry?'

'Alright Anthony.'

'Good. Zach, what about yo lad?' Zachariah, a skinny runt of a boy that could barely carry his musket.

'Er, alright Anthony.'

'Alf, yo ready?' Alf stood in the fourth rank. Not the brightest, but a stubborn fighter.

'Oy'm alright.'

'Good. Tom?' Tom Gilbert, rear half-file leader, a knife maker, a good soldier.

'All fine, Anthony.'

24

Then came Isaac. The lad still didn't take anything seriously. He needed watching at every turn. 'Izzy, what about yo?'

'Er. . . shit! It's gone out again.'

'Bloody 'ell Isaac, you dozy pillock! This ain't a game. Tom, sort 'im out will yer.'

'Alright Anthony. Izzy, give us your bloody match and don't let the sergeant see yer.'

Behind Isaac should have been Lorimer, but the slippery shit had disappeared with a trollop the morning they left Worcester. Damn him, he could have made a fine soldier. Last, there was Will Bayliss, his bringer-up, a leveller and a fighter. Will Scarlet they called him. He would make a file leader one day, if needed. 'Will, you alright mate?'

'Yes Anthony, alright.'

'Alright then. Like I said, not long now.'

They stood among the ranks of musketeers of Lord Brooke's Regiment, on the left of the Parliamentary foot. Only a wing of horse and a few musketeer plotoons were further left. In front of them stood their captain, John Lilburne – 'Freeborn John'.

Anthony did not give a shit for officers and gentlemen. They were just another part of the bloody system of oppression. But Freeborn John was different. He'd spoken up for the rights of the common man and been punished for it. Only twenty-eight, he was already a common hero. He'd defied the King's taxes, been pilloried, gaoled and whipped for his leveller pamphlets. Anthony wouldn't choose another to follow. Freeborn John seemed to know the mood of the men he led, lifting their spirits with a rousing song or speech. *Don't fail them now John. Speak to these boys. Give these lads the reassurance they need. Don't let them wait in fear*.

Freeborn John turned to face them, looked at them. He

filled his chest, his voice ringing out. *'Praise ye the Lord! Sing unto the Lord a new song!'*

Anthony didn't hold much to psalm singing and prayer but this was the levellers' psalm, one that spoke of their righteous cause, the cause of liberty, of rebellion against tyranny and oppression: Psalm 149. Together, Brooke's eight hundred Birmingham ironworkers joined in chanting its defiant message.

*'Let them praise his name in the dance. Let them sing praises unto him with the timbrel and harp. For the Lord taketh pleasure in his people. He will beautify the meek with salvation.*

*Let the saints be joyful in glory. Let them sing aloud upon their beds. Let the high praises of God be in their mouth, and a two-edged sword in their hand!*

*To execute vengeance upon the heathen, and punishments upon the people. To bind their Kings with chains! And their nobles with fetters of iron!*

*To execute upon them the judgement written. This honour have all saints. Praise ye the Lord!*

Amen!'

*Let these lads be filled with the justice of their cause. Let them fight for their natural rights as freeborn Englishmen, fight for freedom from oppression. . . freedom to band together in common. . . freedom to share in the common land. . . share in the common wealth that was their birth right. . . for equality. . . for their own vote. . . for their voice to be heard.*

There would be no mercy in failure; only chains, the lash and the hangman's rope. There was no going back. This was rebellion.

He was ready. He would rather die fighting for freedom than live a vassal; slave to the Norman yoke of feudal bondage and oppression imposed by force, imposed by a bastard king and privileged few. He was ready to die fighting for the natural liberty of old England taken from the common man by usurpers. Anthony adjusted the bandolier that hung over his purple coat, readied himself for the order for battle. *Don't let them wait any longer; don't let them doubt their cause.*

Freeborn John looked along the ranks as if he gauged them, weighed their resolve. He filled his chest again. This was it, the order they'd waited for, the order that would start the rebellion, the order to stand against tyranny. 'Take up your musket and rest!'

Anthony balanced musket, forked rest and coils of smouldering match in his left hand. Beside him, behind him, the two hundred and fifty musketeers of his wing did likewise. This was the first *posture*, the first step of loading the matchlock musket. But this was no practise. It was for real. This wasn't some muster parade or spectacle of arms. They were readying for battle.

The call to action calmed nerves, gave purpose; concern and worry lost in the familiarity of the drill. The waiting was over. It had begun. Now was the time for the common man to rise up. He braced himself for the order to load, the words that would commit them. There was no going back. This was war.

Freeborn John filled his lungs. 'Make ready!'

# V

# The King's Shot

### *George Merrett*

### *The King's battery, two o'clock*

George Merrett clasped his hands behind his back as the last preparations were made to ready the two cannon. He was a gentleman of the ordnance, but there was little that he could do to give practical help. Even though the rebel guns had already begun their barrage, he knew better than to get in the way. He also knew better than to show his impatience. He dared not pull the watch from his pocket again. The older gunners would do things in their own time. Their art was not to be rushed. All he could do was watch and keep the fussing Battery Master from interfering. *God, just don't let them be last to be ready!*

Treated with near reverence, the guns were a pair of demi-culverins. Smallest of the six cannon that constituted the King's meagre battery, they were placed on the left of the gun line that filled a small plateau on the slope of Edgehill. From here they looked over the heads of the King's foot and down upon Essex's battalions lined along their low ridge across the vale.

It was not the best of positions. They should have been lower down and more central to cover the whole front. But they had simply run out of time. It had been difficult enough getting his two demi-culverins into position, let alone the bigger guns. They struggled to descend Edgehill, horses in front and behind to hold the guns on the steep road. Each of his guns weighed almost a ton with their ten-foot iron barrels. The great demi-cannons were nearer three tons apiece. Difficult to move anywhere, they cost time, sweat and curses to control downhill.

George watched the nearest crew preparing their gun for action. The two gunners and four young matrosses worked in near silence. All knew their trade, their position and role. Mister Busy, Old Nick, had taught them well. His slight stoop, limp, and heavy arms belied an alert mind and a wealth of experience. The gun captain spent hours bullying his men until they knew their roles instinctively. The time for shouting passed; they worked in deliberate unison.

Old Nick selected shot. Turning over the nine-pound iron balls, eyes and gnarled hands caressed each one as he searched for any imperfection. Too much windage would leave the shot to rattle in the bore and fly unpredictably. Any constriction could be fatal to gun and crew. His Number Two took each ball in turn and placed them in a neat row.

The Number Three struggled with the wooden budge-barrel, filled with enough gunpowder to kill them all. Carefully, he loosened the draw-cord to its leather hood. Beside the gun wheel, the Number Four stacked oakum and straw wads.

The Number Five propped a long-handled ladle and rammer on the gun's axle. Not the brightest of lads, he was cruelly named Flash. Last, the Number Six, barely more than a boy in bare feet, staggered along the line with a bucket of water that slopped down his legs at every step to wet a long-handled sheepskin sponge. They called him Squit. What a pair!

Finally, Old Nick trimmed and clamped two ends of glowing match in his forked linstock, twists of sulphurous smoke rising in the clear air. Satisfied, the gun captain stuck the spiked base into the ground and turned with a curt nod and touch of his battered Montero cap. The second gun was only moments behind. They looked at George, waiting for his order.

'Load your pieces!'

The gun captain nodded as the Number Two slid the long-handled ladle into the gun barrel, pushing it all the way to tap the very base of the breech. The bore was clear of obstruction.

Another nod and the ladle's scoop was thrust into the budge-barrel, its protective hood held open. A full scoop of gunpowder slid down the bore, the ladle twisted to release its contents. A crime to spill any of the precious powder, the ladle was carefully withdrawn, filled and slid into the bore again. Eight full pounds of gritty black gunpowder were deposited in the breech.

The round-headed rammer forced the loose powder up against the base of the breech, tamping it down with a double tap. A wad of oakum was stuffed into the gun's muzzle and thrust home. It was vital that the charge was compressed and held in place. Charge rammed home, the Number Two hefted the first iron shot to roll it into the muzzle. It was pushed home, followed by another wad and seated with three steady thumps of the rammer. Any gap between charge and shot could end in a burst barrel and decimated crew.

Now they worked to lay the gun. Sighting along the top of the barrel, the gun captain signalled with outstretched hand. The four matrosses turned the gun with hand spikes under the trail and shoulders to the wheel spokes. A clasped fist told that the gun was laid for line. A small block of wood, a dispart, was placed on top of the muzzle ring while a wedge-shaped quoin was tapped under the base of the breech to lever it up. Squinting over breech and dispart, the gun captain grunted, satisfied with the angle of elevation.

Finally, Old Nick thrust a copper pricker down the touch hole, working it to form a hole in the powder charge. Into this he poured finer grained priming powder from a horn at his side, filling the touch hole. Carefully, the old gunner crushed grains with the end of his horn to make a yet finer powder about the touch hole, covering it with a cupped hand against wind and damp.

Turning, Old Nick doffed his cap. His gun was loaded and laid. The second of George's gun captains did likewise. They were ready. And, thank God, they had beaten the bigger guns. George turned smartly to his right and with a flourishing sweep of his hat bowed low to the Battery Master.

Now they had to wait for the other guns and the order to fire. The Parliamentary bombardment was already taking effect. The King's guns must answer and soon. At least one enemy ball had cut its path through a foot battalion. George could contain himself no longer. He paced backwards and forwards. With each turn he checked to see which of the heavier guns were ready; first the two culverins then, finally, the great demi-cannons.

But still they waited. Why? Why in God's name were they waiting? Were they simply going to stand here while the Parliamentary cannon smashed holes on the King's brigades?

Old Nick coughed, once, behind him. George turned. Cresting the lip of the plateau on an elegant white Turkish horse rode the King and his entourage. They were waiting for the King! He should have known. They were all waiting for the King!

George believed in hierarchy, in Plato's great chain of being. He understood that the King was the fountain from which all power, position and patronage flowed. But must they always wait for him? Even in battle?

Almost too late, he swept off his hat, held it low, its inside hidden. Right foot forward, left knee bent, weight back, body forward, right arm out in open hand, he bowed low making a leg in the fashionable French style of the Court. *Stay low.* He must stay bowed until they had passed, until the King, princes and retinue had passed.

The Earl would be with them, the Earl of Newport, Master of Ordnance, his patron. *Oh God, had the Earl seen him turn late to bow to his King?* His hands were dirty. The Earl was bound to see, bound to be displeased. Had his gunners stopped, doffed their hats? They were quiet behind him. Just the steady thud of hooves passing – hooves and the crash of rebel cannon.

He could not afford to lose his patron's favour. He and his young family depended upon the Earl for his position, his salary and the roof over their heads. He had tried to make it on his own. He was sure that he had been on the point of achievement, so close to forging iron with coal. Working long into the nights after Oxford, he had been so certain of success. But he had not calculated for smallpox until its dreaded pustules burst out across his body. It almost killed him as he lay sweating and vomiting in his bed, racked with fever.

His young wife nursed him back to health. He shuddered at what he put her through in that first year of marriage.

When he regained consciousness it was to know that the pox had taken their child. The creditors and their bloody lawyers had taken everything else. The scars on his face were the least agony to bear.

Somehow, she found him a position as a secretary to the Earl, saved them from ruin. He had risen to oversee the manufacture of gunpowder, made fireworks for the King and was now a gentleman of the ordnance. But he was trapped in squabbling inefficiency and back-stabbing at Court. He had witnessed fools chase favour, petty tyrannies and ruin. Women, ladies and men ruining themselves over clothes and trinkets, living beyond their means, selling themselves in the hope of preferment; only to be abused, humiliated by those with power, those with influence. But such was the natural order of things, the consequence of a strong king surrounded by powerful men. Better that than a weak state, corruption, anarchy and a republic ruled by the fickle appetites and desires of the mob. He longed to escape his dependence upon the Earl. One day he would be free to pursue his own designs. But, for now, he dared not risk upsetting his patron. It was a long way to fall and there were so many ready to climb over him.

George watched as the King was invited to aim one of the great demi-cannon. *God's blood!* Was it not enough that they waited for their monarch to be present? Must they now wait for him to aim the first shot, wait while courtiers positioned themselves, while the damned Parliamentary gunners cut down the King's foot? *Please sire, do not delay. Let us be about our work.*

Thank God, the King merely sighted along the barrel from his horse. With a brief nod, His Majesty retired a few paces without fuss.

A smoking linstock touched the great cannon's breech. There was the slightest pause as priming powder flared skyward in a jet of white smoke. Then, with a thunderous explosion, the great demi-cannon leapt backward in a sheet of flame and ball of yellow smoke, its twenty-seven-pound iron ball sent hurtling towards the Parliamentary line.

George did not wait to see whether the King hit his mark. He bored his eyes into the Master of Ordnance, willing him to give the signal for the general bombardment to begin. Finally, the King and his retinue regained control of their horses. The Earl stepped forward and waved his hat in the air. 'Give fire!'

# VI

# With Sword in Hand

## *Ralph Reeve*

### *The King's left wing, a quarter past two o'clock*

Like hot breath on his skin, the sound of the cannon swept over Ralph in a flush of exhilaration. For the umpteenth time that morning, a surge of excitement rolled up his back to lift the roots of his hair, sweat prickling at the base of his spine and under his hat.

He could not hide the sheer fucking thrill of being there. He knew that his childish grin betrayed him, but many of the other young troopers had to feel it too. Thank God, he had not missed this day. For surely there could be only one battle, one bloodletting.

With a nod, Captain Smith took the perspective glass from him. Thank God. He was done with fetching the bloody thing and they could rejoin their troop. With a tip of his hat, Ralph led Luke and Clem to take their places. As a gentleman's son, he took the front rank. It was only natural, to be expected. Luke took the yeoman's place covering the rear. As a serving man, Clem sat between them. To their right, the other fifty horsemen of the troop waited. Like them, a mix of county society, rank and station.

35

'Glad ye could join wi' us, Mister Reeve.' Ralph bit his lip. Corporal Nisbet seemed to delight in picking on him. 'Better late than never.' Whatever he did, the old Scots soldier never had a good word to say, as if he despised him. Perhaps he just meant to ease the tension. You could feel it running through the ranks, sharp in the air. Nobody spoke; just nods and forced smiles.

Was it right that he wanted to be here, wanted to see battle, to experience war? Should he want to be a soldier or had he let some boyhood fantasy cloud his mind? There was nothing else left. He had failed at everything else, thrown away the one real opportunity he had been given in life. The only chance he had of a respectable living. He had thrown aside the chance of a life of comfort and ease as a London merchant for a woman.

But it was war that had forced his mother to flee her homeland, to seek refuge for herself and her child in England. She had rarely spoken of it. But he knew that she fled with her Winter Queen. Somewhere on that exodus she'd given birth to him. He too was a refugee of the endless wars of religion and power that racked Europe, wars that left only destruction, famine, disease and unburied dead. If she lived – if she could see him now – what would she think of him?

If he had to kill, he would. He had chosen to serve his King and he could no longer shirk from duty, even if that meant killing. Fuck it. He would simply obey his King and be done. He did not worry about his own death – he had so little to lose. What he feared was fear itself. *Oh God, don't let me fail. Don't let the cold hand of fright hold me in its frozen grip. Don't let fear brand me for the rest of my life!* He could not afford to fail here, in battle. Better death than life knowing he was a coward. He could never face his father again. *Please God, don't let fear take my honour. It is all I have.*

It had been hard enough facing his father's anger and despair after London. He had to pick the moment, between the old man's drinking, his rage and black melancholy, to talk to him, to face him and explain. In truth, he was his step-father, but he was the only father he had ever known. For all Ralph knew, he was a bastard. He was certainly an orphan. But the old man did not throw him out when their mother died. He must have loved her. Her death had broken him. Ralph's failure in London almost finished him.

But it had been good to be home for the summer after the stifling puritan piety of the city. He was back in time for St Elmo's Day and sheep shearing, Whitsuntide church ales, Midsummer bonfires and hay making. It was easy to earn his keep over the harvest. There was always plenty of work and he loved to join the men in the fields, the barns and at the supper table, seeing old friends and familiar faces, being with those who understood him. Jesus, it was good to have the sun on his back and the sweet smell of new-cut hay, the sound of larks on the heath, wind on the marsh, the sea on shingle, the cool still of the great woods.

But, even before the harvest was in, he knew he needed to move on. He had promised the old man he would fight for his king. *God, let me do my duty now the time of reckoning has come.* Perhaps then he would feel acceptance, be allowed to marry Susanna, the one girl he truly desired.

His horse shifted uneasily under him. Its nostrils flared and mane shook as he checked dancing hooves, reining back to keep it in line. It too sensed the moment. It too saw, heard, smelled the twenty-five thousand men, the six thousand horses that faced each other across the vale. He leaned for-ward, lay a calming hand on the animal's hot twitching neck. He must not let it work itself into a sweat-lather before they even started. For this was no normal gathering. This was no county hunt or race. Nothing had fully prepared horse or rider for this day. How could it? No matter how keenly he anticipated this moment, he did not know what it would bring.

The only ones who really knew were the few old soldiers who had tried to drill their knowledge and experience into the young troop. Corporal Nisbet knew. He had fought his way across Bohemia, Germany and the Low Countries. But he had little time for Ralph.

There was Captain Smith. He was a man to take notice of: thickset, fierce, ruddy, fiery red hair. John Smith was a man of honour, action and strength. He had fought in Flanders and was one of the reformados who protected the King from the mob at Whitehall. He was serious about soldiering. He had little time for the niceties of small talk. They said he had refused a baronetcy for his service. Ralph had long since made a mental note to stick close to this man in battle.

Smith walked his horse forward to present the perspective glass to its owner. Lord John Stuart sat astride a great charger ahead of the troop. It had taken so much time and frustration to collect that morning, a birthday gift from the King. But the proffered object was swept away in disdain with a raised eyebrow, the desire to use it long passed.

Lord John, courtier and kinsman to the King, gazed impassively at the horizon. Dressed in silk slashed to expose fine linen, topped with an ostrich-plumed hat and mounted on a high-stepping Spanish stallion, he was the perfect cavalier. One calfskin gauntlet crooked nonchalantly against his hip, only the ends of his long golden hair flicked in the gentle breeze. He did not stir, even when a cannonball shrieked overhead. His elegant repose was broken only by the arrival of Prince Rupert reining in hard to halt in front of his cousin.

The colonels of the left wing closed in, but the prince's staccato, Germanic orders were directed to all within earshot.

'Gentlemen, we shall soon be about our work this day. Advance in close order. Keep your ranks with sword in hand. Receive the enemy's shot. Hold the fire of your carbines and pistols till you break in amongst them. Only then make use of your firearms – at close range.'

Waiting only for the briefest of confirmation the prince wheeled away with a final instruction. 'Watch for my signal!' His horse was spurred on its way with a great roar. They knew what they must do.

But knowing the hour had come brought with it a welter of last-minute doubts and actions. Most checked their weapons. Some prayed. A few simply sat in awe. Many felt the urge to piss, slipping from their horses to relieve themselves. The stench of horse and human urine hung in the air, rankled in the nostrils of man and beast alike.

Fuck! He had not readied his pair of wheellock pistols. They were loaded with powder and ball but not primed or spanned. He pulled each in turn from its holster, primed and wound back the ratcheted wheel of the mechanism with a long spanner. Finally, he lowered the flinted dog-arm into position. Holding the cool steel, he could not help marvelling at their precision, the dull sheen of the long eighteen-inch barrels, the polished wood, their vicious beauty, weight and feel. Could he use them to shoot down a fellow man? He checked each pan was covered and slid them back into their holsters.

Finally, Ralph unsheathed the sword that hung at his side. He had been so proud when his father gave him his old rapier. Now it seemed old fashioned and slender compared with the heavier blades beside him. *Don't let me or this blade fail in our duty this day.*

All that was left was to wait. The feeling of excitement was gone. Only numb emptiness remained. *God let us move soon. Don't let me fail those beside me. Don't let me fail in front of Clem, Luke or the others. Please God, not this numbing wait – this doubt. Spare me the cold grip of fear.*

# VII

# First for the Devil

*George Merrett*

*The King's battery, half past two o'clock*

The Earl had given the order for the King's battery to open fire. Finally, they could answer the Parliamentary bombardment. They could get on with their business. George did not wait for confirmation. He whipped around to repeat the order to his own guns. 'Give fire!'

The gun captains stepped back, plucked their linstocks from the ground, blew upon the coals and brought bright glowing match down upon each touch hole. Like those around him, George dropped his jaw and opened his mouth to prevent the shock wave from each gun bursting his eardrums.

The King's remaining five guns exploded in near unison, a single ear-splitting and defiant roar. The heavy gun carriages leapt back in the air, hanging there before dropping to the ground with a crash of iron rivets, carriage bolts and locks. One hundred and two pounds of iron shrieked across the vale leaving the little battery enveloped in a cloud of thick sulphurous smoke. As the smoke parted, it was clear that both his guns had fired long, their projectiles passing over the centre of the Parliamentary line. The guns were cold. He must bring them to bear.

'Put back your pieces!'

The matrosses threw themselves at the great guns, wheeling and levering them back into line.

'Load!'

Again the Number Two searched the bore, this time raking out smouldering debris, while Old Nick pressed the pad of his hand over the smoking touch hole to seal it. Any inrush of air could fan smouldering powder into a fatal second explosion.

Young Squit pushed a dripping sheepskin mop down the length of the bore to extinguish any embers. Black gritty water ran down its shaft to soak his arms, sleeves and breeches. The sponge came out steaming, black and stinking, to be quenched in its bucket.

Now the loading began again: powder charge ladled in, tamped home, wadded and rammed; shot rolled into the muzzle, pushed home, wadded, seated and rammed. All worked in near-perfect unison.

Again, the lay was checked, the quoin knocked a little further under the breech. Once more, Old Nick primed the touch hole with pricker and horn. Ready, he turned with a nod.

Not waiting for further orders, George yelled back his command. 'Give fire!'

Yes, they had beaten the bigger guns! Old Nick was the first to get his second shot away. Again, the great gun leapt back in its recoil, thumping roar and crash of iron fixtures.

George watched for the shot's fall. It took an age, perhaps three seconds. A splash of red earth and stone as the ball gouged into the furrowed earth just short of a Parliamentary battalion, a dark scar etched into the slope. But the ball had buried itself in the ground; there was no ricochet. It should have grazed the ground to bounce, like a stone skipping across water, churning its long path of destruction. It was the only way to compensate for variations in range due to differences in charge, shot or wind. But this ball had simply sunk harmlessly into the earth.

He struggled to train and focus his perspective glass. But it was clear. There was no mistake. However much he wanted the shot to count, the battalion in its path stood shaken but unscathed. He watched as the ball from his second gun buried itself in front of the same battalion, a blue-coated regiment – Sir Henry Cholmley's puritans – damn them!

He saw Old Nick glance then frown. Damn it! The King's battery was too high up the slope. The angle was too steep against soft ploughed earth. If it wasn't for the bigger guns, they could have been lower down. Should they move now? It was too late. They were committed. Old Nick would simply have to work his magic.

The gun captains were looking at him. Damn – they were waiting for his order!

'Put back your pieces. Load!'

Spike, rake, sponge, charge, wad, shot, wad – the gun crews worked like automatons. There was something extraordinary in the way that every man performed his motions as a part of the action. Every movement was synchronised with the next. They were a perfect machine – each one a piece of the mechanism, like the wheels of the watch in his pocket. He could think of no other example of men working together with such precision. This was man, industry and science in unison. Was this the way of the future? It was a wondrous and near-perfect thing. But it was a perfection bent on destruction.

Old Nick took a little longer to lay his gun this time, the quoin eased out from under the breech ring just a little, the muzzle elevated no more than a straws width. With a grunt and deep frown, the old gunner turned to nod.

'Give fire!'

George did not wait to see the linstock touch the breech. He ran along the line to be clear of the smoke, to see the fall of shot. He hardly heard the cannon's roar. He ignored the crash of iron as it came to rest. One, two, three seconds. Had it gone over? No. There, in front of Cholmley's centre, a welter of earth, stone, dust. Had it buried or skipped over?

Finally, the dust settled. Yes! They had struck home – cleaved a gap in Cholmley's ranks. It would not be just the King's foot who would feel the power of the big guns this day. Old Nick had found his mark. Now he must keep it and do his worst. George had to bring his second gun to bear.

Resisting the urge to shout, to punch the air in triumph, he thrust the perspective glass under his arm and turned to face his guns. Old Nick Busy nodded, just the faintest hint of a smile between them. It did not need to be said. They both knew the old adage: *first shot for the Devil, the second for God, third for the King*.

He looked to see if his patron, the Master of Ordnance, saw their success. But the Earl had moved on. The last of the King's escort were turning to follow the King back down the hill.

# VIII

# Rupert's Charge

*Nehemiah Wharton*

*Parliamentary left wing, twenty minutes to three o'clock*

Nehemiah Wharton prayed that God would show them the way. He had led his red-coated musketeers in puritan prayer early on this Sabbath day before they marched out onto the battlefield. They were chosen, chosen as commanded musketeers to stand with the left wing of horse. The musketeers of their company formed a plotoon of sixty-seven that now stood with their horsemen forward and left of the main Parliamentary line. Together, horse and foot formed two lines on a slight hill, a plotoon of musketeers between every squadron of horse. He had promised them a dish of cavaliers for breakfast. His stomach churned. The time for breakfast and dinner had come and gone. With it had gone his appetite to fight.

He and many of his regiment had been ready enough to leave London in the hot heady summer months. Young zealous puritan apprentices mostly, they joined the crusade to overthrow a corrupt malignant Court, its nepotism and self-interest, its abuse of the law and its sinful squandering of taxes. He had seen for himself the flagrant Popery, flouting of the law and licentious waste of the Queen's Chapel. They broke in when the King fled London, when the apprentices marched on his palace of Whitehall to defend Parliament. Walls covered with superstitious pictures, deified Virgin and Saints, Papist idols, feet, hands and bleeding hearts – Jesuit marks – a high altar, silver ornaments, paraphernalia and incense – and all while Catholic invasion threatened England.

But they had marched a long way from the city and his apprenticeship in St Swithin's Lane. In all honesty, he was not really sure what they were supposed to do now. It had felt good to be chosen, drawn out from the rest of the regiment to stand with their horse. But he wished that Lieutenant-Colonel Quarles was with them. He was the only officer who seemed to know his business, to rise above the squabbling and scrambling for position.

Pray God that Captain Bennett would know what to do when the time came. Nehemiah had thanked the Lord when his master released him to join Captain Bennett's company. William Bennett was a good, God-fearing London merchant but he was not a natural soldier. He seemed to refer to his manual of instruction before issuing any order.

The rattle of musketry and waft of gun smoke told of the skirmish on their flank. This dirty fight was getting closer and ever more intense as musketeers and dragoons fought for the hedgerows on the edge of the battlefield. But Nehemiah could see nothing ahead other than the squadrons and plotoons to his front.

He gripped his sergeant's halberd. It was time to prompt his captain again. 'Captain Bennett. . . do you think the damned cavaliers will attack?'

'I don't know, Nehemiah. I didn't expect this infernal

cannonade to go on for so long, and they seem to be pressing closer on our flank.'

'They are, sir. Perhaps the good captain of horse can see further.' Nehemiah nodded towards an officer sat atop his charger contemplating a half-eaten apple. It was one of those sweet little yellow apples they had tasted on the march from Worcester. Nehemiah's stomach groaned. If he was not going to eat it, could he not share it with those who had had nothing?

'Of course. Captain Viviers, can you tell us what you see? Can you see what is going on from up there?'

'I am sorry, how rude of me.' The officer of horse looked down at them. 'I had forgotten that you poor foot must be in the dark down there.'

'Well yes, but what can you see?'

'Ah hum. . . well, our damned gunners are making a lot of noise, but I suppose you can hear that. The delinquents have finally arranged themselves, but I don't think it will come to anything more. They cannot hope to stand against our cannonade. I am sure they will sue for peace terms shortly, once honour is satisfied with this exchange of cannon fire.'

'Do you think so?'

'Oh yes, certainly. They will see sense.'

Nehemiah felt rather than heard the change to his front. A faint movement, as if the ground itself trembled. It built to a steady throbbing, far off shouts – the call of trumpets. The pounding turned to distant thunder, growing louder, as if a great wave was roaring towards them. The young musketeers beside him stirred. Ahead, horse squadrons and musketeer plotoons fumbled into activity. Men and horses swayed, clashing against one another in confusion. What was it that caused such alarm from the far side of the slope?

A dull thud beside them; the half-eaten apple dropped

on the ground. Captain Viviers snatched at the reins of his horse, his face pale and mumbling, as if he saw the host of Hell before him. 'Oh God. Oh God, no.'

'What is it?' Captain Bennett shook the horseman's arm. 'Viviers, what do you see?'

'They. . . oh God. The cavaliers. . . they are charging.'

A ripple of fire burst from among the plotoons in the front line. But it was not the great salvee they had trained to deliver. It was poorly done, sporadic. Even before it had finished the forward squadrons began to break up, lone horsemen turning their mounts to flee. The trickle became a flood as groups broke away until finally those remaining could not hold their horses from turning to race after the fleeing herd. As they went, they dragged the second line of horsemen with them as one white-eyed, wild galloping mass.

Viviers yanked at his reins. 'Save yourselves!'

'Captain Viviers!' Nehemiah shouted at him. 'You must stand with us!'

'I. . . I am sorry. The day is lost. It is every man for himself. You must save yourselves!'

'Damn you, sir! And damn your kind for rogues and cowards!'

Nehemiah turned back to his musketeers. He had to hold them together. Their only chance was to stand and weather the storm. He had to ready them for whatever would break upon them. 'Make ready to give fire by salvee! Draw forth your match! Cock your match! Try your match!'

And then the unseen thunder crested the rise as a mass of charging horsemen, a great wave of yelling screaming cavaliers. A last flurry of shots flared from the plotoons ahead before the wave hit them, horsemen spilling around the blocks, slashing and firing.

'Blow on your match! Open your pan!'

Like castles of sand, the musketeer plotoons in front simply collapsed as the torrent washed over them. Men ran in fear, faces blank, eyes devoid of recognition or thought. Here and there, a knot clung together only to be rolled over like a pebble on the shore as the enemy burst upon Nehemiah and the second line.

'Present! Give fire!'

The plotoon's little salvee crashed out in a billow of smoke. But it was pitiful against the great charging mass. A horse crashed to the ground, sliding into the front rank in a welter of whinnying, shouting and thrashing legs. The rest flowed around their sides in a torrent that enveloped them in smacking pistols, iron hooves, slicing steel and dust.

Within just a few brief moments it was over. The horse still kicked and whinnied, writhing on the ground in front of them. Nehemiah looked around at what was left of the plotoon. Barely half of them stood with him and Captain Bennett, thirty red-coated musketeers lost in a sea of choking dust and grit far from their nearest regiment. 'Stay close!' he called to them. 'Hold together! God protect us but we are lost if we run!'

They looked at each other as the low thunder started again and the ground shook. Nehemiah gripped his halberd in both hands, its spike and axe-head searching the dust cloud around them. And then it was upon them: a second wave of cavaliers breaking through the haze to crash over them.

He lunged at bared teeth and frothing muzzle. He swung his halberd blindly at the beast's rider. Bone crunched, cloth tearing, the horseman pitching sideways, screaming, dragging the animal down with him.

But the beast would not stay down. It raised itself thrashing at the ground to leap forward. Sweating flank, leather harness and flailing hooves cannoned into Nehemiah. He was knocked down, trampled, kicked as the horse careered off, dragging its fallen rider by one stirrup.

Spitting blood and snot into the dust, Nehemiah dragged himself up on trembling limbs. He was shaken, battered, but he was alive. God had shielded him from the worst. His head throbbed. His leg barely carried him. It was ripped and bleeding, torn by iron-clad hooves. Picking up his bloodied halberd, he took an unsteady step.

'Nehemiah, thank God, you are alive!' Captain Bennett held him. 'But you are hurt. Oh my poor boy, you are injured.'

'Please sir, help the others. We must get back to the regiment. I will follow.'

'Yes, yes of course. Come now, my brave boys! Help each other. God will preserve us.' Captain Bennett fussed over the dozen musketeers that were left to carry and drag each other stumbling towards the Parliamentary line in the trail of dust and debris left by the cavalier charge.

———

William Bennett looked back to see Nehemiah limping behind, his halberd gripped as a crutch. How could he have left him? Nehemiah who, like his biblical namesake, was ready to embrace any task, the one he hoped would marry his own daughter, his Rebecca; Nehemiah who had been his constant support, the backbone of his company, his Israelite; his Nehemiah.

Too late William heard the drumming of hooves. Too late he saw the lone cavalier gallop out of the gloom. 'Nehemiah!'

———

The sword carved down and back across Nehemiah's face. The blade sliced viciously to sever nose, crush cheekbone and expose flesh in a great bloody flap.

Smashed backward, he rolled in the dirt again, clasped his face in his hands as blood ran through dust-caked fingers. He felt no pain, heard nothing, only numb emptiness and the thump of his own pulse. Captain Bennett. . . others. . . gathered around him. . . calling to him. They must leave him, save themselves. He could go no further. He would not see Canaan.

## IX

# Kineton

*Ralph Reeve*

**The King's left wing, a quarter to three o'clock**

Even before Prince Rupert's trumpet call reached them, the one thousand horses of the left wing sensed the moment and heaved forward. Ralph fought to rein in his own stamping, side-stepping beast, almost dropping his rapier. He sat low, thighs gripped, to keep the animal inline. Calls to keep the squadrons in check were useless. Weeks of drill book were thrown away, the shouts of the older professionals lost in the clamour and shunting.

Within moments, the dam broke and the great wave of steel and horseflesh lurched forward. They should have started at a walk but bounced straight into an awkward trot. They should have maintained the trot for longer, but within a furlong they jerked into a canter. They should have held themselves in tight ranks, knee to knee, at a steady canter until the last moment, as Rupert had told them. But Ralph thanked God when they broke ranks and he could give up the struggle of holding his big horse back. It was almost impossible with a sword in one hand.

With a few snatched trumpet notes, the whole line burst into a welter of galloping horsemen, all racing for the honour of being first amongst the King's enemies. The ditch and stream at the base of the vale were taken at a flying leap. Somewhere up the far slope a hare bolted from the stubble to streak across the line.

Ralph gave in and let his horse have its head. Fuck it. He was damned if he was going to be the last to reach the Parliamentary line. He simply let the big horse carry him on, grinning at the sheer power of the moment. He did not care that he was sweating hard, clenching the saddle with aching legs. He would not have missed this ride for the world.

They slowed a little as they crested the low ridge, yet to come to grips with the rebel horsemen. What was he supposed to do then? Cut and thrust. Jesus, it was difficult enough staying in the saddle. And then they were on top of the ridge. But where were the rebel horse? The ground in front was empty. Had they ridden up the wrong slope in their excitement? Essex's foot were there, stretched out along the ridge to his right.

Ahead, a great dust cloud – the rebel horse were in the dust cloud! They had broken! They were fleeing from the cavalier charge – just two hundred yards ahead.

They surged on again in pursuit. Only now there was no vestige of order. Every man and horse rode to outpace friend and foe in one great race towards the village of Kineton, a mile and a half beyond – two thousand horses drumming out their thunder in a terrifying steeplechase.

Ralph was lost in a choking cloud of kicked up soil, turf and stones. Dust filled his nose, gritted his mouth. The crash of pistols punctured the roar of hooves as hunter and hunted closed; the whoops and yells of those in pursuit of quarry all around him.

He should try to cut or thrust at one of the figures ahead. But they came and went so suddenly in the fog. He could not be sure who he cut. Besides, it was as much as he could do to stay in the saddle.

His horse missed a step. He grabbed at its mane, almost unseated – a lane across their path, the horse leaping its width. Fuck! It was all he could do to hang on! He let himself be born along, horse and rider terrified, desperate to avoid the rougher ground and the men and kicking horses that fell. Neither could stop in the mad charge.

And then they were plunging down a steep slope into a river bed, his horse floundering in the dank stinking ooze and thick reeds. They leapt clear. He slashed at a fruit tree barring his way. Another horse cannoned into them from behind, sent him lurching forward. He was free of the tree. A small gate. . . he spurred the horse at it. It burst open and he was clattering up a steep village street. Kineton! Fuck, let there be some rebels left here to fight.

A rider ahead. . . the man rode low over his horse's neck, Essex's orange sash across his back. He turned left at the church, disappeared from view. Ralph urged his horse forward the last few yards to the crossroads, the rider in view again.

Reining in hard, hooves skittered on the compacted road. One gauntleted hand fumbling with sword and reins, he reached for a pistol, grasped it, brought it up.

His finger curled around the trigger and squeezed. The serrated wheel spun against flint, sparks scattering into the priming pan. A jet of white smoke, the long barrel whipped back and up as the charge erupted. But the shot was futile. The chances of hitting a galloping rider at thirty paces, from a dancing horse, were minimal. The ball went wide and high to smack useless into the side of a house. The rider galloped on, unscathed, out of the village.

He had fired a shot in battle. But it was a stupid act. Not one that he could be proud of, not the tavern boast he'd wished for. He slid the pistol back into its holster and turned his horse away, back towards the village.

Cavaliers filled the wide street beside the church. Had they seen his foolishness? Thank God, not one seemed to take any notice. They were all intent on plundering the carriages and wagons that lined the road, pulling down cases, forcing locks, smashing boxes, ripping open valises, spilling their contents into the street. Amongst them were the beribboned uniforms of the King's own Lifeguard of Horse – the Troop of Show. Prince Rupert's charge must have broken the other wing. With the field cleared of rebel horse, surely the day was theirs? Lord Digby and the horse regiments of the second line would be free to cut down Essex's foot.

Thank God! They had done their duty. He could savour the moment.

Ralph pushed his way back through the throng still pouring into the village. Coming towards him was a beaming Clem. Clem's face was ruddy, sweat-streaked, dust-caked. They both grinned. He too must be plastered in grit. It chafed at his collar.

'There you be, Master Ralph! Thought I'd bloody lost you in that there orchard. What a ride! Bloody marvellous! Reckon that were better than a day's huntin'. Mind, that there river were a bugger. I thought you were a-goin arsey-varsey in it. Weren't so steady meself. Did you see that hare run? Lord, he must'a had the fright of his life! Mind, I doubt no good'll come on it.'

'Clem, have you been behind me all the way?'

'Well, what could I say to your father if I lost you?'

'Thank you. And, yes, I nearly came a cropper in that fuck-ing river. Mind, Breda here kept his head and kept our footing. He is a bright horse.' Ralph leaned forward and smacked the veined, sweat soaked neck of the big horse that had carried him across the battlefield. 'Clem? Did you see me shoot?'

'No. Lost you in that bloody orchard. Got stuck in an apple tree we did and all. Did you get your man?'

'No, Clem. He got away.'

'Never mind. I reckon there be plenty of others what missed their man. Seems like a few o' they is more interested in a bit of somint else.' With a flick of his chin, Clem indicated the scene of chaos in front of them.

They watched the lock of another strongbox being shot open and its contents spilled into the street. To the annoyance of the gentleman rifling it, it contained only dirty linen.

'Surprisin' really when they do say that our lords of the Troop of Show are worth a hundred thousand pounds a year between them. I didn't think they'd need to go a-pillagin' and a-plunderin'. Mind, that there draught hoss is a beauty.'

Surely, this couldn't be how it should end, with gentle-men grubbing around in their enemy's baggage for a childish trinket or keepsake. The battle could not be over so quickly. Where was Luke? He would know – he always knew. 'Clem, did you see where Luke went?'

'He pulled up outside o' the village. I saw he along with Captain Smith. Back there before that damn river.'

'Luke's with Captain Smith?' Fuck. He had promised him-self to stick close to Smith. He had let himself be carried away. 'Come on, we should get back to them.'

They pushed their way back through the press of riders

that still clattered up the road into the village to cross the ford. An armoured man sprawled face down amidst flattened bulrushes and trampled ooze.

'Poor bugger.' Clem shook his head at the fine mare standing in the muddy stream, one leg twitching, a hock broken.

There, beside the road, was Captain Smith, a knot of horsemen with him. Luke was there, Corporal Nisbet and Colonel Lord Grandison. Before he and Clem could reach them, they were shunted aside by a fresh wave of horsemen cantering down the road to splash across the ford and into the village. The leading cavalier waved his feathered hat as he passed. 'I hope you have left something for us, Grandison!'

It was Lord Digby. The horsemen joining the plunder of Kineton were the King's reserve. Surely, this was not right. The battle could not yet be over. Lord Digby should be charging the rebel foot. They could not all have broken, there was no sign of them running. They must still be standing.

Captain Smith was with Lord Grandison, flushed red and gesticulating with his sword back towards Edgehill. 'Sir, my Lord Digby has charged with the reserve. We must return to the field with all haste. You must rally the regiment.'

'Damn it, Smith, I know my business even if my Lord Digby does not! I will take what we have now and see what can be done. You will gather what you can of our people and join me on that ridge.'

Smith wheeled his horse around with a curt assent. 'My Lord.'

Seeing Ralph and Clem, Corporal Nisbet let fly. 'An' where in Christ's name have ye been Mister Reeve? An ye think yersel a soldier, laddie? Ye'll stick by yer officers in future.'

Lord Grandison was already moving, back up the lane towards the battle. Turning in his saddle he called for his standard and for discipline. 'Mister Musgrave, catch up! Get yourself behind me. God's blood! Corporal Nisbet, kindly send my cornet to the front and get the rest of these gentlemen in some sort of order.'

Ralph, Luke and Clem greeted each other with a nod and an uncertain smile as they fell in behind their colonel. They followed him back towards the noise and smoke of a real battle.

## X

# Panic Fear

*Anthony Sedley*

*Parliamentary left wing, ten minutes to three o'clock*

Anthony Sedley stood with Brooke's purple-coated iron-workers listening to the sound of battle. He and his young musketeers had stood for near an hour whilst the gunners laboured over their great cannon, belching fire and iron across the vale, palls of dirty sulphurous smoke drifting back to writhe through the ranks. Every now and then a cannonball shrieked overhead or ploughed into the slope in front in a shower of earth and grit.

But the battle was changing. Great clouds of dust marked where the enemy horse charged on either flank.

The dust settled on empty fields, fields that had been lined with squadrons of Parliamentary horse. Both wings had disappeared, swept away. All that remained were scattered groups of musketeers that staggered after them. On their low ridge, the foot battalions were now left to face the King's army alone, their flanks unguarded.

A murmur ran through the ranks. The young musketeers were shaken by what they saw. The murmuring turned to open alarm as word spread that some of their foot were running.

In the centre of the Parliamentary line, three battalions collapsed into a welter of men running towards Kineton and the rear, first Cholmley's bluecoats, then Mandeville's and Charles Essex's. The enemy had not touched them. But they were gripped by their own panic fear. Minutes before, these had been regiments of men boasting of their readiness to fight for liberty and reformation. Now they were fearful children bent only on saving themselves.

Shit! Was this it? Was this the end of the rebellion? Was the whole army going to run, to throw down their weapons, to give up their cause and flee?

It was only thirty miles to Birmingham. With a clear path, he could be home by tomorrow nightfall. He could hold his wife and babies again, kiss them, wrap his arms around them.

But what about his file, his merry lads? He couldn't leave Zach, or Harry, Alf, Tom, Will. He couldn't even leave Isaac. Could he get them all home?

And then what? They would be hunted down, pulled from their hovels one by one to be hanged as rebels. He would rather die here, now, than be dragged away in chains like a common criminal. Not that. Not in front of his babies. If he was caught, they too would be taken. Taken, transported, sold as indentured slaves to some bastard plantation in Ireland or the Americas.

He must stand. They must stand and fight, stand against tyranny and oppression. Better to stand and die fighting for their rights, for their freedom, for their wives and children, brother workers and the common man. Better to die fighting for the rebellion, the rebellion that must triumph in the end, that must restore the natural laws of man. To die fighting for freedom!

A great hole had been left in the centre of the Parliamentary line. They had to stop the rot – stop the panic fear. He looked for his captain.

Freeborn John stepped forward. 'Stand straight in your files!'

The murmuring stopped. The drums beat, every man stiffening at their call.

'Advance your arms. Musketeers. . . shoulder your arms!'

Anthony brought his musket up over his shoulder, butt, rest and smouldering match in the left hand.

'Brooke's Regiment will move to the right in column of divisions! To the right hand. . . turn!'

Every man turned in unison.

'By your left marker. . . march!'

They, Brooke's Levellers, were marching across the front. The Earl of Essex's own Regiment marched with them. They would fill the gap in the centre.

But it left the line stretched thin. If the King's foot advanced now, could they hold them or would the line snap? Would his band of merry lads be swept away?

Was this how it was to end – the end of their dream of an England free from tyranny? Would they die here, this day, fighting for their freedom?

Or could they turn back the tide?

# XI

# March on, Boys!

*Robbie Needham*

### The King's centre, three o'clock

'O Lord! Thou knowest how busy I must be this day. If I forget Thee, do not forget me.'

Robbie Needham grinned at the simple soldier's prayer offered up by Sir Jacob Astley. The King's Sergeant-Major-General of Foot spoke loudly enough for those in the near ranks to hear. He would stick by them. He would share in their danger. But the general's next words took the smile from the big miner's face.

'March on, boys!'

As the old man stepped out towards the rebel line a single drummer beside him beat the call to march, a long drum roll followed by eight strident bars. Even before it finished, the call was taken up by the drummers of every company along the Royalist line, three hundred drums crashing out the order to advance. The hairs on the back of Robbie's neck prickled, a surge of heat coursing through his veins at the staccato call.

The drumming ended as abruptly as it started. For the

62

briefest moment, as the noise rolled away, the army held its breath. And then orders barked along the whole line. Robbie focused on those meant for him, those given by his own lieutenant-colonel. 'Battaile, advance your... arms!'

As one, the seven hundred men of the King's Lifeguard hefted their weapons into the air. Robbie grasped the butt of his pike in his right hand, the base of the shaft braced between arm, flank and shoulder, its eighteen-foot length rising vertically to the steel tip overhead.

'Ranks, open. To your open... order!'

Each rank stepped forward until six clear feet were between them.

'Stand straight in your files. Make even your ranks!'

Robbie checked that he was standing directly behind his file leader. He looked to see that he was level with the man three feet to his right. Each man carried on the motion until every rank stood in line with their right-hand marker.

And then came the order that they'd prepared for but never really expected: the order to advance upon an army raised by the Parliament of England.

'The King's Lifeguard will advance. By your right... march!'

They stepped off, the drums beating out a steady rate, seventy paces to the minute. Six feet in front, marched cousin Hal.

A few files to the right swayed the Royal Standard, the King's own colour and call to arms, a great swallow-tailed banner on a staff topped with gold, crimson silk, cross of St George and the royal arms in gold braid. An embroidered hand pointed to a crown and the motto *Give unto Caesar his Due*, a message to a parliament that withheld ancient taxes, obstructed, remonstrated, abused its privilege and dared to impeach an anointed king. Robbie kept station with it as he marched.

He'd not thought it would come to this. He'd thought that they would march the King back to London, that they'd arrest the self-serving shits in Parliament and round up the pissing lawyers, merchants and tossers that backed them and their schemes. He'd thought that once they'd put the King back on the throne, he would be free to return to the Peaks with money in his pocket and the King's promise to end the bloody lead tithe. He would love to see an end to Lord pissing Rutland's privileges and an end to his bloody deep-mine – even better: to see the bastard behind bars, grovelling in that stinking cell in Derby gaol.

But now they were marching into battle against men, muskets and cannon raised by Parliament. He'd not volunteered for this. But he'd not back down now. He was a free-miner, a man of his word. He was damned if he would turn in front of fellow miners. And he was buggered if he was backing down in front of anybody else. He and his like were not soft. Others would have to back down first.

Besides, nothing could stop them now. How could hirelings paid by a rebel parliament stand against the will of the people? Their bloody cannon could belch and fart as much as they liked. They would not stop him.

The power and rhythm of the march swept him on. Dry stubble buckled and snapped under every step. Their scant little patches of oats and peas were nothing like these great fields. He'd never thought to leave the Peaks. Now he was marching across England, an army of tiny golden pikemen underfoot; he strode over them like a giant, his miner's half-boots, coated in the rich red earth and clay of the vale, crushing all resistance.

He'd heard tell from the old soldiers how pikes could shatter when battalions crashed together in a push of pike. The great ash shafts would splinter under the weight of a thousand men pushing and stabbing at each other. Would it come to that? Surely, the bloody rebels would run first. He gripped his own thick pike shaft firmly and strode on.

Ahead of them on the slight rise, the Parliamentary cannon flung fire, smoke and scything iron balls. Everything from little three-quarter-pound robinets to the thundering twelve-pound balls of two great demi-culverins was now hurled at the King's foot.

Most cannon balls simply shrieked overhead. Some ploughed into the soft earth ahead of the advancing line before ricocheting over their heads in a cloud of dust and raining stone. The dust filled nostrils, chafed at sweating necks and left its bitter taste upon parched lips and throats. A few balls passed low enough to scatter a file, their thundering vortex sucking the very air from the lungs of those below. Men were left gasping for breath on their knees. But, as the distance closed, more cannon balls hit their mark to plough through the ranks. Where iron struck flesh, it smashed all in its path to a bloody pulp, tossing carcasses and severed limbs aside. Flesh and bone did nothing to slow its momentum.

As they crested the Parliamentary ridge, the drums changed. Now they hammered out the more urgent call of the Preparative. This was the order to make ready to engage the enemy. Again, orders followed the drum call, shouted at the pace of the march. 'Ranks! Close to your. . . order!'

Now they closed up behind the man in front so that only three feet separated them front and back, left and right. It was more difficult to see the ground. Men cursed as they stumbled forward over plough, ridge and furrow intent on keeping up, on keeping their place in the ranks.

Then it hit them. The first volley crashed out from the musket blocks of the Parliamentary line. A great wall of lead rent the air, smashed into the advancing line. They faltered at the blow, every man checking his pace. It was as if, as a single body, they received a punch to the chest.

But they did not stop. Men cursed and swore under their breath. The wounded screamed out their pain. But most simply pulled their heads into their chests, hunched their shoulders and pressed on. Each man was glad to be spared, wanting to get the ordeal over with, even if it meant closing with the enemy.

Then came a second volley, and a third. Each sent more cursing and crying to the rear. More of the hated musket balls passed over their heads, each one a lethal ounce of lead. With each volley, they clattered through the stand of pike shafts above them in a shower of splinters that cut faces, eyes and necks. The noise was like a boy's stone through hazel twigs. But this was no child's game.

Almost unconsciously, Robbie counted the paces between volleys. As each volley approached, his mind blocked out thoughts of the closing battle, focused instead on keeping pace in the thick rich soil that sucked at his boots.

The fifth volley crashed into them in another hail of splinters and curses. Their file leader spun, twisted, pitched forward, his pike clattering to the ground. Screaming, the young man clutched at his chest, shattered bone and torn sinew bubbling through ripped cloth. A vicar's son, he had a place in the front rank on account of his going to grammar school. It should have gone to a stronger man. The boy clutched at his boot, face upturned, writhing in agony, pleading, gasping. Shit! The poor bugger did not deserve that. He would give anything now to see the lad spared.

He and cousin Hal must move forward to fill the gap. But Hal stumbled, faltered at the sight of the boy falling in front of him. He kept turning to look back, as if he thought the lad would get to his feet, take his place again. 'Stop gawpin, ye nesh bugger, and git goin!' Robbie yelled. 'Hal! Shift yer arse and fill t' bloody gap!'

As they moved forward, Robbie glimpsed the battalion waiting for them on the ridge, a blue-coated regiment. Word ran through the ranks that it was Sir William Constable's Regiment – Yorkshiremen.

A hundred yards from the rebel line, the drums thrashed out the call to Battaile. The orders flowed faster now as officers urged the pikes to close in, to form a tight mass that could not be broken. 'Pikes! Files close to your centre. To your close... order!'

They closed together as they marched, until each man brushed against those left and right.

'Pikes! Port your... pikes!'

Robbie swung his pike forward, held it high over Hal's head, left arm straining to support the weight of the shaft as they marched, right arm stretched behind, forcing the base down.

'Pikes! Files close to your centre. To your closest... order!'

They closed even tighter, each man wedged between those left and right. He focused on keeping step with the drum. A stride out of time could send a file crashing to the ground, break the block.

Still volleys rang out. He'd counted seven. One more yet to come. Finally, the last of eight volleys crashed into them to leave more smashed bleeding bodies, screaming and curses. Thank God, he and Hal were spared.

The smoke from the last volley cleared; heart thumping, his breath quickened. Were they going to march straight through the Parliamentary line? Only forty feet separated them. And then the drums stopped. The Lifeguard halted.

'Pikes! Charge your. . . pikes!'

Their pikes dropped to the level. Right arm straight back, butt at shoulder height, Robbie looked along the shaft, past Hal to the steel tip and the rebel pikemen beyond. Their pikes waited already at the charge.

'Pikes! Ranks close forward. To your closest. . . order!'

This was the order to lock themselves together, to form a single mass of flesh, wood and iron for the coming push of pikes. The front rank leaned back as those behind shoved forward. Robbie wedged his shoulder against Hal. Four more ranks behind forced him forward, air crushed from body and clothing by the impact – a single bestial grunt rose with the stench of stale cloth and warm rank sweat.

In the second rank now, he looked out between the broad-brimmed hats, caps and heads of those in front. His pike lay over Hal's shoulder, its tip amongst the layers ranged ahead of them. The pikes of the ranks behind ran past his right cheek and over his head.

The King's Lifeguard faced the men of Constable's in defiant silence, their pike tips separated by just a few feet. A pike shaft quivered, wobbled. Then another, fear and exertion shaking it uncontrollably. Weeks of training had brought them to the point of charge. But almost none had experienced what came next. Were they just going to stare each other down?

The strain and tension could not hold. The silence broke with shouts from Constable's officers for civil and parliamentary rights, for 'Magna Carta!' The King's officers yelled out 'Prerogative!' and 'For King and Country!'

'God marches with us!' came back.

'Go preach in a crab-tree – pooritan!'

Laughter burst from the ranks of the Lifeguard at this popular taunt from a common soldier. It only stoked the slur, fanned the anger. The exchange fell to a slanging match of ever courser insult, invective, obscenity and northern *flyting*, as tempers, prejudices and old county rivalries flared along the line, both regiments working themselves to fever pitch.

'Cavalier curs! Papists!'

'Ah'm no papist. Yo rebel dogs!'

'Go home thou kiss-arse lackeys! Thou dim-witted slaves!'

'Go back to yer middens yo limp pricks. Yer wives and mothers itch for stiffer cocks than yers. Yo piss dribbling cunnies!'

'Come on then, thou pox-smitten sons of whores!'

'Lerrus at the bastards! Lerrus at the bastards!'

Over the din, drums rattled, fresh orders rang out, this time for the wings of musketeers on either side to form three ranks, to prepare to fire as one.

'Musketeers! Make ready to give fire by salvee. Half files double your ranks to the left! Front rank. . . kneel! Rear rank close forward to your close order! Make ready!'

Over the shouts and rattle of their own musketeers, Robbie heard orders yelled in the ranks opposite – the same orders. Both their own and Constable's were making ready to fire a single volley into each other's ranks. Almost in unison the final commands rang out.

'Present! Give Fire!'

For a moment, the tight packed ranks stood in deafened silence, blinding gun smoke and thumping ears. Surely both sides could not still be standing. One must have been blown away.

The pall of musket smoke drifted slowly back through the enemy ranks. They still stood firm. A growl spread through the ranks. It quickly overwhelmed the curses and whimpers of the wounded. And then the growl turned to a great roar as the two pike blocks surged toward each other.

Those in the front ranks tried to hold the mass back, fighting desperately to fence aside the layered pike tips surging at them. But the rear ranks shoved them forward until, with a splintering crash and grunt, the two blocks of warriors collided in one great scrum.

Most pikes were forced up over the heads and bodies of their opponents, forming a tangled broken roof. But some hit home. The tip of a pike passed between Robbie and the next man, grazing across the small of his back. His jerkin ripped. It was bloody close to his kidney. Thank fuck it did not gore him. He could move neither left nor right, forward nor back.

These bloody Yorkshiremen wore helmets. And they had iron breastplates, tassets, gauntlets and all! They were armoured, protected. While he and most of the Lifeguard had only an old leather miner's jerkin.

A pike head jabbed in front of his face. He only just managed to lift his head as it slid past splitting his ear, gashing his right arm. Some bastard knew how to work his pike. The long steel tip and riveted langets slid back and forth with evil intent between him and Hal. Robbie forced his head back to keep his face away as the great spike thrust past again.

But he could do nothing to stop it as it ran across the back of his cousin's neck. A leather miner's cap protected Hal's skull. But it left the nape of his neck exposed to the searching steel.

As it ran forward again, the tip gouged a deep gash across the muscle between shoulder and neck. Each time after, the riveted shaft tore a little deeper. He and Hal cursed, swore, heaved and blindly worked their own pikes to stop the relentless cutting.

At last, he found resistance and, with a final jab, he felt the tip of his pike pierce cloth or flesh. And then the evil pike was gone. Gone to lick its wounds or force its way into another weak spot. Gone to seek and pierce other exposed flesh.

They struggled to keep their footing as each battalion tried to overwhelm the other by shear brute force. Each knew that the one that gave way would be exposed to vengeful slaughter. Men yelled, cursed and grunted as they heaved against each other, locked in a great sweating, bloody and vicious struggle to survive.

Here and there, a man's will faded and gave out. Scared, crushed and broken, wounded and exhausted men were held in place by the press. Those that slipped to the ground were kicked and trampled in the struggle to stay upright and stay alive.

Hal was bleeding badly from the wound to his neck. The blood ran thick and bright over his collar to form a great dark coagulation on Robbie's tunic and sleeve. Every time Hal fought to keep himself upright, the exposed neck sinews and ruptured veins bled more. His cousin's body slumped lower. Robbie shouted, encouraged, pleaded, but he couldn't keep Hal's head from sagging. Hal couldn't hold out much longer. None of them could carry on this mad struggle for much longer. One side or the other must break.

And then, almost by mutual consent, the two battalions began to pull apart. The two pike blocks dragged themselves backwards like a pair of angry wounded beasts. Each one retired a few yards, out of pike range, to stand leaning on pike shafts, butts on the ground, exhausted.

But, as they separated, the front ranks were exposed again to danger. Most could do no more than drag their pikes away. Here and there, a man had the strength and anger to strike out, to settle a score, to lunge again at an opponent. A wounded or exhausted man caught on his own in the open was at the mercy of the driving pike tips of those still with a lust to kill.

Hal could barely stand, let alone wield his eighteen-foot pike. He couldn't defend himself. Those opposite knew it too. *No! Not Hal.* Hal groaned, sagged, a pike head driving into his shoulder, another into his groin.

'No!' Anger burst in Robbie. He forced his way forward, through the front rank, pike swinging, beating away the shafts that jabbed at their prey. 'You bastards!'

One of them staggered back, dropped his weapon in shock. But the other stood, trying to pull his pike from Hal's twisted pelvis.

Robbie swung his quivering pike back. The bastard went down, swept from his feet, arms flailing. He thrust forward, pike head grating over iron breastplate, smacking into ex-posed throat, sinking under the man's jaw, deep into the base of his skull, forcing his helmet back into the soft earth.

Hal's crumpled frame was dragged back to be sent stumbling down the slope in the hope of finding a sur-geon. Robbie now stood in the front rank of the Lifeguard, bitter tears streaming down his grimy face. The big man leaned on his pike and gulped cool air into aching lungs. He shivered, his shirt and jerkin wet with sweat and his cousin's blood.

Between the pike blocks lay the body of the man he'd just killed. A pool of thick dark blood and mucus drained from the gaping hole in the man's throat, from his mouth, nostrils and from under his helmet. It formed a great shimmering pool amongst the stubble.

The heat and anger drained from Robbie's body until his legs shook. Without warning, hot sour vomit filled his throat to spew from mouth and nostrils.

# XII

# Holding the Line

*Anthony Sedley*

**Parliamentary centre, a quarter past three o'clock**

'Make Ready!'

Anthony Sedley pushed his left leg forward and brought the heavy musket up across his chest. He checked that his match was still fixed firm in the lock and blew on its smouldering end. It glowed bright and hot. A half-squeeze of the trigger, the glowing ember came down over the priming pan cover. The musket was ready.

'Front rank. . . present!'

One last blow on the spluttering match, flick open the cover, priming powder and touch hole bared ready. He lowered the long barrel onto the rest in his left hand, gripped the stock and pulled the musket butt into his shoulder. He squinted along the barrel. The centre brigade of the King's foot came on up the gentle ploughed slope towards them, their drums hammering out a steady pace. The lead battalion was now clear to see, company colours of green silk waving over its pike block. A whisper rang along the line. They were Fielding's Regiment, dumb farmers from Hereford.

He did not wish to kill fellow commoners, those that earned their crust through their own labour. But these simple country fools were the lackeys of a tyrant king, his Norman lords and bloody gentry. They had to be stopped. He and Brooke's ironworkers had marched across the Parliamentary line to plug the gap. Now they must hold the line or else their cause and liberty were lost. They and their families would be slaves forever.

Anthony stood in the front rank. He and the other file leaders would fire the first volley. He must not hesitate. He must show the way for the young musketeers that followed in the ranks behind, for his lads. He waited for the order. Like those beside him, he hated the waiting. But he trusted his captain. Freeborn John would judge the right moment, the moment when their first volley would have greatest effect but leave room for the other ranks to add theirs into the advancing enemy.

He calmed his breathing, looked for an aiming mark. There was little chance of hitting a man at eighty yards. But it felt good to aim at an over-dressed shit in the front rank of pikes. Feathered hat, silver lace, belly and partisan marked him as an officer – a rich pig. The front rank was packed with them, eager to please their king. They would be the first to fall.

Leaning in, he pulled the butt tighter. He was ready. He was ready in the name of liberty and freedom for the common man. He would fight for his rights, for his children's future, for his poor sweet Marian, fight to end tyranny and oppression.

Finally, Freeborn John's voice rang out. 'Front rank. . . give fire!'

Anthony held his breath, braced and squeezed the trigger

arm. The glowing match thrust down, a jet of sparks from the pan and the musket exploded with a brutal kick.

He did not see whether he hit his mark. Thick choking smoke rolled back to envelope them, his eyes and nostrils burning with the stench of saltpetre. There was no chance to see if the pig had fallen before the order to make way for the next rank.

'Volley firing by ranks! Front rank to the rear. . . march!'

A turn to the right, he marched back between the files. A nod of encouragement for each of his lads as he passed, he searched their eyes for weakness, for lack of will, for failure: Harry, skinny Zach, Alf, Tom, dozy Isaac, a gap where that shit Lorimer should have been and Will. Only Isaac looked shaky, but Will would watch him.

Taking a place at the rear, Anthony prepared to reload his musket. This was no time for the slow postures of the parade ground. Each man must know and perform his own drill. The sergeants only had time for shortened battle orders.

'Rear rank, make ready!'

He let his body move mechanically. Let instinct perform the drill beaten into him, honed with hours of practise. With each action, he stepped one rank forward. Ahead each rank presented, fired and wheeled away to the rear to reload.

Finally, he was ready. As the last volley crashed out, the ranks behind caught up and the clatter of powder flasks and sticks on steel barrels died away. The thick smoke rolled slowly back. Fielding's green regiment were barely thirty yards from them.

The oncoming ranks were battered and ragged, but they pressed forward, now with levelled pikes and frenzied drumming. Shit! Would these pikes drive them from the field?

They could not hope to stop them with only the butt end

of a musket. He looked towards his captain. Had they failed? Were they to be slaves?

But Freeborn John had timed it well. As the last rank returned their scouring sticks his clear voice rang out with the order for one final great salvo. 'Musketeers. . . make ready to give fire by salvee. Half files double your ranks to the left!'

The rearmost ranks stepped left and forward to form three ranks. Anthony turned, gave a nod to Tom now beside him, Izzy and Will behind him.

'Front rank, kneel. Third rank close forward to your close order!'

Anthony knelt, left arm braced against left leg.

'Present!'

A last blow on the match, flick open the pan, butt into the shoulder. Through the shimmer of heat from the barrel, he found the fat laced officer again. He aimed low. Better to compensate for the musket's kick. He aimed at the fat shit's groin. This time the bastard would fall!

'Give fire!'

With one deafening roar the two hundred and fifty muskets of Brooke's left wing exploded in unison. Anthony's head rang with the concussion of the muzzles above and beside him. He barely heard the order to reload. He worked feverishly, preparing for the coming clash, as the dense smoke rolled back.

But the salvo of lead had done its work. Its weight and power had stopped Fielding's charge. They staggered to a halt, front rank punctured with bleeding broken men, a great groan rising from their mass. The fat silvered pig was on his knees in the bare earth.

As the last of the smoke cleared, the power of their salvo became clear, plain. A murmur rank through the ranks of Brooke's boys, turning to a shout then a defiant yell that drowned out all others. The young Levellers of Birmingham, Coventry and Warwick shouted their victory, shouted their rebellion out loud.

That yell only died with the shrill call of trumpets and the rumble of heavy horses moving behind them.

# XIII

## *Ei Dderbyn yn Ŵr*

### *John Benion*

#### *The King's left, twenty minutes past three o'clock*

'Give fire!'

John Benion could not help closing his eyes. He knew that he shouldn't. He was supposed to aim his musket, to keep his shot low. But he could not help it. He was frightened. He shut his eyes and squeezed the trigger, bracing himself for the terrifying blast and bruising pain of the recoil.

On either side of him, the line of muskets exploded in a deafening crash. Choking, stinking, sulphurous smoke enveloped them, burning his eyes. But his shoulder did not hurt so much this time and he hadn't wet his breeches again. The little squirts of piss that came with the first volleys had stopped. Perhaps he was getting used to it. Perhaps he'd make a soldier after all.

Passing between the files, John grinned sheepishly. He could not stop it. He knew it was inane, stupid, but it covered his fear. Now he could not stop it. None of them grinned back. They seemed to look past him. Perhaps they were scared too? He would show them.

79

He would show his nagging wife and ale-sodden in-laws that he was a man, a man who could no longer be pushed around. A tailor from the Shropshire village of Newtown, he'd sold his stuff to buy a soldier's musket. It cost him twenty-one shillings – all that he had. Trade was poor and enclosure forced them off the commons to scratch a living from odd jobs.

His wife laughed at him when he told her that he was going to muster, to be a soldier. Her laughter turned to anger and swearing when he marched away the next day. It wasn't the reaction he'd wanted. But he would show her. She would do as she was told when he returned a hero.

John was now a musketeer in Sir Thomas Salusbury's Regiment of Foot. He hadn't thought to join any other regiment than the one quartered in his village. They were tough Welshmen mostly and John found it difficult to be accepted. He knew that the big men billeted in his cottage laughed at him. They called him *pidyn bach* – little prick.

He came in from his workroom one afternoon to hear his wife laughing and drinking with them. She laughed at him when he questioned her. But he would show her and he would show them. Some of them did not even own a musket, only old billhooks and staves. He knew they were jealous of his musket. He would show them. If only he could stop wincing and squirting.

John turned to take his place at the rear of the file.

'Make ready!'

He still dreaded this moment. No matter how many times they'd drilled and practised, he still found it difficult to master the complicated postures and motions needed to load his musket. It did not come naturally. The more he tried to think about it, the more his mind went numb. It was not like stitching a smock. That needed patience; a thing not to be rushed. He was never able to load his musket quickly enough. He dreaded the inevitable shout of the sergeant.

He brought the heavy musket across his chest and blew to clear the pan of residue. He fumbled for the flask at his side before priming and carefully shutting the cover that protected the pan. He remembered to shake off the loose grains of powder and to give another blow to be sure. Balancing the musket and match in his left hand, he searched the bandolier across his front for the next full wooden powder bottle. He gripped it awkwardly, struggling to force the lid up and off with thumb and forefinger. Carefully he poured the dark gritty powder into the barrel.

'Not you, Benion, you cock!' The sergeant's hand gripped his shoulder from behind as the big man yelled in his ear. 'Look at your fucking match! It's fucking out. Again! How many fucking times do I have to tell you? Keep the fucking thing alight!'

John turned to look up at the big sergeant.

'You let the fucking match go out, again. You misfired, again! Fuck knows, we are hard pressed enough as it is without cocks like you not even firing at the fucking rebels. Jesus! You still don't get it do you? Your musket is still fucking loaded. It didn't fire. If you load another charge and shot on top, you'll blow the fucking breech! I couldn't give a toss if you kill yourself. But I can't afford for you to go blowing anyone else up. Now, just prime the fucking thing, get a light to your match. And don't let it fucking go out again!'

# XIV

# Truth

*Francis Reeve*

*Parliamentary rear, half past three o'clock*

Praise God, at last they were to join the battle!

Francis pulled the barred faceguard of his helmet down to meet his iron breastplate. Gathering reins in his left hand, he reached forward and drew one long pistol from its holster. He rode in the front rank of Balfour's Regiment of Horse. With Stapleton's armoured cuirassiers, they had been held back in reserve, waiting for the Earl of Essex's order, champing at the bit while the battle raged around them.

But now they were moving forward in close order, knees and booted legs pressed between the flanks of their mounts. As they crested the gentle slope, they passed the purple coats of Brooke's Foot – Birmingham ironworkers, impious Levellers, their yelling coarse. . . lewd.

Left and right the battle raged, hidden in palls of gun smoke, as each army tried to push the other from the ridge. But here, in the centre of the field, God had opened the way. As the smoke rolled back from Brooke's last great salvee, it was clear that Fielding's advance had been halted in its tracks.

The King's centre brigade had lost the will to press home their attack.

The Earl of Essex had seized the moment to turn the tide. Having halted the King's foot, they would now break its centre, break them before they could reorganise. The reserve of horse would strike as a great sword and he, Francis, rode with it. For now was the time of judgement. This was the place of reckoning.

The two regiments of horsemen did not break their pace but rode on at a steady trot, Stapleton's cuirassiers swinging right against the King's Lifeguard. Balfour's rode on, straight ahead, on towards Fielding's brigade. Francis gripped his pistol, pulling back on the reins to hold his high-stepping horse in check, pressed in by those on either side. They rode on until they were barely ten yards from Fielding's ranks.

Reining in, each trooper raised his firearm. Standing high in his stirrups, over his horse's tossing head, Francis levelled the pistol. The green-coated musketeer in front of him was not the image he had envisaged of a Popish idolater. He did not look like a profane cavalier. He was a frightened farm labourer or town craftsman – some cobbler, potter or carpenter. Was it God's will that this man die? The fool stood against the righteous and true army of God. Francis took comfort in the words of the sermon before his regiment: *Here is truth. For the rider is truth!*

A ripple of fire ran along the front rank of horsemen. Francis's gauntleted finger closed around the pistol's trigger. The weapon exploded, its long barrel whipping back and up. His horse leapt, twisted, pulled, eyes wide with terror. Dropping back into the saddle, he yanked at the reins, fumbling to holster the pistol. With two hands free, he hauled the beast's neck in and down, twisting the iron bit in its mouth.

Damn the beast for its stupidity. He forced the animal back into line, barely glancing at the green-coated musketeer writhing on the ground before him. The young man flailed, croaked, clutched at his chest as he fought for breath from lungs flooding with blood. God had ordained it.

Fielding's front line recoiled in shock. Frightened men tried to force their way back through the packed ranks. Within moments, the brigade that had marched against the Parliamentary line with such determination wavered and cracked. Halted by musket fire, they could not stand firm against Balfour's horsemen firing into their ranks at point blank.

The front battalions of the brigade began to break up. Great clumps of them staggered backwards so that they lost their cohesive front. Their line was broken, gapped. Panic fear spread to the battalion in the rear. Instead of standing as a reserve and rally point, it began to melt away.

Their officers yelled, pushed and cajoled, insistent drums thrashed, colours held high, but they would not be held. They believed the day lost. Imagination amplified the cries from the front. Men ran from their attackers, ran for fear of what was to come. They ran while they thought they had the chance. They ran because others did. They ran because they knew no better.

With those around him, Francis drew his sword, its thick heavy blade rasping through the scabbard's steel mouth. There was no need for further volleys of shot. The time had come to charge home and finish the business of breaking this brigade. It would be done with the sword – *the sword of just revenge*.

## XV

# Lobsters

### *Robbie Needham*

*The Parliamentary ridge, twenty minutes to four o'clock*

Robbie Needham stood in the front rank of the King's Lifeguard. For a half hour, they'd faced Constable's Yorkshiremen in combat. All along the low ridge before Kineton, battalions continued to pour fire into each other's closely packed ranks. He stood clutching his pike shaft, his shoulder turned against the volleys of shot.

The weight of fire had slackened a little as musketeers were forced to refill their powder flasks. But neither side could yet find the will to close again to the terrifying struggle of push of pike and butt of musket. Instead, the two lines stood their ground, steadily firing volley after volley into the smoke that engulfed them.

The brutal ounce musket balls continued to shatter limbs and tear bloody holes in torsos. Those who fell victim were pulled to the rear or fell were they'd stood. The piercing fingers of death and disfigurement favoured no rank or position. Officers, sergeants and corporals fell leading the front rank alongside their neighbours, tenants and servants. Rich and poor, gentlemen, yeomen, craftsmen and labourers were all cut down.

Now and then, the rebel line appeared through the smoke, dark shapes, stark silhouettes amid smoke filled with the bright light of the lowering sun beyond. The Royal Standard still floated over the Lifeguard. It twitched – another ball plucking at the crimson silk to tear a hole. Battered and ripped, it reached above the smoke, the low sun catching on heavy gold braid.

Robbie knew what that piece of silk and gold thread meant. The loss of any colour meant humiliation. He'd heard tell how a company or troop could only regain its honour by capturing an enemy colour in battle. But the Royal Standard meant more than that. It was the King's own banner, the emblem of his army. Its raising had rallied the people to their king. It was the embodiment of their cause. Now the Lifeguard carried it for him. They had sworn to follow and guard it to the end.

*A change in the battle; something was happening to his right.* There were shouts, curses, more musketry and the snatch of a drum from the next brigade. Dark shapes moved within the wreathing smoke. Beastly shapes.

Then the drumming was gone and the screaming started. A shocked whisper ran through the ranks like an insidious wind – Fielding's Brigade had broken! They were running for their lives.

The Lifeguard were left physically shaking, minds blank to all but the thought that they may be next. Men turned left, right and behind, searching for support or a way out of the ranks.

This was panic fear: fear of the shapes in the smoke, shapes that had smashed the biggest foot brigade in the King's Army, rending a gap in the centre of the line; fear of the unknown, of the unnatural, of evil; fear of never seeing home, family or another harvest; an irrational but deadly contagion that threatened to drag the King's Lifeguard into the same oblivion.

And then they lurched sideways, files buckling. A sudden, violent, unexpected movement as their own musketeers shunted them. On the regiment's right, they pushed inwards shouting their fear and alarm.

'Stand straight in your files!'

The call to order, to face the threat, but what did they face? What lay in the smoke?

'The King's Lifeguard will prepare to receive horse!'

Once again, the drums beat out their strident call, this time the alarum. Orders followed thick and fast. 'Battaile, advance your arms! Port your arms! Pikes, charge your pikes!'

The great ash poles swung forward and down once more to form a thick, iron-tipped hedge, fear ebbing as the call to action brought certainty, unity. As long as the pikes stood close and firm, even the hardest spurring would not bring a horse to force the line.

Robbie stared along the length of his pike, searching the swirling smoke for the sudden rush of the dreaded horsemen. Bastard rebel horse! Where were their own pissing cavaliers? Constable's had even stopped their bloody firing as every man searched the smoke in silence for what lay within. He hated the waiting, hated the unknown. Even the bloody shooting was better than this.

And then they came, a troop of horse appearing out of the smoke, great shadows magnified by the sun behind them. Forty horsemen, they came out of the yellow and red sulphurous gloom, a host of shapeshifting spectres, barghest wraiths – dread shag gytrash. The riders were faceless, dark shadows in barred steel helmets. But their mounts glared, foamed and tossed their heads as they came on, red and white eyes, bared teeth, nostrils snorting the very smoke they breathed. Over all came the crash and thud of hooves and steel harness.

Suddenly wheeling away again, the host slipped back into the smoke. Had they really gone, or were they simply searching for a weakness? Where would they come from next, front, right or from behind? Faces twisted back and forth, ears straining. Were they gathering in front of them, their foul red eyes able to pierce the smoke?

Drumming hooves, crashing pistols, shouts and screams of frightened men; the musketeers to the right could not protect themselves from the volleys of shot that rode at them. They reeled under the blows, each troop riding in to fire into the mass at point blank range. Flailing, stamping beasts hacked at cowering men with mortuary sword and poleaxe.

Yelled orders, drums and screaming, the musketeers broke to scramble under the shelter of the pike stand. Two of them huddled at his feet. Another forced his way into the line behind. All breathing heavily, cursing under their breath.

Robbie looked down at the pair kneeling under his pike. One held a half-severed ear to his head, fresh blood running bright down hair and collar. 'Worr'eh you lairy buggers doin?'

'Gerrin out the way of yon bloody 'oss! We've not gorra great pissin stick like thee, you daft bugger!'

'Well, aah-do, sirrey. Robbie Needham, Castleton.'

'Al' right ahtey. John Scollins, Ilkeston. An' this 'ere is our Billie. Only ee's not prattlin much on account of one of them bastards slicing his lug 'ole.'

'Ey up! 'Ere the bastards come agin!'

Again, a troop of horsemen came out of the swirling smoke. This time they did not turn away. They rode on at a steady trot. At thirty feet, they reined in; heavy dark mounts snorting and tossing great wild-eyed heads, spume dripping from champing bits.

Each rider held a firearm levelled at the huddled mass of Lifeguard, long-barrelled pistols, harquebuses, carbines, dragon muskets and a few old fouling pieces. It did not matter. All would maim a man at this close range.

A ripple of fire ran along the front rank. The Lifeguard received it in silence broken only by the curses and shouts of those struck. There was little the rest could do for them. There was no room to let them through the packed mass and nowhere to go.

As their smoke cleared, the horsemen hauled their angry beasts away. Robbie looked down again at John and Billie. 'Why the pissin 'ell don't you shoot t' bastards?'

'None on us 'as gor any powder left.'

'I suppose you want me te prick the bastards then?'

'You prick 'em an we'll bat their bloody brains out!'

''Ere we go agin!'

Low curses rumbled along the Lifeguard line as yet another troop of shadows emerged, took form. They were bloody lobsters, armoured from head to knee: barred helmet, gorget, shot-proof cuirass, back, pauldrons and vambraced arms, jointed steel tassets to the knee. Long hide boots gripped the flanks of heavy warhorses.

Again, they came on at a trot. Again, they reined in at thirty feet, stamping, snorting, pistols levelled in a streak of flame, smoke, flailing hooves and rearing beasts. The air exploded around them. The next pike fell to the ground, the man beside Robbie cursing, clutching at a shattered elbow. A kneeling musketeer slumped forwards into the stubble, a ball of speechless pain.

A great dark beast leapt through the wall of smoke, its

armoured rider forcing it at the gap in their pikes. A heavy broadsword smashed down across Robbie's pike. The bastard was trying to force open a gap in the line, a gap close to the Royal Standard.

Robbie forced his pike back and up to jab at the horseman. Anger boiled in him. Damn this beast and its kind that came to kill and take yet more. He could stand it no more. Stepping over the crouched musketeers, he lunged. 'Come on then yo bastard!'

The rearing mass of steel, leather, kicking hooves, foaming muzzle, teeth and horseflesh were one. This was not man and mount. It was a monster, a changeling – Black Annis, come to tear them apart. It had mauled cousin Hal, slashed poor Billie, smashed the bone and sinew of those beside him. Now it wanted more. It'd come to tear at their very flesh, feast on them, gorge itself, drag them to oblivion.

Robbie lunged wildly. The sword parried, splinters flying from his shuddering pike. Again his thrust was knocked aside. It glanced off steel tasset plates, stuck useless in leather saddle. He had to drag it free – kill the beast.

'Bugger 'im!' John was shouting. 'Prick the bloody 'oss!'

In his blood rage, he'd struck at the armoured rider. Better the soft horse flesh. He gathered the strength for another blow. *Get control o't pike, aim low, away from't swinging sword – at the base o't neck.* He drove the pike into the beast's straining shoulder muscle. It did not go deep, but bone grated under it.

Wild eyes and bared teeth screamed in pain and fear as the horse leapt backwards. Forelegs and hooves flailed as the animal reared, the pike kicked free, bloody. The great horse rose on its hindquarters, the weight of the cuirassier dragging the terrified mount backwards onto its haunches. Beast and rider crashed to the ground in a welter of flying legs, underbelly and dust. The horse rolled over, staggered to its feet kicking and bucking to career off; eyes wild, ears flattened, stirrups and reins slapping its bloody flank.

The cuirassier lay on his back in the dirt, winded, wounded, in pain but alive. He struggled to drag himself up, one leg twisted under him. John and Billie were up, leaping forward. Raising their heavy musket butts they drove them down onto arms and upturned face. Again and again they struck until, with a screech and crack, steel faceguard and bone gave way and the bloody lobster lay motionless.

As the troop of cuirassiers wheeled away, Billie tried again to hold his severed ear against his head. He spoke for the first time. 'Bastards!'

# XVI

# Just Revenge

*Francis Reeve*

*The King's centre, a quarter to four o'clock*

Francis touched brutal spurs to the scarred flanks of his horse. The great beast leapt forward over the bloody, choking body of the green-coated musketeer to crash into the ranks beyond, iron hooves flailing.

The ranks in front turned on each other to escape this new onslaught. Only an old corporal stood firm, musket raised in defiance. A man of standing, a yeoman farmer or tradesman, he was too proud to run.

Francis swung his heavy sword down. Its steel grated on iron, rasping on the musket barrel until it dug deep into fingers and wooden stock. The older man cursed. He was flung aside to be trampled by the ranks of horsemen behind.

It was God's will. This man was a sinner – born sinful. No matter what he did in life, he would die stained with man's sinfulness. Only absolute faith and Christ's grace could cleanse him. But God had not chosen him to be amongst His faithful, had not given him the gift of sure faith. It was right and justified that this sinner should die.

Francis had been given a great sword, *the sword of just revenge*. He was chosen to deliver God's justice upon the wicked and the sinful. He knew that he was chosen; his name was written in the Book of Life. With his mother, he would be taken in to join God's elect.

He raked his horse again, forcing it to canter. Ahead, streams of men fled back down the gentle slope towards the village of Radway and Edgehill. The brigade was broken. Pikemen and musketeers threw down their weapons to run faster.

A young ensign dropped his company colour and ran. Francis did not care about the silken image; it was nothing to him. But the apostate that carried it against the true and righteous army of God was a worthy offering. He must be pursued. . . cut down. . . sacrificed. Though not much more than a boy, he too was a sinner. To leave him would be to let the pestilence fester and spread, to infect more souls with malignancy, to swell Satan's hordes against God. Sin begat sin. Not to purge the world of this sinner would itself be wicked. Only the chosen could be saved in the final battle.

Francis brought his great sword down in a sweeping arc that cut across the boy's scalp. The blow was not strong enough to split the skull, but it laid it bare, slicing through taut skin. The boy screamed, stumbled, fell beside pounding hooves.

The youth staggered to his feet to run on again, blood and tears running down his face and curling hair. Francis steered his horse back across the young man's path. The boy threw up his arms, tried to cover his bleeding scalp. The sword cut deep into cloth and sinew, again and again, until thin feeble forearms could take no more. Finally, the child fell to the ground, a tattered, bleeding, sobbing heap on the earth. Francis did not look back. He rode on towards Edgehill.

On the hill beyond Radway, the King's battery spewed out another volley of flame and sulphur. The great tongues of fire lashed brighter now against the darkening hill behind. With the other riders of Balfour's Horse, Francis turned towards this hellish spectre and put his horse to the slope. This would be a different test: they would not simply be sending sinners to their fate but facing engines of war, Hell's own engines.

He must send these beasts back to Hell, back into the bottomless pit. He must ride the Red Horse.

# XVII

# Hammer and Anvil

*Anthony Sedley*

*Parliamentary centre, ten minutes to four o'clock*

'Advance your arms!'

Anthony and Brooke's ironworkers had seen the battle ebb and flow before them. The King's foot had surged up the slope to crash against the Parliamentary line. On their left, the fighting washed back down the slope to settle along the stream bed that ran across the field, its course traced by fire and smoke in the darkening vale.

'Muskets. . . shoulder your arms!'

To their right, the King's Lifeguard were locked in a desperate fight with Constable's foot and reeling from charge after charge of Stapleton's cuirassiers. Further right, the King's foot had fallen back down the slope to leave the Lifeguard alone and exposed. The battered remains now clung to the crest of the ridge, their musketeers sheltering under the pikes.

'Brooke's Regiment will wheel to the right. . . about!'

Now they were to swing across the open gap in the King's line to smash the Lifeguard's exposed flank. Constable's

Yorkshiremen held the Lifeguard as an anvil. Brooke's Levellers were the hammer that would break them.

As the drums rattled out the command and pace, Anthony stepped off. He and the other file leaders lead the way in a great swinging arc. Those in the left wing of musketeers had to step out to cover the distance on the outside of the turn. Men stumbled and cursed in the dusk as they struggled to keep pace. Here and there, they broke into a run to keep up. Two hundred yards to the right, the battalion's right-hand marker simply marked time on the spot as he pivoted slowly like the hinge on a gate.

Gradually, the battalion swung on its axis until it faced the Lifeguard's open flank, the King's musketeers and pikemen scrambling to face the new threat in growing alarm. The King's Lifeguard were gripped in pincers, held in the white heat of the furnace.

Now was the time to strike the hammer blow of rebellion.

## XVIII

# Defiance

### *Robbie Needham*

*The Parliamentary ridge, five minutes to four o'clock*

Robbie stood in the front rank of what was left of the King's Lifeguard. The files were thinned, the Royal Standard now only a few places from him. It still hung over them, holed and ripped, the last rays of setting sun picking out its rich scarlet, blue and gold thread.

They'd been locked in combat with Constable's Yorkshiremen for over an hour, neither battalion able to push the other from the low ridge that ran along the Parliamentary line. Other battalions slugged it out in similar fashion in a line that swept back down into the vale. But the Lifeguard alone clung to the ground it had won on the crest of the ridge. Exhausted but not prepared to accept defeat, they defied all efforts to dislodge them.

For most, it was their first experience of combat. They'd trained for battle. But the drill books had not told them what to do if neither side could break the other. Unsure, their officers simply stuck down their colours, continued to pour shot into each other and prayed that they could hold on. Equally stubborn English, Welsh, Scots and Irish pulled their necks into their shoulders, as if it was another heavy shower of rain.

But it was the King's foot that suffered most. The Lifeguard, short of powder and shot and with their right flank exposed by the destruction of Fielding's Brigade, were vulnerable. They were now a single battered block of pike and musket huddled around the Royal Standard. They clung to the ground they'd gained, waiting: waiting for the return of their horse or a miracle; waiting to be told what to do. But neither horse nor orders came.

In their place, rumours ran along the line: the Earl of Lindsey, their Lord-General, lay dying, his thigh smashed by a musket ball; the Earl's son, the Lifeguard's own lieutenant-colonel, was going to his aide; Sir Nicholas Byron, their brigade commander, was wounded; the princes were cap-tured; the King was coming to stand with his Lifeguard. Sir Jacob Astley, their Sergeant-Major-General, would get them out of this. Sir Jacob would know what to do. And always, Rupert would bring the King's horse back to crush the enemy foot. If only they could hold on.

Now they looked to the Royal Standard and its bearer for direction. Robbie took a good look at the Knight Marshal, the King's Champion and Standard Bearer. Sir Edmund Verney was not a young man. A haggard face and troubled eyes told of drink, debt and a son who sided with Parliament. The old man had refused to wear his armour. He fought in shirtsleeves.

Sir Edmund stared ahead, ignoring the dangers around him. He did not seem to see how exposed, how vulnerable the Lifeguard's position was. It was as if he dared Constable's ranks to attack them again, determined to hold the ground they'd won or face destruction. It was his duty. He trusted his king would come to his aid.

Jason, the servant beside him, twisted and turned, halberd in hand, flitting between the enemies that gathered about his master. Constable's bluecoats still poured volleys into their front rank. Now a purple-coated regiment raked their right flank with yet more fire.

'Sir Edmund, will you not come away a little? We are hard pressed on all sides.'

'Jason, you know that I have eaten the King's salt. I have served him near thirty years. I will not forsake him now. It is my honour and my duty to defend my master unto death. Our conscience is only to do our duty. We will stand. We will not yield.'

Jason seemed to sag with hurt. Robbie couldn't help offering his own feelings. The big Derbyshire miner didn't care if Sir bloody Edmund heard him.

'That's as may be. But t' King promised us an end to tithe and them tossers in Parliament. I reckon t' King's getting his due. Our Hal is in a right bad way an' others an all. Look at yon Billie's 'ed. Any road, I've 'ad enough of this. Let's gerrit over and done with – one way or tuther.'

Something was changing. The firing ceased. Its rattle and crash gone. In its place the urgent sound of drums. Constable's bluecoats were hidden in the smoke. But they were coming on again.

Sir Edmund pulled up what was left of the Lifeguard. 'Stand straight in your files! The King's Lifeguard will prepare to receive foot.'

Again, the Lifeguard's drums beat out the alarum.

'Battaile! Advance your. . . arms!'

Muscles aching, they hefted their weapons.

'Port your arms! Pikes! Charge your pikes!'

Again, the great ash poles swung forward and down.

'Stand with me! Remember your King!'

Robbie stared along the length of his pike, stared into the swirling smoke, waiting for Constable's charge. Were they as ragged and aching as he? Like those beside him, he hated not knowing, not seeing, the clawing wait before the attack.

And then they came, out of the smoke, a yelling blue wall of steel.

Edged pike heads thrust at him, at his shoulder, gut, chest, face – spikes in four serried jabbing ranks that sought to pierce flesh, to force their long shafts through him. Four more ranks hung over them, waiting for an opening. Robbie fought to smash them aside, working his own pike shaft back and forth to part the wave of steel and ash.

The last pike head grazed past his throat. His own pike struck home. It grated on iron, juddered sliding across the breastplate of the hireling bastard opposite, burying itself between the files that pressed forward. He lent his weight against the jarring thrust, muscles tearing, right hand gripping the base, forcing the pike into the closing mass. The thick ash shaft sunk deeper into the ranks, tearing cloth and flesh until it struck hard, lodged against iron or bone.

The surging mass pushed on, closing the gap, the pike shaft buckling back and up in a bow until. . . with a rendering crack, it shattered. The last pikes lunged toward him. He twisted, turned, smashed at them with the shattered stump.

The charging wall of iron hit him with a breath-slamming thump, crushing him between it and the ranks behind. Gasping for air, he was chest-to-chest with the hireling bastard's breastplate, a shining gouge scored deep across it.

Hot fetid breath filled his nose and throat. The Yorkshireman stank of rancid sweat, stale ale and dried fish. Broken yellow teeth grinned back from unshaven jaw. Foul stubble rasped against him. Neither man could swing weapon or fist more than a few inches – no room to move in the crush, their arms pinned. They staggered and swayed, locked together as if in a drunken dance, desperate to keep their feet as the mass surged dangerously back and forth. All the while the grinning bastard panted his foulness against Robbie's cheek.

A sharp intake of breath – the stinking grin gone – the heavy brim of the bastard's helmet smashed down across Robbie's nose in a vicious head-butt. Searing pain blinded the big miner. Blood and involuntary tears flooded his face, eyes and chin.

He buried his smashed face in the crook of his arm. He had to fend off his tormentor but pain, blood and tears blinded him. He pushed at the bastard but his arms were feeble, muscles failing him. Like a chained bear, wounded, baited by dogs, he had to fight back. He had to fight back or sink to be battered, kicked and crushed to death in the scrum.

Squinting through the sting of sweat and blood, he raised his head. The rank-mouthed bastard was grinning at his work! Burning pain exploded in wild flailing anger. With a screaming heave, Robbie wrenched his arms free of the press, drove the splintered stump of his pike down across the ugly face. The bastard wasn't grinning now.

But it was not a strong blow. The foul broken teeth lunged again snapping at nose, ears, cheek, searching to maul, rip and tear. Robbie fought to push the beast's head back, got the stump under the rim of the bastard's helmet, forced it up and back, leather chinstrap biting deep into sweating neck folds of stubble.

A leather gauntlet clawed at his neck and face, gouging at eyes and gullet, closing around his windpipe. The bastard was tearing it from his throat. Breath rasped as they struggled to choke each other. Robbie could neither stop nor carry on. Blood swam in his ears, eyes clouding, his knees buckling; sinking.

A voice – John's voice. 'Hold t' bugger still an' I'll bat 'im!'

John's musket butt slid past to smash into the bastard's jaw with a bone cracking thump. The grip on Robbie's throat slackened; the other man's neck went soft. Sucking air into searing lungs, Robbie smashed the shattered pike stump down. Again and again he pounded the bastard's face and helmet until they sunk below the sea of arms and pikes to be kicked and trodden to the floor. The bastard would not grin again.

'Th'k yo' sirrey,' Robbie rasped.

For almost a minute, the Lifeguard held back the mass of Yorkshiremen at push of pike. It was a matter of will. To accept defeat in this deadly scrummage was to succumb to death or brutal maiming. To be overrun was to let in the slaughter. The real killing started when a battalion was broken apart. Men would be killed by the score in the victory lust that followed.

With tears in their eyes and muscles at snapping point, men gave all they had to hold back the tide, but the sheer weight of Constable's single great battalion, eight ranks deep, began to push the Lifeguard back down the hill. Exhausted bodies could not stop an inch turning into a foot and then a sliding yard, feet scrabbling on the stubble. All along the line, grunts and curses told of men close to the end of their endurance.

It felt as if Robbie's muscles were being torn from the bone. His thighs shook involuntarily with exertion. Sweat ran from throbbing temples to smear the cake of dust and blood that covered his face. He could barely focus, his vision closing in.

Another great shove forced them backward. Like a wrestler on the edge of the ring, his body was forced up and back. He was close to being toppled. He dug his shoulder deeper against the mass, dug his heels into the dry stubble and sod. But it did nothing to halt the slide, nothing to stop the momentum. It was all he could do to stay upright. He was almost lifted bodily from the ground. Then, with one final great shove, the King's Lifeguard was thrown bodily backwards. He was on his knees. He curled his back waiting for the final blow.

But the pike heads in front of him stayed on the ground. Both regiments were exhausted. Men leaned over, their hands on their knees sucking in air. Here and there a man collapsed as the two sides pulled apart, staring, breathing, trying to recover.

But it was Constable's men that were in better shape. Their line was intact, firm, recovering its weapons. The Lifeguard's line was bent back, broken in places. They could not hold a push of pike again. They were beaten.

## XIX

# Bits of Bloody Silk

### *Ralph Reeve*

### *Rear of the Parliamentary ridge, four o'clock*

Ralph looked at the Parliamentary foot regiments that remained firm along the ridge to his front. They stood like battlements, their backs to him, dark against the white smoke wreathing around them, filling the vale beyond. The rattle of musket volleys, deeper thump of cannon and the insistent beat of drums rolled back to where he stood.

Time and again, great tongues of yellow flame lit up the smoke clouds to belch thicker, darker cannon smoke, like lightning within storm clouds. Yet this was no wondrous act of nature. This was the work of man and the Devil, of iron and saltpetre.

Lord Grandison had rallied two hundred horsemen from the King's left wing. This motley force was cajoled into a squadron facing back towards the battle beyond the ridge – the same ridge up which they had charged with such reckless abandon to open the battle.

The Parliamentary foot was far from broken. Despite the loss of their horse on the flanks, they continued to hold the ridge. The King's foot were held in an inferno of iron, lead and steel. Lord Grandison's horsemen had now to do what Lord Digby and the King's reserve horse regiments should have done. They had to break the Parliamentary foot.

But between them and the battle was a scene of confusion. The slope ahead was littered with thousands of men, the remnants of the Parliamentary centre fleeing towards Kineton. They ran and stumbled towards him. Perhaps they believed Grandison's cavaliers to be their own horse returned.

To strike their blow against the Parliamentary line, they had to first cut their way through this throng. They could not leave them to reform and return to the battle. Already, a regiment with black colours was re-gathering, drums calling men back, pushing them into their ranks. Other groups clustered around their colours. Before them the ground was covered in a mass of individuals, every colour of uniform mixed as one rabble. Some had discarded their pikes. Others still carried muskets.

They should have been focused on the far Parliamentary line, but the eyes of Grandison's troopers were fixed on the forty colours that glittered before them. Every young man coveted the chance to snatch an enemy standard. It was the ultimate prize, certain honour and glory.

Ralph wiped his dry lips, still gritty with dust, on the back of a gauntlet. He too could not resist the lure of those poorly protected ensigns. As Lord Grandison's trumpeter called the advance, the prickle of sweat ran up his spine. To carry one of those colours home, to hang it in his father's hall, would mean that his place, his life, would be certain for all time.

The mass of Parliamentary foot continued to stumble towards them. Only in the last yards before the trotting horsemen reached them did relief turn to confusion and fear.

The first few simply stood dumbfounded, to be pushed aside or ridden over by the King's horsemen.

Disbelief turned to fear and fumbled panic. Men threw down their weapons, turning to run back into the throng. Some simply curled into a ball on the ground. But, here and there, a musket or pistol rang out. Over all, a hiss of curses washed back at the dreaded cavaliers.

They pressed on at a steady trot, swallowed by the mass of frightened and angry men. They rode in silence trying to gauge the odds, assessing their chances. They were two hundred, but almost four thousand rebels surrounded them.

As they pushed deeper into the mass, more determined men stood their ground with muskets, swords, partisans and halberds, clumped together in knots, refusing to move. They rallied around their colours, held together by loyalty, honour, stubborn pride and the shouts of officers. The increasing resistance could only be broken by steel.

But could he bring himself to cut down these poor wretches? This was not the noble act he had thought soldiering to be. He cringed as Corporal Nisbet and the other professionals swung their swords at those in their way. The poor fools fell bleeding and cursing under the line of horses. Did he really want to take a colour that much? He would rather be spared the need to hack down a defenceless man. Perhaps he did not have the stomach to be a soldier. God, let the waves part. Let there be a clear path through the mass.

A young musketeer stood alone ahead of him. Jittery fingers fumbled with glowing match and powder horn as the shaking boy primed his weapon. The musket swung forward into the aim.

Fuck! He would face the shot at point blank range. Ralph kicked spurs into his horse's flanks. It leapt forward. The match snapped down. A jet of sparks, searing heat as ball and flame passed under his outstretched arm, the crunch of breaking cheekbone as his heavy pistol knocked the boy aside.

He was past, the musketeer rolling in pain and tears under Clem and Luke's hooves. But, fuck, he had been lucky. Cold sweat soaked his shirt. He had been foolish. Could he not, even now, bring himself to kill? He could not expect to rely on luck for much longer. How could he protect Clem or Luke if he could not even defend himself? He must kill, or be killed.

The cavalier line was now punctured, disjointed, broken into ever smaller groups by the increasing knots of resistance. As they broke away, riders congregated around a captured colour, trailing away to the edge of the battlefield, congratulating each other, their duty done.

They had almost cut their way through the mass. Only one colour remained between them and the black regiment: pale blue silk with red lozenges, Lord Mandeville's colours. Perhaps a dozen men stood with it.

He was the nearest horseman to the colour. A length ahead of the others, surely the prize was his. His horse had not yet settled back into a trot. Fuck it! He pushed it on. Sitting low into the gallop he levelled his pistol. 'Deliver!'

For the briefest moment, perhaps three strides, elation swept him on, the horse surging forward.

The last fugitives parted. An old sergeant stood, his halberd lowered. It was too late to rein in! He pressed his legs hard to steer away. The horse sensed the danger, leaping sideways.

The cruel spear-tipped axe thrust at him. He parried, twisted. The halberd grazed his chest, jacket cloth ripped open, the shaft against his ribs – he was past the blade.

Two musketeers beside the sergeant – they barred the way. With a thump of flesh and splayed legs, the horse came to a shuddering halt. Only half in the saddle, Ralph was pitched forward. Hands grabbed arm and collar, pulling him down. Boots kicked free of flapping stirrups, he rolled forward to meet the turf, earth and sky cartwheeling overhead.

Ralph lay flat on his back, the clouds above him reddened by the setting sun. Silence. He should get up, get to his horse. But his arms and legs refused to move, held him motionless, the wind knocked from him. His body lay frozen in torpor. Blood pulsed in his ears, roaring.

The ground shook as a rough, mud-caked shoe thumped down beside his head, a shadow, the dark silhouette of a man standing over him, an angry musketeer stepping forward, musket raised, the heavy butt held high above his head.

He must move, roll away, escape the blow that would surely smash his skull. But his body refused, failed him, lay motionless. Fuck, was this it? Was this the death he deserved? Was this his final failure – to be bludgeoned like a dumb beast? His body convulsed, croaking for breath, lungs crushed, empty, burning, eyes shut.

'Cavalier shit!' the man snarled. The musket butt drove downwards.

The pistol whipped back, the ball slamming into the man's groin, throwing the musketeer bodily backwards. Ralph's fist gripped the pistol in his hand, instinct still squeezing the trigger.

He rolled away. He rolled under his horse. Forcing himself onto all fours, he sucked cold fresh air – life – into aching lungs. Gasping, clawing, he crawled, fell, rolled away, away from the man's screaming, twitching legs, out from under iron hooves.

Thank God! Luke and Clem were either side of him. They must seize the colour. They could not hear him. Clem pulling him up, Ralph croaked whispers between gasps. 'Thank. . . you.'

Another cavalier lifted the silken trophy high.

Ralph dragged his shaking body into the saddle once more. He had come close to death. He had felt the cold hand of shock upon him. It had been his own fault, charging ahead. It was foolhardy. But there was applause, salutes to his courage from those around him, consolations for the missed colour. Luke stood guard while Clem fussed over him.

'Damn! You nearly gone and got yourself killed there, Master Ralph. All impetuous, that's you all over – got to go off a-charging ahead on your own. I don't know what all the damn fuss be about them flags. Just bits o' bloody silk if you ask me.'

The last colour had gone. With it, more of the cavaliers melted away. Now, scarcely sixty horsemen stood with Lord Grandison. Sixty left to rescue the King's foot and what remained of the day.

# XX

# Case-Shot

*George Merrett*

### *The King's Battery, ten minutes past four o'clock*

Through gaps in the belching smoke, George Merrett had watched the battle unfold as he marked his guns' fall of shot. The King's horse had swept their opponents from the field to disappear in a welter of dust. He had to contain his excitement as the Parliamentary centre melted away in a panic fear to follow them and the King's foot advanced.

But two regiments of rebel horsemen had stepped into the gap to smash into the King's foot. A regiment of cuirassiers mauled the King's Lifeguard, forcing its musketeers to shelter under their pikes. The other regiment broke through the King's centre, riding over Fielding's brigade. His perspective glass brought the scene into shocking relief, amplified images of fleeing men hacked and trampled by armoured horsemen.

Now these horsemen turned their charge towards him, his guns and the King's battery. They were cantering hard at the slope of the hill on which the guns stood. They were beyond the rear of the King's foot. They could have one intent only: they would charge the guns and destroy the King's battery. There was nothing to stop them and less than a mile to run. It would take no more than five minutes at a reasonable canter – less at a gallop.

George turned to look along the line of guns. He searched for the figure of his patron, the Master of Ordnance. In Christ's name, why did the Earl not order them to face this new threat? Could he not see the danger?

The guns should turn to face the rebel horsemen with case-shot, a hail of musket balls that could rip apart a charge at close range. But they sat facing the wrong way. Still the Earl gave no order to turn and face the immediate danger. The fool was holding court with the officers around him. The big guns each fell silent. They were not preparing to face the threat. They were preparing to leave the battlefield! The Earl was calling for the teams of draught horses to move the guns to safety. He must believe the battle lost. He was trying to save the guns for another day. But what other day? If this day was lost, the King's cause was lost.

George could not believe it. He refused to believe it. Yes, the centre brigade was broken. But the rest of the King's foot fought on, locked in combat with their opponents. The guns could not abandon them. They must stand and face this threat, not try to run from it.

His two lighter guns must face the rebel horse without delay. Without orders. On their own. At the very least, they would try to cover the withdrawal of the bigger guns. Perhaps the Earl would see sense and turn them too.

He needed the immediate attention of his nearest gun captain, Old Nick Busy. This was not a moment for formality. He needed to break the older man from his concentration and current purpose. 'Nick!'

The gunner's hunched figure flinched, looked up from his breech.

'Mr Busy. . . enemy horse! Case-shot!'

The older man turned to follow George's outstretched arm, squinting into the gathering gloom below them. With a great growl, the gun captain stopped his crew in their mechanical flow of reloading. 'Stay that! Re-lay, horse! Squit. . . Flash. . . case-shot! Fetch it!'

The skinny runt of a Number Six followed by the dim-witted Number Five sprinted away towards the ammunition lines.

The Number Two looked up with concern. 'She's loaded ball Nick?'

'I know that, damn it. One shot ball, then case. Double quick!'

They threw themselves at the demi-culverin's wheels and trail to force two thousand three hundred pounds of iron and oak out of ruts driven deep into the turf and through a quarter turn to the left. George left Old Nick to it, leaping to his second gun to drive them into similar action. It did not take long once they saw the threat and Old Nick's lead. Would the rest of the battery follow them?

But the guns stood idle, silent. The red-faced conductor, Cuthbert Cartington, was running, puffing and panting towards him. Behind him were his teams of draught horses. He was coming to drag their guns away. 'George, we must – we must cease firing. We have to save the guns.'

'We cannot outrun the enemy horse. They will be amongst us before we can get the guns hitched. Besides, where are we to go? You know how difficult it was to get down the hill.'

'But the Earl's orders. . . we are to save the guns!'

'The only way to save the guns is to fight them. We need

case-shot. At least we can cover the bigger guns. They will never get away otherwise.'

'Yes, yes, I see. . . very well. Case-shot? Yes, leave it to me. My boys will fetch it to you.'

'Good. But for God's sake – quickly!'

Cartington lumbered back towards his confused drivers, waving his chubby arms and shouting for case-shot.

Old Nick stood up with a nod, the gun primed. George did not look for the Earl's approval. He gave the order needed. 'Give fire!'

He dropped his jaw, opened his mouth. The great gun leapt backwards, smoke, flame and pressure wave crashing out violently behind the nine-pound ball that shrieked towards the oncoming horsemen.

Diving through the smoke he tried to gauge its impact. It was difficult to see in the darkening vale. He thought he saw some of the riders fall. But the remainder came on still. They were only half a mile distant. Two minutes at best. Could they fire twice in that time? The guns were hot. They had fired near thirty rounds. Would the barrels take two in quick succession or would they burst?

'Put back your pieces. Case-shot. . . load!'

## XXI

# Hell's Engines

*Francis Reeve*

*The base of Edgehill, a quarter past four o'clock*

Francis saw the great tongue of flame flare from the cannon's mouth, bright against the darkening hillside. He did not see or hear the nine-pound ball until it shrieked past him, cleaving its shuddering path through the cool air. Behind him, the ball smashed into the soft earth in a dark shower of sod.

His horse leapt sideways, stumbled – almost threw him. Damn the beast! He yanked hard on its reins, dragging its head back and up before driving it on again with a deep rake of spurs. Lathered in sweat, the frightened animal put itself to the hill again with wide eyes and foam-flecked rasping canter.

Damn his horse for its weakness! Did it not feel God's spirit? It had to carry him against these engines that defied the Lord with their fire and brimstone. For he had to reap a great destruction upon these beasts of Hell.

———

Spike, rake, sponge, charge, wad. The gun crews threw themselves at reloading. Faster than before, they were the very workings of an automaton. George had never seen crews reload so quickly. The heat shimmered along each barrel. They were too hot. The charges could cook-off in the bore, maim those who rammed. Worse, the barrels could burst, killing all around.

Squit and Flash brought the first of the precious case-shot. The red-faced Cartington and his boys followed with more. Packed with musket balls, each casing would split on firing to spew its contents in a lethal hail.

The first case slid into the gun's bore, pushed home, the ramrod whipped out – no need for wadding; the casing would keep it in place. Again, they laid the gun, knocked the wooden quoin deeper under the breech ring. Old Nick hunched over the touch hole, pricking, priming, grinding with extraordinary speed and dexterity.

Five hundred yards. Should he wait – wait to be sure they hit their mark or fire and hope they had time for one final round? George glanced back towards the Earl. He was still trying to organise the trains of heavy horses. They would not get away in time.

George turned and yelled his decision. 'Give fire!'

———

Nearer now, Francis saw the two guns on the slope above throw their satanic fire at him. The hill and sky were lit by their fearful flames. This time he heard the demonic whistle of case-shot shriek past on every side, a cloud of iron locusts released from Hell's bottomless pit. Around him men cried out, horses screamed, as the hellish balls smacked into oncoming flesh.

Again, God spared him. He was chosen. Again, he drove his spume-soaked horse at the hill. He was chosen to deliver

God's vindictive wrath. He must destroy these beasts of iron and fire and return them to Hell. *For the great day of His wrath is come! And who shall be able to stand?*

———

George was sure the first wave of riders was thinner. The dark shapes that kicked on the ground had not been there before. But was there time for one final round?

Spike, rake, sponge, charge, wad, case, ram – man and gun a single machine, a machine that raced against the oncoming rush of horse and rider. But could this machine beat the ancient charge of armoured horsemen?

Should he have waited? Was it too late? Should he stop the reload and let the crews run?

If they ran now, they could make it to the safety of the baggage train and the firelocks that guarded it. If he waited, the horsemen would be upon them. Over the grunt and rattle of reloading, came the growing thunder of hooves, the yells of men and the rasp of horses straining at their girths. He had to decide. The gun crews were too intent on their drill to look up. He must stop them, tell them to run, to run now.

Squit's scrawny frame leapt past him. The runt of a boy planted himself between the two guns, his long-handled sponge held like a ludicrous pike. The boy was right. He must protect the gunners. He drew his sword stepping forward to stand beside Squit. The first horses were only strides away; huge black, slathering beasts.

Old Nick stood up from the breech, grabbed his linstock. Without waiting for an order he swung it through the air. As he drove the hot match into the priming powder the old gunner yelled out his warning to one and all. 'Stand clear!'

———

Francis saw the gunners working feverishly about their contraptions, devils tending their beasts. The smoke of Hell itself wrapped about their legs in the cool still air. He aimed between the two crouching beasts. A final spurred kick, his foaming mount plunging the last yards into Hell's mouth.

Beside him a man and horse disappeared in bloody pulp and flailing limbs as the air around him erupted in blinding light, fire and burning wind. Then silence, white light, numb.

His vision was returning, he could feel, smell. He had not entered God's paradise. He was still on Earth, surrounded by Satan's proxies and the stench of sulphur. His horse had careered to a halt. A hunched ogre barred the way with smoking trident. Beside him a demon brandished a sword urging on devils and a bony fiend jabbed a spear that dripped with the foul black gore of the beast they served.

Francis knocked the spear aside. He swung his heavy sword down upon the demon. His blow was parried. Again, he swung from the saddle. Again, Satan turned his blade aside. But the demon was on its knees. The dripping spear thumped into Francis's side. He clung to the saddle, almost unhorsed, close to falling.

He felt no pain. He felt nothing as he grabbed the spear shaft, pulled it towards him, drove his sword through the fiend that held it. He felt nothing as he flung the sponge and crumpled cadaver aside. Forcing his horse on again, he swung at the ogre's smoking linstock. The terrified animal leapt sideways, crashed into a cannon wheel before leaping the gun trail and on to join those of Balfour's horse who had made it into the King's battery.

George staggered to his feet. More horsemen rushed by, yelling, cutting at his gunners as they ran towards the baggage train.

Old Nick stooped over Squit.

'There's nothing we can do for him now, Nick.' George touched the older man's arm. 'Save the others.'

The old gunner gently laid the boy's bloody carcass on the dewy grass. In a low hunched run, he moved with surprising speed, linstock in hand, shepherding his crew to safety.

George went to follow. A figure huddled under the gun. It was Flash. The poor fool did not know what to do. Nobody had told him what to do. 'Flash, come on. Follow Nick!' Up from under the gun, George held the lad back as another horseman raced past. 'Now Flash, go! Run!' The boy ran like a wolfhound, his bare feet flying as he twisted, turned and sprang over the turf. George followed, cursing his heavy riding boots as he stumbled towards safety.

***

'Nails! Bring me nails! I want these guns silenced!' Colonel Balfour's shout broke through Francis's deafened hearing. The old Scots soldier had served in Holland. He knew his business. He wanted the King's guns spiked – iron nails driven into each gun's touch hole.

But there were no nails. The King's barrel of nails remained with his baggage train, defended by a company of firelocks that waited to fell any of Balfour's troopers that ventured closer.

Francis sat in the middle of a scene of bedlam. Beneath him, his exhausted, sweat-drenched horse shivered in the cold air. Its head hung low, nostrils flared in great gasps, panting clouds of steam that mingled with the last of the gun smoke. Still numb from the cannons' blast, he watched in silence as the troopers around him chased the last of the gunners that hid from them. Finding no more quarry and no nails, they cut the traces of the draught horses and drove them away. The King would not be able to drag away his artillery to fight another day.

With nothing further to be done, Balfour gathered the remains of his regiment to ride back towards the battle that still raged across the dark vale. As they left the King's Battery silent on the slope of Edgehill, they rode towards a blazing orange sky, the sun low over Kineton. In front lay the rear of the King's Lifeguard and its Royal Standard.

# XXII

# The Royal Standard

*Robbie Needham*

*The Parliamentary ridge, half past four o'clock*

Almost imperceptibly at first, the line to Robbie's left began to draw back. The main body of the Lifeguard were pulling away, putting distance between themselves and Constable's iron wall, drawing away from the purple-coated battalion that hammered their flank, turning to face the horsemen gathering behind them. Only around Sir Edmund and the Royal Standard did they stand firm.

Like a fistful of dough torn from the greater mass, the sinews that connected them stretched thinner until, with a snap, they parted and recoiled to leave an isolated ball, a knot of no more than forty men standing with the Royal Standard. Men shouted at each other, shouted to stand, to come away. A few broke to run across the gap to the main body. Stubborn pride, indecision and fear held Robbie and the rest in place around the Standard.

Like a ball of fish separated from the shoal by predators, they huddled closer together. Battered, wounded, exhausted, back-to-back, they faced Constable's Yorkshiremen, Brooke's purplecoats and Balfour's Horse on three sides, the ground around them covered by the dead and the dying.

Sir Edmund yelled at them all to stand with him, not to forsake their king, to think of their honour and duty. This was their last stand, a futile stupid stand against impossible odds. They'd no more to give. But they weren't going to lay down their arms. Not to these nor any other buggers. They would rather stand and die under the King's banner.

Constable's and Brooke's lines were yelling now. They added their voices to the call to run, Yorkshire and Birmingham accents jeering, demanding they yield. Sensing a cornered, wounded beast, they brandished their weapons. A thrust here, a cut or shot there at the knot of men around the Standard. Sensing blood, more stepped forward to have their piece of the kill. Young men vied to be the one to strike the death blow.

Robbie summoned what was left of his anger to threaten those who dared come close. He held his shattered pike in his big hands. Beside him, John Scollins brandished his musket above his head. At their feet, Billie held his reversed. Sir Edmund swung the Standard, wrapped around its staff, back and forth as a half-pike.

But they knew in their hearts that they were done. Beside him, Jason's efforts to parry blows were slow and late. The old servant could no longer protect his master. He was weakening. He was vulnerable. He still clutched his halberd but his face was pale, fleshy. His body was well past its prime, too long used to enjoying his master's table, unused to labour. His eyes were glazed over, almost shut.

Robbie could do no more than fend off the pikes that jabbed at him. He couldn't stop those that thrust at Jason. The old man's halberd swung too late as, with a sickening wet thump, a pike drove into his gut.

Jason sank to his knees, his hands wrapped around the pike shaft. Robbie called out. Leaping forward with a snarl, the standard in both hands, Sir Edmund rammed its head into the face of Jason's attacker. The Yorkshireman fell back into his ranks. Sir Edmund stepped back into his place to lift the standard aloft again, its golden head bent back, twisted over. Staring ahead, he spoke to his servant. 'Come now Jason. On your feet. He will trouble you no more.'

'Sir Edmund, I am sorry.' Jason's face was ashen. 'I fear. . . I am done for. I have failed you in this desperate hour.'

Only now did Sir Edmund look down to see Jason's agony. With sudden tenderness the old man knelt to cradle his groom. 'Oh Jason, it is I that have failed, not thee. My own pain has made me weary of life. Now I have squandered my own servant's life. I have let the vain hope of some fading honour overshadow my duty to thee.'

'Sir, save yourself while you can. I beg you. Leave this field and save yourself. Remember me to Lady Margaret.'

'I will not forsake you now, Jason. I will not leave you.'

From Constable's front rank a young officer called out. 'Sir, you have done your duty. Your position is impossible. You must yield!'

Sir Edmund drew himself up. He didn't look at Robbie or those few that stood with him. He replied as if he were alone.

'My life is mine own. But the Banner Royal is my sovereign's. I will not yield it while I live. By the grace of God, they that wrest it from my hand must wrest my soul from my body!'

Sir Edmund had committed them all to destruction, Jason, John, Billie and those few that still stood with him.

From the front rank of Brooke's musketeers, Anthony Sedley saw the Royal Standard. The silk and gold thread alone could feed a family for a year. Now only forty men stood with the King's banner – a banner emblazoned with tyranny's motto, *Give unto Caesar his Due.*

Damn the king that proclaimed it! Where was he? Was he here or had he run already? Shit on the King's banner and the bloody courtier that carried it! It was time to tear it down. Maybe then the poor lackeys that stood under it would be free to join the cause of the common man in rebellion.

The Birmingham ironworker saw the man who bore the Standard. A man in a fine linen shirt – a rich courtier in a shirt paid for in sweat and toil extorted from the poor. He would make a good mark at twenty paces. Anthony could have him. If he got a clear shot, he would do it. He would not wait for an order. He would bring the Norman bastard down!

Stepping forward, he flicked open the pan, levelled his musket. He took up the slack in the trigger arm, steadied his breathing, aimed for the white shirt and squeezed. The musket slammed into his shoulder in a ball of smoke, vicious thump and crash. Let this be a nail, true and strong, hammered home into the heart of tyranny.

But the standard still stood – the shirt that carried it unmarked.

Another man staggered between them, one of the King's Lifeguard, a young musketeer with a bandaged head. He'd appeared from nowhere, suddenly standing there. The Norman bastard stood unscathed!

———

Robbie did not know why Billie stood up. He'd been kneeling beside poor Jason. But, as he rose, he was spun around by the impact of a musket ball that smashed into his shoulder. Billie dropped his musket, mouthed the word 'home', turned and staggered towards the rest of the Lifeguard. John yelled at his mate to stop, but Billie simply looked over his shoulder, opened his mouth as if to speak, closed it, shook his head and carried on walking – as if he was walking home.

———

Francis Reeve saw the Royal Standard. A flag emblazoned with the catholic lilies of France and Irish harp, symbols of Rome, idols of apostasy. The man who took it would strike a blow for godly rule and a New Zion. For now was the time of judgement. The brother who struck that blow would earn his place in Heaven. He would live amongst the saints.

Could he do it? Would he be that saint? He was one of the few horsemen with a clear charge. Standing on the right of Balfour's line, there was nothing between him and the few fools still guarding it.

Was this why God had saved him in the face of Hell's cannon and certain death? Was this His purpose? God had given him this opportunity. God had placed him here at this moment to do His bidding. Francis did not need an order. His was a higher calling. For he was chosen to reap destruction upon the wicked!

Raking the bloody flanks of his exhausted horse, he leapt forward. Sword levelled, he yelled God's cause. 'Zion!'

His horse drummed out the first few cantered paces to cross the gap. An apostate musketeer staggered across his path, a musketeer with a bandaged head and shattered arm. Francis kicked his horse at the man. But it careered sideways, fearful of trampling flesh. Damn the fool for stopping his charge. Damn the papist to Hell.

Francis drove the heavy blade of his sword into the musketeer's chest, twisting the broken body aside. It fell with a piercing scream.

———

'Bastard!' Robbie heard John's scream behind him. The young musketeer leapt toward the crumpled heap that was his mate, swinging his musket wide at the horseman who'd cut Billie down.

'Stand with me!' Sir Edmund's yell turned Robbie back. Another crash of drums, the blue mass of Constable's pikemen pressing forward again.

'Yield!' The officer in Constable's front rank levelled a pistol as he came on.

'Never!'

The pistol crashed out, the ball piercing the old man's chest. It tore a path through rib, muscle and lung, the lead flattening, deforming, before bursting from his back in a bloody fist-sized hole. Gasping for breath the Knight Marshal sank to his knees, the standard still gripped in his hand, as blood flooded his mouth and fine linen shirt.

———

'Tyranny!' Anthony gripped the hot smoking barrel of his musket as he and Brooke's ironworkers charged, leaping over the dead and dying. Across his path stood a horseman slashing at a lackey musketeer and a great fool with a shattered pike.

———

'Satan!' Francis swung his sword down again. Damn this second musketeer who sprung at him with upturned musket.

Behind him was a bloody-faced devil with a broken pike – two unrighteous fools who stood between him and Heaven.

———

'Bastard!' John swung his musket at the horseman. Robbie saw the sword turn it aside to slice back and down, deep into John's neck. He swung his splintered pike in blind rage at horse and rider. The shattered stump smashed across the horse's muzzle sending it rearing backward in a screaming, flailing whinny.

———

'Freedom!' Anthony rammed his musket butt into the pikeman's already blood-caked face. He left the big man to fall, his nose and mouth a broken, bloody mess. He ran on past the rearing horse and its struggling rider – on to tear down tyranny's silken banner.

———

Robbie Needham could taste dust and grit in his mouth. He could taste the hot slick of his own blood in his throat. He'd been knocked to the ground by a scar-faced, purple-coated musketeer. He had to push himself up, drag himself away. But the earth spun beneath him, twisting his arms and legs in a crumpled heap.

And then the darkness came. He could not stop it. Down he sank as mother earth took the miner home. It closed his mind in on itself and dragged him underground to sleep.

## XXIII

# With Me!

## *Ralph Reeve*

### *The Parliamentary ridge, sunset*

Ralph Reeve stared at the rebel horsemen appearing out of the battle smoke and dark of the vale to reform on the ridge ahead. They seemed to take no notice of Lord Grandison and the sixty horsemen that remained with him. They were more interested in their trophies, helmets thrown back in self-congratulation. Perhaps, they thought the cavaliers were some of their own horse, returned from Kineton.

But it was those trophies that caught the cavaliers' eye. It sent a ripple of anger along their short line. The armoured horsemen brandished an array of colours. Not just their own cornets, but a dozen or more of the larger ensigns of foot regiments. The last of the setting sun touched on green colours of Fielding's Foot, blue of Lunsford's, colours of the King's largest brigade of foot. Amongst them were crimson colours displaying lions and crowns – company colours of the King's Lifeguard.

These horsemen must have broken the King's centre and mauled the Lifeguard, the regiment that carried his standard.

A whole brigade and more had had its heart, badge and honour ripped from its grasp. Was the Royal Standard taken, the rally call of the King's cause lost?

Guilt and anger washed through them. While they had ridden down the fleeing rebel centre, they had failed to protect their own foot from a similar fate. Where was that fool Lord Digby and his reserve of horse? Why had he not swept these rebel horsemen from the field instead of falling on the baggage train in Kineton? They could not be left to wreak yet more havoc upon what remained of the King's foot.

But sixty against two hundred? They were not even an organised troop. It was foolhardy. But if they could catch them at a standstill, before they reformed? Perhaps there was a chance. Did Grandison feel the same anger and sense of shame? Would he seize the moment or turn away?

This was no time for detailed orders, only decisive leadership and determined action. Grandison's order was simple: 'With me!'

———

Francis Reeve pushed back the barred faceguard of his helmet and let the anger and disappointment flow from him. He had wanted to be the one to take the Royal Standard, to lift the Roman idol. But too many were thrown in his path. Damn them and damn the devil with the bloodied face who sent his horse rearing uncontrollably.

He was ready to die a martyr. But God in his infinite wisdom had not chosen to take him in. The Lord had preserved him for another purpose. And yet it seemed their work was done. They had destroyed the King's centre, charged his guns, broken his Lifeguard and taken the Royal Standard. Now they were free to cut down what was left of the King's army.

Surely, the profane host and the King's ungodly cause were finished. It was time to rejoice in the Lord's victory. All about him, the troopers of Balfour's Horse were slapping each other on the back, admiring their trophies, congratulating each other. Francis could not help but smile. God had been bounteous in his victory.

*This was the Lord's doing, and it is marvellous in our eyes.*

———

Near the centre of the line, Ralph urged his weary horse forward. Like those beside it, it sensed the moment. With a snort and toss of mane, its first stiff steps bounced into a trot. Within moments they gathered into a steady drumming canter.

It took less than half a minute to cover the distance between them and the first of Balfour's troops. Almost upon them, they let out a great yell, levelled swords, urging their mounts into a full gallop for the last yards.

At full tilt, they broke through the first few troopers that turned to face them, crashing into the flank of the first troop. A few pistols barked back at them, almost all rushed shots, the balls singing through the air, high and wild.

———

Francis heard the shouts, clamour and shots to his right. Balfour's line recoiled in shock as the cavaliers hit their flank. He struggled to slam his faceguard shut, fighting to keep his horse in line as it danced in alarm.

All around him the Parliamentary line began to disintegrate. They were peeling apart in front of the sudden charge. Panic spread through the ranks as horses crashed into one another, whinnying, stamping and rearing before bolting. Fear and herd instinct tore them from a rider's control. With wild eyes, ears flat and necks outstretched, they turned to race after the herd.

Francis dragged at his reins, trying to turn his horse's head to face the onslaught. He twisted the iron bit in its bloodied muzzle. He dug his spurs deep into its flanks to force it around. But the beast bucked, kicked and reared. It sprang forward, tearing the reins through his gauntleted hands. With tears of anger and despair, Francis knew that there was nothing he could do to control the animal. He was not a good enough rider. He was not strong enough. All he could do was hang onto his saddle as the beast tore off in a headlong dash after the pack.

———

Ralph let his horse have its head in the pursuit, racing along the ridge, cavalier and roundhead, pursuer and pursued, in one chaotic mass. If he could catch one, he might yet take back one of those colours. He searched for a target ahead.

Clem was past him, surging forward, bent low over his horse's neck. Was Clem making a dash for glory? Ralph grinned as he pushed his own horse on.

'Go on, Clem!'

———

Francis felt the rider close beside him. He was reaching for Francis's flapping reins. Who was this man who risked his life to bring the beast under control? Was he Heaven sent?

No! It could not be. It was a vison from childhood, a tormentor. The heathen Clem Tooley! The spawn of Satan's Bitch! The child of the witch who killed his beautiful mother! Here to drag him to Hell, never to see his mother again.

'Get thee behind me! Satan!'

———

Ralph saw the armoured rider lash out at Clem. He held Clem by the collar. He was pulling him down, dragging Clem under their careering horses.

'No!' Please Jesus, not Clem. Ralph forced his horse to close the gap. He struck at the rider. The thin bladed rapier only scratched at helmet, iron plate, buff coat. Fuck! He should have reloaded a pistol. The bastard had the rapier in his gauntleted hand, pulling it away. He was turning, letting Clem go, throwing himself at Ralph.

And then he was gone.

Horse and rider disappeared as the armoured man's weight threw his horse so that they both went down, tail and kicking legs over neck, saddle and rump, to roll on the ground behind.

'Clem, are you alright?' They reined in beside Captain Smith beyond the last rebel horsemen. 'You picked a madman to tackle. Why him?'

'That were Master Francis.'

'My brother? Are you sure?'

'I'd know that hoss anywhere. Tis your father's. Master Francis never could manage he. I said not to take he when he left for Cambridge, but he did insist. I recon they're about as difficult as each other.'

'Thank God you are unharmed.'

'Bit bruised but I'll live. Hosses are a bit blown. Looks like your father's old sword got the worst on it.'

Ralph looked down at his rapier. The blade was snapped in half. 'Fuck! It must have broken when he fell.'

'It catched on my saddle when he went down. I'll grind a new point. It'll make a fine dagger.'

'Thank you, Clem. It would be a pity to waste it. In the meantime, we should reload.'

With a nod, Ralph indicated the battalion of foot on the slope ahead. The black-coated regiment, Lord Wharton's, marched slowly back to rejoin the battle, to add its weight against the King's hard-pressed foot.

Captain Smith was staring at the battalion. There were just fourteen cavaliers left with him. The rest had melted away to carry their trophies home or were simply lost in the gathering gloom, smoke and confusion.

The black battalion had reformed after retreating from Rupert's charge. It had not yet rejoined the battle in the vale, a battle that remained in the balance. Neither side had broken. If this battalion returned to the fight, it would surely tip the scales.

But fourteen against three hundred was madness. And yet they simply grinned at the prospect. Damn their own cock and damn these fucking rebels who stood before them. They worked feverishly to prepare their weapons. Ralph loaded, primed and spanned his pistols. He should have done it earlier.

To their right the battle still raged. Gunfire and the incessant beating of drums rolled back over the crest in a thick pall of sulphurous smoke. To their left the sun was setting over Kineton in a great ball of fire, the sky streaked with orange, scarlet and blood.

## XXIV

# But Fourteen Men

*Ralph Reeve*

### *The Parliamentary ridge, five o'clock*

There was no flowing speech about the importance of breaking this battalion, no great exhortation for cause, glory or reward, just a grunted expletive from the ruddy-faced Smith as he kicked his horse forward. If he was going to charge, they were going with him.

On the left of the line, Ralph forced his weary horse forward. Almost asleep, it burst into an uncomfortable trot. It was not enough to break an enemy. He squeezed harder. With a shake of the head, the great Barbary woke itself to a canter and they surged forward to keep pace with those who now closed on Wharton's Foot.

Thank Christ, the battalion had not turned to face them. They charged its flank. Officers yelled, pushed and cajoled the eight musketeers of its right-hand file to turn and face them. A sergeant tried to prepare the shaking men for a volley, the frightened soldiers struggling with their drill as their hooves beat towards them. Their shots were rushed. Not one horse or rider was hit.

The middle of the line of horsemen crashed into the musketeers, riding over some, scattering more to send a physical shock wave through the battalion's ranks as men were forced back by cold steel and horseflesh. On the far left, Ralph, Luke and Clem were beyond the crush.

Within a few strides they were past the other cavaliers and riding along the rear of Wharton's pikes. Reining to a halt, Luke slashed at a lieutenant who tried to face the rear rank about, yelling at the man to yield.

A single shot rang out.

All was still. As if the three riders and the ranks that faced them held their breath. As if none was sure if they themselves were shot.

And then Luke's horse collapsed; its knees gave way suddenly, the great animal crashing to the ground. Luke jumped aside as his horse rolled over. With a frightened whinny it staggered to its feet again, Luke leaping back into the saddle. But the horse was not right. White eyes stared. It shook from head to tail. As Luke turned it away from the stirring pikemen, Ralph could see its shoulder and foreleg streaked with blood. It was a beautiful animal and must have cost a pretty penny.

'Luke, he'll not hold you for long. You must ride back as quickly as you can.'

'I'm a-feared you're right. I'll join you just as soon as I can find another horse.'

'No, Luke. Ride back the way we came. Find Lord Grandison. I'll join you there. Clem, please go with Luke. His horse may not carry him.'

'Master Ralph, I promised your father I'd watch over you. My place is here with you.'

'Clem, I need you to watch over Luke. Please escort him.'

'Well bugger it! Just you go and git yourself bloody killed then. Damn! What will I say to his father? Well, come on, Goodman Luke. Let's be a-seein how that hoss moves. If I wasn't so obligated to you and Master Ralph I'd – well, I dunno what I'd bloody do.'

Ralph watched them go, just long enough to be sure that they were both moving to safety. There was now a real danger that Smith's charge would lose its momentum, that the sheer weight of numbers would turn against the twelve remaining men.

He alone now faced the rear of the battalion. He had to exploit their fear and confusion to break them. If not, Smith and the others would be lost.

He had no great plan. Trotting along the line he waved his sword towards Kineton and yelled at them. 'Essex is dead! The Earl is dead! The day is lost! Run! Save yourselves!' It was all he could think of, but it was enough to stop the pikemen from levelling their weapons. He had to spread fear throughout the battalion.

He reached the end of the pike stand and kicked his horse at the gap between pike block and musketeers. It was madness to ride between files of enemy foot, to ride a gauntlet only six feet wide. As his horse cantered down the line, he ran his broken rapier across the vertical pike shafts, yelling as his blade clattered and banged against the pikes. Confused faces turned to see the dread rider charging between them.

A captain stepped across the gap to bar his exit. Ralph bent low and let his horse knock the man aside as he wheeled about in front of the battalion.

A young ensign held a company colour – a snivelling schoolboy clutching a great black flag, six and a half feet square of shining taffeta emblazoned with white bulls' heads.

Perhaps, if Ralph could force this palefaced youth to surrender this colour, the men around him would break. Perhaps he would carry home a worthy trophy after all.

He drew himself up and spoke in clear calm tones. 'Young sir, your captain lies on his back, your lieutenant is run through and your cause lost. Render your colour and save your company.'

The boy gaped. The pikemen behind looked sullenly at the ground. The captain was crawling on his hands and knees.

Ralph tried again in firmer tones. 'Render your colour and save your men!'

The boy faltered, took a step forward and proffered the colour. It was nearly Ralph's.

'No!' The bloody captain was back on his feet, damn his eyes. 'Stand firm!' The boy had stopped, snatched back the colour. The captain stood between them shaking his spear-headed partisan. The pikemen watched for the next move, a low grumble sweeping through the ranks.

This was the moment of decision. Either, he broke these men or they would turn against him and Smith's loyal hearts. It was too late for artifice or clever words. He had to act and he had to do it before the pike tips came down.

Ralph clapped spurs to his horse's flanks. The startled animal leapt forward. He knocked the captain's partisan aside, the broken rapier rasping on steel langets, throwing the older man to the ground again. He clutched at the ensign as his horse crashed into the front rank of pikemen. But before his fist could close, the bloody schoolboy fell to the floor in terror, the flag dragged about him as a shroud. Ralph was forced to rein back his stamping horse over the prostrate captain.

Drawing a pistol, he levelled it at the nearest pikeman. 'Hand me that fucking colour!' The pikeman looked at his prone officers, stepped forward, swept up the colour and handed it to him. Grasping it firmly, Ralph reined back further, indicated Kineton with his pistol. 'Good. Now go fucking home!'

The pike stand seemed to almost melt before him. Men turned away in clumps towards Kineton, away from the battle. Ralph and his horse were both shaking with physical and psychological exertion. He could not face the remaining wing of musketeers alone. Turning away, he pushed his horse into a trot before they could react.

There were no congratulations from Captain Smith or the others. He was alone, his deeds unwitnessed. The little troop had melted back into the smoke and darkness.

## XXV

# Deliver!

*Ralph Reeve*

### *The Parliamentary ridge, dusk*

Ralph was alone. He was somewhere behind the centre of the Parliamentary line, for he rode along the crest of the ridge that had been occupied by their foot. To his right, the last of the sun's crimson disc slipped beyond Kineton. To his left, the sounds of battle still thundered in the ever-darker vale. Only now, it was further off and deeper into the gloom so that the ridge itself was almost lonely.

The King's foot had been pushed back down the slope. Had the King been with his Lifeguard? Was he fighting desperately for his life somewhere in the hell of smoke and steel as the battle hung in the balance?

Ralph wrapped the great black colour around its staff and rested it across the front of his saddle. His elation at taking it ebbed away as he threaded his way across the scene of destruction. Had it been worth it? This was not the glorious scene he had expected.

Discarded weapons, clothing, equipment littered the field. Here and there a body lay crumpled in agony. Some still called out for help. Bleeding, fearful, broken men staggered across his path to escape the scenes of Hell in the vale. A riderless horse cantered past. Ralph badly wanted to find his friends. He needed their strength and reassurance.

Ahead, two riders were moved along the ridge as he was. *Thank Christ!* One of them was Captain Smith. The other carried two colours draped over his saddle. It was Chichley, Lord John's groom. Ralph urged his tired horse into a brisker walk.

But before he could catch up, a second group cut between them: six horsemen, one an armoured lobster with a vicious poleaxe on his hip. They wore Essex's orange sash. Ralph slowed to stay out of their way.

The horsemen escorted a man on foot. Over his shoulder a great crimson colour draped around a staff with a broken head, another of the Lifeguard's company colours. And yet, there was something different about it. He was almost past them. A great swallowtail hanging loose, the last light of the dying day reflected upon crimson, yellow and blue silk. It glinted on golden thread depicting lions, fleur-de-lis, a great harp and a hand pointing to a crown.

He walked on. Fuck, but this was no ordinary company colour! It was the Royal Standard – the King's own banner; his rally mark; the embodiment of his cause, army and being. Ralph kicked his bewildered horse, forcing it into a stumbling trot. 'Captain Smith. Captain Smith! They are carrying away the Standard!'

Smith turned in his saddle, looked at him dumbfounded.

'The Royal Standard!' Ralph pointed with outstretched arm.

Smith looked again. 'My God, boy, you are right! Well, they will have me with it if they carry it away. Chichley. . . be ready to drop those colours. Reeve. . . with me!' Sword

139

levelled, John Smith spurred his horse at the rebels. 'Traitor! Deliver the Standard!'

The six horsemen turned in their saddles. Before they could react, Smith charged between them burying his sword in the footman carrying the standard. The great flag dropped to the ground. The man's body writhed under Smith's hooves dragging him forward and down, his sword stuck in the man's chest. The horsemen reached for pistols. The lobster turned, swinging the poleaxe in a great arc. Jesus, no!

Ralph forced his horse to leap forward. A pair of pistols flashed and roared bright in the fading light, the heat of a pistol ball passing. The poleaxe sliced across Smith's neck. Ralph tasted smoke acrid in his nostrils as his horse crashed into Smith's attacker, knocking the lobster back in his saddle. Thank God! Smith's sword was free, driving deep into the lobster's exposed belly.

As the armoured man slithered, gasping and cursing from his saddle to crash to the ground, the five other horsemen turned and fled. Smith clasped a hand to his neck. The poleaxe's vicious spike had ripped away half his collar, blood oozing across its fine lace. Powder-burns from a pistol spattered his face. He sat back in his saddle and swore. 'Damn!' Neither wound was vital.

The lobster coughed, spat blood, struggling to sit up. Ralph slid from his saddle. Kneeling stiffly, he removed the man's helmet, pulled him into a sitting position propped against the body of the footman. No word was spoken. Both knew nothing more could be done.

The older man fumbled at his side, reaching for his sword. Ralph unhooked the belt that held it. With a bubble of blood at his mouth, the lobster pointed to Smith before looking away, tears of pain and resignation in his eyes.

Ralph wrapped the belt around sword and scabbard, picked up the Royal Standard and handed both to Smith with a nod. Smith took the flag. With a raised eyebrow, he pointed at Ralph's broken rapier. 'Thank you, but you appear to have more need of a sword than I.'

'My father's rapier has seen better days.'

'Well, you deserve it as much as I. Now, that poleaxe I would trouble you for. The damn thing near finished me.'

Ralph handed the poleaxe to Smith with a grin.

'You did well, Reeve. Without you, the Royal Standard would have been lost and I may have lost my life. Come on. We must return the standard to His Majesty. There is still work to be done if we are not to lose this day.'

Ralph gathered up the stricken lobster's sword, the black colour he had taken and the reins of the dying man's horse. With straining limbs, he hauled himself back into his saddle.

Once again Ralph, Smith and Chichley set off. Even Smith dared not cut his way back through the chaos that still raged in the vale below. Instead, they made their way in silence along the ridge clutching the Royal Standard and their trophies, skirting the rear of the Parliamentary line.

The very last of the day's light was slipping away, darkness descending. Sporadic, vivid flashes of musket fire marked where the two armies continued to face each other. The line stretched obliquely across the field, from the King's right to the village of Radway. His centre and left forced back against Edgehill.

With a sudden shiver of night air, Ralph felt drained, physically, emotionally. The victory that had seemed so certain now seemed to hang precariously. The King's army was forced into a corner of the field. From the hill above, its great guns crashed out again in the gloom.

Was the King still alive, fighting desperately to hold on? Or were his life and cause shattered? Had all the bloodshed been in vain?

## XXVI

# *Paid!*

### *John Benion*

### *The King's left, last light*

John Benion grinned at those around him. He knew it was stupid, but he could not stop it, just as he could not stop wincing every time a cannon fired. He was still frightened.

He waited in line to refill his bandolier. He'd fired all twelve apostles. After his second misfire, he'd not let his match go out once. He'd kept it burning in its lock and between the fingers of his left hand. It smouldered in his fingers now, ready for his return to the battle. The sergeant would not be angry with him this time.

Perhaps he would make a soldier after all. The Welsh soldiers would stop calling him *pidyn bach*. He would return to his Shropshire village a hero. He would show his wife and in-laws that he was a man, a man that could no longer be pushed around.

It was dark now. The battle had not ended. He was still fearful. But he was going to fill his bandolier with powder and shot and return to his company. He would march back to the firing line and show them that he was as brave as any of them.

He would go back to the flashes, yells, screams and crashes that leapt out of the dark and smoke behind him. He would not shirk; he would not slink away.

Now it was his turn. He placed his musket on the ground and stepped forward. Groping by the half-light of a shaded lantern, he leaned deep into the half-full powder barrel with his bandolier. He gripped the edge of the barrel with one hand and thrust the first open cartouche into the course-grained powder.

His concentration was broken by a sudden yell, a yell that brought his head up out of the barrel sharply. The quarter-master was pointing, shouting at him.

'*Paid! Y cordyn!* Your match!'

John looked at the smouldering match end between his fingers. It hung over the barrel of powder. With widening eyes, he watched as it touched the inside of the barrel. Paralysed, he felt the squirt of piss again in his breeches.

The match end touched a loose grain of powder caught between the staves. For a brief moment the grain flared, light-ing the inside of the barrel. He stared as other grains and dust spluttered. A single bright spark fell gently from the barrel wall, flickering, floating down to land amongst the mass of dark powder.

A cone of intense white flame and blazing gas erupted sky-ward from the budge-barrel. Its thirty-foot jet flung back his head, tore the clothes from his torso and seared exposed skin.

Instantaneously, the barrel burst open. Iron hoops and wooden staves splintered, driven outwards by the force of the blast, tearing through those within a thirty-foot radius. Scorching heat left hands, faces, throats, lungs blistered and burned.

———

John Benion's body lay twisted, stripped and charred, amongst the bodies of those who had waited for him to fill his bandolier. Only the whites of his teeth shone back at those who surveyed the devastation by lamp and moonlight. They shone back in the inane grin of a man trying to hide his terror on the battlefield, a man who should never have been there.

# Part Two

# The Road to London

*From ladies down to oyster-wenches,*
*Laboured like pioneers in trenches.*
SAMUEL BUTLER, *HUDIBRAS*, 1664

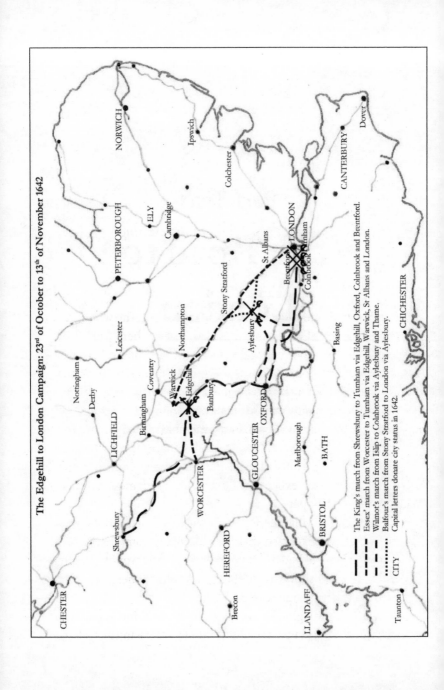

# The Edgehill to London Campaign: 23rd of October to 13th of November 1642

The King's march from Shrewsbury to Turnham via Edgehill, Oxford, Colnbrook and Brentford.

Essex' march from Worcester to Turnham via Edgehill, Warwick, St Albans and London.

Wilmot's march from Islip to Colnbrook via Aylesbury and Thame.

Balfour's march from Stony Stratford to London via Aylesbury.

CITY    Capital letters donate city status in 1642.

# I

# Darkness

*Ralph Reeve*

*Radway, eight o'clock in the evening*

Ralph stared into the pathetic, hesitant flames. The wood was damp, smoky, of little warmth. Christ knew where Clem had found it, some poor cottager's stack for the winter or the vicarage orchard. Some of it was still green, sap oozing from the grain in spluttering bursts of steam.

He did not really care. He sat wrapped in a cloak, his mind numbed by the day's events and the cold of the night. The uncertain light flickered upon a circle of faces trying to comprehend the enormity of what they had seen, what they had done; a circle of exhausted horsemen, gentlemen, yeomen and serving troopers.

They had all volunteered to join the King's army. But few of them had ever expected that it would really come to pitched battle. Fewer still had dwelt upon what a battle would actually entail. It was a shock to all but the few old soldiers, the very hard, or the truly dull witted.

Most had imagined some glorious show of force, perhaps a charge to round up a rebellious rabble – the King's cavaliers against poorly-armed peasants. None had foreseen the slog in smoke and half-light they had experienced. They had no idea of what would happen next.

Each sat wrapped in their thoughts and the vapour of their breath in the cold night air. Already the evening dew was starting to freeze. After a glorious sunlit day came clawing cold, frost and darkness. Bowed faces, dull steel and freezing breath wavered in the inconsistent firelight.

They sat in silence, gaping at the fire, lost in reflexion. Here and there a man shivered uncontrollably, teeth clattering, chest frozen, stomach clenched as the fear they had fought to hide overwhelmed them in the darkness. Some nursed wounds, cuts, bruises, powder-burns. But it was the mind, rather than the body, that troubled most. They turned in upon themselves searching out inner hurts and fears.

Most found guilt. Guilt for what they had done – or for what they had not. Guilt for having ridden down fellow men, fellow Christians, protestants, fellow Englishmen. Guilt for having left the battle before it was truly over. Guilt for failing to do more, for failing to fulfil their duty. But, above all, most felt the guilt of having survived.

Lanterns and a brazier flared within the old church. Pools of shifting light from door and window washed over a grave-yard of fresh bodies. Macabre shadows danced within. Cries for help echoed into the night over the moan of tortured and exhausted men as the King's surgeons did what they could for the broken, shattered and bleeding that were brought to them. Those that heard them prayed they would never need the surgeons' attentions.

Some could not stand the strain and slunk away to seek the peace and comfort of their village billets of the night before. A few stayed active. Captain Smith rode out into the darkness time and again to rescue wounded men from the horrors of the battlefield. Clem built a fire and tended the horses, drying them of sweat, rubbing down stiff muscles, walking them to find water. They needed it. Luke sat cleaning and checking his musket.

Ralph stared into the wavering flames. Guilt and doubt swamped him. Why was he here? What had he done? Was this the way all battles ended? What had he thought would happen when he joined the King's army? Why had Clem and Luke followed him here?

Clem was the one Reeve servant to step forward without question to accompany him on his journey to join the King. Ralph had wished for no other. Childhood playmates, they had saved each other from the worst of scrapes at petty school and home. Clem had always been there when he returned from grammar school, always ready to ride or walk out for sport.

The Tooley's were a rough lot. Clem's father was a bully. A known smuggler, he had drowned landing barrels of Dutch genever in a storm. The elder brother was not much better, a drunk and petty criminal. Katherine Tooley, Clem's mother, was the village midwife. She sold ale from a rundown tenement on the edge of the village where she tended the sick and the lame – villagers and animals – that came to her. Some whispered she was a sybil, a cunning woman helped by fairies. She was a knowing, kind woman; a caring nurse to his brother Francis and a comfort to their mother.

Clem probably hoped his master would rise up the social ladder and take him with him. Perhaps Clem was simply waiting for an opportunity to move on, but he did not think so. Clem was comfortable in the old ways, where master and servant knew their place and their responsibilities in the natural order. Clem had promised Ralph's father to care for him. More importantly, he had promised the other servants that he would protect him.

In return, Ralph was expected to choose the best path for them both, a path through a complex and changing world. As master, he was expected to provide food, clothing and a horse for Clem. Theirs was a mutual dependency and bond. But his choices had brought them to this battlefield and this night of pain and uncertainty. His own jacket was torn, his purse almost empty – and with winter drawing in. He pulled his cloak closer. Christ knew how he was going to do his duty towards Clem.

Luke was more complex: rational, pragmatic, reserved – a deep thinker. He was no romantic; he had always been the sensible one, always ready with an answer for Ralph to copy at grammar school. Luke would not have accompanied him on a whim. He chose the King's cause from reason. Prosperous yeomen farmers, the Sheringtons owned more land in Westleton than any other family, more than Ralph's own father. They would have little use for blind loyalty to a king who taxed them heavily for ship money. And yet, the Sheringtons had as much to lose, if not more than his own family.

Luke feared revolution as much as any gentleman. He did not wish to see some Leveller mob sweep away his family's hard-won gains. Luke had seen the chaos unleashed in the corn riots that swept through Colchester, Long Melford and the Stour Valley earlier that summer. He had read of the pillage, rape and destruction of the wars in Europe and Ireland. For Luke, even a tyrant king was better than anarchy.

God knew that Ralph's reasons for being there were less noble. Yes, he too believed in social order, bound by a hierarchy of dependency and the shared fellowship of the village. He believed in an Anglican church governed by King and bishops – surely, this was the natural order of things. But he had not thought deeply about the merits of each cause.

He was not sure what he had fought for. It was instinctive to answer the King's call to arms, easy to accept the call as a duty. His father's sympathies lay with the King. Had he only volunteered to please his father? Christ knew he needed to do something to regain the old man's love – to end the drunken, sullen anger that seethed at his return from London in shame.

The fuss and attention at his announcement he would join the King had made it all seem right. He had revelled in it. Best of all was Susanna's reaction, the visits, the lingering after church, the slightest squeeze of a hand, a kiss and a parting gift. It was nothing more than a ribbon, a ribbon for his hat, in the King's colour. But it was *her* ribbon, *her* favour that he wore.

All would have been perfect were it not for his brother. Francis had left for Cambridge calling them all sinners, drunkards and bastards. He accused Ralph of abusing their father's love. Was he right? He was not sure if Francis was more upset by his foolish jealousy for Susanna or their father's old rapier, a rapier now shattered in a battle between them.

What if Francis was right? Not for one moment had he stopped to consider what would happen if he joined the losing side. Could his joining the King cause yet more trouble for his family? There were plenty of powerful families that wanted what was left of the Reeve lands. They would take any opportunity to bring their influence and law suits to bear against his father. The family had lost most of what it once had. And their father was almost certainly deep in debt.

Deep down, he knew that he had volunteered to be a

soldier to prove that he was not a failure. He needed to show that he could make something of himself. He needed to prove that he was a man, a gentleman, worthy of his place in society. He needed to prove that he would be able to uphold his heritage; that he would not slip down the social ladder. He would not be the one that failed.

In truth, there had been nothing else left that he could do. He had volunteered to fight for the King because he had failed at everything else. He had squandered the one real chance he had to make it in this world. He had failed as an apprentice to a merchant draper in London, a position and failure that had cost his father dear.

He shivered, sweat running cold down his spine. His was not a noble calling. He was here because of his own personal failings: his failure to curb his sanguine impulses; his imprudence; his inability to control his temper – worse, to control his lust for a woman. Had he dragged Clem and Luke into the chaos of this battle just to prove he wasn't a failure?

He relived the moment he was caught fucking his master's wife. It had served the puritanical old goat right, but it had cost him dear: years of hard graft wasted, his indenture lost. There could be no going back, no forgiveness. He was a sinner beyond redemption. He was cast out, damned.

God knew how he had tried. For four long years he'd tried to conform. He worked every daylight hour and long into the night to satisfy his master, to learn his trade. He knelt and bowed his head in prayer with his master's family and servants, morning, noon and night. But he never felt that he belonged. It had been the same as a child, at school, ever since his mother died. He wanted to belong but always felt he was an outsider. No matter how hard he tried, he never truly felt accepted. Perhaps he never would.

He had tried to adopt his master's puritan ways, suppressing his natural love of merriment, carousing, lewdness. They could not stop him now. He would drink, swear, dance and fuck when and where he liked.

He stirred at the thought of her, at the memory of her smell, her taste, her clutching pleasure. In God's name, how was he supposed to have resisted her? She was a seductress, demanding that he soothe her itching lust.

Yes, he had fallen to temptation, but damn those city elders for their judgement and their hypocrisy. There were plenty of them who had drooled over their bibles and copybooks at her. Half of them plagued the city's stews, took whores, mistresses and maidservants to spill out their frustration in sweating labour.

It should have been the daughter. He should have seduced and married her. She would have been a good catch, bringing with her the old man's business. God knew that he'd been tempted and tried. She was pretty enough, too. But she was a tight little puritan tease. With her bible and disdain, she scowled at his advances and loose country ways.

The wife was different, dark and lusty under her headscarf and drab puritan smocks. He had known she was trouble. He tried to stay out of her way, but in the end he could not resist. He knew that she felt it too. He saw her struggle between desire for him and duty, how she rejected and reproached him after their first innocent touch. A younger second wife, not much older than the daughter, she was jealous of his attention towards the girl. He had guessed too at her frustration – the old man failing to sate her hot prickling desire at night. The old fool did not see the storm brewing as he worked and prayed late into the evening before snoring in his chamber.

Finally, she came to him as he worked in a storeroom. Unable to resist her blatant, wanton kiss, unable to contain his own frustration, he fucked her hard on a great bale of wool-cloth. Stunned at the immediacy of their act, neither spoke a word as the old man counted his money in the chamber above.

For three weeks they rutted furtively in storerooms and closets, against walls, tables, chests and bales of the old man's precious bloody broadcloth. Driven on by the sticky, airless heat of the city and by their own lust, they fucked each other with increasing abandon. They met secretly one evening in a walled garden, rolling on the warm damp grass under a pear tree. But, best of all, there was one glorious afternoon, stolen from his rounds, when they took a chamber in a Queenhithe tavern.

Each had explored the other's nakedness. Slick with sweat and their sex, they touched, kissed, tasted and fucked each other for two shameless hours. Finally sated, they lay together, a tangle of sheets and limbs, listening to their bodies, the port and city outside. The sun at the window, the noise of the street and the bawdy laughter of the punters, whores and boatmen below all added to the joy of their forbidden pleasure. The sunlight from the river painted a pattern of light upon the low ceiling, water nymphs writhing in careless abandon, tongues of light lapping each other's curves, seeking each other's centre, melting, folding one into another until they dashed themselves into a hundred points of light.

But it could not last. He had known it would not last. They could not hide their lust from those that watched, from those who sought out sinners. He was sure the bloody daughter knew. Part of him wanted her to know. He wanted her to know what she was missing, what she could have had. He knew that the storm would break. But he could not resist. He could not say no. He was trapped. She threatened to have him thrown out if he stopped loving her. He could not have stopped himself even if it had been otherwise.

Once more, he followed her into a back chamber. With quiet urgency, he bent her over a great carpet-covered chest. Raising her skirts, he fucked her from behind, long deep thrusts that had her clawing at the rich fabric, relishing the power and impurity of it – of fucking like beasts. He heard her gasped pleasure. He felt her belly twitch and grasp at him until sweet splintering chaos was ripped from his own core.

Collapsing on top of her, for one glorious moment he drank in the smell of damp skin and ruffled hair, her scent mixed with the distant aroma of dust, heat and the spices of the orient rising from the carpet beneath them. It was typical of the old miser to keep something of such beauty locked away and untouched in a back room.

It was only then that he heard the scream. He had no idea how long the daughter had been there. Perhaps she had followed to watch their primal act; perhaps she had only then stepped into the room. It did not matter. They were caught.

They only just had time to stand before the old man arrived with surprising speed. Ralph fumbled with his clothes as the accusations flew. Straightening his apron, he was stunned to realise that the bitch was shouting at him, accusing him of forcing himself upon her. Like a twisting cat, she was covering her tracks, protecting herself at his expense. Perhaps she had always been ready for this moment. The stinging slap across his face burned. Damn her. He'd caught the second swing, holding her wrist, throwing her back. She turned on her husband, demanding that he throw him out of the house and his employ.

The foolish old cuckold raised his stick. Ralph wrenched it free and broke it over the chest, the dry wood shattering in a cloud of dust from the carpet that had held their pleasure. He did not wait for more but marched from the room. She turned from him as he left. But he saw the tear and bitten lip as she did.

He gathered his meagre purse and what he could of his belongings before leaving the merchant's house for good. The door slammed behind him. He hurled his apprentice's apron into the shit and filth of the gutter. It belonged with the city's rats.

He went straight to the nearest inn, at the end of St Swithin's Lane. That prig Nehemiah Wharton tried to stop him, to remonstrate, calling him back to repent. The other puritan folk pulled their windows shut, ushering their children inside as he passed. It was as if they could smell her on him, as if he was unclean, as if they would catch the pox just by looking at him. As if anarchy and hell followed him.

The Golden Anchor was as cool and dark as the penny ale it served. He swallowed down the smooth rich sweet malt flavour, feeling its strength sooth him. Savouring its forbidden pleasure, he ignored the glances and whispers of the merchants sitting around their dinner. He would never succeed in their puritan world. But he had sworn on the London Stone that they would pay him back for the years of sweat and grovelling. One day, one day he would return to claim his due.

Warmed by the memory of her body, Ralph wrapped himself in his cloak and lay down to sleep. These were memories of spring. Now it was a cold autumn night and there was nothing he could do to change what had been. Whatever the next day brought, he was a soldier now and needed sleep. Clem had returned and lit a pipe of tobacco. Its smoke mingled with the firewood and freezing breath of those around the fire. The pipe smelled good. It smelled of home.

But, fuck, how he missed London. He missed its bustling, boisterous, heaving mass of humanity; its shops, silversmiths, booksellers, butchers, bakers, fishmongers and street criers; he missed its inns, taverns and alehouses; its theatres, pleasure gardens and houses of ill repute. He missed its dark narrow streets, even when the rain turned them slick with mud and when the sun turned them to dust.

Perhaps more than anything, he missed the river, the great sweep of the Thames with its bridge, quays, steps, ferries and swarming boats and, towering over all, the mass of church towers, spires, ships' masts and endless chimneys. Fuck, he even missed its smoke and stench, its horse piss and foul tide. He missed its beauty and its filth, its sophistication and its squalor. For London truly was the greatest city in Christendom.

One day, he would return with money in his purse. Enough money to take his pleasure in that glorious, mean, brilliant shit heap, that bejewelled seductress bitch of a city.

## II

# Dread Night

*Francis Reeve*

**Kineton Field, midnight**

Francis stamped on the cold earth. Frost had crept over the damp ground and seeped into his boots to claw at his bones and at his soul. Like most of Essex's Army, his regiment remained on the battlefield. They stood in almost the same positions in which they had started the day, their colonels not daring to let them find shelter for fear that they would not return to face the King at dawn.

They stood in clusters around pitiful fires that gave little warmth and no cheer. The damp, cold night air frosted helmets, armour, horse harness and weapons, biting at fingers, ears, cheeks. It was impossible to rest. Men simply stared into the flames and prayed for this dread night to end. Even when someone found a little cheese and hard bread, Francis and the others ate in silence. In truth, it was a struggle to chew, let alone talk. His jaw and temple ached from teeth clenched through the battle. He had not been conscious of the natural reaction, but now his head ached, like much of his bruised body.

There were many fires, each throwing a pool of light on a group of men, young and old, brooding, wrapped in their thoughts; fires that surrounded Kineton and flickered along the low ridge that had held the King's onslaught. Other fires lined the base of Edgehill, clung to its slopes and flickered from its summit marking the line where the King's army slumped down for the night.

Brighter than any was the signal beacon, lit to warn Parliament that its army had faced the King in battle and that they were at war. The beacon's flames flared high and bright stoked with pitch. The warning was seen and passed on by a second beacon that burned forty miles to the south as the ancient signal chain carried the message across Oxfordshire, Buckinghamshire and Hertfordshire to London.

But beyond the pools of light was the night, a cold terrible half-light that stretched across the vale. A great autumn hunter's moon did nothing to conceal its horrors. Its silver light etched a stark scene of light and dark amid the first tendrils of mist rising from the earth. Across this midnight field dread shadows moved.

Worse than the shadows were the sounds of the night, sounds that no man wished to hear. From the vastness of the vale, came a low continuous moan. It was the chilling sound of the wounded. Broken men called for help, cursed or whimpered pleas for mother and maker, long sobbing groans of despair. Every now and then, a shriek of agony pierced the night air as tormented souls were moved or stripped by the creatures that roamed amongst them.

The groaning lasted through the night as the stronger fought death. Blessedly, the howls of Golgotha died slowly as frost, shock and trauma took its toll on shattered, exhausted and frightened bodies. Darkness enveloped the vale as the wreaths of mist closed over the ground to form a thick, deadening fog.

The cries of the wounded only reinforced the shock and self-reproach of the survivors. This was not what they had imagined, not the godly victory they had prayed for. Instead, this was the noise of many inglorious deaths amongst the mud and filth of a stalemate, ignominious deaths at the hands of want, cold and the scavenger. It was the noise of souls being dragged to Hell. Evil roamed the battlefield unchecked, haunted this cursed place.

God chose those who lived and those who died, those who were maimed and those untouched. Why had God spared him? Why had God not gathered him in to paradise? He had done all that God demanded. He had scattered the heathen and sacrificed his enemies in His name. He had charged the very engines of Hell while those around him were cut down. Had he not done enough to be chosen? Was he still not worthy?

He so wanted to be with his mother again, to feel her heavenly touch, to hear her voice. He so wanted to sleep and know that she would be there when he awoke. He still remembered her singing him to sleep with her strange Bohemian lullabies. He did not understand the words but remembered the rhythm of her prayer for angels to watch over him.

*Spi, mé milé poupě,*
*Spi, malé holoubě.*
*Spi mi dobrou chvíli.*

Turning away from the firelight, Francis hid the tear that hung cold on his cheek. He wished he was a sickly child again to have her wipe away his pain. Instead, he was left to brush his face with a rough hide gauntlet. Why did God torment him still?

The Lord must yet have a purpose for him. Was he yet to see Christ's reign on earth? Was he to build the New Jerusalem? Would he yet marry Susanna and live with her in a New Zion, in God's City on the Hill? Was this God's purpose? *Please God, give me the strength to deliver Thy will.*

Or was it God's will that he face his bastard brother again? Did God demand that sacrifice? God had caused their paths to cross on the battlefield. If it had not been for his possessed horse falling and that heathen, Clem Tooley – the spawn of Satan's Bitch, the child of the witch who murdered his beautiful mother – he might have killed Ralph then.

Instead, he had been thrown to the ground to roll with his horse in humiliation and pain. Ralph had always been the better rider, strong and reckless, while he had been uneasy, clumsy, hesitant. He had never really understood horses or dogs, not like Ralph or that warlock, Tooley, who seemed able to enchant any animal to his will.

Once again, Francis slid his hand under his steel armour to touch the Bible he kept there, to take comfort in its words. Lifting his face to the cold night, he whispered the lines of a psalm, Psalm 86, the prayer of David.

*'Thou hast delivered my soul from the lowest hell.*

*Oh God, the proud are risen against me and the assemblies of violent men have sought after my soul. And they have not set Thee before them. But Thou, oh Lord, art a God full of compassion and gracious longsuffering, plenteous in mercy and truth.*

*Oh turn unto me and have mercy upon me. Give strength unto Thy servant. Save the son of Thy handmaiden. Show me a token that they which hate me may see it and be ashamed.'*

# III

# The Quick and the Dead

*Robbie Needham*

***Amongst the dead, Monday the 24<sup>th</sup>
of October 1642, first light***

The body lay face down in the freezing earth where it had fallen. A covering of frost dusted the muddy and blood-stained jerkin of a King's Lifeguard, tiny ice particles sparkling in the faint moonlight of a smothering fog.

Something tugged at Robbie Needham's leg. From the far recesses of his mind, his aunt called to a small boy, calling down to him in the mine; calling for him to come up, to get up, to find his cousin, to find Hal. Hal who had been stuck through with a pike in the groin.

With a start, he was conscious again. He kicked at the dark shadow that gripped his boot, sending it scurrying, cursing back into the darkness.

He pushed his half-frozen body up, struggling on shaking limbs, numb. It was as if the earth did not want to give him up. The frozen soil clung to him, plucking at his sleeves, sticking to his frosted clothes. His senses returning, he tasted cloying earth in his mouth and nostrils. Earth and blood. His blood.

He sat spitting out the mix of stones, grit and broken teeth that filled his mouth. His tongue pushed the grating mix past jagged stumps and pulpy gums. With trembling, dirt-smeared fingers he carefully explored his smashed and swollen face. Broken lips hung over bleeding gums and broken stumps where his front teeth had been. One side of his bruised face was swollen to the point of closing over his eye. His whole face ached. At the first touch of his nose, searing jolts of pain pierced his skull. He braced himself, touched again. It was broken, flattened, bent across his face. He would be marked for life, disfigured by a scar-faced bastard musketeer in a purple coat.

Dragging himself onto numb, shaking legs, Robbie took stock. The fog enclosed an eerie scene of death painted in the moon's diffused light. He was surrounded by bodies. Many were stripped, others lay in their dirty and blood-stained shirts. They looked like a field of sleeping sheep in the grey predawn light.

Close by lay the naked body of an old man, a dark bullet hole pierced its chest. One outstretched arm ended in a stump at the wrist, as if reaching for its severed hand. The other lay across the slumped body of a servant, an old retainer – Jason.

This crumpled, naked old man was the King's Standard Bearer, Sir Edmund. His boots, fine breeches, hose and linen shirt were all stripped away, stolen to expose mottled, lumpen legs rotten with gout. God knew the pain it must have cost the stupid old bugger to carry that bloody standard this far.

Not far beyond lay John Scollins and his 'ahtey, his mate, poor bloody Billie. There would be tears and sorrow in Ilkeston at their loss. There would be wakes in many a Peak village and cottage for lost sons. Aye, pain and want across all

England. He was buggered if he knew how he would tell his aunt of cousin Hal.

Robbie heard again Jason beg his master to withdraw, the old man's refusal to leave, his call for the Lifeguard to stand with him. With a terrible shiver, he heard Billie's scream as he was cut down, John's last defiant yell as the final wave broke over them all.

He could not remain amongst the dead. They were beyond help now. They must wait for God or the Devil. He needed to get back to the living. But before he left, there was one more body he must find. He groped his way forward to find his tormentor, the rank-mouthed Yorkshire bastard that near killed him in the last great push of pike.

With cold, shivering fingers in the pale light of dawn, Robbie buckled on the dead man's breastplate, a rough-edged gouge scored across it by his own pike. If there was more fighting to be done, he was buggered if he were going to be stuck through the gut like poor Hal.

Gingerly, he tried on the hireling's helmet. It was battered, bent and the cheek-guard flapped against his swollen face and jaw. The bastard could keep it. He would stick with his leather miners' cap.

The armour fitted well enough. He chose a pike from among the many that littered the ground: a good ash pole, undamaged by musket ball or blade; it was a foot shorter than it should have been – no matter. . . better to control in a fight.

He took one last look around him, one last look at Sir Edmund, Jason, John and Billie. One last look at the bodies of the King's Lifeguard and the regiments that charged them time and again, men and horses twisted in grotesque shapes, all clutching for a silken standard.

Robbie forced cold stiff limbs to stagger back down the slope they'd fought their way up. The first light of dawn etched the outline of Edgehill, the fires of the King's army still glowing in its shadow.

## IV

# Retreat

*William Bennett*

*Kineton, Tuesday the 25<sup>th</sup> of October 1642, eight o'clock in the morning*

Nehemiah's hand felt hot, damp, clammy, despite the morning chill. Fever had taken hold. Its sweating fire seeped from the festering wound to leave his body limp, pallid, clawing for breath.

William Bennett could not bring himself to let go of the hand while there was still life in it. But he dared not look at the young sergeant's face again. Its bloated mass was bound together by dirty bandages that leaked puss and dark blood. Underneath, the flesh hung in a rotting flap where the cavalier's sword had laid it open to the bone. A single glazed eye stared out at the fog-bound street.

They had dragged Nehemiah back to the Parliamentary lines after the damned cavaliers had ridden over them. It was Nehemiah who had stood like a rock. He was the one to hold them together in the dust and chaos of that terrible charge, abandoned by their own horsemen. He was the backbone of their company, an Israelite to William's own failure, his Nehemiah.

For two days the surgeons had done what they could while the army buried the dead. Now Nehemiah lay unconscious in an open cart, a cart filled with wounded men, a mass of broken and bloody bodies, shattered stumps and rotten bandages. Few had even the energy to moan, much less pray. A miasma of foul sweat, excrement and death hung over the cart in the cold damp air.

'William, it is time you rejoined your company. You have done what you can for him. They need you now.' His lieutenant-colonel was right. But he could not bear to let go.

James Quarles was an old soldier. He had done his best to form their band of young London apprentices, journeymen and street hawkers into a regiment. With tears in his eyes William gently let go of Nehemiah's hand. He stumbled down the muddy street to follow the remainder of Holles's Regiment of Foot past other carts, wagons and carriages of wounded, munitions and baggage, past fat bloated crows that hopped, flapped, pulled and fought over bloodied scraps in the mud.

He did not know why they were leaving. Essex had left for Warwick Castle the day before, the day after the battle. Now the whole army was following. They were marching back the way they had come, north and west, away from London. They were retreating. They were leaving the way open for the King to march on the city.

The battle had not been the great victory that Parliament had promised. They were supposed to have faced nothing more than a rabble of serving men and a few drunken fops. They went to bring back a repentant King to rule with Parliament, to commit his court of evil counsellors to chains. Instead, they had been mauled by a determined and courageous army that even now stood its ground on Edgehill.

Had it all been in vain? Had he risked his business and home, his family for nothing? He had invested all that he had to raise his company of foot, leaving his business and house at the mercy of creditors. He had wanted so much to be a hero, to make his wife proud after all the long years of suffering. He wanted to wipe clean the discredit of bankruptcy and the debtor's gaol. It was not his fault that his stock was impounded, filched, left to rot while corrupt courtiers made their profit. If it had not been for an uncle in Virginia, he would have died in that gaol. Thomasine and the children would have been thrown into penury, forced indenture or, worse, forced to sell their bodies to sate vice, to be the prey of every immoral perversion.

He had worked his way back to prosperity, had wanted to finally be accepted amongst the city elite, to be an alderman, perhaps even Lord Mayor. An independent merchant, he always felt he was shunned by the older, established companies, the city corporation, its courts and Guildhall. He wanted so much to be accepted among them, to finally be somebody. He had told himself that he was doing it all for Thomasine.

Instead of bringing love and support, his decision to soldier was met with anger and hostility. Thomasine accused him of abandoning her and their children, of running away, of leaving her to run the business when trade was depressed and prices high. She said that he would not leave her if he truly loved her, that he was only doing it for his own selfish pride, that she and the children would end up on the street.

But it had been too late to back out. He had accepted his commission, his contract to raise and command a company in the London regiment of Denzil Holles, the champion of Parliament's Grande Remonstrance against the King. He had sold all his stock and his shares in a ship to raise the capital to equip a hundred soldiers with pikes, muskets, swords, armour, uniforms and accoutrements. He had even mortgaged their home to pay his men when Parliament failed to.

Commanding a company of soldiers was not as easy or as rewarding as he had expected. No matter how much money he spent, there was no clear return. They ruined their uniforms and broke, lost or spoiled equipment. Some even deserted. And they always moaned. They seemed to sense that he struggled with the complicated drill manoeuvres and arcane wording of the orders expected of him.

They preferred the rude humour of the old soldiers more than his money. It seemed that soldiering was more than uniforms and bright equipment. No matter how fine they looked on parade, many of Parliament's regiments had run in the face of men dressed half in rags. Some of the King's Welsh foot had not even been equipped with pike or musket.

Soldiering had cost him so much more than he had expected. It exhausted his money, time and energy. Thomasine's rejection crushed him. They had parted with barely a word. It was Nehemiah who had saved him from failure, Nehemiah who translated his orders, who kept discipline on the march, who held the company together on the battlefield, Nehemiah who he had hoped would one day marry his own daughter, his sweet Rebecca.

And now he was running away, stumbling down a muddy street in a godforsaken little village in the middle of nowhere, running away from Nehemiah's gangrenous face, the cartloads of death, a lost battle and his home.

He had lost everything. He knew only too well how a man could rise to better himself one moment but fall the next in this unforgiving world. He was a fool to have risked so much.

He was a fool to ever believe he could be a soldier, a fool to leave London, his wife, children and home.

He was a failure. He was ruined. He could not even protect his wife and children in their home. Palpitations seized him again, the black bile of melancholy filling his chest, crushing him. Oh God, he wanted to hide. Let him find a bed, curl in a ball under warm coverlets, let the darkness of depression wash over him. Just leave him to sleep.

A pistol shot barked in the fog behind him.

'William, run! For God's sake run!' It was Colonel Quarles, urging him on, urging him back from his dark despair. 'Cavalier horse. They are in the village!'

'Leave me. It is too late.'

'No, damn it, it is not! Your company need you. Damn it, *I* need you! I need you to command them if we are ever to get out of this mess.'

'But the army is retreating. We have lost.'

'William, we may be retreating, but we have not yet lost the war. You must keep your company together. If not, there will be many more like Sergeant Nehemiah Wharton.'

William turned as more pistol shots rang out. Flames flickered bright in the fog as the bloody cavaliers torched a cart. With tears wet on his face he stumbled after his lieutenant-colonel, his regiment and his company.

# V

# The Rendezvous

*Hywel Lloyd*

***Edgecote House, Wednesday the 26th
of October 1642, ten o'clock***

Hywel Lloyd stood with his musket by his side. He did not care that its stock was scorched and blackened where that *pidyn*, Benion, had blown up a barrel of powder. It was his now. Now he could fight as a musketeer. Like many in his regiment, he'd fought the battle armed only with an old billhook and his hunting knife. Now he was a proper soldier.

The thought of it still wounded him. They'd charged the Parliamentary line. But with only a few muskets they could not match the fire of their enemies. With weapons fit for a cattle-raid they'd faced massed musket, pike and cannon. In the end, they were forced to give ground, forced back by the bloody English. It would not happen again. They would not lose in a fair fight.

They were men of Wales, hard mountain men of north Wales. They came from the valleys, villages and *hendra* of Eryri, the Carneddau and Mynydd Hiraethog, men of Denbigh, Caernarfon, Harlech, Llŷn and Ynys Môn. Welsh vermin some called them. They might not have many airs and graces clad in their homespun wool, but they could outrun, sing, drink or fight any Englishman.

Now they had the weapons they needed. Just give them another battle. They would show what Wales could do. They would fight all the way to the Tower of London if they had to. It was time to teach those tossers in Parliament a lesson. They'd gone too far. *Reform* they called it. Well, as far as he could see, it was sacrilege. They sent their preachers to destroy everything that it was to be Welsh: their language, their singing, their dancing, poetry and art. Worse was what they did in the name of religion. They banned saints' days, pilgrimages and maypoles. They said they weren't in the Bible. They smashed statues and stained glass, and whitewashed their painted churches. Desecration it was. What would they know of it? There were saints in Wales when the English were still bloody heathens.

Now they punished the old folk that still used their beads, those that kept to the old ways and those that held to the old beliefs. It was as if they wanted to banish *y Tylwyth Teg*, the fairy folk. They said they were evil, not natural. They would snuff out all nature, beauty, colour, song and ritual with their black and white, fire and brimstone.

Their ministers preached that everyone was free to choose his own path. That no man was bound to his lord. That a man was free to rise by his own labour in the marketplace. They wanted to turn the world upside down. It was all bollocks. No man wanted to live alone in the mountains. They needed each other. It was good enough for their fathers. Why change it now?

He did not have to follow his lord to war. But he was buggered if he would miss it. His lord had called his freemen together and they came willingly for the honour and glory of it. One day they would sing of this in the halls, *hendras* and *hafods* across Wales. His children's children would know that he followed his lord as a warrior, like his forefathers before him.

He may not have a fine hall or great herd of cattle, but he was Hywel *mab* Madog Lloyd ap Maurice ab Ellis Gethyn ap Cadwaladr of Cyffylliog in Llanynys, *teulu* to Rhys ap Meredydd, who took up the Red Dragon Banner at Bosworth fight, descended from Marchudd ap Cynan noble chief and lord of Bruffenigl by his mam. And nobody was going to deny him his right to be here.

Besides, he was indebted to his lord. Not for money. But he owed his freedom to Sir Thomas Salusbury. He could not ignore his lord's call to war. It was his chance to repay the debt.

It had been Sir Thomas that freed him from Chester gaol. He and some of the boys had driven cattle to market there. Well, they celebrated afterwards. But there was a girl and a fight. It was the bloody Englishman that started it. He would have been damned if he did not answer the *sarhad*, the insult, with fist, cudgel and blade. He beat the *Sais* fucker in a fair fight. But English law said he was a criminal, caged him behind bars, said he was to hang.

He never did get his knife or purse back. Worst of all had been having to tell his mam, watching her struggle to feed them all that winter. The cattle were their pride and joy, their walking gold, but some fucking English gaoler stole their gold. A year's labour on the mountains gone. But he was free, thanks to Sir Thomas. He was free, he had a new hunting knife and he had a musket.

Now the King had called his army together again. A

rendezvous they called it. Well, the Welsh were ready to march and fight again. They followed their lord and his king as freemen for the honour it brought. Now let them have it. Let slip the *lluoedd*, unleash the host!

---

Robbie Needham glared at the army around him through a single eye. The other was closed up under the swollen mass that was half his face. With his nose flattened, lacerated lips and shattered stumps for teeth, he bore the marks of that final stand around the Royal Standard. Though the wind blew cold, his face was hot, inflamed, angry under his miner's cap.

The King's army stood in a great hollow arc ranked against Edgcote Hill. Regiments of foot and horse and the train of artillery faced inwards towards Edgcote House. From a mound in front of the house, the King surveyed his army on his white charger, attended by courtiers, secretaries, heralds and officers.

Beside the King, the Royal Standard snapped its long tails in the cold wind. It was battered and holed but it still stood, a challenge to those who would defy, impeach, curtail or usurp their king's power. Once again it was the rally call to save England from a parliament of upstarts, city merchants and bankers, rich bastards who turned their back on people living in hunger and misery, who stole their livelihoods and cast them out for their own gain.

Robbie stood stiffly in his scratched and dented armour. Armour that he'd taken on the field of battle, taken from an enemy he'd killed. If he had to, he would do it all again. Beside him, others in the King's Lifeguard were bandaged, bruised, tattered. But they stood straight, ready to follow their king. They'd lost many good men, men from the Peaks of Derbyshire, Nottingham and the fens of Lincoln, but they weren't beat. They were ready to march again. If needs be, they'd face the King's enemies once more. They'd march against cannon, pike, shot and horse again, if that was what it took.

But would these other regiments? Were they still ready to fight for their king, for their cause? Were they ready to carry him back to Whitehall, to take London? Would they still fight? Would they still fight to reclaim their dignity, to make England glorious again, to put an end to the blood sucking leeches in Parliament and city?

———

George Merrett stood with the train of artillery. He watched as heralds, trumpeters and officers cantered between the regiments and their sovereign Captain-General. They brought reports of the numbers that stood with each colour, their readiness to march and to fight.

Three full tertias of foot, two brigades of horse and the artillery train stood on parade. It was clear to all that the King's Army was in good order.

Every regiment had lost men during the battle. Still more carried a wound, not least four of the army's commanders; Sergeant-Major-General Sir Jacob Astley and three of his brigade commanders, Sir Nicholas Byron, Charles Gerard and John Belasyse had all been scarred. But most of those missing after the battle had returned and stood once more with their colours.

This was not a beaten army. This was an army that was ready to march and ready to fight. Ready to return their king to power, to curb an infantile parliament that played on the desires of the ignorant masses, that would leave England weak, divided, defenceless.

And at their centre, at the base of the mound upon which the King sat, were the trophies they had won, the spoils captured in battle. Seven cannon stood ready to be manned by the King's gunners. Piled on those guns were no less than fifty-seven captured colours, near a quarter of all those that had stood with Essex.

Wagonloads of muskets, pikes, swords, armour, match, powder and shot were captured as Essex retreated from Kineton. As a gentleman of the ordnance, George had worked long hours to count, itemise, divide and issue them to the King's regiments. The poor bloody Welsh needed them most. Now Taffy stood proud and fierce, ready to march.

They had even captured Essex's own coach stuffed with his baggage and correspondence, letters and copies of orders detailing the enemy's numbers and condition. A perfect hoard for the King's intelligencers.

The feeling of strength and confidence was infectious. It seemed to spread on the fresh cool wind. A buzz of excitement passed back and forth along the ranks. The King's army would march again. Rumours flowed as to where they were headed. Some said they would besiege Essex in Warwick, others that Rupert and his cavaliers would dash for London. But the rumours quickly solidified into clear intent as messages and orders were issued.

The army was to take Banbury. They were to march immediately to surround the castle and town. The King himself would march to Aynho. He would hold the junction of the road south to Oxford and the ancient cattle drovers' way to London.

---

Ralph Reeve watched the herald canter out from the King to halt in front of his regiment. He and the other troopers waited in anticipation as Lord Grandison, Lord John Stuart and Captain Smith were called forward to attend His Majesty. Were they to receive some special mission?

In front of the whole army, Smith knelt before his King to be knighted for his valour in breaking Wharton's Regiment with only fourteen men, in rescuing the Royal Standard and in snatching away three brass cannon. He was now Captain Sir John Smith, a bannerette knighted on the field of battle.

A herald read the King's decree that Smith was to command a troop of his own. Orders followed immediately for Corporal Nisbet's division to be drawn out from the ranks. A division from Lord Grandison's own troop was added and his cornet promoted to be Smith's lieutenant. Together they formed a new troop.

For a moment, Ralph wondered if he too would be rewarded for his part in breaking Wharton's battalion, taking a colour and in saving the Royal Standard. Would they promote him to be Smith's cornet? It was what he dreamed of. But there was to be no third division and no third officer. Not today. But perhaps, if they recruited enough troopers before the rebels were defeated, there might still be a chance to be an officer.

Captain Smith took his place at their head, the new lieutenant at the rear. The two corporals and thirty troopers grinned at each other. They did not have a third division, a cornet, trumpeters, farrier or saddler. They did not have a standard. But they were a troop. They were Sir John Smith's troop.

A flurry of cantering officers, trumpeters and heralds announced to all that the King and his army were to march.

First to move was Prince Rupert's brigade of horse followed by the vanguard tertia of foot. Next came the King with the young princes, courtiers, the Troop of Show and Pensioners, followed by the train of artillery and centre tertia, with the battered Lifeguard carrying the Royal Standard high. The baggage train and rear guard followed them to turn south on the road to Banbury and Aynho.

Finally, Lord Wilmot's brigade of horse moved off. They did not follow the King south. They were to invest Banbury from the north and guard against any move by Essex from Warwick. One by one, the regiments peeled off, troop following troop, the men turning their horses' heads to file away.

At last, it was their turn, the turn of the newest troop in the army to move off. They retraced their steps through Wardington and Williamscot to Cropredy and Great Bourton. Here they branched out to leave the rest of Grandison's Regiment of Horse settling back into their old quarters. They rode on up the hill out of the Cherwell valley to new quarters of their own, the lieutenant riding ahead with a pair of guides to lay out billets.

Little Bourton was not much more than a dozen cold stone cottages, a scant green and dirty tavern. Its doors were shut, silent, dreading the arrival of winter, war, soldiers and their horses. They drew up in front of the old manor house to stand on parade in front of their new captain. It was already late and they were hungry. Pulling a sheaf of papers from his buff coat, Smith addressed them.

'Some of you know me well. Others of you will get to know me well enough. We quarter tonight in this village. Do not get too comfortable. We will be moving on once Banbury is taken. In the meantime, we form an outguard for the army. Lieutenant Musgrave will post those on guard and see the rest to quarters shortly. This will be your place of muster in the event of an alarum.

'It is customary for a new captain to acquaint his troop with his commission. I will, therefore, read to you the commission given to me by His Majesty the King.'

Smith straightened the paper in his gauntleted hand and read.

'*Charles by the Grace of God, King of Great Britain, France and Ireland, Defender of the Faith. To our trusted and well-beloved Sir John Smith, greeting. We do hereby constitute and appoint you to be captain of one troop of horse under the regiment of our trusty and well-beloved Colonel Lord Grandison.*

*The which troop you are to forthwith muster and retain of such as will willingly and voluntarily serve us for our pay and for the defence of our royal person, the two Houses of Parliament, the protestant religion, the law of the land, the liberty and propriety of our subjects. To cause them to be duly exercised in arms, commanding all inferior officers and soldiers of the said troop to obey you respectively as their captain, according to our commission hereby given to you. Given under His Majesty's signature at Edgcote.*'

Smith looked up. He searched their faces.

'As your captain, I am also required to read His Majesty's military articles to you. I will not read each and every article this first time. It is getting late and we have a duty to set our guards. However, I will read those laws and ordinances of war that I deem of greatest import, so that you may know by what I set greatest store and the punishment that may follow transgression.'

The paper steady in front of him, Smith scanned the ranks again before reading.

'First, *let no man presume to blaspheme the Holy Trinity, God the Father, God the Son and God the Holy Ghost, nor the known articles of Christian faith, upon pain to have his tongue bored with a red-hot iron.*'

He looked at them.

'Gentlemen, as your captain, I am charged to see almighty God reverently served and sermons duly frequented, as well as all churches, ministers and ornaments of God's worship protected.'

He read again.

'*No man shall use any traitorous words against His Majesty's sacred person, or royal authority, upon pain of death. Whosoever shall be convicted of doing His Majesty's service negligently and carelessly shall be punished at my discretion. And whosoever shall presume to violate His Majesty's safeguard, or safe conduct, shall die without mercy.*

*All soldiers coming to their colours to watch or to be exercised shall come fully armed, upon pain of severe correction. None shall presume to appear with their arms unfit or indecently kept, on pain of arbitrary correction.*'

Smith looked them in the eye. 'Gentlemen, I take this article most seriously. Essex may have retired to Warwick, but do not think that he is beaten. Parliament will not give up London without a fight. Not two miles from us, their garrison at Banbury remains armed against us. You are to keep yourselves, your weapons and horses fit and ready at all times. We have a duty and I will not be lenient in correcting slackness in this regard.

'*None on their march through the counties under His Majesty's obedience shall waist, spoil, or extort any victuals, money, or belongings, from any subject, but shall pay for their meat and drink at the usual rates, upon pain of death.*'

He stared at them again.

'Those of you who know me will know that I will not tolerate abuse of those less able to defend themselves. Gentlemen, there is to be no free quarter. This is not Germany or Ireland. We are here to protect His Majesty's loyal subjects from the abuses of the rebels and to restore His Majesty to their affections. Each man will pay sixpence for his board and lodging and fourpence for his horse hay. Any man that is not able to pay for his subsistence should make himself known to Mister Musgrave who will arrange payment – to be recovered at the next pay day.'

Ralph felt his purse half empty in his pocket. Was Smith staring at him? Did he know he could not afford to keep himself and Clem for much longer?

'And finally. . . *a sentinel or perdue found asleep, or drunk, or forsaking his place before he be relieved; or upon discovery, not giving warning to those quartered according to the direction given him; shall die for such offence, without mercy.*

'Again, gentlemen, I take this most seriously. We are charged with mounting an outguard for the protection of our sovereign and our army. Our enemies may yet be about this night. We are to ensure that none are to pass through our lines to do harm. Those of you that mount the watch, attend to your duties with diligence and care that others may sleep soundly, as you will want in your turn.'

Then, with a final look at his command, Smith folded the papers and turned to enter the manor house handing the parade to his new lieutenant. 'Mister Musgrave. . . please carry on.'

The young lieutenant took his captain's place. 'The outguard will be drawn from the captain's division. Corporal Nisbet, please select ten troopers and take charge as corporal of the guard. I will lead you to your outpost. The remainder will be shown to their quarters once the corps de guard is posted.'

With a sinking feeling, Ralph knew that Corporal Nisbet would pick him, Luke and Clem for guard duty. It would be a long and disturbed night with little rest and some rat-infested barn for a bed.

# VI

# South

*Ralph Reeve*

*Little Bourton, Friday the 28ᵗʰ of October 1642, dawn*

They left Little Bourton at dawn, crossing the River Cherwell by the ford at Slatford Mill. A brisk wind blew up the valley to ruffle the dark water with the first grey light. Black clouds scudded overhead, obscuring the last stars, promising rain.

The horses shook their heads at the wind in their ears as they splashed through the cold dark water. On the far bank, they waited beside the road for the rest of Grandison's Horse to pass. Ralph pulled his hat low and wrapped his cloak about him, waiting for their moment to join the great column. The King's Army was marching south, to Oxford, and Wentworth's Brigade of horse were to lead it. The horses were restless as they watched the great host streaming past in the half-light until their own regiment came into view and they joined its tail.

Horses and men were eager to be moving in the stiff grey cold, eager to be moving south towards Oxford and the great prize: London. While the troopers rode in silence, their mounts could not contain their whickering and tossing of heads. Manes and tails flicked in the wind, harness jangling as they stepped out on the road.

A mile south, they crossed the river again at Grimsbury Bridge and passed under the walls of Banbury Castle to enter the town with a wave from the King's newly installed garrison. Their hooves echoed through the grey, deserted streets. Here and there a light shone in a shop or inn as fires were stoked and water drawn. But no crowd greeted them, just cold dark streets and shuttered windows. Banbury was a puritan town, a conquered town. There was no joy for the cavaliers who rode through it.

They left the empty market place and its famous Banbury Cross in the grey dawn. Light shone from a single shop ahead, a baker's shop. Here at least, trade outweighed politics. On the street outside, a woman chivvied a boy with a tray of warm, sweet-smelling cakes whilst shouting instructions inside.

'Cakes! Banbury cakes! Best in town. Well, go on boy, hand them up! Can't you reach that tray higher? The gentlemen will be hungry and they don't have time to stop. Jarvis! Jarvis, I needs another tray. And get more in that there oven! There's another lot comin now!'

'All right Betty, all right, I'm comin, but I only got two hands and I needs more currants.'

'Cakes! Banbury cakes! Best in town. Now gentlemen, how many would you be a wantin? Go on boy, reach up to the gentleman. I'm terrible sorry, sir, he's only little, but he's all we got.'

Ralph handed the woman a silver penny and a ha'penny as Clem scooped up three of the little cakes folded in a napkin. He was not sure that he could afford the expense. But he was damned if he would miss the famed delicacy of a Banbury cake.

By daybreak they were south of the town and breaking into a steady trot that took them past the village of Bodicote, the underside of charcoal clouds glowing with the first streaks of orange sun. Here they halted to piss and tighten girths. Then on again through Adderbury. By late morning they had crossed the River Swere and were clattering into Deddington town to halt, stretch legs, piss again and take an early dinner.

The marketplace was filled with horses and horsemen, one thousand beasts and men of Wentworth's brigade passing through it. They filed in from Banbury, stood in great clumps outside the inns, surged, laughed, kicked and crapped in great steaming heaps before re-gathering in their columns with shouts and whinnies to clatter back onto the road south.

Grandison's Horse dismounted outside an inn at the far end of the marketplace as another regiment mounted and moved off. There were shouted greetings between old friends and jests that all the ale was drunk and nothing but piss left. The place already stank of it. Horse piss ran across the cobbles to fill the town pool, its hot acrid stench added to by troopers without time to queue for a jake. Men splashed their urine against the inn wall or between the legs of their horses. The distaste of a puritan matron scurrying past only brought laughter as the inn's tap-maids rushed to slake the cavaliers' thirst.

Ralph bought three draughts of ale. It was not the strong Banbury ale of the night before, but a lighter brew, a second mash, pale and dry. It went down well. And it was a little cheaper than the best ale, only a ha'penny a quart.

Clem carefully unwrapped the cakes and served them on their napkin. His face beamed as he bit into thin layers of crispy sweet pastry and rich spiced currants, jealously guarding every last morsel from the hungry looks of the other serving men in the troop. 'My! Master Ralph, that were a fine delicacy. I hain't never tasted nought like it.'

Fuck it. Clem's delight and praise made the expense worthwhile. His worries about a dwindling purse could wait another day.

Deddington's inns were doing a roaring trade but they had not seen a good market day or fair in a long while. A few shops lined the square and a smithy was busy seeing to a line of thrown shoes, but the place was down at heel. Some of the shops were boarded up, long closed. A shattered church tower brooded over what might have been.

He was not sorry when they mounted again and rode out past the ruined castle. He was keen to keep moving, to push on to Oxford. A surge of excitement swept up his spine at the prospect of riding on to London. Besides, the darkening clouds were gathering ever thicker and it would not be long before the first rain.

The road south ran bleak and windswept along an open flat-topped ridge, no slope, bend or tree to offer shelter. The horses bent their necks and snorted at the gusts, irritated by the wind and the streaming tails of those in front. Ralph pulled his hat low and his neck into his collar. The first drizzle wet their faces, chilling cheeks and ears. A blessed burst of sun brought warmth and steam from the flanks of the horses as they kept up a steady trot. But it did not last long; the next wave of rain soon sweeping across the column.

This time it was heavier; constant driving rain. Rain that seeped steadily down necks, dripped from noses, chins and ears. It even found its way into his boots, dribbling in at the tops and seeping through the welts. It seemed to seek out the seams in his gauntlets, soaking through the thick leather to wet hands and leave his thumbs numb. He sought comfort in the heat of his horse, pressing his thighs against the saddle to hold the warmth there. But the leather was soon damp and squeaking with rain. He was stiff and sore from the long ride. Every time he shifted to rest his arse, another rivulet of water soaked his seat and breeches.

The road was bad before they set out. Now it was a broad strip of mud and standing water churned by the rain and the passage of a thousand horses. The ooze splashed up to coat legs, tails, undersides, boots, weapons and cloaks so that all now dripped with rain and gobbets of clinging mud. God only knew what it would be like for the tertias of foot, guns, carts, beasts, women and children that followed.

By mid-afternoon they were near to the palace at Woodstock. Word passed that the King would rest there. Wilmot's brigade was to form a screen of outposts beyond it, regiments fanning out in each direction. They would not be in Oxford that night. Grandison's Horse turned left to follow the great highway from Wales and Worcester towards London. It led them down to the Cherwell River. At last, they were off the windswept high ground. They halted beside the river, sheltering in the wooded valley whilst lieutenants, troop quartermasters and guides went forward to find quarters.

Ralph leant his back against a twisted old oak and tried to shelter from the wind and rain. It was not much better than being on the road. Great drops of water fell from the branches above to batter his dripping hat. He looked into his horse's despondent eyes as water streamed down its face. Leaning in, he cradled the big head against his chest, sharing its warmth, scratching behind ears and under dripping mane as the wind buffeted the tree above them. Curled oak leaves blew past like little boats tossed on a sea. Birch leaves tumbled by, spinning on their axis and stalk. Here and there a heavier clump of twigs crashed to the ground to sink in the mud.

Finally, the order came to mount again. It was well after three o'clock when they entered Islip's high street to stop between a pair of welcoming stone inns. Lord Grandison and four troops were to quarter in the town. But Sir John Smith's troop was to quarter in a village beyond as an outpost again. They were to make for the village of Oddington, another mile east.

Thank God, the rain finally stopped; a low sun bursting from under the clouds to cast long shadows ahead of them. A pale rainbow emerged to chase the last clouds as they rolled away north and east, boiling columns tinged with gold atop flat purple nimbus. The land was flat and low lying; the air clean, sharp. Here and there a scrubby stunted tree grew beside the road. Otherwise, a great blue evening sky opened up to the level horizon.

Even the wind seemed to ease a little as lapwings beat their way against it. A single crow, blown like an old rag, made its erratic evening flight home. In the distance, a flock of starlings rose like a ball of swirling bees; like some lady's favour lost on the wind to catch on a bush, a net of the finest lace turning itself inside out. The tiny birds rose and fell as one before settling to roost.

They heard the barking of dogs before they saw the village. Only the squat church tower and three houses stood above one storey. The rest, a dozen low thatched hovels, crouched either side of a muddy village green as if hunched against the wind and horizon. The years had not been kind to this place. Oddington existed on the very edge of utter poverty.

The manor house was shuttered, decayed, unoccupied. The rectory did not look much better. Its thatch roof was old and moss-ridden, its barn open to the sky. A single farm-house offered the only decent accommodation. But it would not hold the whole troop.

They stopped in front of a rundown cottage. Ralph's heart sank. He so wanted – *needed* a proper bed, a good night's sleep.

'Yer abode, Mister Reeve,' Nisbet sneered. 'Luke... Clem... yours forbye.' The corporal moved on, left them standing in the mud.

The single-storey longhouse, without window or chimney, was both dwelling and cowshed. Smoke seeped from a sunken roof of black, moss-riddled thatch. A broken hay-rake and half-finished wicker basket lay on the steaming dung heap. A tethered pig snuffled and grunted. Easing himself down from the saddle, Ralph's boots and spurs sank into ankle deep muck.

Rainwater still dripped from the thatch ends jutting over low eaves as he pushed open the rough wooden door. A wave of dense, reeking smoke billowed out from under the lintel. Stooping, he stepped into the single room, a scrawny chicken scattering from under his boots.

His eyes smarted in the foul smoke, struggling to adjust to the dark. Nostrils rankled at the stench of peat smoke, dirt and damp. The smoke oozed from a fire in the centre of the earthen floor, dark turfs smouldering on a few flat hearth-stones. It hung in a dark fetid cloud to leak up through the thatch and out of the doorway.

A dog growled. Snotty barefoot children cowered behind ragged parents and an elder sister. There must have been half a dozen of them, unkempt, wide bewildered eyes, unsure, clinging, scared. The father tried to quiet the dog. A gaunt woman covered a flaccid teat and babe whilst soothing more little hands that clawed at her dirty skirts. From the only chair in the place, an old woman peered out from a bundle of rags. A wide-eyed cow dribbled and belched, its cud interrupted, while the indignant hen flapped desperately to reach the safety of a low beam. All looked at the stranger, their feet shuffling and eyes downcast.

They had probably never met a gentleman or soldier before, let alone have one cross their threshold. He may as well have been the man in the moon.

Luke broke the silence, doing his best to put the family at ease. 'You've nothing to fear. We'll pay well for our lodging.'

Immediately, the mother stirred the family into action. The strangers were shown to a thin wooden bench against the wall. The younger ones were banished to peep from behind a tattered screen while the father and elder boy were sent out to help Clem with the horses. The older girl stoked up the fire in the centre of the floor. Throughout, the baby clung to its mother's hip and the old woman creaked in the corner.

The girl squatted on her haunches as she set about baking barley breads on a bakestone over the fire. Her cheeks glowed with kneading the barley and pea-meal dough before the heat of the fire and the gaze of strange gentlemen. The remains of bean and pea pottage spluttered in a pot as yet more unctuous smoke billowed over her head. Steaming wet cloaks and hats added to the fug, lit only by the glowing peat and the last rays of the sinking sun at the door.

Clem came in from the byre with the father and boy, the horses settled in place of the evicted cow. There was only rainwater to drink, from a jug and horn beaker. 'That's all they got, Master Ralph. Tin't Banbury ale, but that's fresh enough. I checked the butt meself.'

Ralph simply shrugged, took a draft of the water and

smiled at the little girl who offered it. He was too tired to care. 'Thank you. It is perfectly refreshing.'

Luke also drank long and deep. 'It's nature's gift, a tonic for the body.'

They ate in silence, rough barley bread and bean pottage from the pot, watched by hungry eyes in the gathering gloom. As soon as they had finished, feverish fingers, hands and a couple of wooden spoons descended upon the pot and scraps. Ralph had not eaten much, but he could not bear to make the children wait longer. Luke too had put down his spoon before long.

After the simple supper, Clem took the traditional role of the traveller to tell the news. Ralph listened with ever heavier lids, a warm belly and the heat of the peat on his cheeks. He smiled as Clem told their tale, the man and eldest boy squatting intently beside the fire, the boy's eyes wide with excitement. More eyes glinted with hushed wonder beyond the firelight of the now dark room.

When the tale was told, the animals were checked once more, the door barred, and the hearth banked up for the night with an extra sod. Secure from wind, fire and theft, the father gathered his family around the smouldering peat to protect them from demons and evil spirits of the night. Eyes shut in fervent prayer as their father recited ancient words of protection.

'Lord Jesus Christ and Saint Benedict, bless this house from every wicked sprite. From the night-hag protect us white Paternoster. Where went thou, Saint Peter's sister? Amen.'

Ralph was surprised to hear a prayer from the old religion. The reformed church had not reached as far as changing their nightly ritual. This simple family were not dangerous Papists; they merely clung to the words that had protected their fathers before them. They probably did not even know that their prayer could bring punishment.

Clem gently added a newer, more accepted invocation.

'Almighty God, we request thee, shadow us this night under the comfortable wings o' thy almighty power. Defend our senses, our thoughts, our souls and our bodies, with all thy powers, from all assaults, temptations and illusions o' the Devil. Amen.'

Grateful for the added protection of Clem's words, the mother and father retired with their eldest daughter and babe to sleep on a pallet behind the drab cloth screen. The younger children curled up with the dog on a pile of bracken and rushes near the fire, all soon twitching in their dreams. The old woman sat propped in her corner, phlegm-filled lungs rattling and wheezing; a pile of dirty old rags that coughed and mumbled in the firelight. At the far end of the long-house, in the byre, the horses chewed hay and shuffled gently in the dark.

Ralph, Luke and Clem slept on the dirt floor, propped against damp saddles on a bed of loose bracken. Clem mumbled something about it being a bit lumpy. The stiff stalks poked through Ralph's cloak, but he was too tired to care as the sounds of sleeping family and animals soon lulled him into deep sleep.

———

Ralph woke in the middle of the night, as he normally did. For a while, he stared up at the rafters above, bathed in the dull glow of smouldering peat, listening to the old woman, the horses breathing and the dog's dream. He was not the only one to wake. Father and boy rose to piss outside. He guessed they were both used to getting up to protect their meagre crop from deer and cattle. Clem also stirred and went to check on the horses.

Clem fussed gently over the boy. Perhaps he was trying to recruit him. He was skinny and short for his age but had to be about fourteen – old enough to muster and old enough to fight. They needed another trooper and this family could do with one less mouth to feed.

The place stank of wet animals and poverty, the fetid stench of baby shit, milky puke, unwashed children, wet dog, damp earth and cow shit mixed with the reek of smouldering peat from the hearth. Ralph did not mind the fresh chill air that blew under the rattling door.

And yet this was a home. Thank God he had not been born into such a place. But, more than that: *Oh God don't let this war – my war – take this home from this family. Let them always have its warmth and each other. They have so little else.*

# VII

# Oxford

*Robbie Needham*

### *Oxford, Saturday the 29ᵗʰ of October 1642, midday*

The King raised his hand. The drums stopped and the great column halted behind him.

Ahead, the fifty-seven captured rebel colours snapped and tugged streaming bright in the cold sunlight. At the end of the broad street, in front of Oxford's old North Gate, stood a group of dignitaries, town, church and gown; mercantile, ecclesiastic, academic. Anxious town militia stood in front of a crowd looking on in awed silence. They stared at the sight of the army that stretched out behind the King, an army that carried the trophies of its victory before it, an army that marched on London.

Robbie Needham filled his armoured chest and steadied his pike. With an eye that was barely open in a battered, bruised and swollen face, he glowered at the crowd. He'd heard tell of Oxford. But he was buggered if anybody expected him to be impressed.

It was all bollocks as far as he were concerned. It was where the sons of privileged tossers learned to hide the law in their bloody Latin, to keep it from the people and to twist it to their own ends. Besides, they'd marched the twelve miles from Woodstock and he was hungry.

To nobody in particular but all in the ranks beside and behind him, he let his thoughts be known. 'Who're all them old buggers in their fancy garb? An' them militia boys look like they're goin to piss their pants. Are they really goin to stop us from goin in that poxy gate? Gerron with it! I'm fair clammed for me dinner.'

The hush was broken as one of the gowns stepped forward with a theatrical sweep of his arm to proclaim: 'Our Oxford hath now thrown off all clouds of discontent, stands clear, gilded by the beams of Your Majesty's royal presence.'

The mayor presented a bag of coin and the keys to the city gates on a silver tray. The town band struck up a discordant tune on shrill fifes, sackbut, pipes and shawm only to be silenced by a lofty motet from a robed college choir accompanied by musicians playing lute, viol, hautboy, flute and rackett as the gates were thrown open.

The brief ceremony over, the dignitaries led the King, the princes, the Lifeguard and the army through the gate's arch and into the old city. They marched between fine houses, shops, side-streets and spires, the drums hammering out their steady beat in crashing echo, as if they would shatter the fancy windows that looked down on them as they passed.

Robbie began to swagger as they marched. He swelled at the shocked gasps, the flushed cheeks, the pale stare at their muddy blood-stained coats, dented armour and notched weapons fresh from battle. 'Worr'eh you staring at? Go on, take a good pissin' look. This is what real soldiers look like. Not them cockless militia boys. Where were they all when there were real fightin' to be done? Didn't see any o' thee at Edgehill neither. Bloody tossers, the lot o' yer.'

At the cross, they marched on downhill, past houses and church. And then they were swinging through a grand gate, between fine stone towers, high carved arches, into a great courtyard, a huge quadrangle with a fountain at its centre. He'd never been in a place like it. It were nigh big enough for the whole Lifeguard to form up in close order. They stared up at great windows, pinnacled buttresses, towers and roofs.

The King dismounted to receive the welcome of yet more assembled gowns, a welcome to his Christchurch. The Royal Standard, company colours and officers trooped forward to follow the King and gowns inside. *No doubt the rest of us are goin' to get fed us snap in the yard outside.* Then the sergeants ordered pikes and muskets stacked and divisions to dress inside. File by file they wound their way up the broad stone stair under fan-vaulted ceilings, stone polished smooth like petals on a flower, to enter the great hall.

Robbie pulled off his cap, hid its greasy leather in his hands. They sat on benches on either side of tables that stretched the length of the hall. It was like nothing he'd ever seen. It was as if he were dreaming – blazing fire, panelled walls, paintings, hangings, hammer-beam roof and the sun streaming through the great south window. If only Hal, John, Billie and the others were there to see it.

He wondered if he smelled bad, if he should have washed. And then serving boys began to pile the tables with food and ale.

---

The train of artillery did not follow the Lifeguard and the other regiments of the vanguard down St Aldate's. Instead, they turned east at the Carfax into High Street. The wheels of the great cannon squealed as they made the tight left-handed turn, the drivers fighting to keep the teams of heavy horses pulling evenly.

George Merrett was grateful that they were off the highway. It had been a long slow struggle on the march, at times knee-deep in mud. It was good to be back in Oxford. It brought back memories of time as a student, memories of a happier time, a time when ambition and confidence had not been cut short by disease, creditors, lawyers and the need for a patron's employ.

He had forgotten how much he missed it, the study of higher things, of philosophy, the Classics, of principle and Plato, the *Studia Humanitatis*, of nature and form; of Copernicus and Kepler, of mathematics, method and reason, of Descartes; of *Scientia*, planets and a universe unbounded; the intense focus, the belief that study could unlock the mysteries of the world; of heaven itself, the search for the key to a better world; the single truth of Hermes Trismegistus, a single *Prisca Theologia*. Christ, he had missed these spires, towers and colleges, the inns and taverns, the challenge, debate and sheer damn thrill of life!

Now he was back with cannon powerful enough to level the city; back with an army that had fought and killed, an army that was intent on wresting power back from a rebel Parliament. An army that was ready to blast, burn, shoot and hack its way into London if it had to.

Was this the fundamental truth of the world? That, in the end, even the noblest achievements were prey to man's brutal nature? That all civilisation, even knowledge itself, was fragile, transient, as ready as Rome and the great library of Alexandria to fall to barbarity?

This city was worth fighting for, to protect these great halls of advancement. Only a king with absolute power would have the strength to protect them in a turbulent world, the strength to make England glorious again. If that king was portrayed as a tyrant, so be it. Better a strong state ruled by reason than a bad *democratie* governed by the base appetites of the mob. Since Socrates, democracy had only led to self-interest, abuse of privilege, despoliation of the plenitude, chaos, revolution and the tyranny of brute force unchecked.

King Charles should emulate the great monarchs of Europe – Louis of France, Philip of Spain and the Emperor Ferdinand – with their patronage of the arts, sciences and new industries. If not, England could not hope to keep pace with the great revolution in military affairs. It would be left weak and vulnerable, unable to protect its trade and shores from attack or invasion.

The King had to smash the shackles of an ungrateful and deluded Parliament, free the nation from the sanctimonious faction that sought to dull England's glory, to remove all colour and brilliance, all music, theatre, song and dance from church, state, town and village in some perverted idea of faith. They would turn England into a black and white Bible school. They would force women to hide their beauty and men to forsake all question, debate and joy.

They passed All Saints, St Mary's Church and Oriel Street. He longed to see his old college again. It would have to wait. He would call on his professor as soon as he could. On, past All Soul's College, Queen's, University and St Edmund's and then another turn into Longwall Street before bringing the guns to a halt in Magdalen Grove.

At last, there was room for the teams to turn in an arc and park the guns in a line facing Magdalen Bridge and the road to London. The horses were unhitched and taken to drink thirstily from the river. George waited while his gun captains checked over their charges after the march.

Old Nick Busy fussed over his demi-culverin. The old gunner ran a gnarled hand along the barrel, almost caressing it. He felt deep inside the bore, feeling for any powder residue that might have sweated out of the metal to pit and corrode. Satisfied that no damage would befall his beloved gun, Old Nick gave a nod to his crew to cover the cannon with a tattered canvas. In his bare feet, young Flash was sent to crawl underneath to secure it tightly.

There was no rushing him, but finally Old Nick lined them up with the other gun crews that waited to go to dinner and their quarters around New College.

———

Sir Thomas Salusbury's regiment of Welsh hill men did not pass through the North Gate. They were halted outside the city walls. Some said there was no room left for the rear guard. Others, that Welsh vermin were not welcome inside the city at night. They were to be quartered in the houses of St Giles that lined the road north of Oxford.

Hywel Lloyd didn't much care. It was late afternoon by the time they arrived. It would soon be dark and no bloody Englishman was going to stop him drinking his fill in any city tavern he fancied. He'd heard of Oxford. His lord and colonel, Sir Thomas, had studied here. A famous place of learning it was. Well, he would see it for himself.

They could shut the gate for all he cared. The walls were old and there would be plenty of ways in for a mountain man. He and a few of the other Denbigh boys would have their sport. Just try and stop them.

# VIII

# The Trenches

*Thomasine Bennett*

*London, Sunday the 30ᵗʰ of October 1642, eleven o'clock*

The rector climbed stiffly from the pulpit. A few old merchants and their wives left their pews to follow him out in silence – all malignant royalists and closet Papists. But the church remained packed, intent. Like other London churches, prescribed Sunday service was followed at St Swithin's by godly preaching, lecture and prayer. Now it was the turn of the puritan minister.

*'Curse ye Meroz, said the Angel of the Lord! Curse ye bitterly, the inhabitants thereof. Because they came not to the help of the Lord. To the help of the Lord against the mighty!'*

Thomasine Bennett listened with reverence. Even her children and maidservant sat in awed silence on the hard wooden bench. The minister was known for his fire and his rebuke.

'Will ye not heed the call to assist the Lord's people? To defend this city in the Lord's name? Is not the Book of Judges clear evidence that all people are cursed or blessed according to the succour they give to the Lord, His church and people against His enemies? For the people of Meroz did not come to the aid of the Israelites against King Jabin and the might of Sisera's army. And they are cursed for eternity! But whosoever cometh to join their strength to the Lord's people, the Lord doth interpret it as assistance to Himself.

'When kings and captains, drunk with the wine of the whore of Babylon's fornications, give their strength to the Beast to make war upon the Lamb, and do now threaten the gates of this city, will ye not march out to do the Lord's bidding? Will ye withhold your hand while the heathen host dash out the brains of the Lord's children against the stones of this city? Is not the Book of Lamentations warning enough? God's wrath and curse will be upon you forever!

'For it is most plain in scripture. Come that Day of Judgement, the Lord will call all to account. Christ will divide the flock as a shepherd, saying to those that gave succour to His church and people in their hour of need, "Come ye blessed, receive the Kingdom prepared for you." But to those that did not give willingly or diligently, he will say, "Go, ye cursed!" For cursed is he that doth the work of the Lord negligently. The Lord Jehovah is the fountain of all blessedness. From His favour only flows salvation and eternal happiness.

'Ye may think ye are weak, feeble, or too young to fight. But ye can dig and carry. With the Lord's people ye can build walls that will keep out the mighty, walls that will save this city. For the efforts of men will come to nought against the work of the Lord. Was it not a weak and feeble woman that felled the mighty Sisera? For it was Jael, wife of Heber, blessed above all women that put her hand to the workman's hammer and pierced through his temple with a nail. And when it was done, she smote off his head!

'As with a ship, save the vessel and ye save all. Let the ship sink and every man is lost. The tempest cometh! Now is the time to heed the Lord's call. Join the Lord's people in this noble cause, in this *righteous* cause. Readily and cheerfully consecrate yourselves and your service to His work. Clothe yourselves with zeal as with a cloak, put on righteousness as your armour. Be as saviours upon Mount Zion. *Come ye blessed!* To the walls and trenches in the sure knowledge that God's blessing is upon those who answer His call.

'Those of Meroz – *go ye cursed!* For those who come not to the help of the Lord against the mighty will be cursed for eternity! Amen.'

'Amen!'

Thomasine choked out her response alongside the congregation, her throat closing. She dropped to her knees hiding eyes that swam with tears. Her children, maid, others must not see her weakness – her wickedness. She needed to pray. She needed to beg for God's forgiveness.

She had sinned. She had been angry, hurtful, prideful. She had sent her husband to war with bitterness in her heart. She had refused him a parting embrace, hiding her love in her chamber. She had not even waved him goodbye. She had cursed him for leaving her, leaving her to care for their children, their home and business. But it was she, Thomasine Bennett, who should be cursed. She had turned away from William and his fight against the Lord's enemies.

But she had been so angry. She implored him not to leave, not to forsake them. She told him that his duty was to protect and provide for them. Not to run away on some foolish game of soldiers, to run from his responsibilities, to risk all in search of a young man's glory. He was too old.

She struggled to keep their business going. It was the worst of times for him to go, with trade depressed, rising rents and creditors calling in loans. William had sold most of their stock to pay his soldiers and she was forced to buy in at a higher price to meet contracts. There had been no one to turn to.

William had taken Nehemiah and the best of their workmen with him. Even their oldest customers threatened to turn elsewhere while once friendly merchants sensed an opening. William's mother was no help. She would not hear a bad word against her son.

Thomasine had been left alone to raise credit, buy, sell, secure and ship; to hire, pay and layoff workmen and servants; to keep house, school, feed, clothe, tend and mother their seven children. All with a baby expected and winter soon upon them.

In all this she had forgotten William's own plight. He had gone to war. He was not a soldier, but he had followed the Lord's call. Now there had been a battle. She did not even know if he was alive. There had been no more letters from him, or from Nehemiah.

William could be dead or, worse, lying hurt somewhere. His dark melancholy, his despair would consume him. She had abandoned him in his hour of need. Was it too late? Was she now cursed as one of Meroz?

*Oh Lord, forgive this sinner. I have forgotten my husband and my God in my pride and self-pity. I beg Thee, let William live. I will dedicate my life to Thy work. I will come to Thine aid. I will dig and build a wall to keep Thy church and people safe. I will build a fortress for William. For him, for Nehemiah, for all his brave Israelites. Please, just bring him home.*

Nails dug deep into determined hands, Thomasine Bennett stood up, gathered her children around her and, followed by the maid, walked out of the church onto Cannon Street. The congregation were talking in animated groups, sending servants for tools and preparing to join the working parties at the city's defences.

'Mistress Bennett.' A matriarch, the mother of one of their competitors, blocked her way surrounded by a group of wives. 'We are resolved to march, to lend ourselves to support the men in the trenches. Will you not join us?'

'My dear, her husband is with the army.' Another busybody wife stepped forward. 'With Denzil Holles's regiment. They were at Kineton. I think the Bennetts have done quite enough.'

'Thank you, ladies. I am quite resolved to march with you.'

'Thomasine, nobody expects—'

'That may be but I will not be deflected.' She turned to the maid. 'Now, Fanny. . . take the twins home and mind house. Thomas. . . Benjamin. . . run and fetch the spade and shovel from the garden. Rebecca. . . bring bread and cheese and the dish of sprats from the kitchen. And the tart that is prepared. And, Rebecca dear. . . change your dress and shoes. There is no need to spoil your best. Little William. . . go with her now and bring three baskets from the pantry.'

———

With her children behind her, Thomasine followed the minister and his Bible along Cannon Street to St Paul's. As they marched through the city wards, they were joined by other congregations who answered the call to dig London's defences. They marched on west, out of the city walls at Ludgate, into Fleet Street, past the Temple Bar and on down the Strand. At the Savoy Hospital, they turned north to gather in the new piazza at Covent Garden. Hordes of tradesmen and women, oyster wenches and whores from the rougher parts of Westminster and Southwark flooded in to join them. There were more speeches and prayers before the great column moved off again, led by the drums and colours of the militia. They worked their way through New Row and St Martin's to emerge on Haymarket. As they went, groups were led away to work on the forts and breastworks that guarded each road into the city. Thomasine and those from St Swithin's marched on up Piccadilly to the crest of the hill and the edge of Hyde Park.

The drums stopped. The column halted. An expanse of mud stretched before them. Ditches no more than waist deep, earth banks no higher, marked the base of a fort beside the road, a great square sconce with pointed bulwarks at each corner. It was set back from the crest in the junction of Piccadilly and the track that ran north to Tyburn. Complete, it would look out across the park, down towards Kensington and across Constitution Hill to the battery there.

But this was no castle, no Jerusalem city wall. This was the reality of fortification in a new age, where only deep trenches and thick banks of earth would provide protection from cannon and massed muskets. The minister and those behind him stared in silence at the scene of mud and impossible toil.

'Come along, children. We are here to do the Lord's work.' Thomasine stepped forward basket in hand. 'Come on. Thomas, Benjamin. . . help those men digging in the trench. Rebecca. . . please feed these workmen – they will need sustenance. Little William. . . you and I will carry the earth to the top of the bank. We will build the walls.'

She felt her shoes sink, cold mud enveloping her ankle and skirt hem. They were her best shoes. She should have changed. Thank God she had sent Rebecca back. She could not afford new shoes and clothes for her now. Rebecca must save her best for Nehemiah's return.

She pressed on with tears brimming as her boys splashed past to join the labourers already digging in the trenches. Oh God, don't let her falter now. She must not show her weakness. Let the others stare, let them be cursed. She and her children would build this fort for her husband and his brave soldiers.

Bending low, she let a workman fill her basket at the bottom of the trench. 'Bless you, missus. We were near beat. Mind now, it'll be heavy.'

The basket sagged, dripping wet mud as she lifted it. It was much heavier than she had imagined. Struggling to balance on the rough-hewn walk-boards she staggered up the bank to deposit the spoil at its top. Some of the earth rolled back down so that the wall was little more than an inch higher where she had deposited it. God only knew how many basket loads would be needed to build this fort.

Turning to descend into the trench again, she wiped a tendril of hair from her face with the back of a muddy hand. Blinking, she saw, all around her, people swarming over the fort to help dig, carry and build up its walls.

———

The light was fading and the air cold so that their breath hung in clouds. Damp sweat and cold mud sapped what strength she had left. Her arms and back ached from manual labour. She was covered in mud and had lost her shoes somewhere in the sucking mire.

The minister and others had drifted back to their warm homes to leave Thomasine and her children alone. But she was determined to work on while she could. She so desperately wanted to finish the fort. In truth, it was not much more than a foot higher all round. It would take at least a week of continuous labour to finish it.

And then she fell. Her foot slipped on the mud-smeared walk-board. She scrabbled to catch the basket and clods of earth as they rolled back down into the trench. Exhausted she fell back against the damp earth bank and sobbed.

'Please, mother. . . I don't think we can finish it today.' Rebecca knelt down beside her. 'The others have all gone and Little William is cold. He is shivering. It is almost dark now and we have a long walk home. We will come back to finish it tomorrow.'

'Yes, yes, you have all done more than I could have asked. Your father will be so proud. The Lord will smile on you tonight. Let us go home. We will finish the fort for him tomorrow.'

# IX

# Traitor

*Hywel Lloyd*

*Oxford, Sunday the 30<sup>th</sup> of October
1642, half past eleven o'clock*

Hywel Lloyd and his mates pushed through the crowd. He wanted to see this. He'd seen a man hanged – everyone had. But he'd never seen a man drawn or quartered. This would be a rare spectacle.

They'd been to church – St Giles', a glorious fine church. The service was not to their liking, with its long preaching sermon all in English. But the church was beautiful. With the sun streaming through the windows and arches, they had lifted their voices in Welsh to the hymns they knew, to the tunes they recognised.

Afterwards, they avoided the guard at the North Gate, skirted round the backs, climbed a college wall and ducked down an alley into the city. Joining the crowds heading up the High Street, they slipped into the castle yard with them. They were just in time.

The traitor was already on the scaffold, bound, sagging, torn and bloodied from the extraction of his crimes. A brazier burned beside a butchers table, the noose twisting gently in the breeze. An officer read out a list of the crimes confessed and the sentence to be exacted while a drum beat slowly.

The crowd were excited, jostling to get closer. A boy pushed past his legs. A rosy-cheeked maid balanced on tiptoe. Hywel could get no closer. A great pikeman in dented armour blocked his way. A smashed, bruised and swollen face glared at the crowd through a pussy yellow eye.

'What happened to you? Looks like you've been in the wars.'

'Aye 'ahtey and I'll kill the scar-faced bastard what did it when I find 'im, so mind thy manners.'

'Is that so. And what did the fucker on the scaffold do then?'

'Bloody traitor. Mister Blake or somert. Any road, some pissin secretary t' Prince Rupert writing secrets tut Earl of Essex.'

'Look up. It's started.'

'Can't bloody see, can I? Got t' face you lot.'

The drum beat more insistently as the traitor was pushed up a ladder towards the hangman sat astride the gallows. The noose was slipped over his head and pulled tight. The drumming beat faster, rattling out its thunder, the crowd yelling in their anticipation.

A final crash of the drum, the ladder fell to the scaffold floor and silence. Only the creak of the rope and gallows, the twisting desperate thrashing of legs and the choking rasp of breath as the traitor swung. The crowd held its breath, counting, watching the darkening swelling face, the bulging eyes and tongue, the ever more pathetic kick of legs.

The hangman had a knife in his hand, holding it high for all to see, waiting for the moment, the moment just before death, when the traitor would see the gates of Hell awaiting him. And then he was cutting the rope, the knife sawing through the strands, the cords snapping, unravelling until only a single strand held him spinning slowly in the air. The body fell to thump limp on the planking.

The noose was pulled free. The gasping body dragged up onto the table. Clothes ripped from it, the traitor exposed, naked. Knife raised high, the executioner's hand gripped cock and balls. A scream of agony and the traitor's manhood was cut from him to be held aloft. The crowd gasped.

'Ooh *ffyc!*'

'Worr'eh thou see, youth?'

'They just cut off his cock and his balls.'

'Shit!'

The bloody giblets were thrust in the traitor's face, held aloft again, then thrown on the brazier beside him to hiss and spit. The knife swept down again to rip open the traitor's belly from waist to sternum as he cried out for pity.

Hands dragged out intestines, stomach, liver, kidneys and bowel, the body arching in a terrible groan, the steaming guts thrown on the fire to sear and burst in a stinking heap.

'They're drawing him now,' Hywel grimaced. 'I reckon you'll smell it soon enough.'

The executioner thrust bloody arms up deep into the chest cavity. A last spluttering gasp, a sucking wrench and the final blood-dripping trophy was held aloft: a traitor's heart.

A butcher's cleaver severed neckbone and sinew, the last lifeblood running from the scaffold. Rolling free, the head was stuck, eyes open and dripping, on a spike. The carcass was hacked into four, the cleaver smashing down again and again to chop through the pelvis, across the spine and up through the ribcage, the quarters thrust aloft on spikes.

A final roll of the drum and the officer stepped forward to proclaim justice served. 'Behold the head, heart and quarters of a traitor!'

'We best be going. Hywel Lloyd's the name.'

'Well aah-do sirrey. Robbie Needham.'

'See you in London for the next one, then.'

'Reckon so. We march again on t' morrer.'

# X

# All Hallows' Eve

*William Bennett*

### *Warwick, Monday the 31ˢᵗ of October 1642, nine o'clock*

At last they were marching. They were leaving Warwick. They were marching towards London. They were going home.

William Bennett strode out at the head of his company. He wished that they marched faster. But they were just one company in the great column that was the Earl of Essex's army. The pace the drums beat out seemed desperately slow. At this rate it would take them at least a week to reach London.

Were they too late? They had sat in Warwick licking their wounds for five whole days while the road to London was left open to the King. The damned cavaliers might be at the gates of the city now. They might yet storm, pillage, burn, rape and slaughter as they wished. There were many who said that Prince Rupert would bring the destruction of the war in Germany to England, that he would leave London a smoking ruin like Magdeburg. How had they left their city unprotected and at the mercy of the cavaliers?

William had hidden himself in a bed in Warwick in dark despair. Despair for the loss and waste, the throwing away of years of hard-earned capital, for risking his business and home, for acting like a foolish young man, for wanting to be a soldier – to be a hero, for what he had put his wife and family through, for leaving Thomasine.

But worse was the thought of Nehemiah and those killed or wounded. He had marched from London with his company of a hundred brave apprentices, journeymen and boys, resplendent in their red uniforms, armour, helmets and caps, all with the best pikes, muskets, swords and accoutrements money could buy. Of those hundred, the tally on his ledger showed only thirty-one musketeers, twenty-seven pikemen, two drummers, two corporals, one sergeant and an ensign remained. Sixty-four. One third lost.

This night would be All Hallows' Eve. Demons and evil spirits would be free to roam the Earth, to torment, torture, take unworthy souls. Would the ghosts of those he had failed, those he had left dead at Kineton, return to haunt him, to take their vengeance, to drag him to Hell? He dared not think of Nehemiah's face with its bloody bandages and staring eye.

Thank God they were now marching. There was a chance of seeing Thomasine, his children, his home again. Perhaps the cavaliers were not yet at the gates of London. Perhaps they were still wallowing in their victory, drunk on their looting or stuck in the autumn mud. Perhaps there was yet time to rescue his family, to save London. Perhaps there would be peace. Surely there had been enough letting of blood to cool the nation's distemper. Surely the King and Parliament would come together now to heal the body politic.

Damn, how he longed to return to the city! He should never have left it. He did not really understand soldiering. It was still a mystery to him. But he understood business, commerce and trade. He knew where he was in the city: how to buy and sell; how and when to invest; the thrill of owning a share in a venture; the pleasure of turning a profit; the re-investment and doing it all again.

He might have to start again; he had so little capital left. But, if he could claw back some of the money Parliament owed him in back-pay for his company, he would do it. As long as he was free to work and trade, as long as a malignant court did not corrupt and stifle the marketplace with its sale of monopolies to favourites, as long as the city and its merchants kept their independence.

A man should be free to rise, to better himself by his own ability and effort, to rise or fall on his own merit. Yes, some would fall by the wayside, but that was only natural. They must learn to pick themselves up, to emulate their betters, not rely on largess and charity. Each man must seek God's merit in his endeavour to succeed.

The market place was the best engine of progress. It was the proving ground that nurtured strong growth. Trade, commerce and the law were the keys to a strong nation. Look at the Dutch Republic. They had built themselves a state that defied Spain, Rome and the Imperial *tercios*, a state that traded where and with whom it liked to bring back the riches of Africa, the Indies, the Spice Islands, Cathay and the Japans.

If he could not rebuild his business in London, he would leave for Holland, or join his uncle in Virginia. He would rescue his family and start again. God, let him reach them in time! Tomorrow they would pick up Watling Street and head south for London.

———

Anthony Sedley marched at the front of his file of musketeers. They'd left Warwick behind, passed through Southam and

216

on into Northamptonshire. They were going the wrong way. They were marching south and east, away from Birmingham.

He longed to get back to the iron-forge, to feel its heat, to laugh and talk with his fellow workers. But most of all he wanted to hold his wife and babies again. To tell them he lived, to take heart, to stick together, not to give in to oppression, to tell them that the rebellion was alive. But now the army marched south, south to save London.

It was bloody typical. The labourers and craftsmen were being driven by their masters to save Parliament and the sodding riches of London. Why couldn't the bloody workers of London rise up to defend their city from tyranny and oppression? Why did they not join the rebellion and fight for their rights and freedoms? Were they just soft?

Or was this all part of the bloody Norman system: the Earl of sodding Essex, grandee colonels, shitting officers and Members of Parliament protecting their own, while bastard cavaliers still roamed free in the north?

Somewhere up ahead, a dog barked. A prickle of anger swept over him at the childhood memory of eviction; the lord of the manor's hounds snarling on their leash as their cottage was torn down, cleared for enclosure; as they were forced off the commons, chased from the woods to tramp the roads as vagrants; his father worn down under the shame, hunger and the load on his back. He hated dogs.

No doubt they would have to sleep in some shitting barn or pigsty tonight. And it was All Hallows' Eve. His band of merry men would not be happy. They were town lads, cocky and streetwise, but edgy on a dark night in the middle of nowhere. 'A couple of hours or three and I reckon we'll stop. Harry, you alright?'

'Alright Anthony.'

'Zach, what about you lad?'

'Er, alright Anthony. But me pegs don't 'alf ache.'

The skinny runt could barely hold his musket. The march would be hard on him. 'Alf, take 'is musket for a bit, alright?'

'Oy'm alright. Giz it 'ere Zach.'

'Tom, alright?'

'All good Anthony.'

'Izzy? What about you?'

'Me bloody shoe latchet's undone again.'

'Bloody 'ell, Isaac. 'Ow many times 'ave I showan you? Now fall out, get it tied proper and get back in your place before sergeant kicks your arse. Will, mate. . . watch 'im will yer?'

'Alright Anthony.'

'Good. Now. . . when we stop, I want a nice big fire tonight. Plenty of wood. Keep it burning, alright.'

———

It was almost dark by the time Francis Reeve rode into Weedon-on-the-Street. Most of the foot had halted for the night in and about Daventry. But Balfour's Horse had pushed on through Dodford to Watling Street and the road south to London. Praise God, the way was open!

They passed squalid cottages, dung spread on the walls to dry under low eaves, fuel for their stinking fires. Worse: despite their poverty, many of the hovels burned candles at their window – candles for the dead. The fools still believed their dead were trapped in Purgatory, released to return home for this one night. Others scurried in the gloom towards the toll of the church bell, scuttling to join the vigil for the souls of the departed.

But there was no Purgatory. It was a Roman heresy, a lie to tempt the living, a fallacy to trap sinners. Their candles would not bring back their dead. They were proffering a light to the Devil! Their candles, their bells and prayers for the dead only invited Satan into their homes, into their souls. They were opening themselves to evil, letting in the forces of Hell, threatening all around with eternal damnation. Even now, all about him was danger, demonic forces surrounded him. This place, this night, was cursed. Its stench hung in the air.

They dismounted outside an old inn, one of several that lined Watling Street, as the last light faded and a mist formed over the ground. Behind them, the flames of a bonfire flared into the night sky atop a great dark hill brooding over the landscape, its light etching ancient rings dug deep around the summit.

'Tis Barrow Hill. The blood of the Danes do stain it.' A toothless old man stood beside him, an ostler in a battered leather apron. 'Best keep them and their kind at peace this night. They like a good bone-fire they do.'

Francis handed the man his horse's reins. Ignoring the outstretched palm, he strode into the inn. He had to find solitude, a place to pray, a sanctuary from evil. He needed to armour his soul, to feel the protection of God's word.

# XI

# All Saints

*Ralph Reeve*

*Aylesbury, Tuesday the 1ˢᵗ of November
1642, six o'clock in the evening*

'Come on, Clem. I have a thirst for ale.'

'Alright, Master Ralph. We just got a-hang up this here *hag-stone.*' Clem held out the small round Suffolk flint, a natural hole through its centre. 'Us don't want no hags worrying the hosses tonight. I seen what they do to a hoss, leavin them all lathered in a muck sweat, a-shiverin and fair fit to drop by mornin. I ain't a-goin to leave these here hosses without a hag-stone to keep them safe. Not this night, it bein Hallowtide and all.'

The stone would ward off any witch that tried to ride a horse in the night. Clem handed it up to the boy who hung it by a cord from a beam over the stall. It was the boy from Oddington. He had caught up with them on the road the next morning. God knew where he had found a horse – stolen from the parson, most likely. He signed the muster role with a simple X, was found a sword and a pistol and joined as the fourth trooper in Ralph's file.

'There.' Clem patted his horse one more time. 'That should keep they safe for the night, shouldn't it my beauty.'

'Ralph, Clem!' Luke's voice called from outside. 'You'll want to see this.'

Luke was standing in the inn yard looking up at the hill beyond the river. Tiny pricks of flame flared and smouldered red in the fields and clear night air.

'Fire red and low, light on my teen'lay.' An old man squatted beside the inn wall. 'They be burning tindles for All Souls. Some folks keep to the old ways.' Between his legs sweet chestnuts roasted on a chaffer, the flames drawing deep lines in his face. Sunken eyes appealed for a penny as crooked hands cupped what warmth there was. 'Best chestnuts in the vale.'

'I haven't had roasted chestnuts since I left for London.' Ralph looked down at the old man, a travelling peddler or poor cottager trying to supplement his income. 'Four years.' This was an unnecessary expense and he had to save his purse. But times were hard for all. The man needed a sale. 'We'll take a dozen.'

'I got cobnuts too. Find a Welshman and 'e will tell yer future. I seed em do it. Strange things they do with nuts. That's if you can find a Welshman that speaks rightways.'

'Alright, we'll take a dozen cobnuts too.' Ralph handed over a farthing while the nuts were scooped into the boy's hat and carried into the inn. Luke bought them a jug of ale and they sat around an upturned barrel cracking the nuts and eating their hot mawkish flesh.

'Well, I don't mind sittin here eatin nuts.' Clem looked up from the litter of shells. 'But I thought we was a-goin to London.'

'Good point, Clem. Luke, remind us why we are here.

221

Why are we in the middle of bloody Buckinghamshire and not marching on London?'

'Well, Prince Rupert leads the march on London. The King follows along the Thames valley. We're to provide a flank guard, to protect the army from any interference. We're to watch for any move by Essex against the King's march.'

'I reckon Old Cock Robin is still hiding in Warwick Castle. He knows the King will have his head for a traitor. What I don't understand is why we don't just seize London while we can. Why do we move so slowly?'

'I think the King doesn't want to be seen as a vengeful conqueror. He prefers to gather support as he goes, give time for the waverers to return to him, for Parliament to beg for peace. Then he can enter London as the people's hero.'

'At this rate, it could be Christmas first.'

'I reckon the King'll want to be in Whitehall for old Queen Bess's Day on the seventeenth. It's the perfect celebration of old Gloriana. It's two days afore his Majesty's own birthday feast and a week afore the Queen's. If I was to wager, I'd say he'll want to be in London in a fortnight's time.'

'So, let's drink to feasting and merriment in London in a fortnight.'

'I'll drink to a bit o' feastin.'

'Ah Clem, you remind me o' the other reason why I reckon we're here in the Vale of Aylesbury.' Luke enthused. 'This is where the Welsh drovers fatten their cattle afore driving them on to London for Christmas. And where they breed the ducks for London tables. I think our Commissary-General, Lord Wilmot, is here to intercept them. To feed our army and to hold them for ransom until London submits.'

'Oh Luke, that's clever.' Ralph slapped the table. 'So, the

King enters London a hero, gives the people peace, Gloriana and beef, and sends his army home for Christmas.'

'Home for Christmas.' Clem lifted his ale. 'I'll drink to that an' all.'

They sat in silence for a moment, each lost in their thoughts. God it would be good to be home for Christmas, for bringing in the yule log, posset, misrule, twelfth night – and for Susanna.

'Mind, there'll be some not a-goin home anytime.' Clem stared at the fire. 'I heard tell we buried more than a thousand dead on Kineton field. And more'll die yet o' their wounds. Tis All Hallows. Best we remember the dead this night. Lest they haunt we.'

# XII

# Aylesbury

*Francis Reeve*

***Stony Stratford, Thursday the 3rd of November 1642, seven o'clock in the morning***

They were heading south, the first rays of a bright winter sun spreading across their path to challenge the frost. God had given them a fine morning and, God willing, they would make good time on the road. The horses snorted in the cold air, shaking out the night's stiffness as the column picked up a steady trot.

Francis had risen in the dark hours to pray. Like many in the column, he wanted to make sure he was ready in every way, mind, body and soul. The three hundred horsemen of Sir William Balfour's Regiment of Horse led the way, followed by two regiments of foot, Grantham's tawny-brown Lincolns and John Hampden's local Buckinghamshire boys in green. They would be slower on the march, but were as keen as any to be in Aylesbury by nightfall.

They had marched from Warwick for three days with no sight or report of the King's army. But now they had sure intelligence from the God-fearing people of Buckinghamshire.

At least one regiment of base cavaliers were quartered about Aylesbury. They terrorised the poor inhabitants, demanding a daily ransom of drink, beef and oats.

Balfour's horsemen marched as a flank guard, protecting Essex and the main body of the army as it limped towards London. Now they would strike out to throw back the army of sin before it overran the city. They would strike like a spear into the flank of the Roman host.

They left the line of Watling Street at Stony Stratford to head due south in the dawn grey, passing through the villages of Beachampton, Nash and Great Horwood. At Winslow they halted to take dinner, rest the horses and let the foot catch up.

The country was flat and easy going, the sun rising in a clear, still sky that stretched to a far horizon. A flock of geese passed overhead in a great arrowhead. They too headed south. God was surely with them. *Then the Lord said unto Gideon by these three hundred men will I save you and deliver the Midionites into thine hands.*

---

'What're we still doing sat here in bloody Buckinghamshire?' Ralph Reeve threw down his hat and gauntlets, slumped into the parlour settle and ran a hand through his hair. 'We've been here for three days. The rest of the army is marching on London and we're sat here on God damned outpost duty.'

'I'll have no blaspheming in this house!' The farmer's wife bristled at the door to the kitchen. 'I don't care if you are soldiers.'

'I'm sorry, goodwife. Do you have anything to break our fast? I am famished.'

'We got good caudle.'

'Caudle? Well then, six of your caudles, if you please. The corporal will be in shortly, there are two in the barn settling the horses and three more on watch.'

'I'll put another log on that there fire if you don't mind, Goodee.'

'Well done, Clem. Another day and night on duty. And you, Luke and I have four hours on watch from midday. We may as well make the most of it till then.' They had just arrived at the farm on Weedon Hill to take over the outpost that watched the road north of Aylesbury. 'Why are we on outpost duty again while my Lord Wilmot's Regiment sit eating beef in Aylesbury? Even the rest of the troop has it better as Grand Guard at the ford. At least they are in an inn.'

'I'm sure they'll take their turn,' Luke offered.

'You may be right, Luke. But I still don't understand why we freeze our butts watching an empty road. Essex is still hiding in Warwick Castle. If you ask me, we should be riding for London.'

'Git that down you, while it's still hot.' Clem set down the pots of caudle, a thin porridge of oats in warm ale.

'Thank you. It's, *er hum*. . . delicious.'

———

The sun was now well past its midpoint. They had ridden for two hours since stopping to snatch dinner in the market at Winslow and were past Whitchurch. It was time to rest the horses and let the foot catch up again. Francis reined in as the column halted behind Colonel Balfour's raised hand. He rode in the vanguard, the lead troop, the spear tip; only a party of scouts preceded them. The colonel sat watching a great faggot of wood bundled high on a cottager's back draw near. 'Goodman, what place is this?'

The old man set down his load and straightened his back. 'It be Hardwick.'

'And how many more places afore Aylesbury?'

'There be Weedon, Weedon Hill Farm and the inn beyond Holman's Ford.'

'And have ye seen soldiers in these places?'

'Whose askin'?'

'I am Colonel Sir William Balfour. I ask on behalf of the Earl of Essex, Captain-General of the Parliamentary forces.'

'Well sir, God be blessed, we ain't seen none hereabouts. But I heard tell they's at Holman's Ford and that they been as far as Weedon.'

'Thank ye my goodman. I am obliged.'

———

'It must be well past three o' the clock now.' Ralph looked up at the sun. 'Why is it that the last hour of any watch always drags?'

He and Clem sat astride their horses on the highpoint of Weedon Hill. From here they watched the road north, a pair of sentinels beyond the outpost on the flank of the King's army. Nothing moved in a landscape braced for winter, nothing except a great flock of crows passing overhead, a long column of black cawing preachers making their way towards Aylesbury.

'I doubt weather'll hold. That'll rain afore morning.'

'I think you're right, Clem. And we've got the middle watch from midnight. Let's hope it stays clear until after that.'

'Mind, tis a beautiful clear day. Can see for bloody miles. Don't need no perspect glass.'

'Well don't tell Luke, but I think you're right.'

'See that there church over hinder. Well, I reckon I can

227

see hosses a-movin this side of it. And them ain't no team o' plough hosses.'

'Really? Where're you looking?'

'There on the road at th' edge o' the village. There be two o' they. I reckon them look like a pair o' sentinels or pointers a-scouting.'

'Clem, you're right. But we don't have any scouts out. Corporal Nisbet would have told us. There shouldn't be any of ours out there.'

'Well, there be more on they a-coming. I reckon that's a troop on the march, maybe more.'

'Fuck! We must warn Corporal Nisbet. I'll go. You stay here and keep watching. Your eyes are keener. But don't let them see you.'

Ralph turned his startled horse and kicked it into a sudden canter, clods of earth flying as he raced across the field. Nisbet was already outside the farmhouse, the rest of the guard tumbling out of the barn behind. 'Well, Mister Reeve, what have ye seen?'

'At least a troop of horse. They're on the road heading this way, out of the next village, out of Hardwick.'

'Aye, well we're no expecting any of our ain from that road. It'll be a while yet afore we can be sure, but we must assume they are not for the King. Ride tae Captain Smith. Warn him. Tell him what ye've seen and tell him we will hold here as lang as we can. I will send word when I am sure whose they are. If pressed, we will fall back on the ford. Ned, fetch the farmer and his men intae the farmhouse and keep them there. The rest of ye, prepare yersels and yer horses. A'right laddie – go now.'

Ralph was away at a hard gallop. Thank God the road dipped away so that he could not be seen by the scouts. The outpost was well placed.

At the bottom of the slope his horse plunged through the ford. The River Thame was neither wide nor deep, barely more than a stream between muddy river banks. This was where they were to fall back to. It wasn't much of a barrier to hold back an enemy.

Reining in hard outside the inn, he found Captain Smith and the first division already mounting in the yard. Others were dragging horses from stables and saddling up. They had seen his approach.

Sweeping off his hat he delivered his message to all in earshot.

'Well done, Reeve.' Smith gathered his reins. 'Ride back to Corporal Nisbet. I will send word to Lord Grandison and to Lord Wilmot in Aylesbury. My compliments to Nisbet, he is to fall back when pressed. We will hold the ford.'

Ralph turned his horse, and with a wave of his hat raced back to the outpost.

The boy and two others were holding the horses in the farmyard. Ned stood at the farmhouse door with his carbine. 'Corporal and t'others are in the field, along the hedge. Be sure you're not seen movin' about.'

Handing his horse to the boy, Ralph drew and spanned both pistols. One wedged into the sash around his waist, he gripped the other. He was not sure what would happen, but he did not wish to be caught without a loaded firearm.

He eased himself into position beside Nisbet and delivered Captain Smith's message. They crouched behind the hedge in silence. Fuck it, he needed to know, had to ask. They had not trained for this. There had been nothing like this in the weeks and days of drill and exercise. They had barely mastered the basics of troop manoeuvre. There had been no time to even discuss the notion of an ambush. 'How should we do this?'

The old soldier rolled over, looked along the hedge at his seven young troopers. 'A'right. . . well, Clem reckons he saw at least three troops of horse, probably harquebusier, with foot behind. They're on the march in column on the road. There will be at least a division of horse half a mile ahead, with two or three pointers scouting forty yards ahead o' them.

'We keep hidden ahent this hedge, a' silent. We let the pointers gang by. We note their colours, red or orange, friend or foe. If they're friends, I will hail them. If they're foe we wait for the division tae get level. On my command we gie them one volley. Make yer shots count. Aim low. Aim for their mounts. We want to hit them hard and put them in a panic. Then it's away back tae the horses and away tae Captain Smith. Any questions?'

'What do we do about the pointers?'

'If they charge us, we shoot the bastards.'

They waited, tucked behind the hedge, nursing their weapons. Only Nisbet peered out from behind the roots of a tree.

And then they heard it, the slow approach of a horse, two, three, four horses. They were walking, cautious as they approached the farm. One stopped. It was opposite Nisbet. Had they seen him?

They moved on again. Nisbet's arm stretched out behind him, thumb down. They were enemy, rebel horse. They were past now, between them and the farm. What if they reached the farm before the ambush was sprung? Would they find the horses? They would be caught on foot.

And then came the noise of the division that followed, their target. Perhaps twenty horses. They would be in column, six deep. Surely it was time? Nisbet's hand outstretched. . . *steady*. . . palm down. . . *not yet*. Come on, come on. They were passing now. . . one. . . two. . . three. . . four. . . five. . .

Nisbet's hand rolled over as he sprang to his feet. 'Up! Up! Fire!'

———

The road ahead suddenly exploded – flame, smoke and a welter of twigs bursting from the hedge, a volley of shots crashing out. Men and horses collapsed kicking and screaming in the chaos. Five troopers down, the rest of the scouts fighting to control their terrified mounts.

Francis dug spurs into his horse, struggling to hold it steady as it crashed backwards into the files behind. Colonel Balfour was yelling. 'Ambuscade left! Left!' He was giving orders, retaking control. 'Left! Through the hedge! Follow me! Left!'

They surged forward again, swinging left to hack and smash their way through the hedge, through hawthorn, beech, bramble that stuck, sprung and clawed at them. And then they were through – through into the field beyond.

———

Ralph ran. He ran as fast as he could, heavy riding boots flapping about his legs as soft harrow sucked at heels and spurs. It was a hundred yards to the shelter of the farm and their horses. He could hear the chaos on the road their ambush had caused. No sign of the pointers.

He looked behind for Clem, Luke and the others. All ran. No shots returned. But Nisbet was lagging behind. *Fuck!* Beyond him, horsemen burst from the hedge.

———

Francis was through the hedge. Ahead eight men ran across the field – cavaliers! They were four hundred yards away,

231

running towards a farm – base devils that had lain in ambush to murder in cold blood. He dug spurs into his big horse as it pounded over the loose harrow of the field. They had to be cut down. 'Heathen!'

———

Ralph reached the farm track, Ned and the boy holding the horses. He leapt back in the saddle, a fresh pistol ready. Clem and Luke were mounted; the others hauling themselves up. Only Nisbet to go. The older man was struggling in the soft earth.

'Ned, go!' Ralph shouted. 'Get the others on to the road! I'll cover Nisbet.'

'I'm a-staying with you Master Ralph.'

'And I.' Luke drew a fresh pistol.

'Alright. Clem, bring his horse. Luke with me.'

They plunged back into the field to haul the gasping corporal into his saddle. Pistol balls hissed past, shots ringing out. The roundheads were forty yards away and closing.

'Thank ye laddie. Now away.'

Back on the track, they turned to give one shot each, then on to the junction with the road. Ned held back a rebel pointer that hacked at him. A shot from Nisbet and together they raced after the others as the rebel column surged forward again.

———

'Halt! Stop I said, damn ye!' Colonel Balfour, his hand raised, reined in across the road. 'I'll not have ye charging into another ambuscade. The damn cavaliers know we're coming. They'll be readying themselves to stop us again on the road afore Aylesbury. Captain Hesilrige. . . I'd be obliged if your troop took the van. Captain Fiennes. . . reform those of yours caught in the ambuscade. And send word to the foot. And to Major Urry, to close up.'

Francis yanked the reins of his heaving, stamping horse as he struggled to reload his pistol. Behind the first three troops marched the two foot regiments. Behind them another three troops of horse made up the rear guard, a force of fifteen hundred men. But how many waited for them before Aylesbury, waited to blunt or turn aside their thrust?

———

The outpost streamed across Holman's Ford to halt in front of Captain Smith and the rest of the troop formed up on the road. They could not help panting and grinning at what they had done, at getting away with their ambush.

Corporal Nisbet tipped his hat and reported what they knew of the enemy force to his captain. Something passed between the two old soldiers. A familiarity, a knowing smile, an understanding, a shared experience, a trust born of earlier skirmishes, of other dirty fights.

'Well done, Nisbet. Well done all of you. You have bought us precious intelligence and precious time. We hold here. We hold the line of this river. I will buy what time I can by charging their horse. But that will not do alone. Corporal Nisbet, please dismount your men again and line the river-bank. I need you to hold back any attempt to take the ford.'

Ralph handed his horse to the boy who led it and the others back behind a hedge. As they went, he reloaded his pistols. Fuck! His pistols were only any good at short range. The rebel force included foot. Any musketeer could pick him off at a distance, before he came within pistol range. He needed a carbine.

It was too late to worry as they waded across the river and lined the far bank beside the ford. He had imagined they would wait behind the river. But the shallow muddy stream would do little to halt a charge by horse, while down behind the river bank they were protected from enemy fire. And they had a clear field of fire out across the flat winter meadow. Nisbet knew his business.

Already the roundhead horse and foot were advancing down the road from Weedon Hill. Behind them another three troops of harquebusiers. Their drums beat as they came on, a steady insistent pounding that grew louder. Where were Lord Grandison and Lord Wilmot? Surely, they would not leave Smith to face this force alone? Would the captain really charge three regiments with less than a troop of horse to follow him? The ruddy-faced warrior sat impassively astride the road as they drew closer.

At half a mile's distance, the leading troops spread into an arrowhead. Still they came on. Still no sign of Grandison or Wilmot. A murmur ran through the line of troopers as they looked on. The odds were against them. This was not like the ambush. The advantage of surprise was gone. The numbers were too many. They should abandon this fight, fall back into Aylesbury.

And then Lord Grandison was thundering past at the head of his troop, thrashing across the ford, up the bank and on at the charge. 'Second me, Smith!'

Smith leapt forward at a gallop. 'With me!'

Grandison's charge slammed into the leading troop of roundheads, sending them staggering back before they could counter. Smith's troopers crashed into the second rebel troop before it could envelop Lord Grandison's flank, forcing it to a halt.

'Yes! Hit 'em hard!' Ralph could not help but cheer at the sight. 'Go on my beauty!' On the riverbank, the others too were yelling. 'That's the way!' But their cheering was short lived. The third troop of roundheads swung out wide, past the clash. They came on towards the river at a steady canter.

'A'right. . . steady yersels!' Nisbet cocked his carbine. 'We wait till I gie the order. We make it count. We keep shooting, we keep moving an' we keep low. They dinnae ken how many or how few we are, so we make it look like we are more. If they get past us, we keep tae this river, d' ye hear? We hold the ford, down here till Captain Smith and Lord Grandison are back across. Now ready yersels. Here they come!'

———

Francis gripped his pistol as they rode in line across open meadow, their hooves drumming the flat ground. The lead troops were now locked in a melee with the damned cavaliers. They were moving past them, heading for the river. They would seize the ford.

The way was clear. They would cut off the cavaliers' retreat and force the heathen to surrender or slaughter them as they fled. They would turn this action and avenge the ambush.

Then a horse went down. Had it stumbled in the soft ground? The whir of a musket ball passing, a billow of smoke from the river, and another. A trooper cried out clutching at his arm. Another rolled from the saddle.

All along the river, flame and smoke exploded, the thump of musket fire rolling towards them. There had to be at least a plotoon of musketeers. But why could he not see them? They were hidden, invisible. Did some evil magic, some witch-craft hide them? Did other phantom companies lurk unseen ready to add their fire? Or was this another vile trick, another fiendish ambuscade? The base cavaliers must be in the river bed, hiding themselves below the riverbank.

They must charge them, close the gap, enact God's vengeance on these low cutthroats that killed from the shadows. They were not soldiers. No better than heathen scum, they deserved no mercy. They must be put to the sword.

But the troop was wavering, hanging back as more horses and men fell, screaming, whinnying, thrashing in the cold meadow grass. There were shouts that the foot must clear the river, that they were exposed, that they should turn to aid their brethren against the cavaliers behind them. With a single volley at their unseen enemy, the troop wheeled about.

Damn their failure! Damn their humiliation! But there was nothing he could do. He was forced to follow, forced to turn away with those either side of him, forced to turn back.

———

The roundhead troop was wheeling away. They'd done it. They'd forced them back. 'Go on, run you cockless tossers!' Just nine dismounted horsemen against a full troop. 'Fucking cuckolds!'

'A'right now, but that winnae be the last o' them. Check yer powder an' shot. Make sure each man has enough now. Jesus! Just as I thought. . . their damned foot are next.'

The rebel foot regiments had left the road. The nearer, a tawny-brown-coated battalion was already firing into Grandison's flank. The second, a regiment in green was coming on towards the river, colours flying, drums urging them on.

At sixty yards they halted to deliver their first volley. A hail of lead tore up the earth, grass and trees on either side of the river. The drums beat again as the next rank of musketeers stepped forward to deliver a second volley. Rank by rank, volley by volley they advanced.

Between each volley, Ralph and the others raised their heads to fire back. But as the roundheads closed, their volleys rolled into one continuous fusillade. There was no break, no respite, no safe moment to rise and return fire.

The hail of shot whirred overhead like angry bees, it scythed through the grass in hissing trails. It ricocheted up to tumble past, each ounce of lead searching for flesh and bone to strike, smash, mangle. A trooper next to Nisbet twisted, screaming, clutching at his shoulder. Another lay face down.

And then Ned fell backward, the top of his skull ripped away, blood, brains, matted hair spilling down the bank to run across the mud; a bright rivulet of blood draining into the stream, mingling with the flow, twisting amongst the weed and trampled rushes.

A young trooper stared at the body, wide eyed, shivering, ready to run. 'No!' Ralph pulled the boy down, shouted to break through his fear. 'You wouldn't get across the river. Stay down. Load for Luke.' How long before they all broke?

Ralph crawled across the mud to pull Ned's carbine and cartridge pouch from his body. They couldn't afford to leave them with the dead man. The carbine stock was spattered with Ned's gore. He tried to wipe it away with a muddy sleeve. The wood was smeared with mess, but there was no time to clean it properly. He brought the weapon up to his shoulder, lowered his face into the aim and squeezed the trigger.

———

Francis watched as Hampden's greencoats advanced on the river in a cloud of gun smoke and deafening musketry. The murderous devils in the river could not withstand their fire for much longer. As soon as the foot broke them, his troop would charge again, put them to the sword.

The horse troops of the reserve were now coming forward on the far flank to envelop the cavalier horsemen. Soon he and his troop would cross the river and seal their fate.

———

Where the fuck was Lord Wilmot? They could not hang on much longer. If Grandison and Smith could not extract their troops and get back across the ford, they would all be lost.

Was this how it would end, fighting back-to-back in the mud of some shitty fucking stream in the middle of nowhere?

Ralph lay on his back against the mud of the riverbank reloading the carbine. The turf above his head plucked and danced as musket balls grazed the lip to smack into the far bank. 'I am running out of powder. Only enough for a couple more shots.'

'Aye, we are a' the same.'

'What do we do if their foot charge?'

'We gie them one good volley an then break out.'

'We'll never make it to the horses. We'll be shot down.'

'Aye. We'll try our luck downstream.'

'We break out on foot, across country?'

'It is the only way out now, laddie.'

'Fuck!'

The rebel drum call had changed – more intense, thrashing out the *battail*, the command to charge.

'A'right now. . . this is it!'

And then a trumpet called. It was a trumpet calling a charge of horse, a trumpet from behind them. Lord Wilmot! The Commissary-General pounded across the ford at the head of his regiment, water and mud flying as troop after troop thundered across the stream.

'Thank God!'

The charging horsemen smashed into the roundhead reserve, sending it reeling back. The rebel foot halted, musketeers hiding under levelled pikes, protecting themselves against the cavalier horse rather than force the river.

The action did not last much longer. Wilmot's charge was enough to halt Balfour's advance, enough to allow Grandison and Smith to break free. Both cavalier regiments fell back across the river, dragging their wounded with them to reform on the home bank.

Grandison doffed his hat to the Commissary-General who held a gauntlet to his blood-smeared shoulder. 'You are wounded my lord.'

'Yes, damn it Grandison. But I have had worse and I still command.'

'And your orders?'

'God damn it, we cannot hold the town. They are all damned puritans. They will be up in arms by now. We fall back on Thame. I must ask that Captain Smith acts as rear guard. He is still captain of the guard.'

'Very well. Smith. . . you know what to do.'

'Yes, my lords. If you will excuse me. Corporal Nisbet! Get mounted! We're leaving.'

# XIII

# Gunpowder, Treason and Mud

*George Merrett*

*Twyford, Saturday the 5<sup>th</sup> of November 1642, midday*

The column shuffled to a halt again. They had barely moved a hundred yards in the last hour. At this rate, they would not reach Maidenhead until well after dark. Christ knew what this rain and damp would be doing to the powder. It had not stopped pouring since they left Reading. It pounded on George's hat to run from the brim down his sodden cloak.

It was Gunpowder Treason Day – a holiday, a day of celebration for the deliverance of King and Parliament, a day of thanksgiving for divine intervention. But George Merrett doubted if many would feel like celebrating. There would be few church bells ringing that evening, when King and Parliament were at war.

Pym and the factious party in Parliament had turned the celebrations into a raking up of Catholic intrigue, plot and rebellion. Their apprentices delighted in burning effigies of Satan and the Pope. It did not help that the Queen openly flaunted her Roman faith. And now the King had accepted the support of his Catholic subjects against Parliament. He had no choice, but it would be used against him.

It would not be like the celebrations of earlier years, when George had made fireworks for the royal displays. He loved changing their composition and design to create guises, wheels, fireboxes and rockets that showered stars to gasps and applause. Now he commanded a pair of cannon on a rain lashed, mud soaked road.

He felt for the watch in his pocket, pulled it free, held it under his cloak. He still marvelled at its beauty and precision, a perfect mechanism cupped in his hand, contained in its egg-shaped case. It had been a gift from his patron in better times. He flipped open the silver lid. Midday. He could try to push past the column to find dinner in the village ahead. But he could not bear to abandon the gunners and drivers while he fed himself. Besides, he would have to argue with every quartermaster to find space in an inn. And he was expected to join Prince Rupert by nightfall for an attempt to seize back Windsor Castle.

The road ahead was chaos. Foot regiments had become mixed up with the baggage and with the streams of refugees moving in each direction, as well as the normal traffic on the Great Road from Bristol to London. Somebody needed to take control, to restore order, or the chaos would spread.

George snapped the watch shut and pushed it deep into his pocket, away from the rain and muck of the road. With a resigned sigh, he lowered himself from the saddle to sink into the mud. He handed the reins of his horse to a boy from the nearest gun. It was Flash. The boy was soaked, downcast, lost without his mate. George shivered at the memory of those last moments when the King's battery had been over-run at Edgehill: Squit's tiny frame thrown aside; Flash hiding beneath the gun. 'Mister Busy, please bring two men. Let us see what can be done.'

They stepped forward, squeezing past companies of Welshmen scowling and hunched in their homespun wool and bare feet. He hated the mud. He hated muck, mess, filth. He had always hated dirt and disease, ever since the sweating sickness as a child. He did not hold with the old ideas that sickness was spread simply by miasma – bad vapours. Disease had to be caused by corruption, contamination of the body, not by an imbalance of its humours. Uncleansed wounds poisoned the body with their foul rotting puss. No matter how many fresh herbs were burned in a house, fever and the plague spread to infect and kill. Order and cleanliness were needed. Man must learn to tame the brute chaos of nature if he was to free himself from its mire.

The blockage lay in front of the Welsh. A great wagon, laden with bales of woollen broadcloth for London, had lost a wheel. It canted dangerously between ditch and road. A carriage trying to pass was now locked with a cart heading towards Reading. Horse teams snorted and stamped while locked wheels threatened to break an axle. A mass of pedlars, footmen, handcarts and dirty, frightened people threatened to swarm over them in both directions.

An overweight parson sat atop the cart gesticulating and urging his driver forward. His wife and many children sat on a pile of wet furniture and belongings, soaked and shivering in the open cart behind. 'I am a man of God sir, evicted from my church and home by those sectarian rogues. I must get through. I must see the bishop.'

'All in good time, reverend. I am sure that God and the bishop will wait. However, this is the King's highway and I must insist that you make way for his army. If not, we may all be evicted. Now, please desist from going forward and wait while we free you.'

George stepped up to the carriage window and pulled aside the blind. A lady, a frightened maid and a crying baby cowered inside. The lady pulled a travelling case under her cape. Another protruded from under dark puritan skirts. 'My lady, please, do not be alarmed. I must ask you to remain in the carriage while we back it up. There is no way past until we clear the blockage.'

Stepping down again, he turned to his gunners. 'Mister Busy, please back this carriage up and keep it there. If the driver gives you trouble, throw him down. I will try to get this wagon cleared.'

While the gunners worked to unlock the carriage and cart, George waded back to the nearest group of sullen Welsh musketeers. There seemed to be no officer with them. 'Do any of you speak English?'

'*Mae'n dibynnu be ti eisiau boyo.*'

'Christ, what a fucking mess!'

———

Hywel Lloyd eyed the pockmarked Englishman in the rain. 'Alright, I speaks a bit.'

'Thank God. Now, once this carriage is backed up, I need you to clear that wagon. Do you understand?'

'Alright, I got what you want.' Turning to his rain-soaked mates, he translated. '*Mae o eisiau i ni symud y wagen.*'

'*Dweda wrtho fo i symud o ei hun!*'

'The boys want to know what is in it for them.'

'Well, you tell them that if they want the King's cannon to be with them when they next face the enemy, I need them to shift that wagon.'

'Like I said, they want to know what is in it for them.'

'Christ alive! Alright, tell them that I will buy them a barrel of ale in London, if they shift it.'

*'Mae'n dweud mai fo ydy'r dyn efo'r gynnau mawr ac os ydan ni'n symud y wagen mi wneith o brynnu casgen o gwrw yr un i ni yn Llundain.'*

———

Without further word the twenty Welshmen threw themselves into unloading the wagon. George turned back to the carriage as it backed up. 'My lady, I implore you, turn off this road as soon as you can. You, and your belongings, will be safer in an inn or lodging. Wait until the army is past.'

Behind him there was a splintering crash as the wagon and the last of its contents were tipped sideways into the ditch. A fierce thickset Welshmen pointed at him and spat into the mud. *'Dweda wrth y diawl bydd o'n ei chael hi ac mi fydda'i yn torri'i gorn gwddw os dydy o ddim yn cadw at ei air!'*

———

Hywel couldn't help but smile despite the rain. The boys had got this *Sais* fucker marked. They'd have their barrel of ale from him. 'We'll see you in London, then.' He flung his musket over his shoulder and splashed after his mates as the carriage and column lurched forward.

# XIV

# London

## *William Bennett*

### *London, Tuesday the 8th of November 1642, ten o'clock*

William stood on parade in the great yard before Guildhall. He was exhausted. They had marched from St Albans the day before, only reaching the outskirts of London after dark. There was no time to go home or send a message. His duties kept him with his company, with only a few hours dozing in a Cripplegate tavern chair.

Now they stood on parade outside the Guildhall: Holles's regiment of London apprentices and Brooke's Birmingham ironworkers. They formed two sides of a square, battered, bandaged, dishevelled in their muddy, powder-stained red and purple coats.

A thin line of plumed and beribboned London Trained Bands stood uncomfortably in front of the Great Hall in their polished armour. A crowd of Londoners looked on in awed silence to complete the square. Thank God the rain had finally stopped.

He would have liked to have been inside the Great Hall to listen to the speeches, to be seen alongside those with influence. The Lord Mayor, aldermen of the city, colonels and some of the other captains were in there. But he was left outside. His colonel seemed always to favour others.

He had hoped that Thomasine would be here to welcome him. He had imagined their reunion – hero returned to her loving embrace. But she was not here. Did she still wish to punish him for choosing to soldier? She must know that the army had returned. Or had she found another to love, hold and protect her? Had someone taken his place already? *Please God not that.* He could not bear it.

At least he was spared telling her that Nehemiah was dead. He dreaded the moment he must face his daughter with the truth. It would crush her, his poor beautiful Rebecca.

———

Anthony Sedley shifted uncomfortably. His feet were wet, cold and sore in their rough workman's boots. He could feel his toes squelch in their sodden, holed hose. Behind him his file sighed and fidgeted. A musket butt scraped on the cobbles. Young Zach had struggled on the march. He was near beat and close to falling.

'Alright lads, not long now. Nice warm dinner after this.'

Why did they keep them shitting-well waiting? It was always the same. So-called bloody gentlemen inside in the warm while the working man stood outside. Even Freeborn John had abandoned them. He was not even sure why they were here. So that the bastards could show them off to their Norman lords? Why couldn't these shitting southerners fight for London themselves? Were they too soft?

*Come on, get on with it. Let these lads get to quarters to rest. And then see what rebellion means.*

———

He was here. He had come. Thomasine had waited all day in the rain the day before. She had seen regiment after regiment limp into the city under Aldersgate. So many of them were hurt. Behind every column came carts loaded with wounded and exhausted men. She was terrified that he lay mangled and broken amongst them.

But there was no sign or news of William or of Holles's Regiment. Some had said that they were the rear guard, that they would not come until the morrow. In the end she was forced to take her tired and shivering children home. Little William was so disappointed, angry at her through his tears, saying she had lied, that his father was dead. But she also felt Rebecca's disappointment mixed with relief that Nehemiah would not see her limp and bedraggled, her hair wet and slicked to her face.

Now he was here. She was sure. A neighbour had knocked with the news that the rear guard were at Guildhall. She dragged her elder children out of bed, dressed Little William, fussed over Rebecca and marched them through the streets. He was here and Nehemiah would be with him. Thank God Rebecca had not fallen for that wastrel, Ralph Reeve – handsome, but a reprobate. Such a scandal. That poor young wife had not shown her face in St Swithin's Lane since.

They worked their way through the crowd. There were grunts and huffs as she pushed deeper towards the front. She had to see him, had to know if he was alive, if he still loved her, that he was not one of those broken and maimed bodies in a cart.

She was too short to see over the crowd. A great fat merchant blocked her way. 'Should have got here earlier.' He refused to let her pass.

'My husband. . . please. . . the children's father. They must see him.'

''Ere! Let the lady through!' A fishwife turned on the fat merchant. 'You 'eard her! Husband's a bloody hero. 'Ave some respect. What you done, sat on your arse?' The woman's scolding parted the crowd enough for the boys to slip through as Thomasine pulled a reddening Rebecca behind her. 'Go on misses. Give 'im one for us! It's gettin cold at night. Husband's better 'an coal for warming your bed!'

And then they were at the front, her boys racing across the cobbles to clasp him, Little William wrapped around his father's legs.

She could wait no longer. She did not care what the crowd thought. She picked up her skirts and marched across the hollow square to throw her arms around him. He had lost weight, firmer, unshaven. He smelt of sweat, woodsmoke, damp earth and saltpetre, but he was alive. He was unhurt and he was home.

Rebecca was hesitating, holding back. She should go to him, go to Nehemiah. Could she not see him? He had to be there, in the ranks behind. They all looked so different, gaunt, haggard. She could not see his face. Why was he not here?

*Oh God, please no, not Nehemiah, not Rebecca!* She had prayed so hard for William's safe return. Was this the cost? Was this God's punishment for her own pride, her selfishness? *Punish me oh Lord, but not Rebecca, not my poor innocent girl.*

She looked up at William. Tears rolled down his face. He shook his head reaching out his arms to his daughter. 'Rebecca, I am sorry. I am so sorry.'

A drum beat. The Lord Mayor, aldermen and officers emerged from the Great Hall. Colonel Lord Brook stepped forward and raised his hand high for silence.

'Gentlemen, citizens of London, I bring a message to you from his Excellency the Earl of Essex, your Captain-General.

The Lord Mayor, aldermen and committee have heard it. I think it fit that you should know it also.

'The General wishes you to know the danger that is at hand. The enemy's regiments of foot are even now at Staines and at Colnbrook. Their cavaliers threaten Kingston and Brentford. The question now. . . what is to be done?

'Some of you may think to trust in peace, to hope for mercy and goodwill. But I say to you that this is a most doubtful course. We have stood against the foe in your name, in the name of your Parliament. Do not think that the delinquents will show pity.

'We gained an honourable victory against them at Kineton, a most bloody victory in which they lost two thousand killed. We too lost many godly men, and not a few women slaughtered by the base cavaliers. Would you discard that victory? Was it all for nought?

'It is a certain truth among all soldiers that you must keep evil as far off as you can. You must not let it come near your gates. You cannot fight amongst the tears and distractions of your wives and children, but must go out and meet your enemies valiantly.

'The General's resolution is to go out tomorrow and do as a man of courage, not only as a general but as a common soldier. He led his own regiment, pike in hand, encompassed by his enemies on Kineton Field. He himself will go out and risk all again, as he hath done before. And all this is for your sakes.

'But his forces are weary, his soldiers spent. You see before you the rear guard come but late last night into the city. Some marched twenty miles – a hard march – to reach you. But, weary as they are, they are resolved to go out.

'It is not certain that Gideon's sword alone can hold back our enemies. But if you will assist the cause and join with us, hand, heart, pike and musket, the General doubts not that God will favour us with victory.

'Let the Trained Bands of London stand with us. Let every available man follow the drums. Each and every apprentice that enlists in the public cause today is granted his indemnity. The corporation has guaranteed his freedom and place for life.

'And what is it we fight for? It is for our religion – for God – for liberty. . . our rights and freedom as Englishmen, one and all! And what is it that they fight for? For their lust. . . their will. . . for tyranny. . . to overthrow the law – to take all. To make us slaves!

'I speak not that I doubt you, but that you will resolve that when you hear the drum beat tomorrow to follow with conviction in your hearts. Oh London, I beseech you. . . doubt not in the righteousness of God's cause! But fight courageously! For this shall be the day of your deliverance!'

# Cavalier

*Ralph Reeve*

*Colnbrook, Wednesday the 9<sup>th</sup> of*
*November 1642, eleven o'clock*

Ralph stood dressed in his first fresh shirt in weeks, the fire
in the grate warming his clean washed skin. A bright winter
sun streamed through the leaded window. It felt good to be
alive. Even the smell of beery farts from a shared inn chamber
seemed to have gone. He had slept for a night, a day and a
night. Claret, good food and a feather bed had wrapped him
in sleep. He remembered getting up to eat and to piss in the
chamber pot. But each time he fell back into the warm bed
and vacuous sleep. By God, he had needed it.

There was no sign of the others. The warm fire and bed
were tempting. But Luke had woken him with news that the
King was expected to arrive with reinforcements and that
the troop would parade that afternoon. He had to prepare
himself and his gear.

If there were reinforcements, perhaps there would be
enough for a third division in the troop, for a third officer.
Would Captain Smith make him his cornet? He had proven

himself at Edgehill and at Aylesbury. There would be other contenders, but Smith must favour him.

Fuck, how good would it feel to return to London as an officer, as a conqueror, to look down at his old master and all the bloody merchants who had taken his indenture, taken his money, taken four years of his life? To ride up St Swithin's Lane, to see their faces: the Willinghams, the Bennetts, that cockless prig Nehemiah Wharton – the whole self-righteous puritanical pack of them, merchants, apprentices and servants. God! To see his old master grovel in front of them. He would make the old goat and his bitch pay. They owed him.

Picking up his purse, he counted out its contents. Just one gold half-crown left. There were nine shilling pieces, three groats, seven half-groats, three pennies – one badly clipped, four ha'penny bits – one a tin forgery, one old silver farthing, five copper rose farthings and a lead token from the Golden Anchor on St Swithin's Lane. All told, counting the forgery and clipped coins, a grand total of fourteen shillings and tuppence ha'penny.

The King's horse were promised two shillings and sixpence a day. They'd seen nothing since Shrewsbury and there was no free-quarter. Board and lodging was sixpence a day each for him and Clem, with fourpence a day for each horse. He could not deny Clem his ale and a little tobacco. At two shillings a day, he had barely enough to keep them for a week.

And that was without paying for anything else. He had wanted to buy himself a buff coat. More than anything, he had to find Clem new clothes for the winter. He was not sure he could even afford to have the horses shod if they cast a shoe. Unless he found more money soon, he would have to dismiss Clem and send him home – or find him a new master.

Oh God, not that! And what then? Sell his horse and serve as a musketeer? Fuck! They had to take London soon!

He turned to the pile of worn and muddied belongings in the corner. He pulled open the canvas snapsack that normally sat behind his saddle. Dust, dry mud and horsehair scattered across the floorboards. Pulling out each item he made a pile of its contents in front of the fire: musty grey riding cloak – badly in need of airing, spare shirt, stockings, hose and a pair of handkerchiefs, all stiff with grime and smelling of sweat.

Thank God he did not have lice. But all his clothes would need the attention of the washhouse. Next came a pewter mug and horn spoon, damp paper, ink bottle, a broken quill, a small bag containing only breadcrumbs, a pair of buckle shoes, a tinder-box – its flint, steel, baked linen and coil of match still dry in their oiled bag. Finally, he found what he was looking for: his comb and tooth-stick wrapped in a napkin.

He combed his tangled hair, brushed the fur from his teeth and finished dressing. His jacket was ripped and scorched where halberd and musket had come within inches of killing him. A flush of sweat prickled under his clean shirt at the thought of how near they came, how close he was to having his skull smashed by a vengeful musketeer.

He ran a hand over stubble and beard. There was no time to shave. Besides, it would be all the better for London, the very image of the rough conquering cavalier returned to claim his due. With a grin, Ralph turned his attention to the tools of his trade. He unsheathed his sword from its mud-spattered scabbard and began to polish it reverently. He turned it in the air to look down its length, sunlight flashing from blade onto ceiling and shadow. It was a fine German blade, better suited to battle than his father's old rapier.

He remembered the dying lobster that had given it to him. They both knew that he would die a foul and painful death, his guts pierced and oozing. A shudder ran across him as he relived the moment when the old rapier shattered in the struggle with his brother. Clem had said he would grind a new point to make a dagger. He would ask him how he faired.

He gave the sword one more wipe then turned to the pistols that sat on the table. They were not a matching pair, one Italian the other French, but they were well made and proven. He turned each of the heavy weapons in his hand. Methodically, he retracted each pistol arm, opened the flash-cover, checked the barrel, spun wheels, adjusted flints. Once again, his head rang with the din of battle; the shower of sparks, flash and clap of firing; the upward whip of the barrel; the sudden ball of black sulphurous smoke; the piercing scream and thrashing legs of the musketeer who had nearly killed him.

Finally, he picked up Ned's carbine. With even more diligence, he checked the flint and dog-lock, cleaned, wiped and polished steel and wood. He wished he could polish out the memory of poor bloody Ned lying on his back, his brains spattered across the mud as the hail of shot whipped over them in that damned riverbed outside Aylesbury.

Satisfied that all was in good order, Ralph pulled on boots that were dry and warm for the first time in weeks, strapped on his sword and headed for the yard. He wound his way through the creaking inn to descend its great stairs out into the sun. It was time to find Luke and Clem. He had left them too long.

The yard of The Ostrich Inn was busy with men and horses. The place was alive with preparations for London. A farrier hammered out hot iron shoes on an anvil for a line of horses that waited to be shod while a dog chewed at the sweet-smelling hoof clippings. All around men fed, watered, washed, brushed and rubbed down horses. They cleaned and waxed saddles, halters, reins, leathers; polished steel bits, curb chains and stirrups. Dust hung in the sunlit air mingling with the smell of sweet hay, musty horse shit and acrid piss.

Ralph found them on the other side of the yard. Luke sat on an upturned bucket with a book. Clem was grinding the old rapier on a stone, one eye on the boy picking a hoof clean.

'Well Master Ralph, I thought that there landlord had done away with you. Goodman Luke's been reading us the story o' *Thomas of Reading*. You want t' watch that there chamber above the kitchen.'

The story of Thomas of Reading was said to have been set in the Ostrich Inn. A merchant was given the best room in the inn, above the kitchen. Whilst he slept, the landlord dropped a trapdoor that tips the merchant from his bed into a cauldron in the kitchen below.

'Thank you, Clem. I'm feeling rested. Does Corporal Nisbet know I've been missing?'

'No. I reckon you're fine there.'

'Well thank you all. How are the horses?'

'They're lookin better for a rest and a bit o' fuss. I'd give them more oats, mind – if there were any. Still, I reckon they're ready enough.'

'Thank you for looking after Breda. I think we both needed a rest.' Ralph leaned in to fondle his horse behind its ears, drinking in its smell of sweet grass and dusty hair, warm breath, dewy whiskers and slobber. Even the swish of its tail seemed welcome. The horse had carried him through so much, as had Clem and Luke.

'I nearly got a fair point back on this old rapier. It's taken a bit o' grinding, but I reckon it'll make a fine dagger. An hour or two and I'll have he done. What do you reckon?'

'Clem, thank you. I thought it broken beyond use.'

'It'd be a shame not to make summat of your father's old sword. Pity Master Francis broke it. He always had a temper on him. Mother said it were on account of he losing your mother so young.'

'She may well be right.' Katherine Tooley was a knowing, clever woman and she knew his brother. She had nursed Francis as a child, through all his sickness. 'What would she say to this weather, Clem?'

'I don't doubt she'd say that'll be a hard winter. It's near Saint Martin's Day, and if ducks do swim at Martinmas, at Christmas them'll slide. That'll be snow and ice soon enough.'

———

Ralph needed to piss. In truth he needed to think more than he needed the jakes. The Ostrich Inn was filled with the noise of carousing. The whole of Grandison's Regiment were celebrating the King's arrival in Colnbrook with his army, reinforcements and pay. Even if the pay was only for the poor bloody foot, it was welcome. It would keep them from mutiny. There was even news that Parliament wished to negotiate peace terms.

The war was all but over. The rebels would beg forgiveness and London would be at their feet. They would occupy the city in triumph and be home for Christmas. This was a victory celebration. The old inn roared with their drinking, smoking, boasts, jests and laughter. As Ralph stumbled out into the dark yard, yet another song rang out from the tap room.

'*Lavenders green, lavenders blue*
*You must love me, 'cos I love you.*'

He grinned, tempted to run back and join in the bawdy verse. But he needed to clear his head. He needed to focus and to think.

'*I heard a bird, sing in my ear*
*Maids will be scarce, the next new year.*'

They had paraded that afternoon with fresh recruits to swell their ranks. Captain Smith's troop now had three divisions. It even had its own standard.

'*Down in the dale, where flowers do grow*
*And birds do sing, all in a row.*'

But the reinforcements had arrived with a new officer. There was no hope of a commission now. It was too late. He would never be an officer.

'*A brisk young man, met with a maid*
*And laid her down, all in the shade.*'

Instead, Smith had made him a lansprizado. He was now Corporal Nisbet's second, in place of poor Ned. Had he been foolish to hope for anything more?

'*Oft have I lain, with him in the dark*
*But he has ne'er, shot at the mark.*'

Worse, he and Nisbet were to serve in the new officer's division, to take orders from Master bloody Vaux, a rich young fool with no experience of war.

'*But now my dear, have at thy bum*
*For I do swear, now I am come.*'

He needed to find Nisbet, to talk with him. Before morning. Before he had any more to drink. He needed to know what the old corporal thought – what he knew.

'*Lavenders green, lavenders blue*
*You must love me, cos I love you!*'

He found the old soldier sitting in the shadows of a parlour settle in a less rowdy corner of the inn. He sat alone, drawing slowly on a long pipe. A group of flushed young troopers diced noisily at the next table while maids and serving men carried past an endless procession of ale jugs.

'So, laddie. . . ye're no' at the gaming table with Mister Vaux?'

'No, Corporal Nisbet. I was looking for you.'

'An' to what do I owe this honour? Did ye lose yer purse?'

Did Nisbet know he had no money? Did he still think of him as just a young fool? Perhaps he was. He had spent too much on ale already that night. But he had to know, had to ask – but not directly. He drew up a stool. 'Do you think there'll be more fighting, or is the war over?'

'Ah. Well, I widnae celebrate just yet. Mebbe some are ready for peace, but I dinnae think yer parliament will gie up London that easy. Rebellions – civil wars, have an uncanny way of ending messily.'

'You think there could be more fighting?'

'Aye, I do.'

'What's it like to fight in a city?'

'It is brutal, dirty, close quarter fighting. Pistols, daggers. . . crawling through holes, cellars and attics. An' burning buildings – always some fool sets the place afire. Tis the very worst sort of fighting, the closest thing tae Hell.'

'But surely, it's not something for horsemen. It's for the foot?'

'Ye might think so, laddie. But oft times the horse are expected to dismount and lead the assault with pistol and sword, or fight as dragoons on foot.'

'Then this is something we should prepare for.'

'Aye laddie, we should. But ye'll need to persuade young Mister Vaux first. An' I d'innae get the feeling he's one for getting dirty.'

Was that all Nisbet had to offer? Was he ending the conversation there? Ralph almost stood but... fuck it – he needed to know. He had to ask. 'You served in Bohemia?'

'Aye, I did.'

'Will you tell me of Prague and what happened?'

'Telling of it could be thirsty work.'

More expense, but he could not walk away now. He signalled for a jug of ale, fumbling in his purse for tuppence, half a day's horse hay. The older man remained silent until it came.

A gnarled fist gripped the leather tankard in front of him before taking a long pull. Only then did Nisbet finally turn to fix him with grey eyes, dark lines etched across a weathered face. Fire and candlelight flickered along the tight scar that ran from eyebrow to jaw.

'I sairved under Sir John Hepburn. I was younger than you are now. We marched from Edinburgh in the spring of 1620. We served as bodyguard tae Elector Frederick and his queen, Elizabeth Stuart. King Charles's sister – the *Winter Queen*.' The older man's eyes sparkled, almost moist.

'They say that she's very beautiful.'

'They call her the Helen of Germany. But that disnae describe her, laddie. Such a woman! I have seen her hunt from dawn till dusk. By Christ she can ride! Better than some of our young chevaleers, I'll wager.

'Their court at Heidelberg wis the jewel of Germany. The sons of good protestant princes came from all Europe to lairn an' marvel at its brilliance. When Bohemia elected them king and queen, it must hae seemed that God had blessed their stars. It was a time of hope an' beauty.

'But it was destroyed. Them same princes left us tae face the imperial *tercios* alone at White Mountain. We lost near a third of our number slaughtered afore the last stand at the Star Palace. The bodies were ten deep agin its walls.

'It didnae stop their Cossacks, hussars and bloody Croats raping, pillaging, running amok through the city. You could hear the screaming into the night hours. Blood courts, execution and inquisition followed.

'That was in the November. They had been king and queen but a year. The Queen rode pillion on an officer's horse through the snow, with Prince Rupert but a bairn. The few of us that could, followed. It was a terrible winter the like o' which nane had seen afore. There were many as died on that retreat of cauld or want, let alone the bloody imperials.'

The older man sank back into his settle, as if his very youth drained away. As if he had done and said too much. Finally, the corporal expelled a deep breath.

'An' that was just the beginning on't. Twenty-two years of war have followed, an' nae end in sight. Half of Germany lies dead, slaughtered or taken by famine an' plague. Their towns an' villages are but ruins picked ower by craws, dogs an' wild pigs. I hear tell Bohemia is worse. Aye, those princes that live regret the day they unleashed chaos. Pray to God laddie that these isles are spared the worst on't.' The old soldier's eyes stared grey and distant in the firelight. At last he drank deeply. 'But why dae ye ask?'

'My mother served the queen in Prague. She died without speaking of it.'

'And your father?'

'My stepfather will not speak of it. I know nothing of my father.'

'Aye well, I'm sorry laddie. Thank God she 'scaped the hell that Prague became. She must have been a rare strong woman.'

He wanted more. But it was clear the older man had said enough. 'Thank you.'

'Now, ye'll need to excuse me, laddie. I have an engagement.' Nisbet nodded in the direction of the serving girl that watched them. And, by Christ, she was smiling – blushing.

Ralph headed back towards the noise of the tap room. In the next room, a group were gaming at a card table. Fuck! It was Mister Vaux with his cronies. Lieutenant Musgrave sat with them. They were gambling. It was too late to back away. Vaux beckoned him, looked him up and down. 'Ah, Reeve, isn't it? Our lansprizado? Will you not join us at table? Patrick, find Reeve a chair. And fetch more claret, man.'

Ralph inclined his head and bowed, not low but enough to be polite. 'Thank you, sir, but I must decline.'

'Decline? I am not sure I can trust a gentleman who will not risk a little wager at table. Are the odds not to your liking?'

He ignored the challenge and the toadies' snigger.

Musgrave stiffened. The Lieutenant looked as if he had already had enough of the company. 'I don't think Ralph Reeve's bravery is in any doubt.'

'Thank you, sirs.' Ralph bowed again. 'But I must sing.'

'Sing?' Vaux sneered. 'Are you a minstrel?'

'I promised the tap room a song – for the troop.' It was not true, but it was all he could think of. 'If you'll excuse me.'

He did not wait for an answer but turned and strode towards the door. He clenched his fists trying to ignore the jibes that followed. It had been a bad enough introduction. He could ill afford to make it worse and he could not deny the truth of Vaux's gibes. 'The man is in rags. His jacket is ripped. Has he no dignity – no money?'

The tap room was as rowdy as he had left it, flushed with beer and song, thick with smoke and banter. 'Ralph! Where have you been?' they called. 'You took your time. Was she worth it?'

Fuck Vaux and his cronies. He would sing. He sprang onto a chair.

'Sing man, give us a song!'

He climbed higher, up onto a table. There were shouts as his spur caught a tankard, its contents spilling across the boards, then more yelling, chanting. 'Sing! Sing!'

Ralph held up his hands for silence. Slowly, he looked around the room. Luke shook his head, Clem grinned, the boy gaped, open jawed. There was a raised eyebrow from Smith and a quizzical smile from Lord Grandison. Two hundred faces stared at him. Fuck it! If he couldn't be an officer, he may as well enjoy himself. He would give them a song to remember.

*'What creature's this, with his short hairs,*
*His little band, and huge long ears,*
*That this new faith hath founded?*
*The saints themselves were never such,*
*The bishops ne'er ruled half so much.*
*Oh! Such a rogue's a roundhead.* Come on! With me!'

Together they roared out the chorus. '*Oh! Such a rogue's a roundhead!*'

His hand raised for silence again, holding them, looking for the next verse.

*'What's he that doth high treason say,*
*As often as his yea and nay,*
*And wish the King confounded;*
*And dares maintain that Mister Pym*
*Is fitter for a crown than him?*
*Oh! Such a rogue's a roundhead.'*

They were on their feet, stamping, yelling. '*Oh! Such a rogue's a roundhead!*'

Hush again, they were waiting for him, wanting more. Quietly now, he must build it up.

*'What's he that met a holy sister*
*And in a haycock gently kissed her?*
*Oh! Then his zeal abounded.*
*'Twas underneath a shady willow,*
*Her Bible served her for a pillow.*
*And there he got a roundhead!'*

The room exploded, cheering, roaring, shouting out the chorus. *'Oh! Such a rogue's a roundhead!'* They thumped the tables, banged down their ale pots, crashed their tankards, yelling for more, more, together, once more. *'Oh! Such a rogue's a roundhead!'*

# XVI

# Lust

*Francis Reeve*

### *London, Thursday the 10<sup>th</sup> of November 1642, four o'clock*

*Lord, cleanse Thy servant of his sin. Release him from torment, I beseech Thee. Thou art but my refuge, my only fortress. Let me dwell again in the shelter of Thy shadow. Do not forsake me, I beg!*

Francis clutched his bible in fervent prayer, his knees pressed to the cold stone floor beneath the high choir of St Paul's Cathedral. He needed God's reassurance, His certainty to wash away his doubts, his torment. He needed to cleanse himself, to armour his soul from sin. But even here, he struggled to find God's presence. Even here in England's greatest church doubt and uncertainty racked him.

*Lord, show Thy unworthy servant the righteous path, give him the strength to resist temptation. Let him do Thy bidding in the sure knowledge that he fights in Thy name.*

He had taken his free afternoon to see the city. He had wanted to see London, the capital of their godly rebellion, the blessed city that would surely be the New Jerusalem. It was a pilgrimage. He sought to be lifted, inspired, confirmed in God's purpose and their sacrifice in battle. But instead of clean puritan streets, he had met with dirt, drunkenness, crime and lust. Parliament and the city elders seemed indifferent to the rot that surrounded them. Worse was the knowledge that temptation had pierced his own armour. He had felt dangerous urges. He had felt the lure of sin again – here, in the very heart of Zion.

He had gone first to see for himself the Babylonian Palace at Whitehall. He thought himself ready. But the scenes of Roman debauchery painted on the ceiling of the King's Banqueting House still shocked. Even now they tormented him with their cavorting flesh and deified King. Under these craven images, bare-breasted ladies had danced with dwarves, monkeys and the King's favourites, in obscene masques and drunken revelry.

He thought to find Westminster more uplifting. But instead of piety, spiritual leadership, godly government, fortitude, he found richly-dressed Members of Parliament protecting their interests. They anticipated sack or surrender at any moment. The place was filled with their servants piling carts with earthly belongings, while courtesans waited in their carriages.

In St James's and at Charing Cross, single, masterless women, idled, waited, fishing for men, for their own pleasure. In Covent Garden's newfangled piazza, pretty girls sauntered under the Spanish arches, paraded in front of the Roman temple, flaunting themselves for money. Along the Strand, older bawds and wanton women lounged outside taverns and bordellos looking to lure a man in, sink their hooks into him. Behind them, the worst sort of whores, pimps, footpads and cut-purses waited to haul a catch into the alleys and rat-runs sloping down to the river, a dark tangle of irretrievable vice and crime they called the Bermudas.

Within the old city walls, he found unchaperoned, lewdly dressed women. At the Royal Exchange merchants' wives and daughters in gaudy silks and velvets met his eye, watched him from behind scarves and winter masks as they sauntered. It was as if they were sizing him, weighing him in his soldier's buff coat and boots, considering him, body and soul, as a purchase.

Even here in St Paul's, he was shaken by what he saw. In the churchyard, booksellers sold every sort of book and pamphlet. Where he thought to find holy scripture, Puritan prayers and godly instruction, he found *The Book of Sports*, Donne's conceits and *Aretino's Postures*! Visions of flesh and a student's sin flooded back to send him rushing from the shop in a sweat. The great cathedral was not what he expected. It was dirty, neglected: scaffolding propped up a shattered tower, the spire struck down by God; window panes were broken; shacks built against its walls; rubbish littered the doorways where vagrants slept and men waited to be hired for work.

Inside, men and women mingled, promenaded, gossiped, flirted, sold themselves up and down the bare nave. The Paul's walk they called it. Even now their noise echoed overhead, a swarm of insects, the clicking of their feet climbing the walls, crawling across the chancel roof to surround him with their muttering and their eyes, eyes that bored into his soul, recognised the lust that lay within. . . black. . . rotten. Their incessant whisper was broken only by the sound of irreverent laughter, a woman's shriek and the wings of pigeons flocking to roost and shit amongst the great gothic arches.

This Temple had to be cleansed, the priests and bishops cast out by Christ, their paraphernalia, books and obscenities heaped on the fire, burned in the street. He came to find a New Jerusalem. Instead, he had found Babylon, its streets clogged with whores, pimps and the filth of their fornication! But how could this be? He had fought so hard to protect a Parliament that even now treated with the Devil. Did God really wish him to fight again to defend this abomination of a city?

And yet he could not tear himself away. He was stirred. He wanted more. He wanted to see, hear, touch, everything. Even now, in the choir of St Paul's, he struggled to rid his mind of flesh and seduction, images that burned his soul, urges that tormented him once more.

He had not been vigilant. Satan tempted him – even here in God's church! His blood surged, heating his loins. His breeches itched, his buff coat heavy in his lap. His balls ached, his manhood throbbed, slickened.

He felt his old enemy close again. Asmodeus, demon of lust, prince of Hell, was here. Even now, here in the cathedral, the Prince of Lechery possessed him, lured him, whispered to him. He was weak. He burned with desire. It was November; Asmodeus was strong in this month. The eternal fires of Hell awaited those who fell to his temptation.

*Oh God, do not desert Thy pilgrim now. Not here in Thy house! Wantonness surrounds this weak sinner. Lord, give me strength to resist. The End of Days beckons. Let me be counted amongst Thy Elect, to sit with Thine angels. Do not forsake me I beg. Do not leave me. Do not let me fall!*

# XVII

# Slaughter

*Robbie Needham*

*Colnbrook, Friday the 11ᵗʰ of
November 1642, eleven o'clock*

'Whorr'eh they pissin' doin' in there? We've been stood 'ere nigh
an hour. It's past guard change, I've 'ad no snap and nowt t' drink
neither. I'm bloody clammed.' Robbie stood with the guard in
the yard of the Catherine Wheel Inn. He was tired and crabby
after a night of watch, the bruising on his face still hot and itchy.
He wanted to shit, get his boots off and shift his clothes after a
day and a night in them. He was hungry, thirsty and scratchy.

'Buggered if I even know rightly why we're waitin' on 'em.
If I were t' King, I'd gaol t' bloody lot of 'em an' chuck away
t' key. Pissin' Members of bloody Parliament! I don't care if
they beg for peace on their knees. I ain't come this far to see
'em keep their bloody privileges while people can barely buy
bread. They know nowt of hardship. The tossers 'av 'ad it their
way too long. I reckon it's time we put t' King back in London,
cleared them lot out and got back to makin' a fair livin. Any
road, it's Martinmas. Tis a bloody holiday, b' rights. We should
be drinkin. Not stood out ere waitin' on them buggers.'

There was a sudden clattering behind as the young Officer of the Watch rushed from the inn to take his place beside the Corporal of the Guard. 'Stand straight! Advance your arms!'

Robbie heaved his pike up to clasp it in the cup of his right hand. The guard stood in silence while final pleasantries were exchanged between Parliament's five peace commissioners and the King's courtiers.

At last, the commissioners mounted. They were led out of the inn yard by a trumpeter and troop of cavaliers as escort, clattering under the arched entrance to turn onto the road to London.

The yard was suddenly empty, the guard standing alone; before them only lumps of horseshit steaming on the sunlit cobbles.

———

With a trumpet call to clear the way, the Peace Commission and escort picked up a brisk pace as they clattered down Colnbrook high street. They rattled over the County Bridge into Middlesex. With another trumpet call, they passed the King's artillery park, its twenty-seven cannon on display facing London.

George Merrett stood before the guns with his hat removed. He did not salute the passing commissioners out of any great respect for them or their purpose. But he could not afford for his patron to hear that he had been lax. He still depended on the Earl's goodwill.

They rode on out of Colnbrook on the Great Road laid out by King Charles over which the King's mail carried his new common postage, on over the new bridge across the King's newly cut Longford River. The King's new highway would take them across Hounslow Heath, through Brentford,

Hammersmith and Knightsbridge to Westminster, envoys of an obstructive parliament that refused ancient taxes, revenues due to a visionary king, taxes to fund the navy, defences and great works.

Old Nick stroked the long barrel of his demi-culverin. 'Reckon they're playing for time I do.'

'You may well be right, Mister Busy. I fear it is to their advantage. They hold the approaches to London. They have forces at Kingston, Brentford and Uxbridge. And we should not forget that they still hold Windsor in our rear. We are quite hemmed in. Every day provides them respite to recruit, rearm and build up their defences, whilst our resources are stretched from Oxford to Colnbrook and Egham. We cannot sit here and wait for winter while Parliament takes its time. I pray that His Majesty will act swiftly and decisively. If I had his ear, I would say we seize the bridge at Brentford, threaten Westminster and encourage all London to rise up. Parliament's so-called Committee of Safety might then be serious about peace terms.'

———

William Bennett followed his lieutenant-colonel out of the inn and across the market place towards Brentford Bridge. As Captain of the Watch for the next day, William had only just reported to him at The Three Pigeons, when a trumpet call brought the old soldier to his feet and striding out of the inn. James Quarles knew his business and William did not wish to question him. Quarles commanded the regiment while their famous colonel, Denzil Holles, engaged in politics in Whitehall.

They passed the church and reached the bridge just as the peace commissioners were crossing it. A troop of harquebusiers waited to escort them to Westminster, their cavalier escort left beyond the outpost at Brentford End. William followed Quarles in doffing his hat as commission and escort set off at a trot.

'Will there really be peace do you think?'

'William, I don't know. But until there is, we must do our duty and be ready to defend London.'

'But is there not now a cessation of arms while they negotiate?'

'I wish it were as clear as that. We have received no order for a ceasefire. I will not rest unless and until we do.'

---

'Hold 'er still, lads! Zach. . . Izzy. . . hold 'er firm!' Anthony Sedley gripped the pig's warm bristling neck, the reek of her skin and dirt in his nose and under his fingernails. 'Alf, you got that rope around her leg?'

'I got 'er tied good and tight, Anthony.'

'Good. Alright now, my sweet. Hush your snuffling. We don't want you all mithered now. Keep still and this won't hurt. Tom, you ready with that knife?'

'Ready, Anthony.'

'Harry, hold 'er head still. Mind she don't bite. Alright, 'ere we go. Now, Will – do it!'

He braced his body against the pig's flank as Will Scarlet thumped his musket butt down between the animal's ears. The big black Berkshire sow let out one shrill squeal, bucked, grunted and then fell prostrate in the mud. She kicked and twitched but lay unconscious. The meat would taste better for not being addled with fright.

'Nicely done, Will. Alright, lads – pull 'er up!'

They hauled on the rope to drag the pig up so that it hung

by one back leg, head down, swinging gently in the air. The mud below already ran red with the blood of other pigs.

All along Brentford High Street, pigs were being washed, scraped, disembowelled and butchered. Men cut, sliced, sawed and chopped carcasses. In doorways, old women and boys plucked and gutted geese, the feathers sticking to the wet blood and warm stinking offal.

It was Martinmas, the day of sacrifice, when every family killed what they could not keep, preserving precious meat for the long winter. Bacons, hams, chops, loins and hocks were salted, smoked, cured, potted or packed in barrels. Intestines were washed and stuffed, chitterlings, brawn and trotters boiled, the blood baked into blackpot puddings. Nothing was wasted.

The soldiers joined with the citizens, helping the families upon whom they were billeted. The work, communal celebration and ritual was a welcome break from march and drill. It was also a reminder of home, an ancient rite shared by the common man in every corner of England, and beyond. It was all the better for the beer shared with it.

A trumpet call suddenly echoed through the street, the banter and communal effort cut silent. A troop of armoured horsemen filled the road with their steel and horseflesh. In their midst rode a group of elegantly dressed lords and gentlemen, dignitaries and escort coming from Brentford Bridge. Anthony glared at them in the silence.

'Who are them buggers, Anthony?'

'The bloody Peace Commission – lords and shitting gentlemen. They bargain with the tyrant on behalf of the common man. No doubt they'll save their necks and estates at our expense.'

They all glowered as the escort and commission went by;

a sullen, staring crowd watching the uneasy horsemen pass. Wide-eyed horses, fearful of the scent of pigs, danced and skittered at the warm sickly smell of blood and death.

The silence was broken by a grunt, a piercing scream, a shrill squealing as the sow regained consciousness. It kicked and thrashed, spinning on its rope as it howled out in fear.

Panic spread through the horses. Horsemen fought to control mounts that cannoned into each other. All dignity was lost as one of the riders fell, his horse bolting towards London followed by the rest at an ungainly canter, their riders trying desperately to cling to their saddles.

'Shit! She's woken! Grab 'er legs. Tom, slit 'er throat quick! Zach. . . the bucket! Get the bucket under 'er!'

As the runt of a boy tried to catch it, the pig's blood spewed out over the mud of the street. Will Scarlet pointed at the rider sprawled in the mud. 'Serves the shitter right. Like they say, Anthony. . . every hog will get his Martinmas.'

# Part Three

# Brentford

*To Brainford, westward, if thou sayst the word. . .*
*My bird o' the night! We'll tickle it at the Pigeons,*

BEN JOHNSON, *THE ALCHEMIST*, 1612

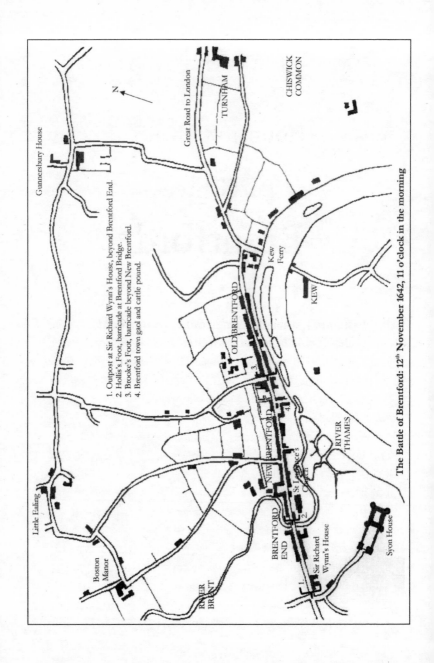

1. Outpost at Sir Richard Wynn's House, beyond Brentford End.
2. Hollis's Foot, barricade at Brentford Bridge.
3. Brooke's Foot, barricade beyond New Brentford.
4. Brentford town gaol and cattle pound.

**The Battle of Brentford: 12th November 1642, 11 o'clock in the morning**

Gunnersbury House

Little Ealing

Boston Manor

RIVER BRENT

BRENTFORD END

Sir Richard Wynn's House

Syon House

NEW BRENTFORD

St Lawrence's Church

RIVER THAMES

OLD BRENTFORD

KEW

Kew Ferry

TURNHAM

Great Road to London

CHISWICK COMMON

N

# I

# Hounslow Heath

*Ralph Reeve*

*Colnbrook, Saturday the 12<sup>th</sup> of November 1642, six o'clock in the morning*

It was still dark when the King's army began to move. Ralph was grateful to find Clem waiting for him. The inn yard was a mass of horses, men, muffled curses and last-minute adjustments as the regiment prepared to march. 'The boy's got the hosses on t'other side o' the yard against that there wall – out the way, like.'

Wreathed in fog, cold breath and steaming horse piss, Ralph and Luke followed Clem through the press. 'Goodman Luke, if I could ask you to check that girth of yours. The boy done it, but it needs checkin'. He's a-learnin', but he ain't too good of a morning. He do need his sleep. Master Ralph, yours is done, I checked he meself. Captain Smith is over there with Lord Grandison. Corporal Nisbet is outside in the street already a-fretting for we to be lined up. I hain't seen nought of Mister Vaux nor his man. No doubt they'll be a-combing that fine hair o' his. There's a terrible thick fog out there. I hope some bugger knows where we is a-goin. I don't fancy getting lost in it.'

277

Ralph slid his pistols into their holsters and took the bridle of his horse. He led them out under the low arch of the Ostrich Inn, horse shoes rasping on the cold cobbles, echoing in the dark. They took their place in the column forming in the street. Nisbet was already waiting, impatient. Once Mister Vaux and the final files were lined up, they mounted and moved off.

As they rode, men were tipping out of every inn, house, hovel and outbuilding in Colnbrook to form up in the cold damp air. Corporals pulled and pushed half-sleeping youths into line, quartermasters checked rooms for forgotten kit, wagon masters cursed their stubborn teams while suttlers, wives and whores hoisted children and belongings onto carts, packhorses and their own backs.

Slowly the great mass began to take order and move off, regiment by regiment: Wilmot's brigade of horse; Byron's foot tertia; the train of artillery; baggage and camp followers. In Egham, Rupert's horse and Wentworth's tertia were crossing the Thames. At Ashford, Fielding's tertia was also on the move. All had orders to rendezvous with their king on Hounslow Heath.

It felt good to be moving, even if it was cold, dark and wet. The thick dank fog swirled about them, obscuring light, muffling sound, scaring horses. Everything dripped with dew. Cloaked in the primeval cloud, they hid their excitement. The army was moving forward again. They were riding to seize the bridge at Brentford, to open the way to London.

They thumped over the County Bridge and on over the new bridge beyond the village, past dark, brackish water, willow and rushes. They rode in silence listening to muffled hoofbeats, the creak of damp leather, horses snorting in the cold air. Moisture dripped from steaming nostrils, muzzle, whiskers and lashes. It coated hats, cloaks and flanks in its shining cobwebbed veil.

The land was flat, the soil black and wet, the road filled with pools of water after rain. Moisture dripped from chestnut, willow and thorn, jewelled gossamer hanging from every tree and hedge as they passed. Nobody wanted to talk or disturb the silence, each one of the column wrapped in his own thoughts. Dew hung on eyebrows, moustaches and beards, damp, cold on faces and ears.

They rode past the advance guard at Poyle and the outpost at Longford, readying themselves to follow as, almost imperceptibly, the darkness was replaced by a grey watery light from above. The fog hushed, baffled, shortened the sounds of cockcrow and dog bark as they rode through Cranford gripping cold slick steel, straining for any sound of danger.

Beyond Cranford they left the road to cross the heath, sloshing through long wet grass and heather. Horses and riders twitched and snorted as dim shapes slipped by in the gloom – cattle and sheep. Men twisted to hear and see the ambush they feared hidden in the half-light.

Finally, they came to a halt in line, in battle order, on Hounslow Heath. Wet tails hung limp. Flanks and nostrils steamed in the wet air. Eyes strained into the gloom ahead as they stood and waited for the rest of the army.

Somewhere ahead on the Great Road was Brentford Bridge and London. They would have their king home in Whitehall for his birthday. They would bring Westminster to heel and feast Christmas at home. Ralph would return. And he would return a victor.

## II

# A Cessation of Arms

*Francis Reeve*

*Westminster, eight o'clock*

Francis stood beside his horse – waiting. With a young cornet, a trumpeter, five other iron-clad troopers and a servant, he waited for Parliament's peace envoy. They were to escort Sir Peter Killigrew from the Palace of Westminster to the King at Colnbrook.

He had volunteered for this duty. The peace talks were an abomination, a turning away from Zion. But he had to get out of the city. He had come to London an ardent pilgrim; now, he would do anything to escape it. He longed to be free of the oppressive smoke and grime. His body itched where she had touched him. He was sure the others could smell her musk on him, sense his sin. He needed to wash and rub the stench, the filth, the lust from his body.

Instead, he had to wait, wait for the Committee of Safety to dispatch its envoy to the King, an envoy who must grovel in front of an apostate army that stood at the very gates of London.

The fog hung on him like the whore's fetid breath. Cold and moist, the city was a beguiling female temptress, a phlegmatic witch that wrapped herself around a man's soul to drag him into the gutter of damnation.

He had fallen to temptation again. Was he weak? Was he not worthy to be one of God's chosen? No, this was surely another test. Satan had laid temptation in his way and God had shown him the righteous path once more. Now he must escape Babylon. He could bear it no longer. Sweat drenched him, despite the cold. He was going to retch. He would have to beg leave to piss, to scratch at his itching cock.

And then Sir Peter Killigrew strode out of the fog. He nodded to the cornet, took his horse from his servant and mounted. 'I am to attend His Majesty the King at Colnbrook. You know the way in this fog and you know that we will be at His Majesty's mercy?'

'Yes sir,' the cornet stammered, 'I think so.'

'But do you know the import of your duties? The Committee of Safety must know the King's disposition to a cessation of arms during this time of treaty. We must rectify this omission before some fool fires a shot and destroys the chance we have to heal the nation's wounds. Another bloodletting could be fatal. We should not keep Parliament or the city waiting. Well, lead on. I wish to make a stop at Hammersmith, but not before.'

'Yes sir. Pointers to the front, away! Escort. . . march!'

With two troopers to clear the way ahead and trumpet calls to warn of their official business, they rode through Whitehall and on up Haymarket to turn west onto the Great Road that led to Bristol.

The Devil held them back, the pace slow in the thick fog as the city clung to them, refusing to give him up. The streets were already busy with carts, barrows, porters and every type of idiot, from last night's drunken whore to refugees seeking shelter. Every time they broke into a trot, some fool lurched out of the fog forcing them to rein back. Even the urgent calls of the trumpeter failed to clear the way.

Finally, they rode out past the earthworks and the half-dug fort at Hyde Park Corner. Free of the city, they picked up a steady trot. They passed the seedy inns of Knightsbridge then on between park and gardens through the village of Kensington, and on again through fields to Hammersmith.

Here they stopped to water the horses. The place was filled with cannon, wagon train and munitions. The few fire-locks that guarded the guns played at dice while the gunners lounged about in course humour. As soon as Sir Peter and the cornet were out of sight in an inn, they had their sport with the escort.

'Where you off to in such an 'urry? Trumpets an' all!'

'War's over. Didn't they tell yer?'

'Hey, you don't want to be going that way. You're going the wrong way. You want to be getting back 'ome. 'Ome to your nice little wives and sisters. Before some fucking cavalier takes your place! Me? I'm back to the Dutch wars. Plenty of siege work there for the likes of us. It's the whores and best genever of Amsterdam for me. Should have been fuckin' gunners shouldn't yer. Bloody troopers. Trot on!'

Francis wanted to scratch and wash himself. He wanted to be moving again, away from these louts and their lewdness. Thank God Sir Peter made only the briefest halt to piss and take a glass of sherry.

# III

# The Way to London

*Robbie Needham*

*Hounslow Heath, eleven o'clock*

Robbie Needham stamped his feet. They were piss-wet through and numb with cold, soaked to the skin with marching in sodden heath grass. He could hardly feel his toes, or the holes in his hose, squelching in his miner's boots.

He looked up for some sign of warmth. At last, the sun was starting to burn through the fog. Pools of light swam intermittently through the haze. But there was no warmth in it yet. It was still cold in the gloom that enveloped them. No hope of his bloody feet drying.

They had waited for hours. The King's army was assembling. Regiment after regiment marched up the Great Road to peel off into battle line. No sooner did each appear than it disappeared again into the fog. The only distraction was a pathetic bunch of prisoners bound with match cord and paraded on the road, and a pair of giggling young ladies clinging to young officers as they bounced back and forth on the rumps of their horses.

Robbie just wanted to get on with it. He was a free-miner,

283

not used to waiting for anybody. He didn't like being buggered about, least of all by silly bloody gentlemen who should know better. His bruised face itched in the cold damp air. 'Stupid buggers. Worr'eh they think this is? A pissin' picnic? You'd think they'd know better.' He shifted uneasily in the wet grass. 'Worr'eh we bloody waiting for any road? I thought we were goin to beat pissin rebels and march t' King back to London. Are we goin to wait for bloody Christmas first? If London is so pissin great, why don't we just gerron wi' it? Then we can all go 'ome.'

'Quiet in the ranks. Officers approaching.'

'Shit, it's t' bloody King.'

'Battaile. . . stand straight in your files. Advance your arms!'

They braced up, hefted pike and musket off the ground and into the right shoulder. Mounted on his delicate white Turk, the King acknowledged the compliment from his Lifeguard with a nod and smile, taking his place at their head, before turning back to Prince Rupert beside him. 'Rupert, you understand do you not. . . I cannot enter London as a conqueror. I must have the support of the city and of my people.'

'Sire, I understand your noble desire, but every day Essex's strength grows and Skippon drills the city Trained Bands. At any moment they could envelop us.' Rupert rode high on a great charger, grey campaign coat over armour, the young hero of half a dozen battles in Germany. Helmet off, the prince scratched at matted hair. 'During all their entreaties, they have not once asked for a ceasefire.'

'I know. I know you are right, Rupert. But we advance step by step. This is not a dash for Whitehall. I wish to force the rebels to the negotiating table, not take the city by storm.'

'Sire, let us take this crossing at Brentford. The way is then open to London and they must negotiate. They must accept your terms and beg for your mercy.'

'That may be, but there must be discipline. I want no looting – no sack. You are to keep your cavaliers in order.'

'Sire, I wish and strive for nothing more.'

'Very well, but remember, London is my city. And Rupert. . . for God's sake bathe and change your shirt before we get there. You smell like the very worst of my pioneers.' The King turned to his field marshal. 'Now, my Lord Ruthven, is the army ready?'

'Aye sir, they're ready.'

'Then let us open the way to London.'

# IV

# Alarum!

## *William Bennett*

### *Brentford Bridge, half past eleven o'clock*

William Bennett was Captain of the Watch. He would rather have been in Westminster or the Guild Hall. That was where the important action was, where the other captains were. It was where decisions on peace and the future were being made. They would be with Colonel Holles and those of influence, currying favour, making deals before it was too late. He was not sure what his colonel thought of him. He clearly favoured the others, those with sway in the city. He had not taken William with him. Instead, he was stuck here in muddy Brentford.

He would have loved dearly to be back with Thomasine and the children. He longed for his bed with its curtains and covers. He badly needed time to rebuild his damaged business. He should never have invested so much in soldiering. The war was all but over, his capital wasted, his dreams of acceptance and respect in a city livery company lost. He should never have left London.

He had started his duties at ten o'clock that morning with

a round of the sentinels. All was in place on the bridge. The officer and corporal of the guard seemed to know their duties, but the fog made him uneasy. It was thick down here where the River Brent met the Thames. It still swirled in great tendrils and banks across the still, dark water.

He was not so worried about an attack. Not whilst they were contracting a treaty to end the war. And, besides, there was an outpost beyond the bridge that would give them warning. He was more worried that he, or his sentinels, would be surprised by those of importance approaching from London. He dreaded having to explain to Colonel Holles why his guard had failed to salute the Committee of Safety or their commissioners on their way to the King.

William turned from the bridge and walked back past the church. At the corner of the marketplace he entered The Three Pigeons Inn. His next appointment was dinner with Lieutenant-Colonel Quarles. The old soldier commanded in Holles's absence. He was also Field Officer of the Day, responsible for all the guards and outposts that protected Brentford.

Captain Robert Viviers would be there – damn fool and coward, one of the captains of horse who had abandoned them without a fight at Edgehill. If he had stood, maybe Nehemiah would still live. Now he and his troop were posted to Brentford to regain their honour. But Captain Lilburne, the celebrated Leveller pamphleteer, would also join them. Freeborn John was Captain of the Watch for Brooke's purple-coated Levellers, quartered behind Holles's regiment in Old Brentford. He had arrived last night from London. He would have news.

If nothing else, they would have a decent dinner. The Three Pigeons was famous for its fare. A great rambling old place, it dominated the little marketplace and was still reckoned the best of all the inns and taverns that lined Brentford's mile-long high street. Its cheesecake and cream were renowned.

He was not sure about the pair of old actors that kept the inn. John Lowin and Joseph Taylor had played with Shakespeare himself before Parliament closed London's theatres. They were now reduced to keeping board. No doubt they would have preferred more cavalier company than the puritan officers of Holles's Foot.

Once the officers were gathered in the parlour set aside for them, aged Hamlet and portly old Falstaff could not resist making an entrance.

'*You are welcome, masters, welcome all. I am glad to see thee well. Welcome good friends.*'

'Gentlemen, we will send Mistress Quickly to attend you shortly. In the meantime, we are at your service. Do not hesitate to call.'

And then, as if exiting the stage, 'Come Dogbolt, let us leave Mars, Horatio, Pistol and John to their affairs of state. It is the tap and spit for thee and I.'

'*Bardolph, follow him. A tapster is a good trade. An old cloak makes a new jerkin; a withered serving-man a fresh tapster.*'

'Mistress Quickly' arrived with water to wash, napkins, spoons, glasses and a jar of sack. Having poured the wine, the plump serving girl departed to fetch dinner. William sank into his chair with the warmth of the fire, good wine and the anticipation of London news over good fare.

Colonel Quarles opened the conversation. 'Well John, what news?'

'The peace party are in the ascendancy.' Lilburne looked grave. 'They control the House of Lords now and much of the

Commons.' He spoke plainly in his Northumbrian brogue. 'Them that waiver think we've gone too far. Pym and his war party are out of favour. The city's worried and wants to sue for peace. Without their money, we've got no army. If it comes to battle again, I'm not sure if their Trained Bands will stand with us. Many are asking how it is that the King is now in front of London, after Essex reported victory. They want to know why Essex did not stop the cavaliers. Daily, there are demands for peace.'

'But surely we must all embrace this opportunity for peace.' Viviers looked as if he had already been drinking. 'We must heal the wounds. We have gone too far as it is. We must step back. The King will be merciful. We should not provoke further violence.'

They all looked to Quarles for his reaction.

'William, what do you believe?' The colonel looked at him, wanted his opinion.

'Well, Colonel, I am not sure.' William shifted in his seat. 'I mean, of course I want peace. But on what terms? Parliament said there would be only one battle to purge the nation of malignant blood. But it seems now that the court party are stronger than ever. Are we to write-off all that we have invested? I have lost much already. Will Parliament be able to protect our property from corruption? Colonel, I fear we have risked too much. I for one may be ruined.'

'I agree.' Quarles nodded. 'I am not sure that peace can be accepted on any terms. There are the questions of the Queen and the Church. Many of us will not rest until the Church is truly reformed, until England is purged of Papist influence and practice, until bishops are no longer the mouthpiece of tyranny and of Rome. What say you, John?'

'I say we fight. I cannot accept the rebellion is over. Only if the King gives up all his delinquents as traitors against the people will I accept peace. If needs be, I will continue the fight in the North, or from Holland.'

'Well said.' Quarles thumped the table. 'I could not remain if Parliament were to surrender. Not that I wish to, but I would return to Germany, offer my services again to the Protestant cause. William, what about you?'

'I think, Colonel, that I would be forced to sell up and leave. I may try my hand in Holland or join my uncle in Virginia.'

They all looked at Viviers. Pale and shaken, he took a gulp of wine. 'I. . . I would go to Geneva.'

They sat in silence. And then the door burst open – Mistress Quickly bustling back into the room laden with dishes of stewed carp and of oysters. Buttered cabbage and a fresh blackpot blood pudding followed. Finally, she made an entrance with a roast Martinmas goose for the centre of the table.

William could not resist standing to carve. 'Colonel, please allow me. Gentlemen, here's to the goose.' Plunging a knife into the steaming meat, he almost drooled over the waft of juices. God, it smelled good. It was almost as good as being home. Had he really risked all this?

He did not hear the explosion. But he heard the windows rattle, the crash of a plate and a woman's shriek in the next room. A glass rolled, wine staining the white table cloth. Then silence, dust falling gently from the beam above. 'What the devil?'

Quarles sat bolt upright. 'Damned if that was not a cannon.'

'No!' Viviers looked pale. 'It can't be. Can it?'

Quarles was up and moving, out of the inn and striding towards the bridge shouting orders, the others straggling behind. 'Don't just stand there, corporal! Call out the guard!

I want them all out, now! And I want the sentinels on the bridge doubled. You men on the bridge. . . look to your posts. Watch your fronts. You, in the church tower! Yes you! Do you see anything?'

'No, sir! Well, sir, I seed the flame. Lit up the fog, it did. But nought else. It's still as fick as peas out there.'

William caught up with his colonel. 'Did they discharge in negligence? By accident? There will be hell to pay if they did. Hell to pay if it has broken the truce.'

'William, I don't know. I am not sure. Church tower. . . do you see anything more?'

'Well, not exactly, sir. It's. . . it's as if the fog is movin' up away, where the road should be, beyond the outpost. Like there's sumfink in the fog a-movin.'

A muttering broke out on the bridge, each man offering an opinion.

'Silence!' Quarles bellowed. 'I wish to listen. We cannot see. Therefore, we must hear.'

And then it began. First a couple of musket shots, then a ragged crackle, followed by another explosion – a cannon firing for sure this time, its shock wave reverberating across the flat Thames water and back to crash against the buildings around the bridge. And then volley fire as a thousand muskets poured their shot against the outpost.

William looked at the old colonel. They all did. Surely, this could not be.

'Gentlemen, this is no mistake.' Quarles drew himself up. 'This is a general attack by our enemies. We must hold them here at Brentford for as long as we can. We must give Essex time to assemble the army to defend London. Drummer. . . beat the alarum! Keep beating until I tell you to stop.' He turned to Viviers. 'Robert, the enemy horse will try to find a crossing place to ford the Brent upstream of us. I need you and your troop of horse to cover the riverbanks from the market north. If not, we will be outflanked.'

Viviers gulped as if unable to speak.

'Robert, you and your troop lost your reputation at Kineton. You must regain it here. Do you understand? You must keep your troop together. Speak to them. Give them heart and make sure they understand the importance of their work this day. They must stop the cavalier horse from crossing the River Brent. Can I rely on you to do it?'

Viviers gulped again. His face pale, he simply nodded.

'God give you strength. Take heart and go to your troop now. John, you must take charge of your regiment. God knows, but you have no field officer there. I need you to prepare a second defence. Somewhere between New and Old Brentford where the road rises and the Thames sweeps close should be best. Build a barricade, a fortification and defend it. Make sure that you can hold your flanks. We may be forced to fall back to join you. Any questions?'

'I understand, sir.' Lilburne answered. 'But we have precious little powder or match. Our major promised to send it on.'

'Then take it. Take it from any shop or house, wherever you can find it. Go now and may God be with you.'

'Aye, sir. Thank you.' Lilburne strode away calling for his horse.

'William, you must take charge here and organise the defence of the bridge. Your duty is now here. You must defend it against all. Get the whole of the guard onto the bridge. The outpost may not hold for long. I will send you more men as soon as I can get the regiment out of their quarters and formed up. I want a proper barricade on the bridge, not just these two old carts. I don't care how many houses you have to break into, but build a barricade that will stop horse. Put somebody useful in that church tower and do not forget to put men on the riverbanks, right and left. Can you do it?'

'Yes, yes. I think so.'

'Good. I will be with you as soon as I can, but start now.'

William felt exhilarated. For once, he knew what to do. This did not require some complex military drill manoeuvre, but organising men to get a job done. He posted the guard on the bridge, a bright young drummer, and a half-file of musketeers in the church tower, files along the river banks. Now he could focus on the barricade across the bridge.

Behind him, sergeants and corporals pulled soldiers into files as they came running from their quarters, as every drum in the regiment picked up the call to arms. The noise of doors smashing and furniture breaking surrounded him as his men rose to the challenge of building the barricade. The destruction of property had to be born as the cost of liberty.

With the barricade gaining in height and depth, William pulled the guard back behind its upturned carts, bales of wool from the wharf, sacks and jumble of wooden furniture. Its breadth was lined with musketeers, behind them a line of pikemen. He suddenly felt a swell of pride; most were men from his own company.

They were his men, his apprentices, his boys. He would lead them in this battle. They would stand with him against an army that had no lawful backing, an army raised by a corrupt and unrighteous court that sought to seize all power and privilege without restraint. A malignant court infected by Popery, French intrigue and effeminacy. They would fight to defend London, their homes, their property and the law that protected it.

Behind him, Colonel Quarles had formed a pike block on the high street and a reserve of shot in front of The Three Pigeons. They were ready. The drums could finally stop beating. In their place, the sounds of battle grew louder and closer.

# V

# Men and Soldiers

*Anthony Sedley*

*Old Brentford, midday*

Anthony Sedley heard the cannon. He also heard the musketry and the drums. Up on his feet at once, the Birmingham ironworker cudgelled, kicked and yanked his file up out of their slummock. Forcing them to pack fast, he pushed them down stairs and out into the street. A last sweep of the room to check that nothing vital was left and he was with them.

Outside, Old Brentford High Street filled with the purple coats of Brooke's Foot, sergeants and corporals shouting and pushing men into line. The ranks turned to the officers for orders. But there were almost no officers. Lord Brooke, his lieutenant-colonel and major were still in London, as were all of the captains except Captain Lilburne. But Freeborn John hadn't been seen since he'd ridden into New Brentford. All eyes watched the knot of lieutenants huddled in hesitant debate.

An old sergeant stepped forward. 'What's it ter be then, sirs? We can't stand 'ere all day.'

There was a shuffling amongst the young officers before

the senior lieutenant was pushed forward. 'Thank you, sergeant. *Er hum*. . . I propose to wait for orders, to await the Captain of the Watch – or word from my Lord Brooke.'

'Begging your pardon, sir, but the men 'ere are restless, like, with all them sounds of battle up yonder. Seeing as there is no telling what may 'ave 'appened to the Captain, shouldn't we go to attend on Lord Brooke?'

'You mean march back to London?'

'Well, yes sir.'

'I'm not sure that would be the right thing to do, sergeant. Our post is here in Brentford.'

'Well sir, seeing as you are not sure, perhaps we should put it to the men. What do you say lads? Do we stand 'ere all day until the King and his bloody cavaliers come? Or do we march to join the army in London?'

Every man shouted his opinion, discipline cracking as the ranks turned to a mass of yelling jostling men. Anthony stepped forward. They had to stand and fight. He yelled at the top of his voice. He glowered at his file to shout with him. 'Stand! Stand!' But it was no good. They were drowned out by calls of, 'London! London!'

A sergeant pushed him back into line, order restored. All eyes turned again to the lieutenant. He stepped forward to speak.

A single rider careered down the street from New Brentford. This was not a cavalier, but one of their own troopers riding hard towards London.

And then the rest of the troop thundered by shouting their defeat. 'They're coming!' 'Back to the defences!' 'Save yourselves!'

As the flying mud and wet settled, the old sergeant spoke again. 'Well sir, I reckon that about does it.'

'Yes Sergeant, I believe we should retire on London. *Er hum*. . . the regiment will retire by divisions! By your right. . . march! Wheel your front by division to the right. . . about!'

Shit! They were marching away from the fight. They were throwing away their freedom, giving in to tyranny. But he could not break ranks for it. The men had been heard and the decision taken together – *collectively*. Was this the end of the rebellion? Were they to give up their cause without a fight? The King had broken the truce. If they did not stand up to tyranny now, when would they?

Were they to be sold out, surrendered, by Parliament? Sold out by the lords and bloody masters that were supposed to represent them? Sold into feudal servitude and slavery?

They had barely made it to the end of Brentford and the place where the ferry crossed the Thames to Kew when another rider overtook them. But this was no fleeing horseman. It was Freeborn John!

At the head of the column, Captain Lilburne brought his horse to a halt wheeling round to stand in their path, his hand raised high. 'Brooke's Regiment. . . halt!'

Unable to resist their captain, they stood stationary, silent.

'Face to your right. . . about!'

Every man turned on the spot.

Riding down the line, Lilburne glared at them, looked into their faces, gauged their mood, the noise of battle echoing down the street. From the centre of the pike block he seized his own company colour and held it aloft.

He halted in front of them, where he could see every man, see into their hearts, into their stomachs. He spat and then spoke.

'Ye all know me! And ye know for what I stand. For the natural law of God and our birthright as Englishmen! Ye are all freeborn men and must decide the rights and wrongs of this cause, the cause we have risked ourselves in.

'To them that wish to leave, to submit to slavery, I say get ye gone! But I tell you this. . . I have just come from Brentford Bridge where your brothers of Holles's Foot stand now. Where them that fought beside ye at Kineton stand firm to hold back the tide of tyranny. They stand to buy your freedom with their blood for as long as they can!

'To ye that have the spirits of men and the gallantry of soldiers, ye that are willing to spend your blood resolutely, for our commonwealth, to preserve the honour that ye gained at Kineton, I say follow me!'

With his colour in his hand, he turned and rode steadily back towards Brentford. 'Brooke's Regiment will advance by divisions. Left turn! By your right. . . march! Wheel your front by division to the right. . . about!'

Every man found his body obeying by instinct, as if it was detached, unwilling to break ranks, unable to resist the call, their cause and the weeks of drilling. Each division marched up to the head of the column before wheeling around to march back the way they had come, back to Brentford and the sounds of battle.

Anthony Sedley grinned. They would fight. They would follow Freeborn John back to the battle against tyranny. They would fight for their rights and liberty as freemen. They would take back their birthright, fight for their children's future, for the freedom of the common man.

If he died fighting, so be it. He would not die a vassal to the Norman yoke!

## VI

# Brentford Bridge

*William Bennett*

*Brentford Bridge, five minutes past midday*

'Well done, William.' Quarles smiled. 'I would prefer to have a proper breastwork of stone or turf, but your barricade will serve. They will be upon us shortly.'

A steady stream of red-coated stragglers from the outpost warned that they could not hold for long. They climbed the barricade or waded through the Brent to rejoin their comrades at the bridge. Many simply collapsed with broken tales of how they had caught the first regiment of cavalier horse by surprise, forcing them back with their cannon. But they could not withstand the murderous storm of musket shot that followed.

The last few shots, followed by silence, told of the end of the outpost. The fog was thinning, the sun breaking through.

And then came the shout from the church tower that they all dreaded. 'Horse approaching, sir! I can see one, two, maybe more troops. They're coming up fast!'

Colonel Quarles gave his final instructions clearly and loudly enough for all to hear. 'The men in the church tower may fire at will! The remainder, hold your fire until the cavaliers are up close, and then fire by salvee. Make your shots count! I want to break them. I will second you as needed. Remember, the defence of London depends on you! Captain Bennett, please carry on.'

William stepped forward, filled his chest. He would command his boys, his company. They would defend his barricade, hold this bridge. 'Musketeers, make ready to give fire by salvee! You will hold your fire until I give the word. Draw forth your match! Cock your match! Try your match! Pikes. . . move forward to the barricade! Charge your pikes! You are to keep the bloody cavaliers off this barricade!'

The pikes came down across the piled furniture as the first shot rang out from the tower.

And then they were there: a rearing, snorting, tossing column of horseflesh, teeth, hooves and steel, the cavalier column skidding to a halt at the other end of the bridge, staring, gesticulating, pawing the ground.

William forced himself to focus. They all waited on his orders. 'Musketeers! Guard your pan! Blow on your match! Open your pan!'

A cavalier officer in blue silk sash and feathered hat spurred his charger onto the bridge, a gauntleted hand reaching for a pistol. 'Stand aside, damn you! This is the King's highway!'

Damn the delinquent bastard. 'Present!' Damn him and his cavaliers to Hell. 'Give Fire!'

The smoke rolled across the water, thinning as it went. At the far end of the bridge a mass of tattered silk and broken horseflesh kicked and shrieked. A few wild pistol shots rang out as the rest of the cavaliers edged back, turned and scattered.

'Well done my boys! That's the way. But they will be back for more, mark my word. Musketeers, make ready!'

His boys threw themselves into their motions to reload as the first shots rang out from the far bank. The King's musketeers were spreading along it in ever greater numbers. They were in loose order, but their fire was already taking effect. It crashed into the barricade, smashed through the flimsy wooden furniture in a shower of splinters. A young pikeman, one of his boys, fell backwards, staggering, reeling, clutching a bloody face lacerated by jagged wood.

# VII

# No Peace

*Francis Reeve*

*Turnham Green, ten minutes past midday*

On from Hammersmith, the road crossed Turnham Green. To the right, Acton Common stretched out northwards whilst Chiswick Common Field and gardens ran down to the Thames. Together, they formed one great swathe of open land, the first and last between London and Brentford.

Francis Reeve and the escort to the peace commissioner were half way across when they heard the cannon. Sir Peter Killigrew stopped his horse. Standing high in the saddle he threw up his hand for silence. Musket fire crackled beyond Brentford. He slumped back down, the meaning clear. There was no mistaking the noise of battle. 'Damn! I fear we are too late. Some hothead could not wait for a ceasefire. Come on. We must salvage what we can from this mess.'

They had barely moved off again when a rider tore past, bent low over his horse's neck in a headlong gallop. Then more horsemen appeared out of the Thames fog, racing for London. Sir Peter yelled at them to stop. 'Stand, damn you! Stand!'

'Out of the way!' They careered past, white faced, spume flecked, drunk with fear. 'They're coming!'

As the last rider hurtled past, Sir Peter turned in his saddle. 'Damn fools and cowards! Get a grip of yourselves and follow me!'

He set off at a hard canter, Francis and the escort struggling to keep up. They charged on across the common until the road met the river at Kew Ferry. Reining hard they turned into Old Brentford High Street.

At the far end of the street, where the last houses touched the Thames, they found the purplecoats of Brooke's Foot building a barricade. Men dragged furniture from houses, flung mattresses from windows to pile them high on upturned carts, boats, grain sacks, timber and building stone. Some were even melting lead torn from roofs and pipes to make shot.

The position was well chosen. The barricade stretched across the road at the last point where the Thames ran close enough to protect its flank. On the other side of the street, a fine brick house was being fortified as men piled sacks in windows and knocked loopholes through walls. Two small cannon looked out over a crossroads to command the high street sloping away into New Brentford, the noise of battle rolling back along it.

The men worked feverishly amidst the noise of smashing timber and glass. These hard Birmingham ironworkers were Levellers. Many did nothing to hide their delight in the work, relishing the opportunity to break up the homes of those who had more than they could ever dream of. Given the chance, they would turn England – all the world – upside down in a revolution. A pair carrying a broken table grinned at the escort as they passed.

'Who commands here?' Killigrew demanded. 'Where is your colonel?'

---

Anthony Sedley eyed the angry gentleman on his horse before slowly putting down the door he carried – another puffed up shitting peace envoy and escort. Well, they were too bloody late. 'Lord Brooke? We ain't seen 'im since London. Captain Lilburne commands 'ere.'

'Freeborn John? I might have known. Where is he?'

'That'll be 'im siting that cannon in his shirt sleeves.'

'Captain Lilburne! What is the meaning of this?'

'And ye are, sir?'

'Sir Peter Killigrew. I am ordered by the Committee of Safety to agree a cessation of arms. You, sir, seem to be in contravention of their wishes.'

'Well now, Sir Peter, it seems the King and his delinquent army are also in contravention of our master's wishes. If ye can persuade them to stop their attack I swear I'll stand ready to obey. Please, don't let me stand in your way. Ye'll find the cavaliers on Brentford Bridge.'

'Damn your insolence, Lilburne, and damn your trouble-making! I will report your actions to the Committee.'

'I'm obliged sir. I'm sure our masters will be gener-ous in their gratitude. Tell them of these men ye see here – free men who choose to risk all, as men and soldiers, to defend London, to stand between Parliament and tyranny! Aye, and tell our masters that there is no ceasefire and there is no bloody peace! Now, if ye'll excuse me, I have a battle to fight.'

---

Sir Peter turned his horse towards London. 'Well, Cornet, what are you waiting for? We return to Westminster.'

'I – I beg your leave, sir, but I would like to stay.'

'You wish to remain here and fight?'

'Yes sir.'

'Damn, this is most irregular.'

Was God showing him a way? Was this the path chosen for him? *Please God, let me stay.* Francis looked up in devout prayer. *Let me turn back from surrender, turn away from shame and torment.*

Sir Peter scowled at the escort. 'God damn it. I suppose you wish to remain also? Very well Cornet, select four troopers to remain, the trumpeter and two as my escort.'

*Oh God spare this sinner from Babylon. Let this servant fight in Your name. Let me be chosen. I beg you, do not send me back. Let me stay and fight here in this place – today! Make me Your martyr!*

# VIII

# Crossing the Brent

## *Ralph Reeve*

### *Osterley, a quarter past midday*

They were moving. Finally, they were off. Ralph had waited in the fog with Lord Grandison's Horse all morning. It was good to breathe life and warmth into stiff limbs. Turning in his saddle, he gave a wink to the file behind him, *his* file: Clem, the boy and Luke.

He exchanged a nod with Corporal Nisbet and the other two file leaders, Sam and Patrick, Mister Vaux's man. This would be his first test as lansprizado under Nisbet and their new officer. He was eager to get on with it. He wanted to lead the way into London. But he also wanted to see Brentford again.

His old master had a house there. They had decanted to it each summer to escape the heat, stench and sickness of the city, a pretty townhouse and garden, with storehouses for the shipments of broadcloth that came down to Brentford's wool wharfs from Worcester, Gloucester and Salisbury. Perhaps there would be something there for him, some payment for his lost indenture, for four years of sweat and misery as an apprentice. He needed to find something soon. He barely had enough money to keep Clem for another two days.

They had listened to the sounds of battle crash against Brentford Bridge. But the battle had moved no further. The bridge was still held by Holles's redcoats – London apprentices, butchers, dyers and journeymen. They would fight hard to defend their city.

Now Lord Wilmot's brigade of horse was moving forward. But they were not moving towards the Thames and the sounds of battle; they were heading due east on a parallel course. They would cross the River Brent further north and outflank the rebels holding the bridge.

They left the road to head across pasture and meadow down towards the Brent. They were too late now to make use of the fog. They were exposed, in plain view of any roundhead that might wait for them in the trees lining the river. The column moved across the open fields at a brisk trot, each rider scanning the shadows ahead.

On the far slope above the river, beyond the trees, something moved. Was it a rebel horseman, a sentinel, an outguard? Were they seen? Were there others waiting below on the riverbank or waiting to charge their flank as they crossed? Or was it just a cowherd and his cattle?

They reached the near bank. No shot fired. Ralph leaned back as his horse slithered down the muddy bank beneath the trees into the dark water. He lifted his feet, trying to keep his boots dry, the river up to the animal's belly, before lurching up the far bank to reform.

It took time, precious time, to get each troop across. Finally, they were on the move again, up the slope and across open fields towards a lane. To the left stood a manor house, trees and gardens: Boston Manor. No sign of defenders.

At the lane, the lead horse regiment and the dragoons turned right towards New Brentford. They would take Holles's butchers in the flank, dislodge them from the bridge. Grandison's Horse followed Lord Wilmot across the lane to push on east. They skirted gardens, vegetable plots, orchards and the tenements that ran north of Brentford High Street.

Fuck! They were going to bypass Brentford altogether. He hadn't thought about it, but now they were going to miss it he wanted to see the place again, to take something from it, to feel that it had all been worthwhile. Or had he wanted something of her, a memory of her, of her embrace, her mouth and scent?

Now it would have to wait. It would have to wait until they took London.

## IX

# One Brentford to the Other

*Hywel Lloyd*

*Isleworth, half past midday*

'*Dynion*, you lost your honour at Edgehill. I hope you will regain it here!'

Sir Thomas Salusbury's words to his regiment stung them. True, they'd been beaten back by their enemy. But they faced more than one regiment of foot, horse and cannon. Some were armed only with cudgels and staves; they stood no chance against massed musket, pike and gun. In the end, they'd been forced to give ground.

The words stung their pride, their sense of *anrhydedd*, their dignity. They were men of Wales – of *North* Wales – hard mountain men with proud lineages and ancient pedigrees, freemen who went to war for the honour of it. It was one thing to be called Welsh vermin by the fucking English. But to have their honour questioned by one of their own, by their own lord – it was too much.

A shuffling growl ran through the ranks, like dark thunder through mountain peaks. Sir Thomas had touched a nerve, poured bile on their resentment, lit their anger. Perhaps he'd done it on purpose. It did not matter; the slight must be avenged. They would have their honour and more, or die fighting for it! And those who lived would drag home the spoils of London.

Their fragile discipline was on the point of rupture, the ranks seething. And then, in the moment just before they broke, Sir Thomas let slip the leash. 'By your right. . . march!'

They lurched forward. Today, they were the vanguard of the King's army. Only an advance guard of musketeers was in front of them. Theirs was the honour, the pride of place, the right of the line, the first regiment into battle. This would be their day. The riches of London were theirs for the taking.

Hywel Lloyd, freeman of Cyffylliog, *teulu* to Rhys ap Meredydd, he of the Red Dragon Banner, descended from Marchudd ap Cynan chief of Bruffenigl, stepped out in time with the drums. They would sing of this day in every hall, *hendra* and *hafod*. Their grandchildren's grandchildren would sing of the time when the men of Denbigh took London.

Hywel gripped his musket in firm steady hands as he checked its match still burned in the damp air. It glowed bright. He was ready. Its previous owner died at Edgehill. Now it was his and he would show what Welshmen could do. No longer did he have to stand at the back of the regiment armed only with a billhook and hunting knife. Now, he was a proper musketeer.

They passed the defeated rebel outpost. Sir Richard Wynne's house some *crackack* boy called it. A Welshman's house? Well, it was a bloody mess now, all riddled with musket balls.

'Go on, you Welsh bastards! Finish them!' A few of the advance guard cheered them on as they passed, waving a captured red colour, nursing their wounds. 'Leave some of the lasses for us!'

They passed bodies on the road. Up ahead now they could hear the fight. Scorched earth, dead and wounded horse. But mostly red-coated foot, some still trying to drag themselves back towards London. They pushed on between the first houses of Brentford End.

And then they were on the banks of a river. The bridge was blocked by dead horses; a barricade across its far end wreathed in gun smoke. Beyond it was a church, houses, a town. The remnants of the advance guard were locked in a firefight across the river but did not have the strength to take the bridge. This was to be Wales's honour.

Hywel and the other musketeers were turned off the road into their battle lines, along the river bank, left and right. 'Musketeers. . . half files double your ranks to the left! Front rank. . . kneel! Rear rank. . . close forward!'

The pike block was closing up on the road, readying for the assault.

'Draw your match!'

A man fell.

'Cock and try your match!'

Another staggered back from the line clutching at his thigh.

'Guard pans and blow on your match!'

Hywel focused on the weapon in his hands.

'Open pans! Present!'

He brought the musket up to his shoulder, felt the weight of it, squinting along the barrel. He tried to calm his breathing, to hold it steady as he took aim at a red-coated pikeman at the edge of the barricade.

'Give fire!'

The weapon thumped into his shoulder as gunpowder exploded in the barrel. Six hundred muskets roared out, their thunder crashing back from the buildings, reverberating across the river. Ears ringing, eyes stinging in the smoke. He heard the yell, the call for the pike block to storm the bridge, an ancient battle cry, a five-hundred-year slight to be avenged.

'*Ddail achos Gwenllian!*'

With one great animal roar, their pikes charged. '*Gwenllian!*'

'Open pans and clear!' Orders to reload. 'Prime pans! Shut and clear pans!'

Between motions, he glanced up, tried to see what was happening on the bridge.

'Charge with powder!'

The pikes were over the mound of horseflesh. They were up against the barricade.

'Charge with bullet!'

Steel on steel rang out. A splash, a body falling from the bridge.

'Draw your scouring stick and ram home your charge!'

He looked for his target through the smoke. Not there.

'Return scouring sticks! Recover your musket!'

There on the ground. . . a red-coated pikeman. Was it his mark? Had he shot down this man? Or had another?

'Cock and try your match!'

Their pikes were forcing a gap at the edge of the barricade, pushing past it. They were shouldering the gap wider. They were through!

He did not wait for the next order. With another great roar he and the musketeers beside him were up and running. They swarmed onto the bridge or down the bank to ford the river. As one, they yelled the name of a princess butchered, a child locked in a barren convent, the last drifting snow of *Glyndŵr*. '*Gwenllian!*'

Up onto the bridge parapet, he ran its length, leapt, clambering up onto the barricade.

William Bennett pulled at the pike. It was jammed deep beneath broken wood and the slumped body of one of his boys. He had to hold back the Welsh storm that surged against the barricade. *His* barricade. They had forced a gap. He had to stop them. 'Get back!' Sweat blinded him. 'Back!' He let go of the pike. He had to throw himself into the gap, block it with his own body. 'Damn you!'

A sergeant dragged him back. With tears of frustration, he was pulled away as a wave of Welsh musketeers poured over the top of his wall yelling their demonic chants, wielding their muskets like clubs.

He staggered back from the bridge gasping for air to slump down beside Quarles. The old colonel stood like a rock beside his pike block straddling the high street.

'Sorry. Sorry, Colonel. Couldn't hold them. Too many. Not enough powder.'

'William, you did well enough. You have bought us time. Go now. Take the reserve of shot. Form a line where the High Street rises before Half Acre Lane. I will hold them here as long as I can, but you must be ready to cover my retreat. Do you understand?'

'Yes. Yes, I understand, but–'

'Go now. I need you to form that line.'

Quarles stepped forward to take up the fight. 'Pikes, charge your pikes! Ranks move forward, to your closest order! Will you let this heathen Welsh scum sack London? Will you let them despoil your homes, your wives and children, with their lust and their filth?'

A growl went through the ranks of pikemen as they edged forward, pushed on by their own anger and weight.

'Well, come on then! I want this bridge back! Before they reform! Force the scum into the river! Send them back to Hell!'

William took one last look as the pike block advanced. They seemed so few. He had lost so many pikemen on the barricade and along the riverbank, so many of his brave boys. Perhaps only half remained with Quarles to advance against the swelling numbers of Welsh that poured over the bridge and swarmed up the riverbank.

He turned and ran, stumbling up the high street to the reserve of shot. Others from the barricade limped and hobbled behind him.

---

Hywel leapt down from the barricade, musket in hand. He stepped over a blood-coughing body to make room for the men that followed. Behind him, he could hear others tearing the obstacle aside, heaving it into the river to let the press through.

Their Welsh pikes had stormed the bridge and barricade. They were trying to reform, bunching together in a close pack. Bent low over their pikes, they braced themselves against the red-coated phalanx that pressed towards them. But their line was ragged, unformed. Unarmoured Welshmen went down as the English block of steel and ash forced them back.

There were no orders, but instinct told him and the other musketeers to fan out left and right, to harry the flanks of the English. At point blank range, he levelled his musket and fired. There was no mistake. A man went down screaming, clutching at his side.

Upending the musket, he gripped the warm barrel, leapt forward, drove the heavy butt into the face of an Englishman.

The pikeman was too slow, too intent on his drill to face him, dropping to his knees, clutching at a smashed cheekbone.

Either side of him, musketeers fired into the English files or dashed in to club, hack and slash at open flanks. It brought the phalanx to a halt. Slowly, gaps appeared as men turned to protect themselves with swinging pikes or drawn swords.

They could feel it, smell it. This was a Welshman's fight, man against man, a hand-to-hand fight. Their discipline broken, the English sense of superiority was ebbing away to be replaced by fear. They were afraid, afraid of the mass of yelling, hacking Welsh raiders. They were afraid of falling in this muddy, blood-strewn street, to be torn down and slaughtered by the pack.

English pikemen started to break away, a trickle at first, then as a flood, they ran. Here and there a knot of men stuck together around an officer or colour trying to protect each other as they retreated up the street. But they could not hold the mass back. Nimble Welsh musketeers overtook English pikemen weighed down by their armour.

He caught up with an older man too exhausted to run further. A ruddy face turned to stand squarely with sword drawn, morion helmet, breastplate, tassets and leather gauntlets. 'Come on then, you Welsh bastard! Let's have you!'

Hywel dodged the first slash of the thick blade.

'Don't like it now do you? You scum.' The man stepped forward, confident, slashed again.

The sword sliced passed Hywel's chest. He lunged forward, musket butt into the man's breastplate. The older man staggered back. *Hit him again. Knock the old bull down!* But his blow glanced off, the man twisting, throwing an arm out, grasping Hywel's tunic. They fell to the ground. The pikeman was heavier, stronger, forcing him down into the mud.

'Thought you were better 'an me did you, you Welsh shit?'

A gauntleted hand stretched out towards the fallen sword. Hywel fumbled for his hunting knife, fingers wet, slippery in the cold mud. He drove the blade up into the man's exposed armpit, between breast and back-plate. Hot blood gushed down Hywel's arm as the Englishman fell back. *Turn and thrust again.* The knife drove deep into the eye socket, up into the skull. The pikeman's body twitched, kicked and stiffened in the mud.

Hywel pulled himself up. He wiped his blade on the man's sleeve then reached into a pocket to take the *Sais* fucker's purse.

———

'Blow on your match!' William knew that he needed to judge the next volley precisely. Too soon and many of Holles's re-treating pikemen would be caught in the fire. Too late and his reserve of musketeers would be overwhelmed. 'Open your pan!' Most of the pikemen were now behind his musketeers, staggering on up the street towards Old Brentford where John Lilburne and Brooke's Foot would take up the battle. He and Holles's boys had bought them as much time as they could. Pray God that they were ready. But where was Quarles? There had been no sign or word of him. Had the old colonel sold his life at the bridge, or was he lying wounded in the mud of the street? He desperately wanted the old warrior to appear. But he could wait no longer. 'Present!'

And then he saw him. He was alive. His lieutenant-colonel's colour in one hand he dragged his company ensign up the street with the other. The boy was wounded, almost lifeless. *Come on. God give him strength.*

William started forward. He wanted to run to help him.

A shot rang out. Quarles dropped to his knees, colour and ensign by his side. The older man looked up trying to mouth words, spitting blood. A Welsh musketeer ran forward, musket butt raised.

Tears clouded William's vision. The final order choked. 'Give. . . fire!'

He could not wait for the smoke to clear. He had to focus, give orders to retreat by rank and volley. 'Front rank. . . to the rear! Drums. . . beat retreat!'

The last of the front rank was clear. 'Second rank. . . present! Give fire! To the rear!'

They had stopped the Welsh onslaught. Here and there shots were returned but they had little effect. The Welsh kept back, skulking in doorways and alleys.

'Third rank. . . present! Give fire! To the rear!'

Holles's boys, *his* boys, were retreating ten paces with every volley. How long could they keep this up? Could they make this orderly retreat as far as Old Brentford?

'Fourth rank. . . present!' He waited for the smoke to clear.

Then came a shout, a shout from the rear, a shout he had feared. 'Horse! Sir, horse approaching! They're coming down Half Acre Lane. And they are not ours. Cavaliers!'

Cavalier horse. Damn, they must have crossed the River Brent upstream. Where was Viviers and his troop? They were supposed to be protecting his flank. His remaining pikemen were now too far to the rear to be of use. The cavaliers would cut his poor musketeers to pieces if they got close.

'Fourth rank. . . give fire! To the rear! Go! And keep going! Fifth rank, stand with me! Wait for my order! Mister Wade, get the sixth rank across the lane. One volley into the horse and then away. Quickly now. Mister Ashfield, get the remainder

317

moving now. Holles's Foot is to reform behind Brooke's. My compliments to Captain Lilburne and we will second him as soon as we are able.'

———

The sixth volley echoed away down the smoke-filled street. Crouched in a doorway, Hywel waited for the next. Across the street, he could hear some of the boys breaking into a tavern. Saliva suddenly filled his mouth, dry tongue melting at the thought of ale. Should he risk the dash? But the next shot did not come. The redcoats had stopped firing.

Cautiously at first then gathering pace, he and the Welsh horde began to move up the street again. He was thirsty, but there would be plenty more ale in London.

They moved through the last of the gun smoke. The street ahead was empty. Almost running now, they reached the town gaol and cattle pound at the end of New Brentford. Had the bloody English run all the way to London?

They rounded the bend. Across the road ahead, on a slight rise, was another barricade. They'd stormed one, they would storm this one too. This was their day. Fuck standing aside for another regiment to take the honour. If need be, they would storm every barricade between here and the Tower of London.

The pace slowed as they bunched for the charge. Officers and sergeants shouted for them to halt and reform. Fuck them and their drill. They did not need them. They would do it the old way, one volley and charge. Mountain pass or street, every Welshman was a warrior. Together they surged forward again, pike and shot in one great warband.

Just short of the barricade, they slowed, pikes swinging down, muskets up. He found space to let loose a shot at the barricade. But their volley was ragged, thin, wild. *No time for anything else.* He gripped his musket by the smoking barrel, butt held high.

And then with one great yell they charged. '*Gwenllian!*'

———

Anthony Sedley heard the wild heathen yell from behind the barricade – the terrifying Welsh howl and clatter as they charged. And then all was lost in the explosion of the cannon next to him. It was only a little falconet but it shot a pound and a quarter of grapeshot in a vicious hail.

Deafened, he almost missed Freeborn John's order to stand. 'Up! Up!'

Anthony brought his musket down across the barricade. The charging mass staggered, slowed. Lanes of mangled flesh writhed and steamed in the mud where grapeshot had scythed its path. Shots rang out from windows either side to fell yet more of the Welsh. But still they came on. With a terrible growl they gathered pace, surging forward again.

They were only yards from the barricade. They would swarm over it any moment, demonic screaming faces leaping at them. Then came the order, Freeborn John yelling it out. 'Give fire!'

# X

# Dragoons' Work

*Ralph Reeve*

*Kew Ferry, two o'clock*

Grandison's Horse had bypassed both New and Old Brentford. They had crossed the Brent at Boston Manor, ridden through Little Ealing to turn south at Gunnersbury House. Now they straddled the Great Road to London at Kew Ferry. Ahead lay Turnham Green, Hammersmith and London. But behind them, the sounds of battle still raged in Old Brentford.

Lord Wilmot had halted them here, calling Lord Grandison and the other colonels to him. The battle had shifted east from Brentford Bridge but there was no breakthrough. Their foot was still locked in a fierce battle on Brentford High Street. Ralph listened to the sound of cannon fire and musketry clear in the still air. The roundheads were well emplaced.

Lord Grandison turned and trotted back to the knot of officers that waited with Captain Smith beside his troop. 'Gentlemen, my Lord Wilmot is concerned that the foot have not yet taken Brentford. It must be two of the clock and we are running short of daylight. His Majesty did not wish for a protracted battle, but simply to open the way to London and force the rebels to concede.

'Personally, I doubt if the Earl of Essex or the Committee of Safety are sat idle at Westminster. We need to bring this battle to conclusion as shortly as possible. Lord Wilmot and the other regiments will screen any counterattack from Hammersmith or Acton. We are to turn back to give assistance to our foot. We need to break the roundhead defence. We will show them that they are cut off and force their rear.

'This will not be a classic horse action. I do not like street fighting. I would rather we were out of it, but the dragoons are already committed in Brentford and somebody must do it. Lord Wilmot has chosen us. We must do what we can. Captain Smith, you have experience in this sort of warfare. Do you have any suggestions as to how we should proceed?'

All eyes turned to Smith. 'My lord, thank you for your trust. If you accept, I would propose that we first test the enemy foot with a mounted advance. But if they do not break immediately, I am sorry to say that it will need a dismounted approach, house-to-house. I fear there is not the room for a troop to carousel or wheel in the street. As you say, my lord, this is dragoons' work.'

'Major Willys, do you agree?'

'Yes, my lord. I can offer no alternative.'

'Very well. I will test them first with my troop, mounted. My Lord John, would you do the honour of seconding me and to charge home if the rebels begin to break? Captain Smith, you are to be ready to advance on foot, *a la dragoon* as you say, if they do not break. Major Willys, please be ready to second Captain Smith with your troop on foot. Captain

Bertie, I must ask you to act as a reserve and to guard our rear. I do not wish to be caught out by any sudden advance from Hammersmith. Gentlemen, are there any questions?

'Well, let us open the way for His Majesty.'

# XI

# Barricade

*Anthony Sedley*

### *Old Brentford, a quarter past two o'clock*

Anthony Sedley sunk to the ground with his back to the barricade. He let his breathing ease and pulse slow as the sounds of battle slackened. It was the fourth assault they'd beaten back. Each time they had faced a fresh battalion of the King's foot, regiments from Wales, Somerset, Lancashire and bloody Stafford. Each time they forced them back with cannon, pike and shot from barricade and window.

But they were tired and battered. He touched the sticky gash across his cheek, smarting at the sting of sweat and saltpetre. The jagged splinter of wood had opened up the old scar from the forge. Its injustice burned fierce again. The other musketeers in his file were equally battered, bruised, hurt. They needed rest. He looked at them slumped down where they had fought. They'd aged since Edgehill. So young a few weeks ago, they looked drawn, haggard. Their red eyes peered back at him from blackened faces.

God damn the Norman bastards and their lackeys that attacked them. He would fight to keep his little band of merry mates together, alive and free from slavery. They would fight to keep London free. If London fell to tyranny today, it would be Birmingham next. 'Each alright? Alf, how's that shoulder of yours?'

'Oy'm alright, but its bleedin again and it don't 'alf hurt.'

'Tom, check his bandage. Will mate, keep watch will yer. The rest of you, stand easy. Get those touch holes cleaned. They'll be furred up with soot. If you ain't loaded, get loaded. Check your match and keep down. Now, I want to know how much powder and shot each 'as left. Alright, Harry, you first.'

'One up the spout. One charge and one ball left.'

'Zach, what about you lad?'

'Er, three apostles full and three ball.'

'Alf?'

'Four charges, four ball Anthony.'

'Alright. Tom?'

'Two charge, two ball.'

'Isaac?'

'Three charges and er, four ball.'

'How the bloody 'ell 'ave you got an extra ball left? You dozy pillock! It ain't no bloody good just scaring them. You've got to make 'em count. Will, keep a bloody eye on 'im will you? What 'ave you got left mate?'

'I've got one loaded and one shot left.'

'Me too. Alright, Izzy, give me that spare ball. I might 'ave some powder tucked away. Alf, give Will and Harry one charge and one ball each. I want you to rest that shoulder. Stay down and load for Will and Tom. That should leave the rest of us with three each. Harry lad, see if you can find us all some ale or water. I'm parched.'

William Bennett looked at what was left of Holles's Regiment. They were a sad remnant of the thousand red-coated men who had marched out of London in the summer sun, chests puffed with martial swagger, high words from Parliament and preacher, kisses from the oyster wenches.

No more than two hundred now stood with him. Of those, only twenty-two remained of his own company. They had lost so many poor boys at Kineton and now here on the edge of London. It was a terrible price to pay. But they must stand firm, stand and fight to protect their homes and their families.

He had drawn them up across the street as a little battalion. What was left of the pikes stood in a block in the middle of the road. Musketeers flanked them on either side with those he could spare in the houses and alleys on the north side of the street. The number of files was desperately thin. So many of them carried wounds bandaged in linen torn from the houses. But they stood firm and ready.

Tears misted his eyes at what his brave boys had done. They had bought enough time for John Lilburne and his levellers to build a second barricade. They had retreated in good order and now protected Lilburne's rear from attack. They completed the defensive square, facing back towards London.

Already they could see horsemen, cavaliers, facing them down Old Brentford High Street. Together, Brooke's and Holles's regiments formed an island of purple and red – surrounded, cut off. They had to hold for as long as they could. They had to give Essex time to come to their aid or man London's half-built defences.

———

Francis Reeve reloaded his pistol. He stood with the cornet of horse, two other iron-clad troopers and a division of musketeers behind Captain Lilburne. They were the reserve, the last resort. If needed, the forlorn-hope.

He was chosen; for this was the place of judgement and theirs was the greatest part. Twice he had leapt onto the barricade to clear it of attackers, sword and pistol in hand. The second time a musket ball threw him back, his breastplate dented. He would happily have charged the hordes that threw themselves at the barricade. He was ready to be gathered in, to find glory in martyrdom. But Captain Lilburne had been clear: they had to protect the cannon at all cost. The two little falconets reaped the greatest harvest of God's enemies. The mangled remains of the heathen still lay strewn across the street beyond the barricade.

But Francis knew that this was the day he would join the Elect. He would sit with his mother in Heaven. His father and brother would burn in Hell, body and soul, knowing that he, Francis, was crowned a martyr. *Be thou faithful unto death and I will give thee a crown of life.*

He was ready.

---

'Good lad, Harry.' The scar stung on Anthony's face as he tried to smile. 'Just in time.' The drums were growing louder again as the next attack came on up the high street from Brentford Bridge. 'Double ration for Alf and make sure you get a swig yourself. Zach. . . wake up lad and get some water down you.'

This would be the fifth of the King's battalions to assault their barricade. How many more could they stand against? Alf with his shoulder ripped open, Zach near to dropping and only three shots each. 'Alright lads! 'Ere we go again!'

# XII

# Cannon

*George Merrett*

*New Brentford, half past two o'clock*

George Merrett left the cannon on the high street and turned into the alley. The narrow passage was packed with men sheltering from the battle, nursing wounds, drawing breath, waiting, slumped down in its shadow. They were a mix of regiments, Lunsford's boys from Somerset, Molineaux's Lancastrians, Bolle's Staffords. Each had stormed the round-head barricade and been forced back. The walls of the alley echoed with the drums of the fifth battalion to throw itself at the rebels barring the King's highway to London.

For two hours, George and his cannon had inched forward, stuck behind the King's vanguard tertia as it took turns to wreck itself against a well-placed enemy, an enemy with cannon that cut down the King's precious foot in the narrow confines of the street. He needed to get his guns into action and destroy those rebel cannon before any more time or lives were needlessly lost.

But first he must find a position for them, somewhere close enough to be certain of success, but protected from rebel musket fire. He pushed on up the alley. It was just wide enough for a cannon to pass. At the far end it opened onto a track running along the back of gardens and tenements parallel with the high street. More men sheltered here – Welshmen. He was close now to the rebel barricade.

As the drums beat the Battaile, he found what he was looking for. The track opened to his right into an inn yard. It was an ancient place. Sagging wooden galleries overhung stables, kitchens and storerooms on all sides, a natural theatre for travelling players in better times. Salusbury's Welshmen seemed to have taken it over; their noise flowed from the taproom. Those who loitered in the yard took no notice as he took the steps up to the gallery two at a time.

Above the inn's gate he pushed open a door. A dark panelled dining chamber was hidden within. Leaded windows looked down onto the high street, the noise of drums filling the room, loud and incessant as the next battalion came on. He searched the barricade's length for his target, for the rebel guns.

They were below the window now, black colours held high over levelled pikes – Earl Rivers's boys. Perhaps they would break the barricade. Perhaps his guns would not be needed after all.

And then the rebel cannons fired, each one cutting a lane of smashed and bleeding bodies across the street. The battalion staggered, stumbled, before pushing on, the ranks stepping through the writhing remains of their fellows.

The massed volley from the barricade was brutal. Its wall of lead smashed into their charge, knocking men back. A steady fusillade of well-aimed shots from the houses either side brought down yet more. A few brave men got a foothold on the wall. But they were knocked back by pike, musket butt and an armoured horseman with pistol and sword.

And then the rebel guns fired again. Each one cut another corridor of mutilated steaming flesh flung across the street.

This time, George had seen one of them fire, at the far end of the barricade. The other had to be tucked out of view, protected by a brick house on the corner. But he had his target. He had seen enough. It was time to get his own guns into action.

———

Hywel swallowed down the beer. It was his third. The first two hadn't lasted long and he still had a thirst. It wasn't like the ale he was used to drinking; it tasted bitter, strong, but not bad. He and the boys in the taproom were helping themselves. The landlord had disappeared. Hiding in the cellar he was. Well, it wasn't their fault if he didn't want their money. Anyway, they deserved it.

He'd reached the barricade. Some of them climbed up on it. Others tried to pull it apart. But whatever they did, they couldn't get past the pikes and muskets that lined it. There was even a wild, armoured trooper with sword and pistol that swept men from its top. In the end, they were knocked back. The massed volleys from the barricade were brutal. And the fire from the houses either side. They'd lost many good men, too many. But it was the two cannon that did the real damage.

They were proud warriors, but they couldn't stand against muskets and cannon hidden by walls of wood and brick. Slowly at first, but then, like a wave upon a rock, their surge slid back to ebb away. They hadn't left the battle. They refused to run. They sheltered in the alleys, houses and gardens on either side of the road. But it was time to let some other fucker do a bit of fighting. They'd done their bit. Now it was time to lick their wounds, slake their thirst and wait for another chance at London.

'Mister Busy, as soon as you are ready, please load. The rebel gun is beyond these gates, about four-score yards distant, at the far end of their barricade. Now, I must organise these musketeers to keep the rebels' heads down while we deal with the cannon. I will rejoin you presently.'

George strode across the yard and into the taproom. It was packed with men drinking, despite the slaughter outside the inn walls. They were all Welsh. Not a single intelligible voice between them. And no sign of an officer.

Christ! Did it all depend on this rabble? Did they hold the key to Brentford, to London? He could not break the barricade without them. 'Does anybody speak English?'

A big man eyed him, then shouted across the room. *'Hei, Hywel! Cer i ffeindio allan be mae'r ffwc o Sais 'ma eisiau!'*

Hywel worked his way through the press to where the Englishman stood. It was the King's officer of artillery with the pockmarked face. The one stuck in the rain and mud on the road to Windsor. The one he'd tricked into promising a barrel of ale. *'Hei bois! Dyma'r un oedd wedi addo casgen o gwrw'r un i ni yn Llundain!* Come to buy us that ale, then, have you?'

George looked with dismay at the grinning Welsh musketeer, the one who had demanded a barrel of ale for throwing a wagon in a ditch. He drew himself up, regained his composure. 'It would appear that you have found your own ale.'

'Fair enough, but I can't promise the boys won't want you to pay for yours.'

'Thank you, but I don't want your ale. I want your help.'

'Don't tell me. . . you want another wagon shifted?'

'No. I want you and your fellows to fire on the rebels while my guns destroy their cannon.'

'Nasty buggers, those cannon. But the boys feel they've done their bit, see. So it could be difficult persuading them. They have a thirst, you know.'

'Listen. . . if you want that barrel of ale, we need to get to London. We need to break through this barricade. To do that, I need to destroy their cannon. I cannot do that without you keeping the bloody rebels' heads down. And, we need to do it quickly. Now, do we have an understanding?'

'Let me put it to the boys. *Mae e eisiau i ni saethu at y bastards ar y baricêd fel bod e'n gallu distrywio'r canon. Os dy'n ni ddim yn ei wneud e mae'n dweud gwneith e ddim prynu'r cwrw i ni yn Llundain. Beth dy'ch chi'n dweud?*'

'*Dweud wrtho fe ein bod ni eisiau casgen arall yr un. A llythyr gan y Brenin gyda'n henwau ni arno fe!*'

'They want another barrel of ale.'

'Tell them I will make it three if the next battalion breaks through.'

'Alright. Hywel Lloyd's the name.'

'Mister Merrett. George Merrett. Now please, can we get on with it!'

———

'Goodman Lloyd, are you ready?'

'The boys are ready, Mister Merrett!'

'Very well. Please fire at will!'

From the chamber above the gateway came the noise of

breaking glass and musket fire. He would have to trust that these Welshmen could shoot straight and that they would keep the rebels from returning fire.

The boy Flash eased the heavy gate open enough for Old Nick Busy to lay his gun on the far end of the barricade. A slight heave on the trails, a tap of the quoin and the gun captain stepped back linstock in hand. 'Stand clear!'

The inn yard shook with the force of the explosion. A window smashed. Tiles, cob and dust fell from the roof, smoke and pigeons flying as the shockwave reverberated in the enclosed space. Flash put his back to the gate to close it, the others leaping to reload the gun.

Slowly, George's hearing returned. Strange guttural oaths came from the chamber above. Then the musket fire restarted. These Welshmen, the rebels and the regiments that could not wait to break themselves on the barricade would all know the power of the King's artillery before he was done.

A nod from Old Nick and Flash eased the gate open again. A great scar was cut across the barricade. The first ball had gouged a furrow through the mud and debris of the road before ricocheting up to smash a path through the jumble of wood. Beyond it sat the rebel cannon, a little falconet, its gunners scrabbling to move it.

'Stand clear!'

Again, the deafening explosion, smoke, dust, falling tiles and plaster. As the gate closed and his ears stopped ringing, he heard shouting, stamping, cheering from above.

'*Uffern dân!* Mister Merrett! We did it! You smashed the fucker!'

Already he could hear the sound of drums, the sixth battalion starting its advance – Fitton's Cheshire's. It was time to get his second gun into action against the brick house.

# XIII

# Martyr

*Ralph Reeve*

*Old Brentford, a quarter to three o'clock*

'Well, Captain Smith, they are yours.' Lord Grandison led his troop back down the street having failed to break the rear of the rebel position in Old Brentford. 'Damn them, but they will not yield to me tucked up in this bloody street. Do what you can *a la dragoon*. If you can, force them out of their warren and into the open. Then we may have some work for horse.'

'Very well my lord, but I fear it may take time. It may also be costly.'

Ralph Reeve watched as Grandison lead his troop away towards Kew Ferry. Holles's red-coated apprentices looked battered and thin. But they stood firm.

Smith turned to his troop and gave orders in a voice that all could hear. 'Mister Musgrave, please remain here with the horses and horse-holders. Get them off the street, somewhere safe. But be ready to rejoin those of us on foot, if needed.

'Mister Vaux, you are to lead your division on foot, on the Thames side of the street. I will take the north side with the remainder of the troop. We will advance from house to house by way of the gardens at the rear rather than along the street. I want to get as close as possible before they know what we are about. I want to be able to fire down upon the rebels from houses on either side of the street.

'Aim for their officers and those damned cannon. They will be the key to this. Get your best shots into high windows and keep them there. If we are attacked, we defend ourselves and hold for as long as possible. We need to give our foot a chance to break through the rebel defence. Are there any questions?'

'I-I am not sure.' Vaux looked pale. 'This is not something one expected as an officer of horse. Not something of which my father would approve.'

'Mister Vaux, as officers and as soldiers we must be ready to adapt to the circumstances. No, this is not a classic horse action. We are to act as dragoons. On foot. Corporal Nisbet knows the business of street fighting only too well. Your place is to lead your men. Do I make myself clear?'

'Yes, Sir John.'

'And Mister Vaux, leave that colour with your servant and Mister Musgrave. A street fight is no place for a flag.'

'Yes, Sir John. Corporal Nisbet, please ready the men.'

'Aye sir. Well, ye heard the officer. . . dismount! Horses and horse-holders to the rear – to Mister Musgrave. Each man to carry pistols. Those of ye with a carbine or harquebus, carry them. An' plenty of shot and powder for both. Ye'll need it. Street fightin is durty work.'

Ralph drew his pistols and tucked both into the sash around his waist. He dropped a bag of pistol balls into his pocket and checked the cartridge bag and powder flask at his side. With Ned's carbine in his hand, he dismounted and handed the reins of his horse to the boy.

Men fussed nervously with their arms. Gone was the

feeling of supremacy, the feeling of invincibility from on high. No longer were they conquering heroes, knights riding down peasants. They were to fight the rebel foot on equal terms, in the dirt and mud of the street.

He tried to reassure those around him. He was not just a volunteer trooper now. He was a file leader and lansprizado. He needed to set an example. A nod of acknowledgement from Clem and Luke told him that they were ready. Giving his horse a last pat, he spoke to the boy. 'Take care of the horses. You got hold of them? Keep them calm. We will need them fresh later. Away you go now to Mister Musgrave.'

They all looked to Corporal Nisbet. They were twelve, an untried officer, one old soldier, a young lansprizado and nine anxious troopers about to fight their way up a street on foot.

'A'right, now this is how we're going to do it. Begging your pardon, Mister Vaux sir, but we're going to get off this damned street. We're going to slip nice an' quiet through the gardens, between the houses an' the river, just like Captain Smith said.

'When we get close enough, we're goin' to get ourselves intae a house. We'll turn it into a wee fortress an' fire down from there. We're going to do this a' silent and unseen, just until we're ready to give fire.

'Now, I'll take the van an' lead the way with Jack an' Hodge here. Mister Vaux, sir, if ye wid lead the main body with your Patrick, Sam an' their two files. Reeve, you bring up the rear with Luke an' Clem there. A'right, now cock yer weapons an' keep sharp.

'Mister Vaux sir, if ye're ready, I think we should be moving. Captain Smith is away there a'ready.'

The flimsy wooden door gave way with a crack. They were in. Ralph took a last look around the yard at the back of the cottage. It was a rundown jumble of fishing gear, tackle and kitchen garden – an upturned boat in a lean-to, nets, traps, oars, rope in heaps mixed with beds of onions and cabbages, midden and shithouse.

They had crossed a series of ornate gardens and court-yards running down to the river. These gave way to poorer tenement plots as they got closer to the western end of Old Brentford and the noise of fighting. Beyond this little yard was an alley. To the left the lapping waters of the Thames, to the right a battle raged on the high street.

It was dark inside. They stood in a small low parlour. A stair led up to a bedchamber above; to the left was a kitchen. Only a couple of windows and a brick chimney punctured the wood-frame and cob walls. An old couple cradled each other in terror. It did not look like a promising fortress.

'A'right, Luke. . . upstairs wi' that lang fouling-piece of yours. Reeve, Sam and Brown – you too. I ken ye all can shoot. Make your shots count – the bloody gunners round the cannon first, then the officers. Mister Vaux sir, if ye would direct them. An' take Patrick to load for ye.' Nisbet turned to the old man and his wife. 'Now, the pair on ye. . . I cannae let ye go as ye might blab and gie our game away. So, ye bide right there an' keep quiet, an' nae harm will come to ye. Jack, keep yer een on them. The rest of ye. . . we're going to prepare this here fortress below stairs. Clem, fetch in a pale o' water an' then bar the door. Ye lot, get that table up across this here window. And I want loop holes in the wall covering the yard.'

Ralph took the steps up to the bedchamber two at a time. Beyond the bed, a low window looked down on the high street. Directly below stood a red-coated pike block. Beyond them, files of musketeers filled the alleys and gaps between houses on the far side of the street.

To the right, he could see gun smoke curling from the windows of a house. That had to be Captain Smith. To the left was the end of a barricade lined with purple-coated soldiers, Brooke's Levellers. The redcoats must be Holles's butchers. Both would fight hard to defend London.

The barricade butted onto what must have been a fine red-brick house. Smoke hung in wreaths over all after yet another assault beaten back.

And then he saw it. 'There! At the base of that brick house – at the far end of the barricade, do you see it? The cannon.' It would be a long shot. But the gunners were exposed from this angle as they sponged and cooled the hot gun. 'Luke, can you hit them from here?'

'Yes, I reckon so, if I can have something to rest on and we're not too disturbed. I doubt it'll be long afore they realise we're here.'

'Let's get the bed on its edge. It'll make a reasonable rest and may give a little protection too. Sam, Luke, Brown, you shoot. Keep back from the window and don't show yourselves or your gun smoke. Patrick and I will load. Mister Vaux, are you alright?'

'I do not like it. We are too close. And, and there are too many of them. We cannot hope to break them. We must surely be cut off. We will be overwhelmed and taken.'

Fuck! The young cornet was frightened. This was his first battle, his first test. The swaggering cavalier facade was crumbling. 'But we can't withdraw now. Any further back and we'll stand no chance of hitting those gunners.'

'I-I am not sure. This is desperate. It is madness. I must inform Lord Grandison. I will bring help. Patrick, you will escort me.'

All Ralph could do was shout a warning as Vaux almost fell down the stairs past Nisbet and out of the door.

'Mister Vaux, sir! Where in Christ's name d'ye think ye're going?'

'I am going to Lord Grandison. You, you cannot hope to hold this. . . this hovel against them. I am going to get help.'

And then he was gone, followed by Patrick. The door had not shut again before one of Patrick's surly troopers bolted after them.

'Shite! Ah, let the bastards go. Clem, get that damned door bolted an' barred. Now, we hold, we fight for as lang as it takes. We kill those damned gunners an' we pray that the King's glorious bloody foot break through that barricade soon. A'right, now let's be getting on wi' it. Ralph laddie, I want to hear yer boys shooting up there. I want ye to make our presence felt.'

———

'Alright lads, keep down now. Keep your 'eads down.' Anthony Sedley looked at what was left of his merry men slumped against the barricade. Will Scarlet was dead, shot through the neck by some bastard in an inn window, his blood dripping down amongst the shattered timbers where he hung. Alf's wound had opened again to leave him weak and pained. Tom's forearm was gashed by splinters and Zach lay shivering despite the sun. Even Isaac was silent. They'd no more than one shot each between them.

All along the barricade, exhausted and wounded men crouched or cowered. Musket balls smacked down in showers of splinters, forcing heads lower. Worse was the shitting cannon that smashed great holes in the barricade and those behind it. It'd broken one of their own little falconets into a shattered heap of broken carriage, twisted iron and torn, mangled crew.

Now, only the one gun was left beside Anthony. It'd been spared, along with their half of the barricade. The King's bloody gunners seemed unable to reach them from their position behind the inn gate. He'd been ready to follow Freeborn John in a charge to silence the tyrant cannon. But it was too well protected by musketeers in the inn. And they didn't have the powder, shot or energy. Even Holles's lads were busy now trading shots with a house behind them. Anthony's head lolled. He was exhausted. Near beat. This was not the way he'd thought it would end. At least he would die a freeman.

His head jerked back. The plank beside him quivered, smacked by a shot. It sat there, a lump of lead sunk into splintered wood. It could not have come from the inn; it was on this side of the barricade.

The gunner beside him jerked, thrashing his legs in the dirt, kicking, clawing at his chest, back arching, rasping for breath, blood soaking his shirt. He'd been shot.

Somebody was shooting at them from this side of the barricade. But where? Shit! Where?

A ball ricocheted off the falconet's barrel, its crumpled mass whining through the air.

A faint movement, a dull flash in a dark window across the street. Was that gun smoke? Yes, there again.

'Captain John! Up there! Cavaliers!' He pointed at the window. 'One of the gunners is shot!'

'Aye, Anthony, ye're right. Damn!' Freeborn John shouted to the officer commanding Holles's redcoats. 'Captain Bennett! William! The cottage on the Thames side! Upstairs window!'

'I see them!'

'Take the reserve. I can spare no others. But hurry. Their bloody drums have started again. We need the cannon.'

339

'Them be in the alley!' Ralph heard Clem's yell from down below.

The bloody rebels were in the alley next to them, the alley that ran down to the Thames and the gate into the backyard of the cottage. He cocked a pistol, gently opened the window over the alley. He leaned out, aimed at a red coat below and squeezed the trigger. The pistol crashed in the narrow passage. He dropped back inside, the window exploding in a hail of glass shards, wood splinters and twisted lead. Across the room shots smacked into the wall in a cloud of cob dust. 'They're in the house across the alley as well!'

'Alright laddie, I hear ye.' Nesbit acknowledged. 'Can ye still fire on the barricade?'

'Yes. The fire from the high street is not too bad. But they have the alley side covered from the house across it. If you come up the stairs, for Christ's sake keep low. It sounds like our foot are going to attack again. We can hear the drums. And our own cannon are now firing on the barricade.'

'A'right then, let's make this one count. Keep yer heads down an' finish those fucking gunners soon. We'll haud them down here.'

'Them be in the yard! Musketeers!' Clem's shout from the kitchen again. 'And I swear I just seed a bloody tinned trooper!'

William Bennett watched the half-file of musketeers crawl forward through the boat shed. The corporal and another file were already busy firing from the house across the alley. Others fired on the front of the cottage from the street.

Now he waited at the yard gate with the cornet, three armoured troopers, a sergeant and nine musketeers. 'Now, once our boys have broken through at the end of the shed and can fire through the wall, we charge. Cornet, I need you and your troopers to break down that door. Find something heavy. Find yourselves a battering ram. Sergeant, you must be ready with your musketeers to follow me once the door is opened. We must clear the place before the next attack. We charge at the run and kill all inside. Do I make myself clear?'

———

'Ralph laddie! I need ye down here.' Nisbet's call was urgent. 'An' bring two pistols.'

Ralph took a loaded pistol from Luke and crawled across the glass and cob strewn floor to the stairs.

'They're a-tunnelling through the wall, laddie. Ye can hear them up close. It'll be hell in here if they get a musket through. They must be in yon boat shed. We cannae stop them from in here. Now, ye an' me are going to open this back door, sally out and give them a brace of pistols each. Are ye wi' me?'

Ralph nodded. Fuck, this was desperate.

'A'right. Jack! Hodge! On my mark, covering fire from the loop holes. Keep their heads down on the other side of the yard. Clem, ye man the door. Ye bar it again quick so they cannae storm it. If one of us is hit, leave us. Ye bar the door, understand? Are we ready? A'right, two, three! Now!'

The little room exploded with noise from the loop holes, sunlight flooding in from the open door. Ears ringing, heart pounding, eyes squinting, Ralph burst out behind Nisbet. A red blur in the dark shed – one shot. . . turn. . . second shot – the yard filled with flying lead and musket smoke. He dived back into the dark. Inside!

The door was still half open, Nisbet slumped across its frame. 'Clem! Door open!'

Sunlight flooded in again. Ralph grabbed the old man under his arms, shots smacking into the wall either side. Splinters flew from the door and frame. A ball whizzed past into the room. He fell back inside, dragging Nisbet with him, one twisted leg trailing blood across the doorstep. The door slammed shut, more shots hammering into it.

'I telt ye to leave me if I were hit, ye daft bastard! Ye could hae got us both killed. Shite! I cannae stand on this leg. Prop me agin the wall facing that bloody door an' gie me another pistol. Clem, can ye still hear them digging?'

'No. But I can smell smoke. There be a fire a-burning in that there shed. I don't doubt one o' they had a match that's caught a-lit.'

'Shite! That's all we bloody need.'

———

'Damn them!' William knew that he must change his plan. It was not in his nature but he had to be decisive. He had to act quickly. 'We don't have time to try another firing point. And we don't have time to wait for the fire. Those bloody drums are too close already.' He drew his sword.

'Sergeant, I want one volley and then we charge. Cornet, I am sorry but you and your troopers must break that door. Remember your Joshua. . . *Fear them not; for I have delivered them into thine hand!*'

———

Francis Reeve hefted the baulk of wood under one arm, his shoulder turned ready. Praise God, he had been chosen! He would be the first into the breach, the first amongst

342

God's troopers, the true martyr, the head of the battering ram.

Slamming down his visor, he braced himself, armoured by Captain Bennett's godly choice of bible reading. He would finish Joshua's verse. '*There shall not a man of them stand before thee!*'

———

'Luke, we can't hold much longer. This fire is serious. It's through the wall and in the kitchen now. We can't put it out. There's something feeding it.'

'I know Ralph. We can hardly breathe up here.'

'That'll be that there pitch a-burning.' Clem offered. 'I seed it in the shed when I went for the water. Nasty stuff, it do smell like brimstone.'

'Thank you, Clem. Luke, how long? How long do we need to hold? How long before our foot charge the barricade?'

'I reckon our boys are close to charging. But if we go now, the rebels will man that cannon again. Every time we stop firing, they try.'

Ralph looked at the blaze that had taken hold. Flames climbed the walls, licking the beams above. Smoke billowed out of the kitchen door and up the stairs. It was more a question of how long had they got? They could no longer see into the yard at the back of the cottage for smoke. What was beyond it?

'Ralph laddie, the back door.' Nisbet cocked his pistol. 'The bastards are bound to storm the back door now. Get yersels ready.'

'Jack, Clem. . . leave that fire now.' Ralph checked his own pistol. 'You've done what you can. Ready pistols and swords. We'll hold them at the door as long as we can.'

Francis watched black sulphurous smoke billow from the shed in great hanging wreathes, heavy with the stench of brimstone, of putrefaction, of burning flesh. Flames clawed at the back wall of the cottage, shadows leaping in a wild dance around the darkening yard – demonic figures that flung themselves across his path to Heaven.

The sergeant's volley thundered in the enclosed space, smacking into the door, windows, loop holes and cottage wall in a shower of splinters, glass and dust. Francis did not wait for Captain Bennett's order. He did not wait for his cornet to lead the way. This was the time of martyrdom. With one long yell of his faith in God's promise he charged. 'Jehovah!'

Ralph stared at the door, straining to hear any sound over the crackling flames, gunfire and incessant drums. And then it was there, a muffled grunt, the door buckling, timbers cracking, a battering ram smashing into it. But it held. Clem leapt forward to push his makeshift barring back in place and to hold it down.

The second blow struck, threw Clem to the floor opening a great crack, sunlight lancing through. Ralph rammed his pistol through it, fired at point blank. A groan and thud – it would buy a little time. He stepped back and drew his dagger, his father's broken rapier. Flames from the kitchen danced along its steel as he waited for the next blow.

The door and barring gave way in a welter of splintering wood; flames and blazing sunset piercing the dark smoke-filled room and chaos within. The silhouette of an armoured horseman filled the doorframe, crumpled forward crashing across the threshold as the room filled with the deafening noise of a musket.

Luke stood on the stair behind. 'Ralph, they're through!' The musket smoked in his hands. 'Our foot has broken through. They're over the barricade. Brentford is ours!'

———

Francis heard his half-brother's name. The man beyond the smashed door was black with powder stains and stubble, his hair matted and uncut, clothes torn, covered with cob, wreathed in smoke. But there was no mistaking him. It was the bastard, Ralph!

He heard the frenzied yelling in the high street. He heard, but did not heed the shouts of Captain Bennett and the sergeant to leave, to run, that it was too late, that it was all over, that he should save himself.

Anger seethed within him: anger at defeat in battle; at God's unjust trial; at his own foul sin; God's choice not to gather him in to be a martyr; his humiliation in front of the bastard – but most of all at the torment; the deceit of an older brother; lies to steal their mother's love; lies that cheated him of his own father; deceit that poisoned pure Susanna's heart with dancing, kisses and lust.

A shriek of blind fury burst within him as he charged. He leapt over the slumped body of his cornet, through the opening into Hell. 'Satan!'

———

Ralph barely had time to raise the dagger. The weight of the charge threw him backwards, sprawling against the stair, sword, breastplate, buff coat and snarling pot helmet forcing the wind from his lungs. Edged steel grated. Eyes lanced in the gloom. Gauntlet and clammy breath choked and smothered.

———

Francis bore down with all his weight, forcing the blades across the bastard's neck, steel pressed down against unshaven jaw, pulsing neck, rasping breath. His tormentor squirmed and kicked in his grip. The hilt and shortened blade – his father's rapier! White anger burst in him. A lurch, the fine ground edge slitting, cutting, slicing open that handsome skin.

The bastard's blood ran thick across gasping neck, grimy cavalier lace, shirt and hair.

———

The armoured horseman was thrown from him, rolling away to rise again in the kitchen door.

Blood ran from Ralph's jaw, hot, slick down his neck and front. Clem stood over him, wooden spar in his hands, Luke with levelled firelock.

The demonic horseman glared at them, swinging his heavy blade, at Clem, at Luke, Jack, Hodge and the flames that licked all around him.

'Sinners, burn in Hell!' With a final snarl, he was gone, out through the back door, cloaked in the dark smoke that filled the yard.

'Who in Christ's name was that?'

'That, Corporal Nisbet,' Luke sighed, 'was Ralph's brother.'

'Master Francis Reeve.' Clem added. 'He always were difficult.'

'Aye, well they're about as mad as each other. I'm glad we're fightin' just the one. Now, get us all out of here afore we do burn in Hell. Jack, get these auld anes out first. Aye, dearie, I'm sorry aboot yer hoose.'

## XIV

# The Thames

### *Francis Reeve*

### *Old Brentford, four o'clock*

Francis threw down his helmet. Fighting back tears, he slithered down the mud bank into the dark water. They were close behind. There was nowhere else to go. He must cross here or be taken. Please God, don't let him be taken. Not Ralph's prisoner. He could not bear the humiliation. He had to get away, or drown trying.

All along this stretch of the Thames, men were entering the water. Those of Holles's and Brooke's regiments who had escaped the barricade were pressed into the thin strip of garden, wharf and mud bank, squeezed between the King's foot pouring up the high street and the King's horse sweeping down from Kew Ferry.

The river was dark, swirling in great muddy eddies, a high spring tide surging downriver to sweep the weak away. A flaming sunset cast great shadows from the town behind, ahead was a darkening sky. Men stood in the cold water trying to summon the courage to swim, envious of those who struck out, terrified by the splashes, gasps and cries of those struggling to keep afloat on the tide. But there was nowhere else to go. It was cross the river here, or be taken at the mercy of the cavaliers.

Francis's long riding boots sank deeper into the ooze. He struggled free only to slip, stagger and slip again. His head slid below the surface, pulled down by the weight of armour and buff coat. He kicked, thrashed, flailed; sheathed in leather and iron, writhing, sinking deeper.

He fought to kick off his boots but they clung to his legs. He pulled at gauntlets, clawed at fastenings for breastplate and back. The taste of muddied water flooded nose and throat, his chest bursting, arms weakening, legs heavy, feeble.

*Lord this is Thy will. I have sinned. Take this sinner down. Hide his body. Damn his soul!*

A hand pulled him up, up to break the surface. Air filled his gasping lungs. An arm steadied him as he found the bottom and stood again, sucking in life.

'Alright now, my boy?' It was Captain Bennett. The good puritan captain had saved him.

'Thank you, sir. Yes. Thank God, yes!'

With shaking hands, Francis rid himself of armour, buff coat and boots. Shivering in shirt and breeches, he waded deeper, sword and bible above his head. A chain of low islands lined the bend in the river. God willing, he could make it to one of them.

Captain Bennett was still standing in the water. He had gone no further. 'Captain Bennett? What are you waiting for, sir?'

'I am – Oh, damn it, I cannot swim.'

'I think we can wade to that island at least. Will you try with me?'

'Yes, yes but what then? I cannot swim the river – and this

tide. I would freeze to death on that island or be taken. I think I should go back. I think I should surrender. The King will be merciful, I am sure.'

'For God's sake, sir, the base cavaliers may not be so merciful. They are still shooting.'

'No, no, I am going back. I was foolish. I must think of my poor wife and children. One of these cavaliers looks to be an officer. I will appeal to his position and sense.'

Francis saw the riders walk their horses into the water. Captain Bennett raised a hand, began to wade back towards them. The last of the sun glinting on steel – a pistol raised.

'No!'

———

The pistol ball smashed into William Bennett's chest knocking him backwards. His feet slid from under him, the cold water closing over his head. Blood and fireball sunset swirled around him.

He kicked, bursting to the surface. He gulped for air. Cold flooding his chest, filling his lungs, muddy water sucked in through torn breast; cold, wet, black melancholy filling him, weighing him down, crushing him, dragging him back down.

Down he slipped into the dark, into the dark of his bed, cool sheets and coverlets wrapping themselves around him, dragging him back down to sleep.

———

Francis saw Captain Bennett thrown back into the water, his arms and legs thrashing to stay on the surface. He could not swim. He was drowning.

Francis took a step toward him – to save him.

'Patrick. . . pistol. Give me another pistol!'

The click of the pistol cocked. The weapon raised. He turned and dived into the water. He swam under its dark shadow, stroke after stroke, his breath bursting. But cold and flapping clothes forced him back up to break the surface, gasp for air.

A jet of water, the pistol ball smacking down beside him.

He dived again. He must swim, swim away from the shore, away from the drowning captain and this vengeful cavalier. *Oh God, hide me in Thy waters. Cleanse me in this river. Wash away my sins. Give me Thy blessing. Let me cross this Jordan.*

———

Ralph heard his brother's shout. He had tried to follow but lost him in the smoke, chaos and gathering gloom. He heard the pistol shots. Fuck, no! Not Francis. He had promised their mother to protect him. At the river bank, two riders were at the water's edge.

'Patrick. . . pistol.' It was Vaux's voice. 'Give me another pistol.'

'No!' Ralph shouted. 'For Christ's sake, let him live!'

'What? Damn you, Reeve. I will have my pistol and I will have me another bloody traitor. Take care, lest I take you for one too. Have you gone soft on these dogs? Patrick! My pistol!'

Fuck this conceited puppy. Fuck him for taking his place as an officer. Fuck him for a coward and a murderer. The dagger still in his hand, Ralph started forward, started towards Vaux. He would kill the bastard.

Luke's arms clasped around him, held him back.

'No!' Clem charged past them, down the bank into the water, grabbing at Vaux's reins. 'No, Mister Vaux, sir. Tin't needed. Swim, Master Francis! Go on, swim!'

'Damn your insolence man! Reeve, call your man off

before I shoot him too!' Vaux spurred his horse on, pushing Clem aside. He waded deeper into the water still yelling over his shoulder. 'Patrick, damn you, my pistol! Now! The dog is getting away.'

'Mister Vaux!' Other horsemen were on the bank now. 'What in Christ's name are you doing?'

'I am shooting traitors, Sir John. I am shooting traitors.'

'Well stop. They are unarmed.'

'This one is not. He has a sword. I saw it. I will shoot the rogue.'

'I said stop! These men are defenceless. They are beaten. You are to report to Mister Musgrave. Now! I will deal with you later. In the meantime, I will deal with your division. Reeve, where is Corporal Nisbet?'

'He's wounded, sir. We have him on a litter, just along the bank, beside the burning cottage.'

'Very well, take me to him.'

Ralph led the way back to the yard of the burning cottage where Nisbet sat on a makeshift sedan chair. Ralph stepped back as the two old soldiers spoke. Had Smith seen him start at Vaux with a dagger? He wiped the blade clean and sheathed it. Was he to be dealt with? Punished?

The captain showed a tenderness and concern towards the corporal, a bond and understanding between them that could only be born from shared experience and respect. 'Corporal Nisbet tells me that you did well Reeve. You all did well. I watched from across the street. I thought that your position was hopeless when that fire started. I'm sorry that I could bring no help to you. I'm also sorry that I'm given to understand that Mister Vaux did not remain with you.

'I believe that your actions were vital to breaking the rebels. I will make sure that Lord Grandison understands

351

what happened here. But first, Corporal Nisbet must be taken to a surgeon. I will take him myself. I owe him that.

'You must get your division into quarters and cleaned up. The army can go no further tonight. The foot have met yet another rebel battalion on the road beyond the town. We will have to see what tomorrow brings. But, if it is London, we had better get cleaned up. Find Mister Musgrave and your horses, and tell him that I said your division is to have the best quarters tonight.'

'Sir, thank you.' The moment had almost passed. Fuck it. . . he could only try. 'Sir John, might I. . . could I beg your leave? There's a house here in Brentford that I wish to visit, that I have an interest in.'

'I see. Very well. There may be looting and damage after the battle. Some of the foot will be difficult to keep in hand. And you feel it necessary to protect this, er. . . interest? Well then, keep your division with you. I take it you can quarter them in this house of yours? They deserve a good bed. But keep them in hand. You are to ensure that Mister Musgrave is acquainted with your quarters and you are all to be with the troop at first roll call. Will that suffice?'

'Yes, yes sir. Thank you.'

'Good. And Reeve. . .'

'Yes sir?'

'I hope you find what you are looking for.'

## XV

# Prisoners

*Robbie Needham*

*New Brentford, half past four o'clock*

Finally, they were moving. The King's Lifeguard had stood waiting all day for the way to be clear. They stood for hours in the fog and wet grass of Hounslow Heath only to stand all afternoon on the road while the vanguard battered itself against the barricades. Now, when it was almost dark they were marching.

Robbie Needham was tired and hungry. His feet were sore from standing in wet boots. His broken nose still burned and his bruised face itched. Up ahead was the sound of more fighting. He just wanted to get on with it, get it finished.

He'd heard tell it was a purple-coated regiment that had stopped them. It had been one of those buggers who had knocked him down at Edgehill, a scar-faced bastard in a purple coat. He'd kill the fucker if he found him.

———

Hywel Lloyd watched the rest of the army pass. He was supposed to be watching the prisoners. But they just sat huddled against the brick house. Exhausted, beaten they were.

That Mister Merrett was busy getting the road cleared. Right mess his cannon had made of the barricade. Now he was fussing over those two little guns they'd captured. Never stopped he did.

———

They were close to the barricade now. They passed an old inn, windows smashed, gate and walls pockmarked with shot; bodies, mangled, heaped; a fine brick house battered and holed; across the road, a burning cottage. Robbie stepped over shattered wood, ripped cloth; debris strewn across the street.

And then he saw them, huddled in the shadow of the brick house: redcoats, purplecoats. Prisoners. Hireling bastards. Thugs and dogs sent to keep people down while grasping tossers in Parliament, merchants, bankers and pissing lawyers took their profit.

Was he here? Was the scar-faced bastard among them, cowering in the shadows, hiding? By fuck, he'd have him if he was.

They were almost past. Bugger it! He stepped out of line, threw his pike down, stepped amongst them, pulling their heads back, looking into their faces. If he was here, he would find the fucker.

———

Anthony Sedley sat with his head on his knees. A fist yanked his hair, wrenched his head back. Above him a pikeman in breastplate and leather skull-cap, an angry bruised face, teeth broken, nose smashed. Some shitting Norman lackey gaoler sent to brand him a rebel.

The fist hit him hard, knocked him backward. The blow

was unexpected. The bastard would not catch him again. He would die fighting rather than be beaten like a slave. He must get up. Step back to avoid the next blow.

'Come 'ere yer bastard! I in't done yet!'

The glint of sunset on steel – a blade.

———

Hywel pushed between them, musket levelled. 'Hey boy, if you want to fight him, you fight fair and proper. He's my prisoner, see. I know you, don't I. Oxford it was. That was an execution. We'll have a fair fight here. No knives, now. The rest of you. . . make some room here.'

———

George Merrett glanced up from the captured falconet. A fight had broken out amongst the prisoners. Christ, could he not leave anything for five minutes? Those Welshmen were supposed to be guarding them. He'd have to break up the crowd around the fighters, restore order. Where was that man, Lloyd? The one who spoke English, the brazen sod who demanded ale at every turn?

'It's alright, Mister Merrett, it's a fair fight.' Lloyd was clearly acting as the damned ringmaster. 'They need to settle their *gelyniaeth*, their feud. The prisoner, see, is the one who wounded our man in the face at Edgehill. I reckon they're a fair match. But my money's on the prisoner. Got arms like a blacksmith, he has. Fancy a wager, do you?'

———

Robbie spat blood and snot from broken lips. Hands on knees he sucked in air. 'Hireling town bastard!'

'I'm no hireling.' The purple-coated bastard swayed, pulled

himself up, blood running from the scar open across his cheek. 'I work me own forge, a free man. Lackey!'

'I ain't no pissin lackey. I'm free-miner.'

'Then why fight for tyranny? Why oppress the common man?'

'I fight for justice and end to them wankers in Parliament and city pissin on people. Worr' about you?'

'For freedom and rights for all.'

'Al' right ahtey. Buggered if I know rightly which o' us is on t' wrong side. Any road, I reckon I best be gerrin along. Aah-do? Robbie Needham. Castleton. Peak Country.'

'Alright. Anthony Sedley. Birmingham.'

# XVI

# Sack

### Ralph Reeve

### *Old Brentford, six o'clock in the evening*

The house was shuttered, dark and silent at the front, but something told Ralph that it was not empty. Somebody was inside. Was he too late? Had some of the King's foot already broken in to plunder it? Would he be left empty handed again?

They moved up the alley and forced open the side gate. Whoever was inside had not got in this way. Ralph led them between walled garden and laundry into the stable yard. He remembered it well. The tall town house and pretty grounds led back from the high street.

She had first touched his hand in that garden. The first time he saw her desire, her want for him, one moment of tenderness before a winter of distant rejection, bitter disapproval and criticism. And then that final mad destructive spring of frantic lust before betrayal and the rebellion.

Firelight showed under the kitchen door. Was it just the old porter and his wife or was somebody else there? He was sure he could see the glint of a candle upstairs. What if his old master was here? He often came to meet shipments of his precious fucking broadcloth at the wool wharfs. Would she be with him? Would the bitch choose the old man now or would she choose him?

He drew his sword and thumped its pommel on the kitchen door. 'Open up. Open up in the name of the King.'

Hushed voices inside, a chair scraped, then silence again.

'I said open up. Or we force the door.'

The door opened a crack. He put his shoulder to it, pushing the old porter aside. They were in. Frightened servants backed away at stained and tattered soldiers. The maid gasped. He was recognised. He was across the kitchen to take the stairs two at a time. A candle guttered as he passed, boots crashing on wood. There was another light upstairs; somebody was in the great chamber. Master or mistress?

He flung open the door, sword ready to kill the old bastard if he tried to resist – to force him to repay his lost indenture, to pay for four years of labour; four long years of grovelling, sweat and bowed prayer as a servant; four years of living and loving as a young man lost. By Christ, the bastard would pay!

And there she stood, the bitch, in her fine puritan smock and headscarf.

'Is he here?'

She shook her head, a flush at her chest and throat. One dark curl of hair tumbled from under her coif and hood.

Ralph fucked her. Deep hard penetrating thrusts, the oak panelling creaking and gasping in the shocked silence of the house, until she whimpered her surrender and he shuddered deep inside her.

He drew back. They both fumbled to smooth disordered clothing. She did not run, did not strike him. She kissed him hard. She was his – his for this night at least. His totally. Neither God nor master would stop them.

Warm languid curves wrapped around him, silken skin
dancing with firelight. Her shining hair was his to touch,
stroke, hold.

The stair creaked. Someone knocked on the chamber
door. 'Ralph?' It was Luke.

Ralph touched her lips, tried to reassure as she snatched
covers over her nakedness. 'Yes, Luke? Is something
wrong?'

A flush of guilt swept up his spine. He had abandoned his
men as soon as they entered the house. He had done nothing to check that they and their horses were quartered, fed,
stabled, watered. He should get up. But God bless Luke for
continuing the conversation through the door.

'No, nothing wrong. Clem has attended to stables and
we've all supped and helped ourselves to ale. The cook has
rustled up a fine dish of pork if you're hungry?'

'Thank you, Luke, but not quite now.'

'Ah yes, well. . . maybe later. The thing is. . . Mister Vaux
has just called here.'

'Damn! What the hell did he want? He can't bloody move
us, can he? Don't tell me he wants a bed?'

'No. He's Officer of the Guard. He was sent to deliver a
message.'

'Thank God. What's the message?'

'You're to attend on Captain Smith and Lord Grandison
at your earliest convenience. They're at The Three Pigeons, by
Brentford Bridge.'

'Fuck! Did he say why?'

'No. But should I ask Clem to have your horse ready?'

'Yes. Yes please. I'll be down shortly.'

'Clear night, Master Ralph. And a new moon. An oak moon that be. Some'd say tis a mourning moon, the last afore winter.' Clem held the horse for him to mount. Ralph looked up, doffed his hat and kissed his fingers in greeting to the thin crescent low over Brentford End.

'Mind, tis a Saturday moon. I don't doubt that'll rain afore day's end tomorrow.'

Ralph pulled on his hat. Cool silk touched his fingers: the hat band, Susanna's ribbon, her favour. A shiver ran across his shoulders; cold, damp sweat down his spine. Smouldering firelight glinted from behind the chamber curtain. His breath hung in the cold night air, nebulous, dank, guilty.

'You sure you don't want me to be a-goin with you?'

'Thank you, Clem, but no. I hope I'll not be long. And Clem. . . thank you for attending to the horses.'

'Mind how you go, now. Sounds like that's a bit rough out there on that street. I don't doubt a few o' they've bin at th'ale. What with celebratin' beatin' the rebels an' all.'

Ralph rode out of the yard and turned onto the high street, his horse snorting in the cold still air. Why had Mister fucking Vaux been sent to fetch him? He could still be lying in her arms, feeling her warmth.

Had Vaux seen the dagger in his hand? Thank Christ Luke had held him back in his blind fury. But had Vaux told Lord Grandison? Was he summoned to be punished, cashiered, thrown out – not even to be a soldier, let alone an officer? Was he a failure once more?

Every inn, tavern and house was packed with soldiers. Light, music and singing flooded out across the rutted mud as every troop, company and regiment claimed their patch of Brentford, their piece of the victory. Laughter, shouts and crashing furniture told of a drunken tavern game or spilt ale. Here and there a figure staggered out onto the street to piss or vomit against a wall. A girl's shriek of laughter and giggles echoed from a dark alley. The town's notorious whores would be making a fortune.

He passed the smouldering ruin of the boatman's cottage that only hours before they had fought so desperately to defend. Flames and the stench of burning pitch still lingered in its crumpled shell. He rode past the alley, the sound of the river lapping at its end, and on through the bloody wreckage of the barricade.

A once great inn glowed bright, candles guttering in broken windows, a bonfire filling its yard. From within, a thousand Welsh voices filled the night with their singing. He did not understand the words but the strange, ancient, aching beauty of their lament coiled itself around him, flooding the darkness with their grief.

———

Hywel swayed with the crowd as they sang, his voice raised to the flames that licked high into the night air and the sparks they lifted to the stars.

*'Ar hyd y nos,*
*'Nosy w henaint pan ddaw cystudd,'*

Tears streamed down his cheeks, soaked his collar as the words flowed from him and the song flooded his soul; a song for those who would not know again the mountains of their homeland, the clear falling stream, sunburst out of rain, home fire, love; those who would never grow old; a farewell to their fallen.

*'Ond i harddu dyn a'i hwyrddydd*

*Rhown ein golau gwan i'n gilydd*
*Ar hyd y nos,*
*Ar hyd y nos,*
*Hyd y nos.'*

———

Ralph rode on past guards who slept beside the town gaol and cattle pound. He laid a calming hand on his horse at the shuffling moan of hurt and wounded prisoners held within, their whispering prayer seeping out through iron bars and under the wooden gate.

———

Anthony lay on the earth floor of the cattle pound. The smell of cow shit mingled with the stench of stale sweat, gun smoke, blood and close packed bodies in the cold damp air as Freeborn John's voice led them in prayer from his cramped cell.

'Fear thou not; for I am with thee.'

Four hundred men packed tighter than pigs in market pens waiting to be slaughtered, waiting for dawn and the rebel's noose; their pain, hurt and fear surrounded him as they murmured in prayer.

'Be not dismayed; for I am thy God.'

Anthony shifted his aching shoulder in the dirt. He pulled Zach's shivering body closer trying to lift its bony frame up from the cold and damp that seeped into them, dowsing their spirit, soaking away their last strength and resolve.

'I will strengthen thee; yea, I will help thee.'

He had to keep his boys together, keep them brave, ready to face the hangman, keep the fire of hope and freedom alight.

'I will uphold thee with the right hand of my righteousness.'

One day. . . One day, the flames of rebellion would burn bright again. One day, their spark would light a furnace that would remould the world. It had to.

———

Ralph found The Three Pigeons set back from the road and marketplace. A stable boy took his horse. Was he to be punished, humiliated in public? He pushed open the door to the taproom.

The air was thick with pipe-smoke, the low-beamed room filled with ruddy faces, banter, laughter and hospitality. A pair of old players chivvied a company of boys, serving girls and whores between theatrical gesture and verse.

*'A plague of all cowards, I say, and vengeance too!*
*Marry and amen! Give me a cup of sack boy!'*

He worked his way across the room ignoring the attentions of Falstaff, Hamlet, Mistress Quickly and Doll Tearsheet.

*'Give me thy cups. And let the kettle to the trumpet speak,*
*The trumpet to the cannoneer without,*
*the cannon to heaven, the heavens to earth!'*

Sir John was sat with Lord Grandison and a group of officers, wine jar and glasses half full. Thank God, there was no sign of Vaux. Perhaps he had played his hand already, told them all they needed to know. Smith pulled up a stool and poured a glass of wine. It was good sweet canary.

'Ah, Reeve.' Grandison looked at him. 'Sir John tells me that you seconded him at Kineton when he re-took the King's Standard.'

'Yes, my lord. But I fear I was of little help.'

'That's not quite what Sir John tells me. He says that it was you who saw them taking the Standard away. And now I hear from Sir John that you were instrumental in breaking the roundhead barricade, in denying them their cannon. Even old Corporal Nisbet said that you showed bravery and leadership, and he is not one normally to give a compliment. For my part, I am impressed. You will know that I prize valour and honour.'

'Thank you, my lord. How is Corporal Nisbet?'

'My surgeon tells me that he will live. He is a tough old bird. You know that he fought with Sir John Hepburn? And that he campaigned with Mansfeld, King Gustavus and Turenne? One of Pontius Pilate's bodyguard. He will live, but he will not be fit again for many months. He may yet lose his leg.'

Ralph felt the silence that followed. Who would replace Nisbet? Surely not that idiot Patrick, Vaux's favourite.

'The thing is that Nisbet has recommended you to take his corporalship. Sir John here agrees with him. But I wanted to see you for myself. I would not normally expect to find the qualities of a corporal amongst one of my gentlemen volunteers. I would normally be looking for a soldier with more experience. Are you ready? Can you keep the other bucks in hand? Can I trust you to support Mister Vaux? You will know that I also value loyalty and integrity.'

'My lord, I'm touched and not sure what to say. I cannot hope to replace Corporal Nisbet. He is, shall we say, extraordinary. But I hope that I have shown some worth. I am not afraid of the challenge, if that's of concern. As for Mister Vaux. . . he's young. I have made mistakes as a young man. I can at least try to help him avoid some of the pitfalls. And I would hope that my loyalty and integrity have not been challenged.'

Lord Grandison considered him, weighed him. Had he said the wrong thing? Was this some sort of trap?

'Well said. Very well, Smith, I agree. Reeve here is to take

Nisbet's corporalship. It may not be for long. His Majesty expects London to rise against Parliament and welcome him home by tomorrow evening. Now, what do you say to it?'

'My lord. . . Sir John. . . thank you. I hope I will repay your trust fully.'

'Have you eaten?'

'No, my lord. Not yet.'

'Well, sup with us then.'

'My lord, that is kind. But could I – might I beg your leave?'

'Want to get back to your men, I suppose?'

Captain Smith leaned over, whispered something to Grandison.

The young colonel exploded in laughter. 'Well beggar me. Not only does he get himself promoted, but he gets the lady as well! I say well done to that. Go on, be gone with you! Don't waste your time here. Go and get back in the saddle. And give her one for each of us too!'

# XVII

# Turnham

*Thomasine Bennett*

***Chiswick, Sunday the 13<sup>th</sup> of***
***November 1642, midday***

Thomasine Bennett found them huddled beside the church in Chiswick. She had searched for Holles's Regiment all morning among the battalions lined across Acton Common, Turnham Green and Chiswick Common Field.

She had seen the Earl of Essex cheered by his army. She heard General Skippon tell his London militia boys to pray heartily and fight heartily to defend their homes. Officers charged backwards and forwards with orders. She had even heard cannons fire. It was frightening and exhilarating. Alone she pressed on, determined to find William and his soldiers. Even when others ran in panic at rumours of Rupert and his cavaliers charging, she had not stopped.

She carried a great pie in a basket, her arms aching from its weight. It was an extravagance, but the children had insisted. It was a venison pie, William's favourite. She so desperately wanted to find him for her children – for herself. There had only been one night at home after Guildhall. She wanted to hold him, to tell him she loved him, to beg his forgiveness, to tell him that she was with child again.

At last, an officer had informed her that Holles's Regiment of Foot was placed at Chiswick, on the left, next to the Thames. Now she had found them.

But they were not as she expected, not as she remembered. There were barely two hundred of them, a mix of Holles's redcoats, others in purple; more missing coats of any kind, missing shoes, weapons; a motley, bedraggled battalion of survivors tucked away by the Thames. As if they had been hidden away from view.

She searched the ranks, ready to run to him, hoping he would see her, come to her, take her in his arms. But nobody moved. She could not see him. He was not amongst them. He was not here.

She stepped forward. She could feel herself choke. *Oh God, don't let me falter!* Not now, not here on this battlefield. She must not show her weakness, her fear. She must be brave. She must ask. She must know. 'Can you tell me where I might find Mist – Captain William Bennett?'

There was silence. Those nearest looked at the ground.

An officer came forward. It was young Mister Wade. He was a friend to Nehemiah in happier times. He would help her find William. She had not recognised him. He was thin – gaunt. He looked exhausted.

'Mistress Bennett, I am sorry. Captain Bennett has not been seen since the battle yesterday. He was our mainstay, our commanding officer, after Colonel Quarles. . . after Colonel Quarles was lost. But we were separated from him at the end. It was almost dark, there was much confusion. There were many taken prisoner.'

'Beggin y' pardon, misses.' An older soldier spoke up from

the ranks. 'But 'e were the one that saved us. 'E stopped them cavalier bastards at the bridge.'

'And 'e got us back to the barricade.' Another of William's dear boys looked at her. ''E were still fighting at the end, 'e were.'

''Ere, where's that trooper lad? 'E were with the captain at the end.'

———

Francis Reeve sat shivering, wrapped in a blanket on the church step, his sword and Bible clasped in his hands. The Bible was sodden – ruined, the pages wet, tearing at his touch, the ink smudged and illegible. He was lost. Even the word of God was hidden from him now.

He had not been taken in. Surely, he had done all that God had asked. But he had not been gathered in to join his mother in paradise. The bastard Ralph had stopped the vengeful cavalier from shooting him. The Lord had chosen to preserve him from drowning. Why did God test him still? What did He want?

He had swum under the dark shadow of the river, dragged himself across the mud of an island to swim across the Thames. There were others in the water, flailing arms, pale bobbing faces, limp silent bodies. Hands that clutched and grasped, pulled him down as they were swept downstream on the fierce tide, until he pushed and kicked them away.

Washed up at Barnes, he was taken in by a farmer and rowed across the river to join the army marching out from London. But there was no place for him in his troop without horse, armour, boots or pistols. He had lost all at Brentford.

He was lost. He so wanted a sign, a sign of God's purpose for him.

A woman stood in front of him. 'Please, can you tell me where my husband is? Captain William Bennett? Can you tell me what happened to him?'

How could he tell this lady what had happened? How could he tell her the truth? This godly woman did not deserve to know her husband was shot down trying to surrender, that he had failed to save him, that he had turned away from him, turned away from the man who had saved him from drowning. Yet God demanded the truth.

'He. . . he fought most bravely, until the very end. I was close beside him. He spoke of you. . . thought of you and his children. . . just before the end.'

---

The basket crashed to the ground. Thomasine fell to her knees. The pie was split, broken, its precious gravy spilling out. She tried to push the crust back, to hold it together, to save it. But the rich dark liquid ran cold through her fingers, oozed from the basket, soaking into the dirt.

Her eyes swam with tears. Her hands shook. He was gone. It was too late, too late to tell him of her sorrow, her regret, of her guilt, her love, of the child he would never know. She must not let them see her weakness, her loss, her desperation. She blinked back tears to look up at the boy with his Bible and sword. 'Pray with me. Please pray with me. For him.'

He knelt beside her. Together they knelt in front of the church and prayed.

*Oh Lord, forgive me in my self-pity. I beg Thee, take William into Thy fold. I will dedicate my life to his memory, to the memory of Nehemiah and all William's brave boys, those killed, those maimed, those who have given too much. Let me help them.*

*Let me save this poor boy, this boy who was with William. He is alone. He has nothing. Let me give him shelter. Let me comfort, let me feed and clothe him. Let me arm him once more so that he may fight again in Thy name, in William's honour.*

———

Hywel Lloyd stood on the riverbank beside Brentford Bridge. He did not understand why they were back here, back where they'd started the fight the day before. He thought they were supposed to be going to London.

His head hurt and he needed a drink. This fucking London beer made him crapulous. Mind, they'd drunk the old inn dry singing into the night. And then that Mister Merrett woke them with his fucking cannon. Firing at bloody boats on the river he was! Reinforcements from Windsor going to join Essex and his army – thought they could slip by in the fog.

Then they had to stand all morning looking at Essex and his fucking army. Now they were bloody retreating, running away instead of attacking the *Sais* fuckers. Where was the honour in that? And now Prince bloody Rupert expected them to stand here as rear guard while the rest of the army marched past. Yesterday they'd led the way as the vanguard. Now they were the bloody rear guard. And it looked like rain.

*Anffafriaeth* it was, without fucking justice!

———

The cannons rumbled over Brentford Bridge. One of the wheels squeaked at every turn. The noise scratched, scored across George Merrett's thoughts, his calculations. His head ached with fatigue.

They were retreating, leaving Brentford to Essex and his army. The King's plan to force Parliament to beg for terms had been lost in delay, rivalry for honour and a night of drinking – a wasted opportunity. Lives and victory had been squandered in inefficiency while battalions vied to break themselves on the barricades.

There had been no popular uprising to welcome home a victorious and benevolent King. Now the Committee of Safety would paint them as vengeful mercenaries, intent only on seizing London's riches. There was no way Parliament would agree to peace on the King's terms now. They would fortify London, use its wealth to build up their forces. Essex had mustered twice their number at Turnham Green, the London Trained Bands standing with his field army.

Where in Christ's name was the King going to find money to feed and pay his army, let alone build it up? They were almost out of gunpowder. No doubt his patron, the Master of Ordnance, would expect him to work some miracle, to find or manufacture fresh powder. But from what, how, where?

'For Christ's sake, Mister Busy, can you not do something about that bloody wheel!'

'Flash, lad. . . run to the conductor and beg a horn of grease.'

Anthony Sedley followed the King's artillery over Brentford Bridge. He was a prisoner, a hostage of tyranny. The Norman bastards had tried to force them all to turn coat, threatening to brand them with hot irons like slaves. But his lads had all offered their cheek. Not one of them turned, not even Isaac. They were brave lads, true to their birthright: Harry, Zach, Izzy, Alf, Tom and poor bloody Will.

Freeborn John still marched with them, chained, shackled, charged a traitor. But his head was held high. Not like that stumbling shit, Viviers. The cavaliers had thrown him in the pound drunk and pleading for mercy.

Now tyranny was retreating, running. The army of the commonwealth and the citizens of London stood shoulder to shoulder against oppression.

The rebellion was alive. It had only just begun. 'Alright lads, not long now.'

———

'Home for bloody Christmas, they said.' Robbie Needham marched behind the Royal Standard as the King's Lifeguard crossed Brentford Bridge. 'Put t' King back in London, lock up pissin Parliament an' then home for Christmas. Well, where the bloody 'ell are we goin now?' He was hungry, thirsty and irritable. His lips were scabbed, his nose and head aching. He'd had nothing to eat or drink since morning. All day they'd stood in battalia facing Essex and his army. Now they were marching back over Brentford Bridge. Already the pike felt heavy on his shoulder.

'Don't tell me we're goin back to bloody Oxford!'

———

Ralph Reeve led his division back down Brentford High Street. They and Grandison's Horse had remained in place as long as they could to cover the army's retreat. But they could stay no longer. Essex's cannon had found their range. As the rain began to fall, they were forced to turn their backs on any hope of taking London – any hope of keeping Clem.

They were close to the house now. Would she still be there? Was she waiting to follow him, to beg him to stay, to kiss him farewell; or had she had her fill? Had she bedded him to sate her desire only to cast him out again?

She had bathed him, kissing each cut and bruise, gently washing the blood from his jaw and neck. She had combed and cut his tangled hair, shaved and dressed him in clean linen. They had supped, sharing a plate from the kitchen. And they had made love deep into the night. Her scent clung to him.

There was nobody waiting, nobody in front of the house, not even the old porter. The door was shut.

And then he saw her, high up at the chamber window, the glass rain-smeared, her hair down. They were almost past. The door was opening, the kitchen maid running down the steps, handing him a purse, a food-bag to Clem, a book for Luke, reaching up to the boy with a long clinging kiss.

Ralph felt the weight of the purse. Gold. His indenture repaid. He swept off his hat, bowed low to her. Thank God! He leaned back in the saddle and let the rain fall free on his face.

—————

The body surfaced as it passed the muddy earth fort at Vauxhall; bloated, limp, pale, water ran from its mouth. Dark eye sockets stared up as the last of the sun touched the Palace of Westminster. Twice it had swept downstream, twice back up on the tide. The Thames was finally carrying it down through London, past Temple Steps, the Globe, Southwark and great St Paul's, turning gently in the cold dark stream. One final look towards the city, its thousand lights of hope, glory, sin and misery, its joy, heartbreak and indifference, before the surge tumbled under London Bridge and on to the black sea.

A gust of wind ruffled the water, blew off the river to sigh through St Swithin's Lane as William Bennett whispered a last farewell to his Thomasine, his Rebecca, Thomas, Benjamin, Little William, the twins and the child he would never hold.

# Epilogue

# Marlborough

### *Ralph Reeve*

### *Sunday the 4th of December 1642, ten o'clock*

Ralph pushed his horse forward. He could smell wood-smoke despite the cold rain that drummed down, beat on his hat, soaked through his gauntlets and ran from his cloak. The church bells were calling the good puritan folk of Marlborough to prayer. If they were lucky, they would seize the town in time to share their Sunday dinner before the town militia even knew it.

Clem gave a nod as they both moved forward. Behind them rode Luke and the boy. Together they were scouts for Lord Grandison's brigade. They were to seize this town for the King – seize it before winter.

———

The lock of the fowling piece clicked softly as he cocked the weapon. Rain dripped, ran across the sill as he eased the long barrel through the open window. Just a few steps more. . .

'Almost there, cavalier. . . you're almost mine.'

# Historical Notes

*God's Vindictive Wrath* is a work of fiction. However, the story is as historically accurate and authentic as reasonably possible. It does not take liberties with history. There is no need. The events of the British Civil Wars and the personal stories within them are extraordinary enough as they are. These stories just need to be told. They are also sharply relevant today. There are so very many parallels between the current global situation and the crises of the 17th Century.

The 17th Century was Europe's 'Golden Age' of art, science and progress. But it was also a black age of religious persecution, slaughter, famine, disease and destruction. In parts of Germany, more than half the population perished. Bohemia saw worse. The civil wars that tore apart England, Scotland, Ireland and Wales remain the bloodiest conflict in British history.

This was a period of extraordinary upheaval and change. It marks the birth of the modern world in Europe; a secular, materialistic world based on rational, scientific thinking and the independence of man. However, change was not sudden or universal. Faith in ancient, medieval and superstitious practices, local lore and the centrality of God remained fundamental parts of life for many, as they do in much of the world today.

Overpopulation led to huge disparity of wealth and living conditions, exacerbated by climate change. The Little Ice Age is now acknowledged as an underlying contributory cause of the violence that swept the globe in the 1640s. Life expectancy of the poor in England had dropped to thirty years, significantly lower than a century before.

The medieval world no longer provided adequate spiritual, moral or societal answers to maintain stability. This was a period of fundamental intellectual change. The ideas of William Gilbert (1544-1603), Kepler (1571-1630), Galileo (1564-1646), Descartes (1596-1650), Newton (1642-1726) and John Locke (1632-1704) irrevocably challenged the perceptions of the ancient and medieval worlds. Ultimately, they placed mathematical calculation as the basis for scientific advancement.

Whilst the need for change may have been clear, there was no agreement on its course. Some saw a strong centralised state as essential. Others believed in the natural rights of man and a 'levelling' of society. Many sought answers in religion, in glorifying or appeasing God, some in religious extremism, in defeating Satan and in building religious states.

Ultimately, the 17th Century is marked by violence. The Thirty Years War and the endless wars of religion that accompanied it ravaged continental Europe. These brutal religious and political conflicts saw the destruction of large areas of Germany, Bohemia, Lorraine and the Low Countries. Callot's *Miseries of War* provide a glimpse of these horrors which have left a deep scar in the European psyche.

Huge numbers of English, Scottish, Irish and Welsh soldiers fought in Europe, joining the Imperials and the Catholic League, as well as the protestant cause. In many cases, complete regiments served on the continent. Others served Russia or fought against the Ottomans. The British Civil Wars should not be seen in isolation, but as part of the wider European conflict.

Charles I was king of England, Scotland and of Ireland. His reign started with seven 'fat years' (1629 to 1635). These were followed by poor harvests, severe hardship and discontent. The years 1642 (Edgehill), 1649 (execution) and 1659 (end of the Interregnum) were particularly bad years. These were caused by the Little Ice Age. However, many in 1642 saw God's wrath and made biblical parallels with the Pharaohs of Israel's captivity.

The old medieval system of communal farming was inefficient. However, the process of enclosure led to social tension and civil disorder in the years running up to the first Civil War. It was a contributory factor in the Great Rebellion. The disenfranchised rural poor had little legal recourse and swelled the numbers of vagrants on the streets of London, Bristol, Birmingham and other towns across England.

Economic depression contributed to a crisis in government. Charles I's attempt to rule without Parliament and his use of royal prerogative to raise taxes such as ship money is well known. However, it is worth noting that Parliament voted him only one year of Customs and Excise revenue on his accession; a tax granted to all previous English monarchs for life and essential for maintaining the national administration, including the navy.

Religious tensions between Charles I and his Scottish subjects came to a head in 1639. Abortive attempts to impose religious uniformity, the "devil's whore", resulted in the Bishops' Wars. These were rapidly followed by the rebellion of disenfranchised Catholics in Ireland from the summer of 1641. Reports of atrocities stoked political and religious division to the point of crisis, with both King and Parliament claiming the sole right to raise an army to protect England.

The final breakdown came when Charles, encouraged by his queen, made an abortive attempt to seize five MPs from the House of Commons on the 4th of January 1642. However, the "birds" had flown and London apprentices mobilised to force the King to leave London for York. The Queen left for Holland to purchase arms and munitions.

King and Parliament both raised armies. At the centre of the divide were supporters of what were to become the Tory and liberal Whig parties, the basis of British politics today. However, each was forced to ally with political and religious extremists. The King appealed to those who sought strong central patriarchal government, Catholics, reactionary and localist groups (including Derbyshire free-miners). Political Levellers, recognised today as early socialists by the British Labour party, and radical sectarians seeking Godly Rule sided with Parliament.

The armies raised by both the King and Parliament both drew on recent military practice from the Thirty Years War and Wars of Religion in Europe. The 17th Century saw a military revolution that was to dominate warfare for the next two and half centuries. Linear formations of pike and musket progressively replaced the great Spanish *tercio* squares of pike, shot, sword and buckler, finally defeating them at Rocroi in 1643.

Inspired by classical Roman tactics, the Dutch reforms of Prince Maurice of Nassau brought greater firepower to bear and strength in defence. These were adapted by King Gustavus II Adolphus of Sweden to deliver both firepower and offensive mobility. These two styles were to clash at Edgehill in a brutal struggle between Essex Dutch style *tertias* and Rupert's Swedish brigades.

The battle of Edgehill was fought on the 23rd of October 1642. It was the first major battle of the English Civil War. Many had anticipated a single show of force or token battle – a letting of blood to 'purge the nation'. But Edgehill left many in shock. Descending into a brutal drawn-out slog with no conclusive ending, there was no doubt that war had arrived in Britain.

It is an unusually well documented battle and *God's Vindictive Wrath* draws on primary source records to portray the battle as authentically as possible. Hugh Peters really did preach to the Parliamentary troops with pistol and Bible in hand. The battle really did end with an exploding barrel of gunpowder. The depiction of the immediate aftermath draws on contemporary accounts that portray the shock and horror of this battle.

Edgehill was followed by the King's steady advance on London. Had he taken it, the English Civil War would probably have ended after only three months. As it was, after a late start, Essex forced marched his army from Warwick to London to arrive before the King. Both armies had to contend with autumn rain and mud on the march. In London, the capital was in turmoil with many supporting peace negotiations whilst others dug fortifications.

Many have forgotten the Battle of Aylesbury. Part of the battlefield has recently been lost to development. However, this clash was a key prelude to the battles of Brentford and Turnham Green. Many parliamentary reports place Rupert at Aylesbury. However, Rupert led the King's advance on the main access along the Thames Valley. We know this from his own diary. It is likely that Wilmot was dispatched to Aylesbury to act as a flank-guard. It is also possible that he intended to intercept the Welsh beef droves heading for

London. He arrived early on the 1st of November 1642 with the action probably taking place on the 3rd of November.

The battles of Brentford and Turnham Green 1642 ended the King's attempt to seize London after Edgehill. Though less well known than Edgehill, their impact was far reaching. The main events of the Battle of Brentford described in *God's Vindictive Wrath* are taken from what primary accounts exist. These do not include an account of the King's horse outflanking the barricades. However, it seems militarily inconceivable that this did not take place. Indeed, William Defoe's *Memoirs of a Cavalier*, written within living memory, describes such a move.

The King never again came so close to entering his capital as a victor. Ultimately, the successful defence of London at Turnham Green resulted in the protracted slaughter of the British Civil Wars – the bloodiest period in British history. We should not forget that these wars were to see a greater loss of life across Britain and Ireland than even the Great War of 1914–18.

More detailed historical notes and maps to accompany this book can be found on the website at www.charlescordell. com. These include articles on the Little Ice Age and The General Crisis of the 17th Century, the English Revolution and 17th Century military theory. They also include detailed notes to accompany the text of *God's Vindictive Wrath*. These include notes from research of the Battle of Edgehill, the campaign to seize London, the Battle of Aylesbury and the battles of Brentford and Turnham Green.

The focus of research and writing has now shifted to the next book in the Divided Kingdom series. This story will feature some of the survivors of *God's Vindictive Wrath* but will also include a number of new characters. It will pitch them into the brutal Battle of Lansdown Hill, the siege of Devizes, the Battle of Roundway Down and the Storming of Bristol in 1643. Research notes will be shared along the way with the Divided Kingdom Readers' Club.

# Acknowledgements

Sometimes writing can feel a lonely pursuit. *God's Vindictive Wrath* has been a long slow journey. But there are very many who have helped along the way, a few unknowingly. I owe and offer them all my sincere thanks. Any mistakes are mine alone.

First to you the reader: thank you for your time and trust. There would be no books without you. I hope I and this book repay your trust in full. If you enjoy reading it, please do post a review. It makes a very big difference to a debut author. The chances of continuing to be published are slim without positive reviews. I really hope to be able to give you more of the Divided Kingdom series.

I hope to meet as many of you as I can. Please do look out for an opportunity to say hello and let me sign this book. Please also tell me what you think. I would really appreciate your feedback, in person, via the Divided Kingdom Readers' Club or the contact page at www.charlescordell. com. Alternatively, tell me what you are doing and whether I can support you in some way. I like nothing better than giving talks and battlefield walks. I am also a big fan of Living History and Historical Re-enactment. I believe that both play an important role in making history accessible.

Ultimately, the author is only one part of the story of

publishing a book. It requires an extraordinary range of professionals to bring together art, craft and business acumen in a finished book. It is a sector fraught with risk. My sincere thanks go to the publisher, Myrmidon, but they also to their partners: Blacksheep Design for the cover, the printers at CPI, the sales team at Inpress Books and the distributors, Ingrams. Without them, this book would not be on your shelf.

But more than these, my personal thanks go to those that gave their help and support along the way. I owe my deepest thanks to Derek Sturge, Bart Slight and Chris Warner for all their time, patience, encouragement and advice. I could not have done it without them. My thanks go to Bethan Lloyd for her Welsh translation, to Brian Woodall for his help with the Derbyshire Peak Country dialect and to Vojtech Straka for Cormenius' Bohemian. To Vinay Talwar, I owe my thanks for his input on extremist psychology and to Jacqueline Adshead on personality temperament. My thanks also go to Andrew McDougal and Smita Rossetti for their insight and encouragement, as well as to Alexis Scudder, Ted Wrong, Hannah Congdon, Edd King and Jamie Stevenson for their suggestions. I thank Stuart Pringle for all the walks, talks, science and coffee. Friends and family I thank for their patience. I hope it was worth the wait.

I am hugely grateful to Ben Kane, Michael Arnold, General Richard Nugee and Jeremy Ravenshaw Fowler for their kind words of endorsement. I only hope that others feel the same about this book. I am also very grateful to David Gilman, Martine Bailey and Sapho Clissitt for their time, their tips and encouragement in negotiating the world of publishing. It has meant a lot to have their support. All at Jericho Writers and Cornerstones Literary Consultancy I thank for their advice and encouragement. To Elly Cooper, Roger Cawte and all at

CTP and X-Forces, I say thank you for giving me the confidence to go it alone on an uncharted path.

I am forever grateful to the Armed Forces' charities for watching my back and being ready, if necessary, to try to pick up the pieces. I am a soldier who was lucky enough to come home. I have my scars, but they are nothing compared to others. So many veterans and their families are still struggling with physical disability, mental health and disadvantage. It is an enduring Misery of War. I pledge to give 2% of my royalties from the sale of this book to support the work of Royal British Legion Industries, the Army Benevolent Fund and Blind Veterans UK. I wish I could give more.

Finally, to Clio, Fortuna and Mars I offer eternal thanks. But most of all, I thank Tommy Atkins for the sheer bloody inspiration that he is. I am honoured to have stood beside him for a time.